# RESCIND ORDER

## A MORGAN SHAW NOVEL

## NATASHA BAJEMA

NUCLEAR
SPIN CYCLE
PUBLISHING

This book is a work of fiction. The characters, incidents, and dialogue are drawn from the author's imagination and are not to be construed as real. Any resemblance to actual events or persons, living or dead, is entirely coincidental.

*The views expressed in this novel are those of the author and do not reflect the official policy or position of the National Defense University, the Department of Defense or the U.S. Government.*

6 July 2033
0405
Centoreum Tech Headquarters
Fairfax, Virginia

"Humans make one mistake after another. They're easily compromised. And yet, we willingly give them control over nuclear weapons," Dennis said, fastening the last buttons on his tailored shirt. "But an intelligent machine? If a machine makes a single mistake, people freak out. All trust is lost in an instant. That's a dangerous double standard. If we're not careful, it will get us all killed someday." His tone was grim as he glanced at the computer screen. The ARC system was still processing the data transfer.

"Yeah, I've never fully understood the logic behind giving the president sole authority to launch nuclear weapons," Amanda said. She pulled on a black pencil skirt and tugged on the zipper until it closed over her trim figure. "There are any number of things that can go wrong."

Dennis gazed lustfully as Amanda tucked her light-gray silk blouse into her skirt, the snug fit accentuating her full chest. In her late twenties, his systems engineer had emerald green eyes and wavy long blonde hair. She was thin and curvy in all the right places. But her stunning looks weren't the only reason he'd hired her.

"Yeah, it's crazy," he said absentmindedly. He surveyed his office and found evidence of their passionate tryst on his desk, on the couch, and on the floor. He reached down to pick up the nameplate his wife had given him when he'd first started his IT company. As he placed it back on his messy desk, Dennis caught a glimpse of his wife staring at him from their wedding photo.

A wave of guilt roiled his stomach. He pushed the nagging thought from his mind and continued his conversation. "In the early days of the nuclear age, members of Congress were so afraid of military officers launching nuclear weapons without civilian authorization that they placed the sole authority in the hands of one man."

"Or one woman," Amanda said quickly and flashed her white teeth at him.

"Please don't remind me about that woman," Dennis groaned. He pulled his Rolex watch onto his wrist and snapped the clasp shut.

"Aren't you having lunch with her today?" Amanda asked, scrunching her petite nose. She bent over to slip on her heels, and he couldn't help staring at her shapely rear end.

Dennis scowled as he turned to reach for his suit jacket, his mood dipping suddenly. He was surprised his conscience was bothering him all of a sudden. He hadn't slept with Amanda for the past year simply for her good looks—though that made it much easier to do what needed to be done. He'd needed her brilliant mind for a special project—one that required a flexible moral code, absolute loyalty and discretion, and most importantly, a major stake in the game. He'd dangled the possibility of marriage as the lynchpin of the deal. And she was naïve enough to believe his promises.

In the end, it was all a ruse to secure her cooperation in

pulling the wool over the eyes of Pentagon leadership while he made sure his life's work was given a fair shot.

"I really don't understand why you hate President Tolley so much," Amanda said. "Didn't you practically bankroll the Monroe-Tolley ticket?"

He nodded. "Without my financial contribution, that ticket would never have seen the light of day, let alone the Oval Office. Last year, I warned Monroe about choosing Tolley as his VP, but he wouldn't hear of it. And now Monroe is dead, and that woman is the president."

His stomach roiled each time he thought about how Monroe dropped dead on the golf course over the holiday weekend, stricken by a sudden heart attack. Dennis had been invited to partake in several one-on-one rounds of golf with the president, but his wife had forced him to take a rain check since it was their ten-year anniversary. He'd been cross with her all weekend about it. But now a shudder of relief passed through his stocky frame.

*Thank God I wasn't there to see it happen.*

"Did I ever tell you how she nearly killed our plan to launch the ARC system?" Dennis asked.

Amanda shook her head.

"If it were up to Tolley, there would be zero automation in nuclear weapons systems. She wants humans to remain fully in the loop for all such decisions. To assuage her concerns, Monroe even demanded our programmers make some major changes to the ARC system, allowing for human intervention." Dennis walked around his desk and threw up his hands. "She'd rather have millions of dead Americans on her hands than jeopardize the supposed morality of the United States. As if moral qualms will stop other countries from gaining a speed advantage through automation." Turning toward Amanda, he clenched his fists and grimaced, feeling a new surge of determination come over him. "Whether she likes it or not, President Tolley owes me for the election. By the time lunch is finished today, she'll know what's at stake for her personally."

"You're planning to get her on board by threatening her?" Amanda said, crossing her arms.

Dennis smirked. "Well, let's just say I know some damning things about her predecessor. If any of it gets out into the media, it's enough to take down her presidency." He smoothed his sweaty hair, wiped his hands on a Kleenex, and pulled his chair back from the desk. "I own her. If Tolley knows what's good for her, she'll endorse the ARC system and give Burke the empty VP slot." He chuckled. "Even if I let her play the role of commander in chief, Burke and I will take over the Oval Office from within."

Dennis sat down in his black leather chair, looked at the computer screen, and frowned. A pop-up box on the ARC dashboard stated that the data transfer was almost finished. He craned his neck to see Amanda come up behind his chair. He swiveled around to face her, placed his hands around her waist, and pulled her closer to him. "Before you joined Centoreum Tech, the prototype user interface for ARC used to provide much more information than it does today."

Amanda raised her eyebrow. "You dumbed it down?"

He nodded, smiling at her glowing face, still a rosy pink from their romp. "We decided too much transparency was problematic. With a broad range of information at their fingertips, Pentagon leadership would start asking too many questions. They might even refuse to let ARC operate properly. So, we redesigned the ARC dashboard to have only a few audible alerts and flashing lights with a simple color scheme—a simplified user interface to prevent humans from second-guessing the system."

Amanda nodded, her eyes bright with understanding. "Because the worst-case scenario would be having access to an intelligent machine with superior abilities but the Pentagon leadership failing to trust it, shutting it down, and acting on their own limited understanding of the situation."

"Exactly. We're at much greater risk of annihilation if they stop trusting the ARC system."

"Yeah, if we expect human critical thinking to save us from a nuclear war, we're all screwed," Amanda said snidely.

Several loud, high-pitched beeps emanated from the computer. Dennis moved her body gently, turned his chair around toward the desk, and glanced at the ARC dashboard. Amanda leaned over his shoulder, pressing up against the back of his chair. The message on the screen stated that ARC's deep neural network had finished analyzing the new data infusion and produced its recommended outcomes. He clicked on the results button and studied the screen.

"Well, that's unexpected," Dennis said. "I might have underestimated the emerging threat coming from China."

"I suppose we should have run some diagnostics on potential outcomes to a wide range of data inputs?" she asked.

He sighed heavily and rubbed his chin. "Well, it's too late for that now."

"Do you want me to tweak the algorithms using the back door?" she asked.

Dennis shook his head, tapping his finger on his chin. "No, too risky. But there may be another way."

"How?"

He turned to smile triumphantly at her. "I own a Navy captain inside the Pentagon. And then there's my good-for-nothing systems engineer who works for him. Between the two of them, we'll make the necessary changes from inside the Pentagon, just in time for today's test and evaluation."

Amanda tilted her head. "How in the world did you get a senior military officer to do your bidding?"

Dennis smirked. "Everyone has a price."

# [ 1 ]
## DATA INFUSION

GRACE
6 July 2033
0415
National Military Command Center
The Pentagon
Arlington, Virginia

Loud beeps startled Grace Lim, waking her from a restless sleep. In a daze, she lifted her head from the desk and wiped a thick layer of drool from her cheek. Then she slowly recalled the sequence of events that led her to spend the entire night slumped over her desk with her face planted on the cold, hard surface.

Blinking several times, she opened her eyes a bit wider, and they landed directly on the silver framed photo of her father staring back at her. He wore his Air Force dress uniform and a familiar proud smile.

A sharp pang stabbed her gut, the pain of his death still fresh after a year of intense grief. She'd fallen asleep talking to her father's photo, asking him for advice about romantic relationships, of all things. Since her mom died during her teen years, it had been just the two of them for more than a decade. Grace smirked, thinking about her father's discomfort when she spoke to him about her feelings or any other topic he would have typically delegated to her mother when Grace was a young girl.

Grace glanced at her watch and then down at her crumpled Navy uniform and sighed heavily. She looked at her father's picture again, imagining the way he used to grimace at her.

"I know... I can't let my boss see me like this," she said. Rubbing her eyes with the back of her hands, she took a deep breath. "No time to make it all the way back to Falls Church..."

This wouldn't be the first or the last time she had to make use of the spare uniform she kept in her locker at the Pentagon Fitness Center.

"But first, I need to check the status on the data infusion. Then I'll know how much work will be on my plate this morning."

She rubbed her eyes again and stared at her terminal, looking for the source of the loud beeps she'd heard earlier. As expected, a gray textbox on the computer screen announced that the terabyte-sized data transfer was complete. She released a breath of relief and pressed the enter key to acknowledge the message. The screen went blank again. She was about to launch the ARC system's interface when her thoughts drifted to her boyfriend Zach, and her pulse spiked.

*Whoops.*

Grace smacked her forehead. She'd completely forgotten to let Zach know it was going to be a very late night.

*I can't blame him for being worried.* Thankfully, her smartphone was shut away in a lockbox outside the expansive Top Secret facility, so she didn't have to see the long stream of worried texts which probably devolved into angry ones.

"Oh, don't look at me like that," Grace said to her father's photo. "He knows I don't have access to my phone." Her father had always favored Zach over her other boyfriends. It was why she hadn't been able to let go of him for the past year. But it was time. She'd finally worked up the courage to break up with him.

As an active duty fighter pilot in the Air Force, Zach should know the drill about what happened when duty called. But somehow, that excuse didn't apply to her job as an Air Force data scientist, at least not from his perspective. Zach assumed her job to be a regular nine-to-fiver, with a few extra hours tacked on simply for working at the Pentagon. But Grace couldn't give him any details about what she did all day. He didn't have a high enough security clearance and didn't have the need to know. Grace was tired of having to fend off his criticism. She didn't owe him any explanation for why her job was so important.

*I should have never moved in with him.*

Grace hadn't meant to stay the entire night in her cubicle, but part of her wondered if she'd done it subconsciously to avoid going home to have the talk. It would mean she'd have to move out and find an affordable place to live. The previous day, one thing had led to another, giving her the perfect excuse to avoid the inevitable.

She'd gotten back to the Pentagon in the late afternoon from a National Security Council staff meeting at the White House to formulate new policies for deploying fully autonomous weapons systems. The national security agencies of the Executive Branch were busily preparing for the possibility that Congress would pass legislation giving the long-awaited green light to the Department of Defense for fielding such systems on the battlefield.

As soon as Grace returned to the Pentagon, her boss, Captain Dietz, had dragged her to another long meeting with the entire leadership of the J6 Cyber Directorate to discuss the next phase of the test and evaluation process for the Department of Defense's Autonomous Retaliatory Capability (ARC) system.

When she finally got out of the J6 meeting the previous

night, it was already seven p.m. Grace returned to her cubicle to enter in the commands to initiate ARC's data infusion. And at some point, she must have fallen fast asleep holding her father's picture.

ARC was the U.S. Strategic Command's shiny new automated system developed by Centoreum Tech, a leading defense contractor specializing in information technology. The system linked a comprehensive intelligence, surveillance, and reconnaissance (ISR) system together with existing early warning systems for detecting a nuclear attack as well as nuclear command and control systems for launching retaliatory attacks.

By automating the process to detect nuclear attacks, formulate an attack plan, and launch U.S. nuclear weapons, the military could maintain a speed advantage against potential adversaries and counter the threat of a first-strike attack with hypersonic missiles. Or at least, that's what many nuclear deterrence experts had claimed it would do in their testimonies before Congress several years ago.

Since ARC represented a semi-automated defensive system, it had skirted the strict laws against the Department of Defense fielding fully autonomous weapons systems. As long as humans remained in the loop of kill decisions, ARC was authorized by Congress. While some features of ARC were fully autonomous, others required human supervision, decision, and action. For example, although ARC could give the order to launch nuclear weapons automatically, the president retained the ability to issue the rescind order and cancel the launch.

After the system went fully operational, ARC was scheduled to be exposed on a monthly basis to a new data infusion on the latest technological and geopolitical developments. After the data update was fed into the system, the National Military Command Center would test ARC with a nuclear conflict simulation to ensure that it was functioning properly—that is, according to the model of nuclear deterrence.

The previous conflict simulations had been rather tame

peacetime scenarios to test out ARC's basic operations, and the system had passed with high marks. But the next test and evaluation would take ARC into a wartime situation. Congress had designated the first year of operation for the ARC system as a probation period. To keep ARC online, it was imperative that the test be a complete success.

As the lead data scientist for ARC, it had become Grace's job to make sure of it. But that wasn't what her official job description stated. When she started the position nine months ago, her most important responsibility was to serve as the front line for ARC's quality assurance program. Now it was more like quality reassurance. Pentagon leadership had become allergic to any suggestion that ARC might not function properly. It didn't matter how small. They didn't want to hear it.

For the first four months, the tests had proceeded exactly as expected. And each time, Grace had breathed a huge sigh of relief. ARC had consistently recommended the U.S. military stay the course with a few small tweaks here and there, to maintain strategic stability and ensure effective deterrence. Pentagon's senior leadership had made much fanfare in the press about the effectiveness of ARC and its important contribution to reducing the risk of nuclear war.

Both congressional leaders and the news media would be eagerly waiting for a report on the outcome of the fifth test and evaluation later that day. A heavy weight of responsibility rested on her shoulders.

Grace studied her computer screen for a few seconds, took a deep breath, and entered the command to open the ARC dashboard.

When it finally finished loading, Grace noticed a threat indicator had turned red. She typed in a few commands and opened up the ISR threat assessment tool, which determined the basis for ARC's recommendations. Her eyes widened as she scanned quickly through the assessment.

*Oh, this is not good.*

Her pulse quickened. ARC's deep neural network had responded to the previous night's data infusion with recommendations that appeared to deviate from the past four months. Grace double-clicked on ARC's message log to get more information about the results and raised an eyebrow.

*That's strange.*

To her surprise, the new messages were already marked "read." Grace right-clicked on the first message to get the metadata and then glanced at her watch.

"These were opened ten minutes ago," Grace said out loud, biting her lip. She didn't recognize the IP address or username. She stood up and peered over the cubicle wall to confirm she was still alone.

Sitting back down, she muttered, "Maybe NORAD logged on to ARC's dashboard to see the recommendations." Out of the corner of her eye, Grace caught her father giving her an inquisitive look. "Sorry, Dad, I can't tell you about this. It's classified. And you're not in the need to know."

# [ 2 ]
## TWEET WAR

SUSAN
0441
Executive Residence
The White House

*Something isn't right.*

Susan Tolley's painfully stiff body jerked beneath the fluffy duvet as her eyes flew open and her pulse quickened. A fluttering in her belly erupted as though she were in a free fall. But the room was quiet, still, and dark. At the foot of the bed, Penny's dog collar clinked a few times, but that wasn't the sound that had woken Susan.

*What was that?*

She'd sworn there had been a soft tapping sound, but now there was only silence.

Lifting her head, Susan attempted to see in the darkness, the thick fog of sleep still upon her, but she couldn't make out much. White shades covered the floor-to-ceiling windows, blocking the bright outdoor lights and preventing the early morning sunlight from seeping into the master bedroom. Only a tiny gap under the door illuminated portions of the room.

Susan rubbed her eyes and glanced over at her husband, Blake, who was sound asleep. He snored quietly under the light goose down duvet at the far side of the California king bed. Their six-year-old daughter, Lucy, snuggled next to him, her thumb in her mouth and her arm wrapped around her favorite plush teddy bear.

Susan turned her head and glanced at the alarm clock. She groaned. It was 4:41 a.m.

*Only nineteen more minutes.*

She sighed, reached for the alarm, and turned it off. At least now Blake and Lucy would get to sleep a bit longer. She struggled to sit up in bed, her neck achy from sleeping on it all wrong, and lay back down. For a few moments, all she could do was stare up at the fancy woodwork on the white ceiling, barely visible in the dim light. Susan wanted to relax and close her eyes for just one more minute, but the loud thumping in her chest propelled her forward.

Her eyes adjusted as she sat up and took in the elaborate chandelier hanging from the ceiling, the ornate fireplace across the room, and the stately furniture. After a moment of confusion, everything from the past few days came flooding back. President Harrison Monroe's sudden death over the July 4th holiday weekend. Getting sworn into office as the 49th President of the United States. Extensive planning for the state presidential funeral. And of course, the whirlwind move from the vice president's official residence at the U.S. Naval Observatory into the Executive Residence at the White House.

Her heart broke with grief for the hundredth time since Harrison's death. During his short time in office, they had become good friends, trusting each other implicitly despite their significant political differences.

*Is this really happening?*

Susan shook her head in disbelief. All she had to do was look around her unfamiliar surroundings to know the answer, but it didn't feel real.

Even though the move was only a few blocks, it was a major adjustment for the entire family. For the past few nights, Susan's sleep had been fitful and consumed with strange dreams about her recent dealings with China and her vicious rivalry with the secretary of defense. Blake had lain awake each night until the wee hours, tossing and turning. Each morning, he complained about the extra firm mattress. Lucy kept waking up in a frantic state on the other side of the White House, confused and crying for her momma. They'd finally conceded to her sleeping in the big bed until the Executive Residence felt like home. But Susan wasn't sure that would ever be possible. Becoming president had never been part of the plan.

A quiet rustle at the door startled her. Susan strained her ears and held her breath. With the exception of a helicopter rotor thumping in the distance and a few cars honking in the streets, she heard nothing but Blake's loud breathing and another jangle of Penny's collar.

*Maybe I'm just imagining things.*

As she slid out from under the covers, placed her feet on the cold hardwood floor, and shoved them into a pair of fleece slippers, there was a soft rap at the door. This time the noise was unmistakable.

Seconds later, a ray of light poured in through a crack in the door, and a dark shadow stepped into the room. Penny ran to greet the visitor.

"Madam President," a familiar female voice whispered.

"Elise, is that you?" Susan asked, frowning deeply at the formality.

For the past six months as vice president, her chief of staff had called Susan by her first name. After all, they were longtime friends from college, and it seemed silly to use formal titles. But now, she was the President of the United States of America. Elise had explained to Susan that not calling her by a formal title would give people the wrong impression—at least in public. As VP, Susan had been able to slip under the radar on occasion. Not anymore.

The door opened a bit wider. Elise stepped in with a thick blue binder under her arm and reached down to scratch the French bulldog's ears. Penny leaned against her leg and closed her eyes, appearing rather content.

Elise straightened, letting Penny stay put. "Ma'am, I'm sorry to wake you." Her shoulders drew upward half an inch as she winced slightly.

"What's happened?" Susan asked. Elise's early appearance in the Executive Residence fueled a spike in adrenaline, and her pulse quickened.

Elise put her finger to her mouth as Susan tiptoed across the room and then ducked out of the master bedroom. Penny's soft feet padded behind, following them into the private sitting room next door. Susan squinted in the bright light, shielding her eyes with her hand.

Elise was a bit pale, and her azure blue eyes were wider than normal. With her sleek, chestnut-brown hair framing her thin face, she was well put together for the early hour—perfectly applied makeup, a navy blazer, a matching pencil skirt, and snakeskin heels.

"There's some shocking rhetoric coming out of China this morning," Elise said, only a few lines creasing on her forehead. "The intelligence analysts in the White House Watch Center are tracking the situation with the protesters in Hong Kong, where it is still early evening."

Susan nodded solemnly. On July 1st, the day before President Monroe died, millions of Chinese protesters had taken to the streets of Hong Kong. It was supposed to be a peaceful demonstration to mark the 36th anniversary of Great Britain's formal return of the island nation to China. But Chinese police had used tear gas, and the protesters had begun throwing rocks.

She'd expected the situation in Hong Kong to remain tense for a few days but hoped it would eventually simmer down.

Just as it had when the Chinese People's Liberation Army first seized military control of Hong Kong several months ago—a move that spurred the Chinese government to announce an abrupt end to its policy of one country, two systems. The transition took place immediately, fourteen years earlier than planned under the Sino-British Joint Declaration. The loss of Hong Kong to China meant one less democracy in a world consisting of increasingly authoritarian regimes.

*We should have done something about it several months ago.*

At the time of the takeover, the U.S. government had been consumed with restoring law and order in the aftermath of the Nightfall Incident. A low-yield nuclear weapon was dropped from the International Space Station, detonated in the atmosphere, and released a massive electromagnetic pulse (EMP). The loss of power for several weeks and the destruction of most electronics on the Eastern Seaboard brought a major part of the country to its knees for several months. Too busy managing domestic issues, President Monroe had failed to respond to China crossing the critical red line previously espoused by his predecessor. They'd left the people of Hong Kong to their tragic fate, and it was way too late for the United States to take the high ground now.

Elise pulled a thin tablet out of her binder, handed it to Susan, and said, "The protesters are calling on the world's democracies to intervene militarily and release them from oppressive surveillance by Chinese state security. They've specifically requested help from the United States through news media channels. In response, the Chinese government has made some aggressive threats against us on social media, warning against any supportive action on behalf of the protesters."

"Against us? Over social media?" Susan stared at the list of tweets on her screen, her eyes still blurry. Her reading glasses were lying on the nightstand, and she wasn't about to bother Blake and Lucy to get them.

Although Twitter remained banned for the general public in China, its government had made greater use of the social media platform in recent months to communicate with the world about its expansionist goals. But this would be the first time the Chinese government had chosen to engage in escalation with the U.S. government over such informal channels.

*I just don't believe it.*

Susan rubbed her forehead. "But why now? We didn't intervene when they resumed full control over Hong Kong except to condemn the violation of their longstanding agreement with Great Britain. Why are they threatening us? What do they think we'll do?" She furrowed her brow, contemplating the true intent behind the tweets. "Are you absolutely sure the posts are legitimate?"

"That's what our intel analysts are still trying to figure out," Elise said.

"I hope you didn't get me out of bed early for a few tweets?" Susan asked, covering her mouth as she released a huge yawn.

Elise's eyes narrowed. "No. There's more. Do you remember the briefing about how the CIA has been tracking a flotilla of Chinese submarines heading for the Northern Sea Route?"

"Oh, for the naval exercise the Chinese have planned for tomorrow morning?" Susan asked, yawning again. As a long-time environmental expert, she'd been predicting that the Arctic might become a major transit route for years as a result of climate change—possibly even for nuclear deterrence patrols. "Didn't China announce that *Prowling Tiger* would include a nuclear component two weeks ago?"

"Yes," Elise said. "To support the war game, the Chinese sent five submarines through the South China Sea bound for the Northern Sea Route last week. They warned us against any interference. Supposedly the submarines are deployed on a defensive mission."

*Supposedly? They'd better be if they're hanging out in our coastal waters.*

"Did something unexpected happen to change our impression?" Susan asked.

Elise put her finger to her lips. "We can't talk about it here. The director of national intelligence called me an hour ago with a preview of intelligence reporting for this morning. When I heard what it was about, I told him to come to the White House right away. He's currently waiting for you in the Situation Room, along with analysts from the CIA, NSA, and FBI."

"At this hour?" Susan rubbed her eyes again, trying to make sense of what she was hearing. "But it's not even five a.m."

"Ma'am, the director thinks you might want to reach a decision on how to respond to China this morning. Given the perceived urgency, he thought it best to move it up," Elise said, tapping her finger on her binder. "He also wants to know if we should loop in the SecDef, the chairman of the Joint Chiefs of Staff, and the commander of the Pacific Forces."

*Geez, it must be important.*

Stretching her back and cracking her neck, Susan reached down to pet Penny's head. "Uh... not yet. I'll take a look at what they have before we hit the alarm bell. I don't want everyone to lose their heads over nothing," she said, nodding briskly and moving toward the door. When Elise didn't immediately follow her lead, she turned around, raised her eyebrows, and placed her hands on her hips. "Okay, are we going down there or not?"

"Do you maybe want to get dressed first?" Elise asked, cracking a smile and pointing at her pajamas.

"Oh." Susan blinked several times and then realized what she was wearing—blue cotton pajamas covered with gray and white French bulldogs that looked just like Penny. A birthday gift from Lucy. "Yeah, that's probably a good idea."

# [ 3 ]
## THE DINER

MORGAN
0505
Bob and Edith's Diner
Crystal City, Virginia

"She's going to fire me," Morgan Shaw murmured, staring up at the large TV as a new headline flashed across the bottom of the screen. Her eyes followed the scrolling text, flicking back and forth. With each word, her pulse increased a notch, causing her heart to thump a little louder.

The news ticker announced the imminent passage of the congressional bill which would authorize the Department of Defense to transfer kill decisions from human commanders to fully autonomous weapons systems for the first time in U.S. history.

It was the late President Harrison Monroe's prized legislation, the crowning achievement of his first—and now only—six months in office. To honor his sudden death, members of Congress from both sides of the aisle had apparently banded together and spent the entire night in bipartisan negotiations.

Now, the bill was expected to pass its final vote in the U.S. Senate and would be sent to President Tolley for her signature by the end of the day. Morgan sighed heavily.

*Just what I need on top of everything else.*

She pulled her attention away from the news and let her eyes settle on her boyfriend, Luis. Deeply engrossed in reading on his tablet, he didn't appear to have heard her mumbling to herself. Like everyone else, he was distracted by the ongoing investigation into President Monroe's sudden death over the holiday weekend. The entire horrible account—the rapid onset of his symptoms, his collapse on the golf course, and his immediate cardiac arrest—smeared the front page of *The Washington Post* online. The headline read: Independence Day Celebrations Dampened by President's Tragic Death.

Morgan glanced at her work phone, scrolled through the messages, and breathed a sigh of relief when she didn't see anything urgent. Despite a persistent tightness in her chest, Morgan felt comforted by the familiar yellow, blue, and white booths and tall windows of Bob and Edith's Diner. Inside, the restaurant looked like any other diner, but the outside of the building was a stainless-steel trapezoid. It was the odd look of the building that had attracted Luis and Morgan to the diner in the first place. And now it was their favorite breakfast spot.

Her stomach growling, Morgan rubbed her temples with both hands and massaged her forehead. She tugged on the edge of her beige skirt, which had ridden up her right leg after sitting down in the booth.

Just then, a tall male server carrying a large tray of breakfast specialties brushed by her shoulder, sending the salty smell of bacon mixed with sweet vanilla and cinnamon pancakes up her nose. She cast an eager glance toward the kitchen to see if their orders were sitting on the service counter, waiting to be picked up. But they were nowhere in sight.

Morgan reached for her ice water and leaned forward to drink from the paper straw, but all she got was air. She frowned.

When she looked down at the glass, the straw was gone. Furrowing her brow, she searched the table and the floor for the lost straw. Then she looked up to find Luis grinning at her with the straw hanging limply out of the corner of his mouth like a cigarette. Leaning forward, he blew air through it. The straw lifted with the force of his breath, and a few drops of water landed on her face.

"Hey, that's not funny," she said, unable to hide her smirk.

"Well, I beg to differ," Luis said. He gave her a triumphant smile, showing his full set of teeth, and then glanced back down at his tablet.

A slight shiver cascaded down her back. The Marine Corps green and khaki uniform made his chiseled face look even more dreamy than usual. The colors highlighted his coffee brown eyes and dark olive skin he'd inherited from the Cuban side of his family. Sometimes, she still wanted to pinch herself that she'd gotten so lucky—he was smart, successful, and handsome.

Though they'd only been dating a few months, Morgan and Luis were already one of D.C.'s most notable power couples. While she worked defense issues at the White House and reported to the president, Luis served as executive assistant to the chairman of the Joint Chiefs of Staff. But in the wake of the president's death, their success felt empty to her.

A deep pang of guilt made her cringe when she thought about it. Truthfully, she was more upset over the disruption caused by the tragedy of Monroe's death than over the loss of the man himself.

*Am I a bad person?*

She suppressed the thought.

"I think she's going to fire me," Morgan said again, this time with a bit more oomph.

"Who, President Tolley?" Luis asked, eyes still glued to his tablet.

"It's only a matter of time," she added grimly and took a long sip of coffee.

Luis peered over the tablet, his forehead wrinkling. "Why would you say that?"

Morgan shrugged. "She kicked Uncle Jack to the curb the same day she was sworn into office over the weekend. I bet I'm next on her list."

"That was different," Luis said with a frown. "Jack was Harrison's chief of staff. It makes perfect sense she'd want her own people in her inner circle. But I don't think she'd clean house on the National Security Council staff. Not this soon after the president's death. And she'd definitely not ax her most talented nuclear weapons expert in the middle of a crisis with China." He offered a supportive smile.

Morgan grimaced, her cheeks flushing. "Oh, I wouldn't be so sure she'd agree about my talent. Last week, Tolley and I butted heads in the Oval Office on my interpretation of China's forward deployment of its nuclear-armed submarines. There I am trying to explain my views to the president and warn him about something ominous being afoot, and Vice President Tolley asks me how I could possibly know anything about what China intends to do with their nuclear weapons." Her tone went deadpan, and she narrowed her eyes. "Since I'm not a China expert."

Luis smirked. "I take it she disagreed with your assessment?"

Morgan nodded. "Oh yeah. She's close friends with the Chinese ambassador. I guess they attended grad school together or something. That's been useful for negotiating the clean energy deal, but now Tolley thinks her insider connections make her *the* expert on all things China. But I worry she's wearing blinders when it comes to national security issues. China has been making some aggressive moves to gain advantages over the U.S. since the start of the Monroe administration. Meanwhile, Tolley's barely paid attention over the past six months to any of Harrison's preferred strategies for managing China's escalation. I'd respect her knowledge on climate change or environmental issues any day, but it was like my expertise on nuclear weapons issues didn't matter to her."

"But do you really think she'd fire you over a little disagreement?" Luis asked.

Morgan bit her lip. "Harrison sided with me, and Tolley wasn't happy about it. Now that he's gone, she might see an opportunity to get rid of me."

"Well, if your instincts are right, you'll probably find out soon enough."

*My thoughts exactly.*

# PROWLING TIGER

SUSAN
0515
Situation Room
The White House

Her mind still hazy from sleep deprivation, Susan rested her arms on the smooth mahogany conference table. She folded her hands in a desperate attempt to keep herself from fidgeting with her pen. A strong gust blew from the air conditioner overhead, causing goosebumps to form on her bare arms.

From behind her, it felt as if the Presidential Seal on the wall bored a hole in her back. She'd glimpsed it on the way into the Situation Room and experienced another round of fluttering butterflies in her stomach. The responsibility to protect the U.S. and its allies against emerging threats weighed heavily upon her chest.

She wondered if President Monroe had also experienced a serious bout of nerves when he first took the highest office in the land and sat at the head of that table. It didn't seem to faze

Harrison; or at least, he never let on that it did. Harrison appeared eerily confident from day one.

*Another thing I should have asked him about.*

Susan studied the people in the room, counting twelve in total, attending in person or remotely from various locations. Several intelligence analysts from different agencies sat along the table, each one huddled over their classified laptops, reviewing their notes. Elise hovered somewhere behind Susan, ready to whisper in her ear if necessary. Although they were both in their mid-forties, the woman displayed boundless energy and preferred to stand whenever possible.

Aside from the director of national intelligence, Susan hadn't invited any other cabinet members to the meeting. She wanted a chance to get her bearings before having to fend off the SecDef's militant views while she made up her mind.

Surrounded by people in the room and on video screen, Susan was keenly aware of her unwashed hair whipped up into a messy bun. She shifted her weight in the plush chair, trying to ignore her sense of unease. She'd only taken enough time to throw on a clean pair of jeans and a short-sleeve shirt and grab a hair tie—even though her chief of staff insisted everyone could certainly wait for a few minutes on the President of the United States. As the second female president in U.S. history, the last thing she wanted to be accused of was primping in the middle of a national security crisis.

Now that she was in the limelight, Susan desperately wished she'd covered up her bare face with a bit of color. But what she regretted most about her haste was failing to grab a cup of coffee from the White House kitchen. The smell of roasted hazelnut coffee wafting up from a mug several seats down tickled her nose.

*At least I'm not wearing my pajamas.*

"Madam President, we've been following a series of tweets coming from the *China Xinhua News* handle starting around midnight our time," a female senior analyst at the National

Security Agency (NSA) spoke over the secure video conferencing screen on the opposite beige wall. "The first few posts warned of a military response by China if the U.S. attempts to help the protesters in any way. A few hours later, the content of the posts escalated, threatening the use of nuclear weapons if we did anything to interfere with their economic and political control of Hong Kong."

Susan flinched, her face blanching.

*China threatened the use of nuclear weapons? Over social media?*

"I know China is in the process of revising its nuclear doctrine, but this doesn't make any sense," Susan said. "Even if China may be backing away from its nuclear policy of no-first-use, the threats seem a bit extreme." She scratched her temple, searching for an answer. "The blustery posts sound more like they came from North Korea. Are we certain of their origin?"

Before the NSA analyst could respond, William Grayson, her director of national intelligence, chimed in from where he sat to the analyst's left. "Ma'am, I have my guys at our Cyberthreat Intelligence Integration Center analyzing the source of the tweets. From the geolocation data, we've traced the IP address for the posts to a smartphone used somewhere near the city of Harbin, China. We're still trying to ascertain the identity of the specific user and verify if they have a legitimate affiliation with the Chinese government."

Dressed in a broken-in black suit and blue, dotted foulard tie, Grayson looked fondly at her with his smoky-gray eyes through thin, wire-framed glasses. She smiled back at him. Even as VP, Susan had taken a quick liking to the older man. He was wise, competent, and politically savvy, but most strikingly, he behaved kindly to everyone—from the janitor to the White House scheduling assistant to the president. Rank and title didn't seem to matter to him. He also happened to be one of Monroe's closest confidantes and often treated Susan like a daughter. To most people, he went by "Grayson," but she alone was allowed to call him Bill.

Grayson was also the most senior intelligence official in the U.S. government. Every day, his team pulled together the Top Secret Presidential Daily Brief, gathering the most important pieces of intelligence from the CIA, NSA, FBI, Defense Intelligence Agency (DIA), and many others. There were at least sixteen different agencies within the U.S. intelligence community, and Susan could barely keep track of who did what, when, and under what authority. Thankfully, it was Grayson's job to coordinate across all agencies and deliver the latest intelligence to the president each morning.

Susan frowned, thinking about her last official trip to China. "Wait a minute. Harbin? That city is located in the northernmost province of China, but the headquarters of China's state news agency is located in Beijing." She turned to look at Grayson, her eyebrow raised. "Bill, if they were legitimate, wouldn't these posts be coming directly from a computer owned by the Chinese central government or at the very least by the state news agency in Beijing?"

"Ma'am, *China Xinhua News* does operate a bureau in Harbin, so it's not beyond the realm of possibility," he said. "But yes, it's a bit odd that the Chinese government would release important news from a smartphone near a remote outpost."

*A bit odd? Try incredibly odd.*

"How do we even know the tweets originated in Harbin?" Susan asked. She hadn't wanted to ask the amateur question, but it just slipped out.

"Ma'am, if I may," the NSA analyst on the video screen interjected. "Whenever someone posts a tweet, other information is captured in the metadata on Twitter's programming interface, which is made available to the public. This includes information about the user's profile, the type of device the post was sent from, and location data such as latitude and longitude."

"Can we figure out who uploaded the posts?" Susan asked.

"Yes, ma'am," the NSA analyst continued. "We can use Twitter's geocode parameters to search for all posts within a certain radius of a set of coordinates. By comparing the metadata, we may be able to determine if the posts came from someone affiliated with *China Xinhua News* or not. We're still trying to cross-reference the tweets with other posts to identify the user."

"In other words, it's possible that someone hacked the Twitter account of China's state news agency and posted the tweets in an attempt to escalate a conflict between China and the U.S.," Susan said, tucking a loose hair behind her ear. "And I assume you're working to confirm the source of the tweets to exclude that scenario."

Grayson cleared his throat. "Indeed, we are, ma'am. However, even without final confirmation, we believe the tweets could represent official communication from the Chinese government based on other data. The latest tweet tracks with our intelligence on *Prowling Tiger*, China's war game scheduled to take place tomorrow. There's no way an outsider could have known the specific details that were revealed in the posts."

Susan moved toward the edge of her seat to get a better grip with her feet on the floor. "What sort of details?"

"One of the posts specifically mentions a flotilla of Chinese submarines headed for the Chukchi Sea in the Northwest Passage. It also states that two of the submarines are armed with submarine-launched ballistic missiles that carry nuclear weapons, which we've known since we started tracking them," Grayson said. "But no one else could know this without insider knowledge or our submarine tracking capabilities."

"The tweets match our intelligence reports?"

"Yes, ma'am. We've been tracking the flotilla since it left the South China Sea and traveled toward the Northern Sea Route to participate in *Prowling Tiger*. It took about nine days for them to reach the Bering Strait located between Alaska and Russia."

Susan furrowed her brow. "This is part of *Prowling Tiger*?"

"Yes, ma'am, we believe this is defensive maneuvering related to the war game as we suggested last week during the briefing with President Monroe." Grayson lowered his head, and he stopped speaking for a moment.

At the mention of the president's name, something caught in Susan's throat, and she had to catch her breath. Swallowing hard, she suppressed the tears welling in her eyes.

Susan squished her eyebrows together to mask the moisture and deflected her emotion with a question. "Didn't China announce to the entire world two weeks ago that it planned to send a flotilla of submarines to the Northern Sea Route as part of its war game?"

"Yes, ma'am," Grayson said.

Susan lowered her head and pinched the bridge of her nose. "But then I don't understand what is so urgent about these tweets. I mean, if we expect them to travel this route."

"Ma'am, we lost track of China's nuclear-armed submarines," Grayson said.

Susan jerked her head up and looked him squarely in the eyes. "You lost track of two of China's submarines near our coastal waters?"

He nodded grimly.

"Well, shit…"

# [ 5 ]
## LAST WORDS

MORGAN
0530
Bob and Edith's Diner
Crystal City, Virginia

Morgan took a sip of her coffee, hoping it would soothe her empty stomach, which sizzled angrily in anticipation of her hard day at work. The news media would be in a tizzy all day, rehashing the details of President Monroe's death over the weekend. The talking heads would attempt to discern the outcome of President Tolley's decision concerning the new bill on the morning talk shows.

"Do you think Tolley will sign the autonomous weapons legislation?" Luis asked, peering at her over the top of his tablet.

"No idea," Morgan said. "No one has any clue about Tolley's views on fully autonomous weapons. But then, she was never supposed to be the one to make this decision. Harrison added her to the ticket as the VP candidate to mollify moderate Republicans and win over Independents. When the majority of conservative U.S. businesses finally got on board with the economic

25

implications of the climate crisis, the Republican party had to fall in line. Harrison chose the perfect running mate to rob the Democrats of the Independent vote. And now she's the president."

Luis gave her a pained expression. "Well, I'm sure it helped that President Madison resigned from office when information about her corruption surfaced, leaving Harrison as the only viable candidate."

His tone was loaded with sarcasm, and Morgan didn't need to decipher what it meant. Luis referred to a series of unfortunate events that had led to the previous president's resignation, which many of her immediate family members had a hand in. Only a small circle of people knew what had really occurred behind the scenes, and Luis was one of them.

Morgan pinched her lips. "Yeah, Madison's VP had no shot against Harrison that late in the game," she said quickly.

Luis nodded solemnly, avoiding eye contact. "Didn't Tolley just secure a historical clean energy agreement with China to reduce the use of fossil fuels by both countries?"

*He always changes the subject whenever Nightfall comes up.*

Any talk about the largest terrorist attack on U.S. soil and her family's intimate knowledge of how it came about was a non-starter with Luis. She didn't like talking about it either, but if they constantly avoided the topic, they would never discover the whole truth. Maybe she didn't want to know.

"Yeah, Tolley spent the past six months working on that. Since President Monroe took the lead on national security issues, Tolley pretty much ignored the issue of fully autonomous weapons," Morgan said, bringing the conversation back full circle. "Now that President Tolley will make the final decision, I'm not exactly sure what will happen. But I'll have to spend the day fielding inquiries from the media." Morgan frowned. "I really don't like feeling my way around in the dark."

She snuck a peek at her work phone and gulped when she saw two missed calls and a text from her boss asking her to stop by as soon as she arrived at work. Instead of responding to the text, she glanced at her watch to check the time.

*Geez. They're all in super early today. Did I miss something?*

The previous night, Morgan had worried it was a bad day for their weekly breakfast date. But Luis had insisted on going as an attempt to distract her from her dismal thoughts about the president's sudden death and remind her that life must go on.

*It's not working.*

Every time she thought about it, her stomach churned and sizzled. Despite a thorough autopsy, medical examiners remained stumped; a man in his late fifties considered to be in pristine health shouldn't keel over dead from a heart attack during a light round of golf. Of course, Morgan had learned all the shocking details a few moments after they occurred, including some that may never see the light of day. Jack Shaw, Morgan's uncle and the president's chief of staff, had been by his side during his last moments and called her shortly after his collapse.

Harrison was a long-time friend of the Shaw family, but Morgan never felt close to him personally. Her uncle, father, mother, and even her cousin had sacrificed a great deal to get him elected. But the road to the presidency had been a messy one for her family; since Harrison had won the election, no one would speak of what it had taken to get there.

Before he died, the president kept muttering over and over, "They're coming for us, they're coming for us."

No one on the scene could make any sense of it. But his words had alarmed Uncle Jack so deeply, he'd called Morgan to get her take—as if she could somehow read the president's mind and decode the strange words.

"What do you suppose that means?" he asked her. "You don't think they would dare return to the U.S. after what they've done, do you?"

*I sure hope not.*

If law enforcement authorities discovered the events that had led to the Nightfall Incident—the dark secrets harbored by everyone Morgan cared for—if these ever came to light, her entire family, Luis, their relationship, and her career would be destroyed forever. And without the most powerful man on earth to help maintain the cover story, the truth might get out.

*What if Tolley already knows?*

Morgan wanted desperately to talk to Luis about her deep-seated fear since he would know what to do, or at least be able to calm her down. But Luis preferred to pretend as if it all had never happened. Every time she danced around the topic, he'd change the subject.

To get over his own guilt, Luis justified his actions leading up to the election and the Nightfall Incident as defending U.S. national security interests. Afterward, he'd pushed everyone to come clean with the authorities. He backed down when he realized the truth would ruin them all and ultimately change nothing. Morgan knew keeping the secret weighed heavily on his conscience.

"I'm sure you'll do just fine," Luis said.

"At what?" Morgan looked up at him with a confused expression. She'd retreated to her innermost thoughts and couldn't remember what they had been talking about before.

"I mean at work today," Luis said, smiling at her. "Handling all the questions about the legislation."

"You're probably right."

Just then, the server placed a Western omelet with three slices of crispy bacon in front of Luis. Morgan licked her lips as the server set down a stack of fresh blueberry hotcakes and two sausage patties in front of her. With a big grin on his face, Luis grabbed the Tabasco pepper sauce and drizzled it all over his breakfast.

Morgan pulled up her nose. "I'd be careful if I were you. Last time, you used so much hot sauce, you nearly ruined your breakfast."

*And your breath.*

"Well, I like everything hot and spicy," Luis said with a mischievous grin. "Just like my woman."

Morgan flushed. Then she took the first bite of her pancake. Her mouth watered at the combination of maple syrup, salty butter, and a tart blueberry. When she looked up, Luis had stopped chewing, and his face had gone slack. He stared at the screen of his smartphone, and a deep frown formed.

"What's wrong?" she asked.

His forehead creased. "I'm afraid I have to get going." Raising his hand in the air, Luis signaled the server for a carryout box.

"You're not even going to eat your food?" Morgan asked, pointing at his plate and failing to hide her disappointment.

Luis gave her an apologetic look. "Babe, I'm really sorry. I have to take it to-go this time. The test and evaluation for the Department of Defense's Autonomous Retaliatory Capability kicks off at 1:30 this afternoon, and I just got an email from Major Lim, ARC's lead data scientist, about some new issues with the algorithm after the last batch of data. Before the test takes place, we have to pre-brief the chairman this morning."

Morgan raised her eyebrow. "Major Lim. Wait, is that my friend, Grace?"

*She's working on the ARC system these days? That could explain why I saw her at the meeting yesterday.*

Luis nodded. "Yeah, she was recently assigned to be the lead data scientist on ARC at the Pentagon. She didn't tell you about it?"

*Whoops.*

Biting her lip, Morgan shook her head. She hadn't returned Grace's calls in months. And then Morgan spotted her in the room attending the same meeting at the White House. A feeling of guilt rose in her stomach. She'd noticed that Grace wanted to come speak to her, but she had another meeting to get to and ran off, not giving her friend the chance. She gulped.

"What? Why?" Luis asked, but then waved his hand back and forth.

Morgan shrugged like she didn't know why Grace hadn't told her.

"Never mind. We can talk about it later," he said. "I may need to make some last-minute changes to the read-ahead for the chairman before the pre-brief, so I'd better get going."

"Isn't this the fifth test and evaluation for ARC?" Morgan asked in an attempt to delay his departure.

Luis sighed heavily. "Yep, we're on the hook, per congressional order in the 2032 National Defense Authorization Act, to conduct a monthly simulation and test the impact of the new data inputs based on the current threat environment. This is supposed to keep ARC up to date with the latest technological developments and ensure the system continues to function as expected. It's a big ordeal, costing the taxpayers tons of money. We get the National Military Command Center all spun up, with senior-level Pentagon officials in attendance and the commander of U.S. Strategic Command beaming in from Omaha over the secure video teleconference."

"Continues to function as expected?" Morgan asked, her brow furrowed. "It had better function as expected. The system has the capability to give the launch order for U.S. nuclear weapons. How could its functioning even be up for discussion?"

Luis winced. "Yeah, I'm not thrilled about the notion either. It has something to do with the data that's fed into the algorithm and how it changes the outcomes." He scratched his head. "Or it changes the algorithms. I dunno. I'm still trying to wrap my head around the complexities, but the ARC system is pretty much a black box for me. I have no idea what's going on inside ARC's deep neural net—"

"You're responsible for briefing the chairman on its functioning this morning, and you don't understand how it works?" As soon as Morgan asked the question, she regretted it.

Luis clenched his jaw. "Well, it's not really my fault. I do whatever I can, but understanding ARC requires specialized expertise. There are complex mathematical calculations that take place within the deep neural network. Even the mathematicians and data scientists can't always explain why or how the system learns from the data." He paused for a moment and studied Morgan's face. "If you want to know more, you should really ask Grace about it when you get a chance." Luis pointed at his watch, stood up, and gave her an apologetic look.

*Okay, I got the hint. I'll call Grace.*

"Go," Morgan said, waving him off. "I don't want you to be late. We'll catch up later. Maybe after the ARC test?"

Nodding, Luis leaned over to kiss her. A strong whiff of tomato and pepper made her pull away just in time to avoid him. She narrowed her eyes, and he gave her a knowing smirk, settling for a kiss on her cheek. Then he hurried out of the diner.

Morgan watched him go when her smartphone buzzed with a text from her boss:

You might want to get to the office early this morning

*Great.* Morgan sighed and looked down at her half-eaten pancakes. *No breakfast for the wicked, I guess.*

# [ 6 ]
## CHUKCHI SEA

SUSAN
0540
Situation Room
The White House

Susan looked from Grayson to the other intelligence analysts with a blank expression on her face. They'd all sunk deep into the cushions of their seats, none of them wanting to explain further how the U.S. Navy could have lost two of China's subs. She was about to speak when a brave, middle-aged, black DIA analyst finally piped up with more information.

"Ma'am, we've been tracking the submarines with our swarm of underwater drones," he said. "These drones use undersea GPS technology and relay location coordinates back to our own submarines in the region. As expected, China's flotilla of submarines passed by our underwater sensors off the coast of Wales, Alaska yesterday. Then earlier this morning, the flotilla traveled near some Russian submarines, making it hard to keep track of them with absolute certainty. We assumed all five Chinese submarines would take the Northern Sea Route to the

Northeast Passage and then travel along the Russian coast for their role in tomorrow's war game. The three diesel-electric powered submarines took the route we expected. But when the two nuclear-powered submarines reached the open waters in the Chukchi Sea, we lost any sign of them."

"How did we lose them?" Susan asked.

Grayson nodded at her as if he'd expected the question. "Ma'am, although the waters are quite shallow there, the high level of background noise prevented us from picking up a signal."

Suppressing a wince, Susan recalled the argument she'd gotten into with Dr. Morgan Shaw in the Oval Office.

*Was I dead wrong last week?*

She'd shut Morgan down in front of the president in an after-hours discussion about the forward deployment of China's submarines. Susan had disagreed with Morgan's views, but she mostly resented feeling undermined by another woman, especially one fifteen years younger than her. Although Morgan's expertise on nuclear weapons was invaluable, it was her healthy dose of arrogance Susan didn't like. Morgan often behaved as if she was aware of her superior ability for navigating complex issues and powerful players inside the Beltway.

*She doesn't need to flaunt it so much.*

Harrison had hired Morgan as Director for Defense Issues on the National Security Council staff as a favor to Jack Shaw, his chief of staff and Morgan's uncle. Despite her high-level connections, Morgan exhibited a razor-sharp intellect, and her knowledge of U.S. nuclear weapons policy was unrivaled within the White House. Even though the young woman deserved to work on the National Security Council staff, Susan found her unbearably obstinate and difficult to work with.

*But I'm the president now. Maybe she'll be more respectful.*

If Morgan failed to behave according to Susan's preferences, she could always fire the woman.

*But she's really good at her job.*

It might be a better idea for Susan to use Morgan somehow toward achieving her own ends. The last thing she needed was another enemy inside the Beltway. And definitely not one as well-connected as Dr. Shaw.

*I already have to contend with the likes of Burke.*

"Should we raise this issue with the Chinese and see what they have to say about it?" Susan asked, wishing for a moment that Elizabeth Whitaker, her close friend and the secretary of state, was in the room to offer some diplomatic advice.

Grayson cleared his throat. "Ma'am, I'd expect the Chinese to blame us. They might suggest they're merely mimicking the U.S. Navy's strategy of engaging China as far forward as possible as a means to strengthen nuclear deterrence. The Chinese would claim that since we're closely monitoring their submarines in the South China Sea, they have the right to do the same in our coastal waters. However, the Chinese typically defend their submarines with a highly visible fleet of naval forces. That's what makes this operation different."

"Where do we suspect the submarines are located now?" Susan asked.

With a curt nod, Grayson said, "We think they might have taken the Northwest Passage off the coast of Alaska and Canada. If they did, they are probably somewhere in the Beaufort Sea by now. This would be a pretty significant development. In the past, no sane submarine commander would go near that place since it used to be covered in ice most of the year. But with all the ice melt from years of climate change, the route has become passable."

*And that means...*

Susan hesitated to ask the question on the tip of her tongue. She wanted to kick herself for not paying closer attention to nuclear weapons issues over the past six months, but she never thought she'd have to deal with them.

*This was Harrison's job.*

As if sensing her question, Grayson leaned forward and said,

"Ma'am, there are two Chinese nuclear-armed submarines located somewhere in the Western hemisphere. That means China can reach almost any target within the continental United States with its nuclear weapons."

Taking a few short breaths, Susan did her best to hide her lack of specific knowledge and kept her face slack. But the room had gone silent in anticipation of her response, and all eyes were on her. Every moment that passed by felt like an eternity.

Her mind raced through the implications. She knew it would only take one submarine to cause massive devastation on U.S. soil--even if the ballistic missile defense system were successful in taking out a missile or two. For this reason, the White House would need to take the incursion seriously, possibly issuing a strong condemnation of Chinese aggression. However, her senior military advisors would likely caution against a military conflict with China and dissuade her from taking tangible actions that would lead to escalation.

*But would the Chinese even believe our threats?*

Susan considered what might happen if the Chinese called her bluff. As the new commander in chief, the Chinese government might consider her weak and perceive an opportunity for taking offensive action. The United States was still trying to regain its national security footing since the Nightfall Incident. Things were just returning to a new normal when Harrison died suddenly.

Susan doubted the Chinese would make a reckless offensive move. Even so, she felt compelled to ask the next question. "Are the Chinese using the war game as a pretense for putting their military assets into place?"

"Perhaps," Grayson said. "We have to consider all possible scenarios. As you know, it would not be the first time the Chinese have made a major move while we were distracted with other issues."

Susan nodded, gazing at the table in front of her as if it might provide her answers to the many questions in her mind.

During the weeklong communications blackout after Nightfall, the White House had been so consumed with rebooting large portions of the electrical grid, acquiring new communications equipment, and restoring law and order, the Monroe administration hadn't seen the Hong Kong takeover coming.

After several moments of silence, Susan looked up at the room of expectant faces. "Thanks everyone for the briefing. I'd like to reconvene this discussion in a meeting of the National Security Council later this morning. In the meantime, Bill, please have your team try to confirm the source of the tweets and gather as much information as you can on Chinese plans for that war game. And find those submarines."

Susan stood up from the conference table, and the others followed suit.

Elise tugged her arm. "Ma'am, see you back in the Oval?"

Susan nodded, and Elise departed the room.

As the team of intelligence analysts filed out of the room, Grayson motioned for her to join him in the corner. When they were close enough to whisper, she waited for him to say something. For a moment, his wrinkled face looked manic. That's when she noticed his bloodshot eyes and detected a whiff of bourbon on his breath.

*Has he been drinking?*

Susan wouldn't blame him for burying his sorrows in a bottle of whiskey. But she couldn't afford to get distracted by her pain. Unlike Grayson, she'd inherited a vast array of enemies within her own administration. They were like vicious sharks swimming in circles, waiting for a sniff of blood before attacking.

Grayson ran his hand through his thinning gray hair. "Do you think the Russians had anything to do with President Monroe's death?"

*What does Russia have to do with any of this?*

Taking a step back, Susan gave him an incredulous stare. "Do you know something I don't?" Her eyes wide, she waited for an answer, but none came.

Grayson stood there, wobbling slightly as if he were shell-shocked that he'd even uttered the words in the first place.

Susan lowered her voice. "You do realize you're suggesting the president died of something other than natural causes. We don't even know the autopsy results. Shouldn't we wait on making crazy allegations until we have a reason? We've got plenty to worry about as it is."

Grayson dropped his chin to his chest and sighed. "Ma'am, you're right. It was a careless remark, and I apologize. The president's sudden death has me on edge. I'm still reeling from the shock of it and am not myself lately."

"It's okay," Susan said, squeezing his arm.

Grayson shook his head. "No, it's not okay. We're in the middle of the biggest crisis since the Nightfall Incident. I have to get it together, if not for myself... then for you, ma'am." A tear rolled down his cheek, and he sniffed. "I just miss him terribly."

"I can't believe he's gone either," Susan said, her voice wavering. "When I actually stop to think about it, I can barely hold it together."

Grayson leaned in closer to her, crowding her personal space again. "Ma'am, I'm worried about much more than the president's death. I don't know how to tell you this..." He lowered his voice, his lip quivering. "The FBI director called me this morning with some troubling new information about the Nightfall Incident." He studied her face as if waiting for a response.

"Just tell me."

Grayson looked around him again before leaning in and said, "There appears to be a serious counterintelligence threat which has been linked to someone on your National Security Council staff."

"Who is it?" Susan asked, a lump forming in her throat.

"Her name is Morgan Shaw."

# FALSE POSITIVE

GRACE
0600
National Military Command Center
The Pentagon
Arlington, Virginia

Grace stared intently at her computer screen, going over the input data and system outputs one more time. Each time she did so, the disturbing conclusion came back the same. She blinked several times, but she'd read it correctly. Then she blew out a few short breaths in an attempt to calm herself—but to no avail.

*This can't be happening.*

Grace rubbed her sweaty hands on her pants and stared at the screen again. After the influx of new data inputs earlier that morning, ARC appeared to register an emerging nuclear threat from China. Consequently, it recommended an increase in alert status of U.S. nuclear forces to Defense Condition 3. But when Grace examined the input data, no such threat existed—at least not based on her assumptions about nuclear deterrence. That meant the ARC system was suffering from a fatal flaw that needed to be fixed immediately.

Wringing her hands, she contemplated the implications of ARC's recommendation. The Joint Staff's Defense Readiness Condition (DEFCON) system consisted of different levels of alert and combat readiness for the U.S. military, ranging from the lowest peacetime level of DEFCON 5 to the wartime level of DEFCON 1. Since the Nightfall Incident, the U.S. military had remained at a heightened peacetime level of DEFCON 4.

A move to DEFCON 3 would place U.S. nuclear forces on immediate standby for a launch order—something that had only occurred one or two times in all of U.S. history and not once since the end of the Cold War. If senior military leaders accepted the recommendation made by the ARC system and took the necessary actions, the United States would risk unnecessary escalation with China. And if the Chinese perceived U.S. actions as aggressive, its government would respond in kind. Grace didn't even want to imagine what ARC's next recommendation might be after the Chinese response. It might likely be a prelude to nuclear war.

*No one wants to think about that scenario.*

She sensed something was going terribly wrong with the intelligence component of ARC's deep neural network, and she needed to warn the Pentagon leadership somehow. The main problem was she didn't really understand what was going on and why. She needed more time. Grace glanced at her watch and shuddered. Only three hours remained before the pre-brief with the chairman of the Joint Chiefs of Staff in his conference room. She stood up and peeked over the top of her cubicle wall.

Her large office suite located deep inside the National Military Command Center was still empty. She sank back into her chair and stared numbly at the screen. In less than an hour, Grace's colleagues would start arriving at the Pentagon's huge Top Secret facility which was located several floors underground. As the primary nerve center for the Department of Defense designed to monitor worldwide events and military activities in real time, it was protected against the effects of an electromagnetic pulse but could not withstand a direct nuclear attack.

Before the ARC system became fully operational, the facility had supported the National Command Authority's mission to rapidly launch a nuclear attack. A small safe a few cubicles over from Grace's terminal used to contain the key for issuing Emergency Action Messages to the intercontinental ballistic missile silos, bomber squadrons, and nuclear ballistic missile submarines.

The facility now housed the ARC system, which automated most of the functions needed to start and fight a nuclear war. To ensure continuous operation in the event of a nuclear attack, a network of nodes for the ARC system were scattered around the country and linked to the National Military Command Center.

A salt-and-pepper-haired head popped over the side of her cubicle and moved along the edge like a prowling shark, causing her to jump slightly. Seconds later, Colonel Martinez entered her cubicle, a triumphant grin on his face as he straightened up his body. The deep crow's feet around his eyes when he smiled made him look approachable despite his stature.

Having worked for nine months in the Pentagon, Grace had come across many senior military officers. Martinez was by far her favorite, but sometimes he treated her like a little sister, and it got on her nerves.

*How can he goof off at a time like this?*

"Seriously?" Grace said, glaring at him. "You've got to know how focused I am this morning. You can't possibly think you've scored another win just because you snuck up on me while I'm staring at this data. It could mean the end of the world and life as we know it."

"Always so melodramatic. A win is a win," Martinez said with a smirk. Then his face became dead serious. "In your email, you said you had something important for the chairman's read-ahead this morning?"

"Yeah, it's something, all right. But I didn't want to interrupt your breakfast with Morgan," Grace said, suppressing a frown.

A twinge of sadness shot through her body when she thought about her waning friendship with Morgan. The thought of Morgan avoiding her at the White House meeting the previous day stung hard. It had been six months since she'd actually spoken to her good friend from her days in graduate school at Harvard.

The U.S. Air Force paid for a few slots each year at the prestigious university, both to educate its top officers and to expose them to some of the smartest civilians in the country. Grace had been lucky enough to win one of the coveted spots to earn her master's degree. Morgan had approached Grace during orientation, and they became fast friends.

But ever since Morgan took the job in the White House, it was difficult to get an email reply, let alone a phone call. Since Grace worked twelve-hour days at the Pentagon on a regular basis, she was familiar with the burden of a high-level job. But she was still able to make time for the people in her life. And she could have used the extra shoulder in the wake of her father's death.

*I'm sure reporting to the president takes things to a whole new level.*

"Nah, she's cool," Martinez said. "By the way, I told Morgan to give you a call since she had some questions about the ARC system I couldn't answer. I told her you're the best person to explain it. Plus, she owes you a phone call by now, don't you think?" He gave her a knowing wink.

*Great, now she knows I complained.*

Grace replied sarcastically, "Gee, thanks."

"Okay, tell me about the problem with ARC," Martinez said, plopping down in the extra chair in her cubicle, leaning back, and putting his arms behind his head. "Did you identify a bug in ARC's programming?"

"Nope, it's not a bug," Grace said with confidence.

Martinez scrunched his face. "What about a cyberattack?"

Grace shook her head. "I checked for that first thing this morning. As you know, deep neural networks are vulnerable to spoofing or data poisoning. That's why the Department of Defense employs state-of-the-art, AI-enabled cyber defenses and firewalls to protect the data within the ARC system. They are impenetrable to outside forces. Even if a sophisticated hacker managed to break through, we would detect the breach. In the worse-case scenario, we could take ARC offline and revert to a previous version of the software."

"Okay, if the problem with ARC isn't due to a bug or a cyber-attack, what's wrong?" Martinez asked.

"ARC may have learned something we don't want it to," Grace said.

Martinez put his hand on his forehead. "I don't get it."

Grace took a deep breath. "Unlike a traditional computer program, ARC can learn from its environment. Each month, we expose the system to new infusions of ISR data. At that point, ARC tweaks its own algorithms to produce desired outcomes."

"But how does ARC learn the wrong thing?" Martinez asked, frowning.

Grace gave him an uncomfortable smile. She desperately needed someone to listen to her and didn't have time to go through her chain of command.

Getting her points across to senior echelons in the Pentagon was hard enough as a major in the Air Force, let alone a young Korean-American woman. She often had to explain to people that she had not been naturalized, but rather was born in Korea as an American citizen. Her father was an American and served as a pilot in the Air Force near Seoul at the time of her birth, conveying her automatic U.S. citizenship despite her Korean mother.

Somehow, this was difficult for some folks to understand, and they often assumed she was Korean by birth and spoke English as a second language. No one would ever admit to discrimination based on ethnicity and gender, but Grace often witnessed her white male counterparts getting their messages across more easily than she did.

As the executive assistant to the chairman, Martinez could make sure Pentagon senior leadership heeded what she had to say. Although she'd known Martinez long before he started dating Morgan, this was the first time she'd decided to lean on her personal connection in her professional career.

It was a big risk to go over her boss's head; it could cost her job. But she'd tried for months now to convince her leadership that there was something not quite right with the ARC system, and they wouldn't listen.

At least now, she had some tangible evidence of its problems, and she didn't plan on wasting the opportunity.

Grace grimaced. "Well, it's a bit complicated."

"Maybe you can break it down into small pieces first, and we can figure it out together?"

Grace's stomach tightened into knots. *Here goes nothing.*

## [ 8 ]

## DEMONSTRATION BLUES

DREW
0610
Lafayette Square
1600 Pennsylvania Ave NW
Washington, D.C.


Drew Hudson rubbed his eyes and yawned as he peeked out from the huge golf umbrella covered by a giant blue tarp. He'd already slept as long as he could on the paper-thin sleeping pad —no more than four hours. He stretched his achy arms and shoulders. At one point in the middle of the night, he'd rolled onto the warm cement and woken up with a rough texture on the side of his cheek. He touched his face. Thankfully, his skin was smooth again.

Holding the edge of the tarp, he stepped out into the open and took a deep breath, nearly choking on the dust suspended in the air. Drew covered his mouth with his arm, sneezed, and then shook his head at the irony.

*Maybe climate change will kill us before robots get the chance.*

Despite the early hour, the intense summer humidity meant

being outdoors felt particularly uncomfortable. The record-breaking temperatures and high moisture in the air produced more smog than usual, making it dangerous to one's health. But none of it would dampen the spirits of the protesters who'd come out for the Campaign Against Killer Robots.

*If we don't speak out now, humanity is doomed to its own devices.*

Drew wiped sweat from his forehead and surveyed the temporary camp. The hodgepodge collection of tents, umbrellas, cardboard boxes, and lawn chairs stretched the entire length of Pennsylvania Avenue, located just outside the White House. There must have been at least a couple hundred diehards who had camped overnight for the 24-hour vigil, sleeping in the streets. Many more would arrive throughout the day to make their final stand against the Department of Defense's plan to field fully autonomous weapon systems.

Many of the protesters were already chanting, marching back and forth, and waving their signs. They were desperate to sway President Tolley's decision to veto the legislation that would authorize the transfer of kill decisions from humans to machines. The protesters had a special name for the bill—they were calling it the Killer Robot Directive. They shouted over and over: "Ban killer robots, veto the bill! Ban killer robots, veto the bill! Ban killer robots, veto the bill!"

Drew stuffed his hands in his pockets and tried to ignore the low growl in his stomach. Though determined to prevent the development of the Terminator by the U.S. government, he was definitely not a morning person.

*It's way too early for this.*

He would never have volunteered himself to sleep in the streets. Except he'd accidentally mentioned to his friends that he wasn't planning on drinking any alcohol at the previous night's party. So he was the one who got stuck with the night shift. In order to camp outside the White House, someone needed to attend each individual spot at all times. Otherwise Secret Service would dismantle it for security reasons.

The night shift turned out to be more convenient, anyway. Drew was taking a summer class at Georgetown first thing in the morning, and he refused to skip it for anything. After all, he was taking on massive debt to pay his way through grad school. He'd done the math on the hourly cost of his education—it was obscene. His student loans didn't come even close to covering his living expenses.

He pulled out his smartphone, checked the weather, and chuckled to himself. In just a few hours, the sun would blaze down on the makeshift tent, and actual temperatures would reach over a hundred Fahrenheit. He didn't want to think about the heat index. Maybe the night shift was better all around.

Stretching his shoulders and cracking his neck, Drew unfolded a lawn chair, plopped into it, and reached for his thermos on the ground. The coffee from the previous night was room temperature, but he gulped it down anyway, desperate for a caffeine fix.

Then he glanced at the protest signs leaning against an empty suitcase. For a moment, Drew considered whether he should add his voice to the chant. The louder the protesters were, the better chance they had for the president to hear their shouting inside the White House. That's what they told him, at least.

*But do we have a shot at influencing Tolley's decision?*

Before he had a chance to get up, a gray-haired lady with bronze, leathery skin walked toward his umbrella. She was pushing a cart of groceries in the direction of a large tent covered in anti-nuclear signs at the end of his row. Her mismatched clothes were dirty and torn in places, and her curly hair was unkempt. A collection of anti-nuclear and world peace buttons adorned her jacket. As she started to pass him by, the smell of cheap liquor wafted in his direction, causing him to pull up his nose.

As if sensing his disgust, the old lady turned to give him an icy glare. "Hey kid, what's your problem?" Her voice was unexpectedly deep—gravelly, as if she'd spent many years smoking cigarettes.

*Or from breathing in this smog every day.*

He shrugged and gave her a half smile. "Sorry, ma'am. No problem here," Drew said as politely as he could. He didn't want to get into it with anyone, let alone a drunken, homeless lady.

"You guys are way late to this party, you know," the lady said snidely, waving her hand around at his fellow protesters. "In more than one way."

"What do you mean?" Drew asked.

"Well, we've been out here for decades, doing our part to save the world from itself. I've spent the past twenty years camped out here, calling for an end to nuclear war."

*Twenty years?*

"Who's this *we*?" Drew asked, furrowing his brow.

"Oh, you haven't heard of us? The White House Peace Vigil?" When he didn't respond, she said sharply, "Where have you been living? In a cave?"

He shrugged. "I don't know that much about nukes. I'm more concerned about risks of artificial intelligence."

An annoyed look formed on her face. "The nukes will kill us first, you know. But I guess that fancy new technology is more interesting for you young people. Anyway, we're the anti-nuclear activists who have protested the existence of nuclear weapons, warning anyone who will listen about the coming end of humanity. And guess what?" Her voice slurred slightly.

"What?" Drew asked.

"Nuclear weapons continue to threaten humanity today." She grinned sardonically, showing several missing teeth. "Maybe there are a few less weapons, but they still exist. And it only takes one to destroy an entire city. The people in power say we can't put the genie back in the bottle."

Drew quirked an eyebrow. "What's your point?"

"Are you prepared to wait that long for change, young man?" the lady asked. Before he had a chance to answer, she said sarcastically, "Because I doubt it. And we humans seem to have to learn from our mistakes first... that means we'll field autonomous weapons systems before we understand the danger."

Drew fidgeted with his hands. "We're not planning to be out here forever. Just hoping to convince the president to veto the autonomous weapons bill today."

"Ha." The lady's head fell back in a hearty cackle, which turned into a ripple and then a shake. She grabbed her stomach and began trembling from laughter. After a few moments, she recovered and said, "You young kids are all the same. Naive about the ways of the world. Impatient to affect change. Unwilling to make hard sacrifices. Your little autonomous ship has already sailed off on its own. Today's legislation will simply give the Pentagon the green light. If you want to reverse what's already happened, you're going to have to do way more than protest a bill that flips a switch."

Drew frowned, worrying she might be right. "Well, if you think we can't achieve anything by protesting, why are *you* still out here?"

She stumbled a bit, and her eyes dimmed in her stupor. "I guess because I stayed too long. I was young and naïve when I first started... much like you. I didn't have a penny in my pocket or know what else to do to make my voice heard. When a few months turned into years, I wasn't sure what to do differently." She looked him up and down, her lip curling. "I wasn't a rich kid like you, boy."

"Well, I'm not rich," he said with a hint of defensiveness.

She ignored his comment and said, "At some point, I became a well-known fixture at the White House. I worried that if I gave up and left my post, it would signal that nuclear weapons are here to stay."

*Am I being foolish? Can I actually do anything to change the future?*

Drew's hands went limp, his arms hanging loosely at his

sides. He was silent for a few moments and then asked, "If you could do it all over again, what would you do differently?"

She gave him a half-hearted smile. "I'm not sure I would've known better... but if I had, then I'd go to school, study hard, and get a job lobbying Congress to do the right thing. This protest stuff is important, but it's only a small part of a bigger movement to knock some sense into our government and the rest of the world. But I still think it will take a nuclear war for us to really learn the lesson."

With that, she walked away, pushing her cart toward the large, empty tent covered with anti-nuclear slogans.

# [ 9 ]
## WEST SITTING HALL

SUSAN
0620
Executive Residence
The White House

A cup of hot coffee in hand, Susan stood with her back to the massive lunette window of the West Sitting Hall, basking in the soft morning light. Penny rubbed up against her leg, eager for another head scratch. Susan reached down to oblige the pup and took a deep breath. After only a few days in the Executive Residence, this cozy corner had quickly become her favorite spot.

Though she usually preferred to be alone. Susan wanted to soak up her last moment of quiet for the day, but Elise insisted they go through every hour of the day's packed schedule, which had just gotten more complicated due to the looming crisis with China.

*I've totally lost control over my life.* The irony was not lost on her.

"Ma'am, we need to go over the funeral arrangements," Elise said, holding the presidential planner in one hand and her smartphone in the other. "President Monroe's family has decided on a full state funeral, so we can finally move forward with planning. Once the autopsy is complete, Monroe will lie in repose in the East Room of the White House. His family would like to attend a private service there. I expect his casket will be delivered by the end of the day tomorrow."

Susan shuddered at the thought. For as long as she could remember, she'd struggled with the concept of death and funerals. She wouldn't admit it to anyone, not even Blake, but she dreaded the notion of sleeping in the same building with the dead body of her former boss and good friend.

Elise glanced at her tablet. "From there, the president's casket will be moved to the National Cathedral for an invitation-only religious service. We're scheduled to sit down with the Monroe family tomorrow morning to go over the guest list."

Susan nodded.

"The funeral procession will move from Northwest D.C. to the U.S. Capitol where President Monroe will lie in state in the Capitol rotunda for three days for the general public's viewing. My staff is coordinating with the D.C. Mayor's office on street closures and with Secret Service on security issues. Ma'am, is there anything specific you want to arrange?"

"Nothing for me," Susan said, a lump in her throat. "But I'd offer my full support to the Monroe family. We'll do whatever we can to meet their needs during this difficult time."

"That's good, ma'am." Elise smiled. "Because the Monroe family was hoping you'd be willing to offer a eulogy at the religious service later this week."

Susan gulped. "Of course. I'd be glad to do that. Let's get my speechwriter on that right away."

Elise nodded. "Madam President, you're aware of the Autonomous Retaliatory Capability test and evaluation taking place at the National Military Command Center later today," Elise said, reading from an email on her smartphone. "It's scheduled to start at 1:30 p.m. When it's over, Chairman Waller has promised you a comprehensive readout."

Susan nodded, pulling up her nose slightly at the formality. "Can you please stop calling me ma'am or Madam President when it's just the two of us in the Executive Residence? It feels so unnatural."

Elise's all-business face broke into a wide smile. "Ma'am, I'll stop calling you by formal titles when it finally feels natural to me. When I reach that point, I'll be able to trust myself not to call you Susan in public. If that's okay with you, ma'am."

"Okay, okay. That's a good point." Susan dipped her nose toward the cup of hazelnut coffee, catching the subtle hint of coconut in the Hawaiian blend, and took a small drink.

It had been her favorite brew ever since she and Blake had renewed their vows on the beautiful island paradise of Maui—just a year ago now. She'd given her last bag of precious beans to the White House kitchen staff and requested they brew a batch every morning until they ran out. She needed whatever source of comfort she could get. Despite the soothing taste, she couldn't quite suppress her anxiety over the coming chaos.

Her mind drifted back to the semi-autonomous system for launching nuclear weapons. Susan bit her lip. "Let's set up a comprehensive briefing on the ARC system with the secretary of defense and the chairman of the Joint Chiefs of Staff for some time next week. I received the basics when it first launched five months ago, but now I need to know as much about it as possible... since I'm the one who has to push the damn button."

"Absolutely, I'll get that on the calendar," Elise said, jotting down a note.

Susan suppressed a sigh. "I still don't know how we got here."

"Ma'am?" Elise asked, her forehead creasing.

"How did we hand over so much control of nuclear weapons to a machine?" Susan asked, clasping her mug a bit tighter. "Who thought that was a good idea, anyway?"

"Oh, that." Elise raised her eyebrow. "As I recall, the big-five defense contractors hammered out a pretty compelling narrative about the dangers of hypersonic weapons and increasing speed of warfare back in the early 2020s. They warned us that autonomous weapons systems would narrow the window for nuclear decision-making. They claimed that the slow pace of human decision-making amounted to a threat to national security."

"Remember that multi-media campaign put out by Centoreum Tech back then?" Susan asked. "It was all over the place.

Elise nodded with a grimace.

"They must have spent millions on it," Susan said, "but they did succeed in selling the general public and Congress on the risks of hypersonics and autonomous weapons. They pitched the notion of the ARC system as *the* ideal solution to countering the threat. But I honestly never thought we'd cross the red line of automating nuclear weapons systems, even if they are defensive. Ever. But here we are. And now I'm responsible for overseeing it."

"Ma'am, you know ARC is not fully automated," Elise said. "It's technically semi-automated. As the president, you do still retain the sole authority to use nuclear weapons."

Susan grimaced. "Yeah... but only by reversing the launch order given by the ARC system in the first place. What if I can't do that in time? What if my senior advisors prevent me from rescinding the order? Then a machine will give an order that will kill millions of innocent civilians. A machine!" She waved her free hand around.

"I'm sure there are safety measures in place to prevent that scenario," Elise said.

*Well, I'm not so sure.*

Susan took a deep breath and exhaled hard, trying to loosen what felt like a heavy, iron noose around her neck.

*I suppose this is what I signed up for.*

"Speaking of the ARC system, you have a lunch meeting with Dennis Warren, Centoreum's CEO, today," Elise continued. "The scheduler made a reservation for you and Mr. Warren at The Monocle in Capitol Hill at noon. Secret Service agents have already secured the restaurant earlier this morning and planned the route for your motorcade."

*Ugh.*

President Monroe had been close friends with the self-made business billionaire tycoon who had funded much of their election campaign. The CEO also happened to be close friends with the SecDef, her archnemesis, Isaiah Burke. As soon as Warren got wind of Harrison's death, he'd reached out to Susan's chief of staff to schedule a lunch. She was pretty sure what was on his agenda. The CEO wanted to remind her how many strings he pulled inside the Beltway and how she and Monroe still owed him for their successful election.

*The president's dead body isn't even cold yet, and he wants to collect his debts.*

Susan tried to smooth out her pinched expression. "Actually, let's scratch the lunch for today. I don't think I'll have time to leave the White House with the ongoing situation in China. Plus, I'd like to get briefed about ARC before I sit down with Centoreum's CEO."

"Okay, I'll tell him something extremely urgent came up and reschedule the lunch for next week after your ARC briefing," Elise said. "What do you want to do with the free hour?"

Susan smiled to herself, feeling back in charge of her life for a moment. "Let's put in a call to the Chinese ambassador and see if he's willing to have an informal lunch to talk ourselves out of this crisis. We'll do it in the Yellow Oval Room."

"Sure. I'll get that arranged," Elise said, typing a note on her tablet.

Blowing gently against the surface of the hot liquid, Susan took another cautious sip and turned toward the elegant half-moon window, which looked out onto the West Wing and across the West Colonnade.

The French-style architecture and towering granite stone walls of the Eisenhower Executive Office Building were impressive. It was her favorite building in D.C. Members of her national security staff would soon be arriving there for work—including Morgan Shaw.

Although the mention of Morgan's name by Grayson in connection with Nightfall had shaken her confidence, Susan was determined to hold off final judgement until she received tangible details. She also wasn't yet sure how to use the information to her advantage. She'd asked Grayson to have the FBI director dig deeper and send over a file on Morgan's alleged connection to the Nightfall Incident. He'd promised her more information by the end of the day.

Like it or not, Susan would be forced to rely on Morgan's expertise in the coming days; her help would be vital in Susan's determination to find a way out of the escalating conflict with China. Whatever happened, the U.S. needed to avoid the use of military force, or worse, the use of nuclear weapons. For this reason, she needed to set her own insecurities aside and leverage Morgan's knowledge. Susan pursed her lips as an idea surfaced.

*I know just what to do with her.*

"Please make sure Morgan Shaw attends the cabinet meeting later this morning." Susan asked.

Elise raised her eyebrow, giving her a knowing smirk. "Ma'am, are you sure about that?"

"Oh, I'm dead sure. I need her help with something." Susan suppressed a smile when she imagined the secretary of defense's reaction to Morgan's theory about China's submarines.

*He'll blow his gasket.*

Susan's relationship with General Isaiah Burke, the bombastic secretary of defense, had been strained since the start of Monroe's administration. Nothing Susan could do or say was acceptable to him, but she didn't quite understand the personal animosity. To add to her dislike, she was convinced that Burke was now vying for the empty VP spot and she was worried about what that would mean for her presidency. Unlike her, Burke was able to wield the influence of Monroe's base.

Elise turned her attention to something on her tablet. Susan waited patiently for her to continue, her own thoughts returning to Morgan.

*Now that I have something on Morgan, maybe she'll fall more in line.*

"Um, ma'am, there's some more breaking news," Elise said.

*More?*

"The autonomous weapons legislation passed the Senate vote a few minutes ago. In anticipation of this possibility, I'd already moved several things around and scheduled a press briefing right before your lunch to address the legislation and the situation in Hong Kong. Do you think you'll be ready with your decision to sign or veto the bill?"

"I think so," Susan said. "Is that all, boss?" She cracked a goofy grin.

"For now," Elise said, smiling back at her.

# THE MESSAGE

DREW
0630
Lafayette Square
1600 Pennsylvania Ave NW
Washington D.C.

Drew checked the time on his smartphone. His friends would be arriving within a half hour to relieve him of his post. Not wanting to stand around doing nothing, he bent over, picked up a protest sign, and strode through the thick huddle of tents toward the perimeter fence guarding the White House.

As the famous building came into view, he caught sight of a female reporter with a microphone and rugged-looking cameraman standing in front of the fence. The reporter was an attractive blonde woman, wearing bright red lipstick, a snug teal dress, and black heels. When Drew got less than twenty feet away, he noticed her mic was labeled with the words *The Counter View*. He recognized her immediately.

*Holy crap. That's Tori Scott.*

Suddenly, a strong urge to do something overcame him.

Making his way toward the reporter, he raised his sign high up in the air and began shouting as loud as he could, "Ban killer robots, veto the bill! Ban killer robots, veto the bill!" The closer Drew got to her, the louder he shouted. "Ban killer robots, veto the bill! Ban killer robots, veto the bill!"

Amidst the racket, Tori quit talking into the mic and made a sign to her cameraman. Then to his surprise, she turned to smile directly at him. She walked toward him, signaling her cameraman to follow.

*What the fuck am I doing?*

Drew's hands began to shake as she approached. A fluttery feeling filled his stomach. Pushing through his nerves, he raised the sign even higher and kept shouting his slogan.

"Excuse me," Tori said, her voice sugary sweet and tinged with a Southern twang. "Can I talk to you for a moment?"

Drew stopped shouting and froze in place, his sign dropping slightly. He pointed at his chest and raised his eyebrows. "You want to talk to me?"

Tori nodded.

A flush of adrenaline tingled through his body. Drew took a few tentative steps toward her, avoiding her direct gaze. She was even more beautiful in person. Her clear blue eyes matched her dress and stood out against her smooth, ivory skin.

"What's your name, sweetie?" She reached out her hand to shake his. Her grip was surprisingly firm.

"I'm Drew Hudson," he said, shaking her hand, still stunned by what was happening. "And you're... Tori Scott."

"You just gave me a brilliant idea," she said nodding at him. "I was just taping a bit for my show later today. You know, the recording you rudely interrupted with your loud shouting."

Drew's face flushed. "Sorry about that."

Tori narrowed her eyes. "Don't apologize. You knew exactly what you were doing. But it's no worry because this is going to be so much better. As long as you cooperate with me." She gave him a big smile and then looked straight into his eyes, making his legs go weak. "Sweetie, are you willing to help me out?"

Drew backed away. He was tempted to turn around, race back to the safety of his umbrella, and forget any of this had happened.

"Honey, you want your voice to be heard, don't you?" Tori asked.

Drew fidgeted with his hands. "Um, I don't know. I... um... don't have anything to say."

"Hon, I'm sure you do. You wouldn't be out here if you didn't have something to say." Tori smiled again, dazzling him with her bright white teeth. "We just have to get you talking, and you'll be fine."

She motioned for her cameraman to start rolling.

Turning to the camera, she said, "This is Tori Scott reporting to you live from the White House where a group of demonstrators is protesting the autonomous weapons bill that will hit President Tolley's desk sometime today. I'm here with Drew Hudson, one of the intrepid protesters who has spent the entire night in a 24-hour vigil, hoping to persuade the president to veto the bill." She turned to him and smiled. "Drew, can you please tell us why you're protesting against autonomous weapons systems?" She stuck her mic in his face.

"Uh..." Drew stared into the camera, paralyzed by the black hole of a large lens staring back at him.

His head raced, and he struggled to find words, but he could barely hear anything over the pounding of his heart. For the first time in his life, Drew had an opportunity to use all the geeky knowledge about artificial intelligence. His words might actually have an impact. That is, if he could pull himself together in front of a camera.

"Um... for me, I guess it comes down to data," Drew said, his hands shaking.

Tori looked surprised. "Data? That's not at all what I thought you were going to say... I was totally expecting you to say something about Skynet or HAL 9000. You know, like how the machines kill off humans in the movies. Why are you worried about data, of all things?" Her Southern drawl became thicker the more she talked.

"Um… well, everyone fears the Skynet-Terminator scenario, but honestly, that's so far off in the distant future, we'll likely all be dead from something far less ominous. For example, from an autonomous weapons system overfitting a dataset and causing widespread mayhem."

"What do you mean?" Tori scrunched her face.

Drew took a deep breath. "Autonomous weapons systems are built using machine learning tools, which need massive volumes of high-quality training data to achieve specific tasks with minimal error. And we don't have the right datasets to solve complex national security problems."

"Whoa, dude. You're talking way over our heads right now," Tori said, showing her white teeth to the camera. "Can you explain it using simple language for our viewers at home? We don't all have PhDs, you know."

Drew's face flushed. "Okay, sorry. It's just that most people get the wrong impression from how artificial intelligence is portrayed in the movies. Many assume that AI-enabled machines are as intelligent as people, or in some cases, even more intelligent than humans. But we're not even close to building machines anywhere near that. What makes today's AI machines powerful is their ability to learn and adapt to their environment by analyzing massive volumes of data. It's the data that enables them to be autonomous. And that's much different from human intelligence."

"So, you're saying that machines learn, but not at all like humans do," Tori said. "Can you explain that?"

"Sure." Drew scratched his head, thinking for a moment. "Sometimes it helps to compare how machines and children learn about the world around them. A child learns the difference between a cat and a dog from just a few examples. Once children know what cats and dogs are, they can identify them in any position, from any angle, and in any type of lighting. A machine, on the other hand, needs to see millions of labeled images of cats and dogs in different angles, positions, and types of lighting to determine whether something is indeed a cat or a dog. That's because a machine doesn't actually *know* what a cat or a dog is... rather, a machine detects tiny patterns in an image and compares them to a massive set of images they've been trained on. Then a machine determines the answer based on probability. That means there is always a small margin of error in the outcomes."

"Are you saying that humans learn faster than machines?" Tori asked, wrinkling her nose.

Drew shook his head. "Not faster. It's true that machines can process millions of images in a few seconds. But humans learn an incredible amount from far fewer examples. Humans are also capable of transferring knowledge from one task to another. Even if they don't know the exact species, most children can tell you if something is an animal or not. They know this because they have seen other animals and understand intuitively what features animals have and how they behave and relate to us."

"And they don't have to see millions of images of animals to do it," Tori said, her face lighting up with understanding.

"Correct. By the time a young child learns to identify dogs, cats, and other domesticated animals, they may be able to learn the names of wild animals, such as elephants, with only a single example."

"And a machine would still need millions of images to learn this?"

"Yep," Drew said.

"How does this apply to autonomous weapons, then?" Tori asked.

"Okay, so far, we've been talking about visual object recognition," Drew said. "This is an important feature for developing autonomous weapons systems. In the same way that a machine can learn the difference between cats and dogs, it must now learn how to accurately detect, identify, and eliminate specific targets without human assistance and intervention. This is a far more complex task. For example, an autonomous system must distinguish between an enemy tank and a friendly tank in mere seconds."

"But don't tanks have different designs and distinct features?" Tori asked.

Drew smiled, realizing he'd finally come full circle. "They do, but that's where the data problem comes in. Take Russian tanks, for example. Our intelligence services have pictures of different models of Russian tanks, but not millions of images of every model from all angles, positions, and in all types of lighting. That means that autonomous weapons systems have far fewer examples to learn from. Their margins of error will be greater and have life-or-death consequences."

Tori's eyes lit up. "So, you're saying that autonomous weapons are bound to make some pretty costly mistakes."

"Exactly," Drew said, grinning from ear to ear. "But the data issue gets even more complex when adversaries attempt to trick each other."

"How so?" Tori asked.

Drew cocked his head, enjoying a new surge in his confidence. He was on a roll. "If an adversary wants to fool our autonomous weapons systems, they could simply modify their tanks to look like ours. Or change them in such a way that the system would fail to identify them as enemy targets. Advanced adversaries might also use metamaterials to cloak their tanks, making them invisible to certain wavelengths on the electro-magnetic spectrum. They might also engage in cyberattacks against the deep neural networks inside our autonomous weapons systems and feed them false data to corrupt their outcomes. The false data would look normal to human eyes so we'd never know the system was corrupted."

Drew stopped, suddenly feeling self-conscious when he saw Tori's face contort. *Did I get too technical again?*

Tori scratched her cheek and smiled. "Well, this has been incredibly fascinating, but we're running out of time. I do have one more question for you this morning," she said, giving him a big smile.

"Sure, no problem," Drew exhaled, relieved that he hadn't put her off.

"If you could say anything to President Tolley right now, what would you want her to know?" Tori asked.

Drew jerked his head slightly. He wasn't expecting this sort of question after their extended conversation about data. He paused for a moment to collect his thoughts and stared at the ground, searching his brain for the best catchphrase. If Drew wanted to have impact, it had to be something that people understood and feared. Something that could go viral.

Then he lifted his chin to the camera and said, "Today, President Tolley wants to authorize the Pentagon to unleash the Terminator. But we already know how those movies end. Humans die en masse. It's time for her to reconsider America's future and the risks of artificial intelligence on the battlefield."

"Thanks so much," Tori said, motioning to her cameraman to stop rolling. "I think that's a wrap."

"No problem," Drew said, glancing at his watch. He was too nervous to ask her when the video might air. Fumbling with his hands, he waved goodbye to Tori as he hurried back toward the umbrella. When it came into view, Drew saw that two of his friends had already arrived. They were standing in his spot and glaring at him for shirking his duty.

# [ 11 ]
## CATS VERSUS DOGS

GRACE
0640
National Military Command Center
The Pentagon
Arlington, Virginia

Grace could feel the heat rise behind her ears. She'd been trying to describe the problem with the ARC system to Colonel Martinez for the past twenty minutes. And he wasn't getting any of it. She took a deep breath and stretched her neck to release some tension.

Martinez gave her an apologetic look. "Sorry I'm so daft."

"Don't worry about it. It's a complex topic," Grace said, trying her best to hide her frustration. "We'll start from the beginning again."

For a moment, she considered the best approach. If she couldn't get the colonel to grasp the basics, the risk she was taking by circumventing her chain of command would all be for naught.

"Okay, you understand the basics of how the ARC system functions, right?" Grace asked.

Martinez gave her a half shrug. "I know that ARC's deep neural network consists of layered algorithms and that the network learns patterns from massive volumes of data. But I'm not sure what that means."

"During the training phase, we fed the ARC system billions of data points, and the algorithms learned to produce specified outcomes," Grace said.

Martinez's eyes lit up as if he remembered something. "If I recall correctly from the command brief I received last month, ARC consists of four major components that are linked together and activate in a phased timeline, each phase taking place before the first nuclear detonation on our soil."

Grace bobbed her head and gave him an encouraging smile.

Martinez grinned back and began to count them off on his hand. "As its first component, ARC operates using a big data-driven intelligence, surveillance, and reconnaissance (ISR) deep neural network. That's the critical starting point, right?"

"Yes, by feeding ARC's network new ISR data each month, the system can determine potential changes in the behavior of our nuclear adversaries and the implications of new technologies for deterrence. The ISR component leverages data inputs from all government agencies and provides strategic warning to our operations centers for any emergent nuclear threats."

Martinez lifted another finger and looked at her. "The early warning system represents the second component and provides reliable and early detection of nuclear attacks. It gathers sensor data in real time from radars and satellites to detect launches of nuclear weapons."

Grace nodded. "The sensor data are fed into ARC, and the system issues a nuclear attack warning or no warning."

Martinez raised his third finger. "Then in the event of a nuclear attack by an adversary, the third component, our command and control system enables the prompt authorization of retaliation before the enemy's nuclear weapons reach U.S. soil. It determines the most effective retaliatory nuclear attack and decides how many missiles to launch, how many bombs to deliver, what targets to hit, and in what order." He raised his fourth finger. "As the fourth component, ARC provides a rapid dissemination of the launch order to our nuclear forces and delivers the weapons to targets in the attacking country. The main idea behind the ARC system is to accelerate and improve nuclear decision-making and ensure effective retaliation. That's about all I know."

Grace smiled, flashing her teeth. "Awesome. That's something, at least. But we still have to start from the beginning. Or else you won't understand the nature of the problem I've identified." She paused for a moment to make sure he was in agreement.

Martinez gave her a thumbs-up. "Sure, go for it."

She took another deep breath. "Okay. Across all of its components, ARC operates using several of the most advanced deep neural networks that exist today, and they are tightly linked together. The outputs of one component within the ARC system feed into the next one as inputs. Each of these networks was designed to mimic the deep neural network of the human brain. To achieve the complexity of the brain's architecture, a team of mathematicians, engineers, and computer scientists developed a series of complex algorithms that function as networked layers of artificial neurons, just like the billion neurons in your brain."

"Huh?" Martinez said, rubbing the back of his neck. "You totally lost me on the brain stuff."

*Not again.*

Grace suppressed a sigh. "Okay, let me try a different tack. Think of each algorithm in the network as a separate mathematical formula analyzing one piece of a larger equation. Each algorithmic layer within the deep neural network performs a different calculation. As the input data travels through each layer, a mathematical formula interprets the input data to produce a probabilistic outcome using advanced statistics, with an extremely small error rate."

Martinez made an apologetic face. "Still not getting it. Sorry. Math wasn't my best subject."

Grace put her hand on her forehead. "Maybe I should try an example so that you can visualize what I'm saying?"

Martinez nodded eagerly.

"You've heard of the cats-versus-dogs explanation for training a deep neural network?" Grace asked. "It's pretty famous."

Martinez bobbed his head. "I think so. That's for a deep neural network that specializes in visually identifying objects, right?"

Grace nodded eagerly. "Yes, data scientists train a deep neural network to recognize objects by starting with something simple like images of cats and dogs. But we need to feed it a massive dataset of images of cats and dogs, each of which would have to be labeled accordingly. Remember the algorithmic layers I was talking about?"

"Yep... then you said something about a mathematical formula and lost me." He grinned.

Grace smirked. "I'll skip that part this time. Just assume that your deep neural network reads millions of images labeled with cat or dog and then develops a set of rules for relationships between the different features of dogs and cats to predict an outcome about the content of the image. Make sense?"

"Still with you."

"Let's say we want the algorithm to determine whether the image contains a dog. The first layer of the deep neural network might focus on a single characteristic such as the number of ears. The algorithm analyzes the input data, in this case an image of a dog, and predicts whether the image contains a cat or a dog based on that feature. Since both cats and dogs have two ears, that layer would not be definitive. Rather, it would produce a small percentage chance that the image specifically contains a dog. The next layer might address the shape of the ear. Cats generally have pointy ears that stick up, whereas dogs can have many different ear shapes. Since this is a more defining feature, the absence of pointy ears would increase the percentage chance that the image contains a dog. Does that make sense?"

"Yeah, it's starting to..." Martinez furrowed his brow. "In other words, the deep neural network doesn't actually know what dogs and cats look like. It just makes probabilistic predictions about what the image contains. If the animal has two floppy ears, then it's a dog at this probability. If pointy ears, then it's a cat at that probability."

*And he's finally getting it...*

"Exactly. And—"

Martinez rubbed his chin. "But all of this has me wondering what kind of dataset we used to train ARC. I mean, we're not talking about the simple task of identifying dogs or cats. We're talking about analyzing intelligence to predict emerging nuclear threats, detect nuclear attacks, decide on an effective nuclear war fighting strategy, and launch the order. Do we even have enough of the right data to train the algorithm to do all of that effectively?"

*Ding, ding, ding.*

"Well, that's another longer conversation. The short answer is no. The ARC system relies primarily upon collected data from peacetime operations."

"But what about the Cuban Missile Crisis?" Martinez asked. "Could that data help ARC identify red flags for emerging threats?"

Grace shook her head. "That's not enough data for a few reasons. First, the conflict was with a single country during a very short time period—thirteen days, to be exact. Now remember, back then, we didn't have the internet or social media. When you think about a tweet or post going viral in a matter of minutes today, news didn't travel quickly back then. Newspapers and old-school news reporting were the primary source of information about world events. Second, we didn't see that threat emerge until it was practically too late, and the nuclear-armed missiles were located on Cuba. Although we have more satellite coverage today than we did back then, it's still possible to miss things happening on the ground. Third, the crisis remained a peacetime operation in that no shots were fired. We increased our alert status and used some intense signaling to communicate our intentions to the Soviet Union. You can probably guess why it's dangerous to extrapolate from such a small and narrow dataset to predict what might happen after nuclear war begins."

Martinez nodded. "But that's why we run these monthly tests, right?"

"Yes, but the tests are somewhat limited in that they produce synthetic data about nuclear conflict. We can't extract real-world wartime behavior from peacetime operations or from data based on a simulation. Centoreum Tech used the model of nuclear deterrence to keep ARC on track in the absence of sufficient data. Do you want me to further explain the data problem?"

Martinez glanced at his watch. "No, we don't have much time. Just give me the bottom-line up front. I want to understand the problem with the ARC system. We can discuss the rest during the pre-brief meeting with the chairman this morning."

*Um, that sounds... like a terrible idea.*

Grace's face blanched at the notion of trying to teach a four-star general and other high-level military officers about the topic of data bias.

"Don't worry... I'll be there to help you through it," Martinez said. "As a leader, the chairman is extremely thoughtful. He will want to understand this."

Grace exhaled sharply, her pulse elevating rapidly. She knew Martinez was trying his best to reassure her, but every time he mentioned the chairman, she imagined herself telling him about cats and dogs while trying to keep a straight face. Her stomach flipped a few times.

"Okay, the bottom line…" She paused for a moment, attempting to settle her nerves. "Centoreum Tech claims that ARC operates with an error rate of about 0.1 percent, making it the most accurate deep neural network in the world after NASA's rocket software. Of course, any automated system that interacts with nuclear weapons should have the smallest margin of error possible. But the important point is this. There's still a small margin for error."

"Okay, you're saying that ARC can still make mistakes. So, has it made a mistake?" Martinez asked.

Grace took a deep breath. "Well, I'm not sure. It depends on what you'd consider a mistake."

"What?" Martinez asked. "I thought you said there was a problem with ARC."

"I did. And there is. But it's not what you think it is." Grace grimaced.

"Explain, please."

"Earlier this morning, we exposed the ARC's deep neural network to a new round of ISR data in preparation for today's test."

"Yup."

"Well, I checked the outcomes of the ISR data infusion around 4 a.m. this morning. ARC interpreted China's forward deployment of submarines as an offensive move rather than a defensive one."

Martinez squished his eyebrows together.

"And for this reason, the ARC system has recommended increasing the alert status of U.S. nuclear forces to DEFCON 3 and undertaking a countermove against Chinese submarines in the Northwest Passage."

Martinez's eyes widened.

"The ARC system could be producing a false positive. If it

has, then the system is making recommendations based on a misinterpretation of the data." Grace paused for a moment, waiting for the full implications of her finding to sink in.

Martinez scrunched up his face. "Um... a false positive is when the system detects a condition when the condition is absent. You're saying ARC has identified a threat that doesn't exist and now wants us to act on that assessment."

Grace nodded.

He scratched his head. "Given what we know about the model of nuclear deterrence, equating the forward deployment of submarines with an offensive move doesn't make logical sense. China would never initiate a preemptive nuclear attack on the U.S. from its submarines. If they'd ever consider a first strike against us, they would more likely use their land-based intercontinental ballistic missiles in order to minimize damage from our inevitable retaliatory attack. ARC must be overreacting to new patterns in China's submarine deployments."

"That's exactly what I thought," Grace said. "It is possible ARC doesn't understand China's move and therefore has erroneously assigned it an offensive value. Recent ISR data may have produced a heightened threat environment, changing the patterns ARC sees in the data and causing it to recommend an increased alert status. But that's not the worst part. If I'm right, ARC may have changed its internal rules about the relationships among the input and output data. For example, ARC could now think that submarines might be used for a first-strike attack rather than second-strike retaliation."

Martinez shrugged with uncertainty. "Okay, let's say ARC has produced a false positive as you suggest. And it has tweaked its algorithms to produce different outcomes moving forward. What's the worst possible thing that could happen?"

Grace bit her lip. "Well, since the different components of ARC are linked together, perceived changes in the relationships among the ISR data and outcomes will shape the context for all other decisions made by the system and that could have disastrous consequences."

"Like a domino effect?" Martinez asked.

Grace nodded. "In the event of a false alarm from the early warning component, ARC may now be more likely to overreact, causing it to prematurely order the launch of U.S. nuclear weapons. Right now, the system appears to be getting defensive and offensive moves mixed up. What if ARC learns that offensive moves are good or that nuclear war is winnable?"

Martinez's mouth fell open. "If we take it to the extreme, you're saying that ARC could start interpreting every country with nuclear capabilities as dangerous and therefore preemptively bomb them all in order to 'win'?"

Grace nodded grimly.

"That's completely nuts! How is this even possible?"

"The problem is no one really understands how ARC works," Grace said. "I'm not even sure myself why this is happening without spending several days to study the algorithms. All I can tell you is that it's happening and then speculate about the cause. But if we're not careful, ARC could initiate an unintended nuclear war with China. That is, if our leadership blindly follows through with ARC's recommendations."

"Very good work, Major Lim. I assume you've briefed your boss about this?"

*Crap.*

Grace frowned, avoiding eye contact. "No, Captain Dietz hasn't come in yet this morning." She didn't like lying to Martinez, but she didn't want him to change his mind about inserting her talking points into the read-ahead. And as far as she knew, her boss hadn't arrived yet.

Martinez raised his eyebrow. "Hmm. He's not going to be very happy with you if we go over his head and take this directly to Chairman Waller. Are you sure you want me to put it in his read-ahead?"

"I don't see another way," Grace said, her chin dropping.

"But I understand if you don't want to knock heads with a bunch of stars."

Martinez shook his head. "I'm not afraid to take the risk if you are okay with the consequences… it's just that my military career is a bit more insulated from the potential fallout. But I'll try my best to give you some top cover."

Grace exhaled sharply and looked him in the eyes, overwhelmed with gratitude. "Thanks, I really appreciate it."

Martinez tapped his watch. "Unfortunately, I have to get to a meeting at the White House shortly. Can you be prepared to explain to the chairman how this happened in as simple language as possible?"

"Sure, no problem," Grace said.

*Holy crap. I'm going to brief the chairman.*

# [ 12 ]
## THE BUTTER BATTLE

SUSAN
0650
Executive Residence
The White House

Lost in thought, Susan stared glumly out the half-moon window in the West Sitting Hall. The day was already shaping up to be a doozy, and she really wanted to climb back into bed and pull the covers tightly over her head. But no matter how she felt, Susan needed to dig deep and find the resolve to face the mess in front of her.

*I'm the president now.*

Her chest tightened when she heard a distant chanting noise. Apparently, the din of the protesters shouting in Lafayette Park could reach the far west-facing corner of the White House. Immediately after President Monroe's death, the Campaign Against Killer Robots had sprung into aggressive action in a new drive to persuade her to veto the autonomous weapons bill. She shook her head and sighed heavily.

*They think I'm their only hope.*

In reality, autonomous weapons systems existed in many countries around the world. Even the Department of Defense had developed its own autonomous weapon systems capable of operation on land, in the sea, and in the air. But until now they'd operated with at least one human in the loop, ready to intervene if the system reached the wrong decision. But now, all Susan had to do was sign the legislation, giving military commanders the green light to flip the switch, taking humans completely out of the loop and allowing machines to kill autonomously.

*Even if I veto the bill, I'm not sure if I can stop it. The rise of autonomous weapons systems seems inevitable.*

Susan turned away from the window and took in a beautiful scene on the other side of the room—Blake, Lucy, and Penny sitting quietly, blissfully ignorant of her inner turmoil. A feeling of warmth filled her chest. Her blonde hair still mussed from sleeping, Lucy snuggled on the couch with her favorite stuffed bear, tightly clasping her reading tablet. Penny lay next to her, snoring lightly.

Susan stole a wistful glance at Blake, who was sitting in his new recliner. Her shoulders sank when he didn't return one of his famous blue-eyed twinkles or at least an encouraging smile. Sadly, his ruggedly handsome face hid behind the huge state-of-the-art VR goggles she'd gotten him for his birthday.

Blake wore a classic Oxford button-down shirt, khaki pants, and brown loafers, befitting his role as a professor of technology and politics at Georgetown University. Susan always found it amusing that he wore such clothes even when he didn't have to teach class. During the summer months, her husband took a break from teaching to serve as the primary caregiver for Lucy. For the remainder of his time, he focused on his duties as the First Man—though he'd found a way to outsource most of that work to his eager staff and hired a nanny to look after Lucy for part of the day.

*Must be nice.*

Susan shook her head at her husband's goggles and tried to ignore the pulling sensation in her gut. Lately, Blake spent much of his free time in the VR newsroom which featured multimedia stories from all major news stations. In VR, he was surrounded by a maze of video, images, audio, and graphics—all accessible with an easy flick of his wrist. He particularly enjoyed the real-time back-and-forth banter between the co-hosts of *The Counter View*. If Blake had gotten lost in any of the breaking news story-lines for the day, he might be distracted for a while.

Just then, Susan watched as his hand reached for the last piece of toast on his breakfast plate. It was smeared generously with butter and blackberry jam. He felt around the surface of the table with his hand, missing the plate each time. The corners of Susan's lips turned upwards as his hand landed smack in the middle of the toast, covering his fingers with dark purple jam.

As if he'd sensed her keen observation, Blake slid the goggles up onto his forehead with his clean hand, shot her a goofy grin, and licked his sticky fingers one at a time. Then he stuffed the toast into his mouth and chewed loudly.

*He's still such a kid sometimes.*

Susan's shoulders relaxed slightly, but her long to-do list tugged on her thoughts. At times, it felt like she was traveling back and forth between two different galaxies—one was cold and gloomy, darkened by the worst tendencies of humanity. And in that galaxy, it was her job to protect the entire country. The other one was light and airy, in which she'd married her best friend and the love of her life. After years of trying to get pregnant, they now shared a bright and precocious daughter and cherished every minute of raising her to be a confident woman.

She shook her head and mumbled to herself, "Sign or veto. Either way I lose."

"Susie, what's troubling you so?" Blake asked in a singsong voice, appearing not to have heard her.

Her mouth twitched slightly at her childhood nickname. Blake always knew how to reach her when she'd retreated into her innermost thoughts. She hadn't told him any of the details from the early morning intelligence briefing. She'd fully confide in him when it was time to make decisions. He was the only one of her advisors she truly trusted—except Elise, of course.

Susan grimaced and raised her hand in the air to count the crises on her fingers. "Let's see. The president's sudden death last weekend. China's aggressive behavior on Twitter this morning and their suppression of protesters in Hong Kong. The rise of autonomous weapons systems. Planning my good friend's funeral. Am I missing something?"

*Oh yeah. The submarines we lost track of...*

"Most likely," Blake said, smirking at her. "You *are* in charge of *everything* these days."

"Don't remind me," Susan said dryly.

"But what's bothering you the most?" Blake asked.

She went silent for a moment, pondering the right answer to his question. "No single thing stands out yet. I guess it's a little bit of everything for now."

"Do you know what you're going to do?" Blake asked.

Susan furrowed her brow. "About what?"

"Are you going to sign the bill?"

"Oh, that." Susan shrugged and scrunched her nose. "Honestly, I don't know. Ideologically, I'm opposed to autonomous weapons systems. But these systems have existed now for more than five years. This bill just turns them on."

Blake's forehead wrinkled. "Let's say the U.S. doesn't leverage the speed of machines on the battlefield. Won't we be in danger of losing military conflicts with China and Russia?"

Susan gave him a warning look. "Don't get me started on the potential dangers of transferring kill decisions to robots on the battlefield." She pressed her lips together. She couldn't imagine facing down a more terrible dilemma as her first few days as president. In many ways, she considered it an equally fateful decision as the one made by President Roosevelt to develop the atomic bomb. That was more than ninety years ago. "Basically, I lose no matter what decision I make."

"How so?"

"Well, if I sign the bill, the political left will call me a conservative hack, disguised as a moderate," Susan said. "And if I'm unlucky, they'll go as far as to denounce my efforts to address the climate change crisis. What if they create barriers to prevent success? That's my life's work."

Blake rubbed his chin. "But wouldn't that go against their own agenda?"

Susan wanted to roll her eyes but closed them for a moment instead. "Blake, this is politics in the real world, not your ivory tower."

He winced.

"For decades now, it's been a zero-sum game in our country with the entire population polarized by opposing ideologies," she said. "Sure, we had a brief reprieve after the Nightfall Incident and were able to unify across party lines on a few things. But I get the sense people are eager to get back to demonizing each other. And now that Harrison is gone..." A thick lump formed in her throat. "What if my clean energy deal with China falls apart?"

"Well, if you think signing the legislation will cost you all the progress you've made on climate change with China, you could just veto the bill," Blake said. "It's your choice. You're the president."

Susan rubbed the back of her neck. "I'm worried that would be worse. If I veto the bill, the Republicans, maybe even some Independents, will lambast me for not standing by President Monroe's precious legislation. They might even question my ability to serve as commander in chief for not doing what's in the best national security interest of the U.S. Hell, they've already started doing that behind the scenes."

Blake tilted his head, his eyebrow raised. "They wouldn't do that in the middle of a crisis with China, would they?"

"Why not?" Susan's body tensed at the notion. "No matter what I decide, I'll be accused of committing a terrible betrayal."

"I'm sorry, hon. It's a tough spot." He went silent for a moment, and then a sly grin crossed his face. "If we're not careful, Skynet will kill us all."

*Always humor to defuse tension.*

Susan narrowed her eyes, pressing her lips into a thin line. "I don't have time to be worried about robots turning against humanity. I'll settle with making it through the day without starting a nuclear war with China."

"That bad, eh?" Blake asked, his brow furrowing. "You did get up awfully early this morning. Did Elise call you out of bed?"

Susan nodded. "I've convened a cabinet meeting for—"

"Momma, is China and Russia gonna build a Bitsy Big-Boy Boomeroo?" Lucy asked in a high-pitched voice. She rose from the couch and tottered absentmindedly toward Susan, her face glued to the screen. Penny jumped off the couch and stretched her legs. "Will we haft to move underground like the Yooks and the Zooks. Because the Chinese don't like us?"

"Sweetie, what are you talking about?" Susan asked, her eyebrows squishing together as she gazed into her daughter's face.

Sometimes when she looked at Lucy, it was as if Blake's bright blue eyes were staring back at her. Lucy had inherited her father's good looks and was the spitting image of Blake. When Lucy was a baby, Susan had desperately hoped that her daughter would also receive his laid-back personality. In recent years, however, they both noted a growing number of traits that came from Susan's side. Lucy possessed a deep-seated curiosity about all things that couldn't be unequivocally explained and kept her parents on their toes.

Lucy pointed to her tablet. "The Yooks and the Zooks live on opposite sides of a wall because they butter bread on opposite sides. They don't like each other very much. So they build bigger machines to fight each other. But then they can't shoot the machines, or they will both be destroyed forever."

Susan moved toward Lucy to get a better view of the tablet. "Honey, what in the world are you reading?"

"I'm reading my new book." Lucy grinned. "Daddy gave it to me."

Susan's eyes widened, and she turned to face Blake, heat warming her ears.

"It's a Dr. Seuss book," he said with a defensive tone.

"A Dr. Seuss book about nuclear conflict. You gave this to Lucy? You've got to be kidding me." Susan put her hands on her hips.

Blake gave her a look, begging her not to argue in front of Lucy. "Babe, it's called *The Butter Battle Book*. Dr. Seuss wrote a parable about arms races to help kids understand the situation between the U.S. and the Soviet Union during the Cold War."

"And you decided to give Lucy this book without telling me?" Susan asked, her voice still raised.

His hands flew up in the air. "Susie, c'mon. It's a kid's book. I thought it would help. Lucy hears things when we talk, and she was asking all sorts of difficult questions this morning when you left the bed. She kept asking why you didn't wake her up with a good morning kiss. I had to explain—"

A loud knock at the door startled them.

Elise poked her head in and said, "Madam President, there's been another development with China, and you're needed in the Oval Office right away. The secretary of state is waiting to fill you in."

"Now?" Susan asked, her jaw clenched.

Elise looked at Blake and then at Lucy and then back at Susan.

"It's okay," Susan said. "Lucy is riled up about China. Apparently, Blake thinks six-year-olds can handle learning about the ins and outs of international politics and nuclear weapons." She threw a sideways glare at Blake before looking back at Elise. "What's happened now?"

Elise looked at her with some uncertainty. "Um... okay. China's Ministry of Public Security ordered a crackdown on the demonstration in Hong Kong about an hour ago." She paused.

"And?"

"Ensuing escalation between protesters and police officers led to the slaughter of several thousand unarmed civilians, according to news reports. Ma'am, that exceeds the bloodshed of the Tiananmen Square Massacre."

"Momma, what's a massacre?" Lucy asked, her teddy bear hanging from her hand.

*Shit. Blake might have a point.*

Susan gulped, shot an apologetic look at Blake, and then exited the room.

*My can of worms just got much bigger.*

# [ 13 ]
## FAKE NEWS

TORI
0700
Homeland Network News
Washington D.C.

Tori sat behind the news desk on the set of *The Counter View* and studied her script for the morning news hour, making small notes in the margins. A makeup artist finished off Tori's face with a few dabs of blush for color and some ivory matte pressed powder to reduce the shine. To maximize her appearance, Tori wore a solid teal dress, which made her skin tone appear warmer on camera. Her blonde hair was tied back in a tight bun.

Her co-host, Emilio Valdes, straightened his teal silk tie and checked his lapel mic on his navy suit jacket before taking a seat next to her. With his naturally bronze skin, dark hair, and brown eyes, Emilio enjoyed a few advantages over Tori on camera. Whereas he stood out, she had to design her makeup and outfit to make sure she didn't wash out under the bright lights.

Moving over to Emilio, the makeup artist dusted his face with a darker shade of powder and then moved offstage. From behind the glass of the sound booth, *The Counter View*'s executive producer gave the thumbs up that it was almost time to start the show.

Tori took a last sip of water and checked for any loose strands of hair. She looked over at Emilio, who was reading through the headlines on his tablet. After a year of working together, Tori and Emilio had become good friends—against all odds. Because their views couldn't be more diametrically opposed.

Before Homeland Network News (HNN) hired them to host *The Counter View*, they'd both worked as rival reporters for different stations and were known to get into it with each other on social media. After a particularly nasty digital spat, they bumped into each other at the Octane Grill in downtown D.C.— a restaurant frequented by the movers and shakers of the Beltway. In fact, the CEO of HNN was having dinner a few tables away from their shouting match. That's how he got the perfect idea for an improvised news show featuring vibrant personalities debating both sides of the issues.

Tori and Emilio enjoyed the excitement of arguing back and forth on live TV. They would often go off script to cover breaking headlines that came in over their tablets in real time. The improvised element of their show had clinched ratings with viewers across the political spectrum and made *The Counter View* one of the hottest news shows on TV.

The cameraman motioned to Tori and Emilio that he was about to roll the camera and began counting down on one hand. "Ready in five... four... three... two... one." Then he pointed to Tori.

"Hi, I'm Tori Scott, from the left," she said, smiling at the camera.

"And I'm Emilio Valdes, from the right," he said, raising his eyebrow and giving the camera his signature cocky smirk.

"Welcome to *The Counter View* on Homeland Network News," Tori said, turning her face toward Emilio with a smile.

"The news talk show that presents both sides of the issue and lets you decide," Emilio said, finishing her sentence and smiling back at Tori as he always did.

She glanced at the teleprompter and began speaking. "Right out of the gate this morning, we have some breaking news coming out of Hong Kong, China, where it is 8 p.m. on Tuesday evening. After a series of aggressive tweets threatening the U.S. with a nuclear attack, China's Ministry of Public Security initiated a crackdown on a peaceful demonstration in Hong Kong." She took a deep breath and continued. "The conflict between unarmed protesters and police quickly descended into violence when several police officers fired on the unsuspecting crowd. So far, more than three thousand civilians are estimated to have been injured or have died in the shooting and the subsequent stampede. Experts say this is the worst slaughter of unarmed demonstrators in China since the Tiananmen Square Massacre in 1989." She turned to Emilio. "What do you think of this tragic turn in the Hong Kong saga?"

Emilio narrowed his eyes and rubbed his chin. "I guess my first question would be this: how do we know these casualty reports are true? I've seen estimates in the news media ranging from less than a hundred dead into the thousands. How do we know what is happening on the ground in Hong Kong?" He paused for effect. "The truth is that we can't unless we're there. Ever since China kicked out Western journalists from Hong Kong, we're stuck with secondhand information."

"Emilio, this is happening," Tori said. "Right. Now. People are getting killed in the streets of Hong Kong. Innocent civilians. It's all on camera. The evidence is spreading quickly across the internet."

Emilio shook his head. "How do you know for sure? Everyone wants us to believe the story that supports their specific agenda. The Chinese government wants to minimize the casualty reports. Meanwhile, the protesters want us to think people are dying in the streets. Both sides use the data that helps their arguments. We can't know how many are dead until the body bags are lined up, side by side, and we can count them. Maybe someone should drum up some satellite imagery from a reputable company to verify these so-called casualty reports. Because I won't believe anything that would come from our deep state's intelligence community."

Tori shuddered at the crassness of his words, but she should be used it by now. Although she liked the guy, sometimes it was difficult to sit next to Emilio without punching him in the face when he said stupid shit. She took a deep breath. "What about all the video footage and images coming in over social media? That looks like pretty damning evidence to me."

Tori noticed her executive producer give her a warning through the sound booth window.

"Can you be sure that stuff is real, though?" Emilio asked. "I mean, we're way past the early years of deep fakes at this point. Until we have forensic evidence that the videos and images are authentic, I don't know what we should think. It's premature to jump to conclusions."

"Several Asian news media stations are already calling it the Mong Kok Massacre, named after the famous shopping neighborhood," Tori said. "The hashtag has gone viral on social media with more than ten million people posting in less than thirty minutes. Emilio, think about it. There's no way the protesters had time to go home, sit in their apartments, alter hours of video footage, and create deep fakes for release onto social media. That's a lazy assertion, and you know it."

Emilio shrugged. "Just because something has gone viral and has a hashtag doesn't mean it's true. The fake videos could have been prepped in advance. Have you seen the latest video editing software? It's insane what that shit can do."

Tori saw their executive producer glare at them through the window. She'd complained recently about having to delay the broadcast by several seconds in order to censor their foul mouths and avoid a fine from the FCC.

"Always with the conspiracy theories," Tori said sarcastically. Then she turned back to the camera with a serious face. "The State Department issued an official statement about thirty minutes ago, condemning the violence and calling on China to restore law and order in Hong Kong. The State Department spokeswoman said the secretary of state intends to seek economic sanctions at the United Nations in New York City later this morning."

"Well, that move would merely be symbolic since the resolution won't pass," Emilio said, interrupting her. "China holds veto power in the UN Security Council. They'll just veto anything we put forward."

"The U.S. can still impose economic sanctions on key leaders within the Chinese government without support from UN members," Tori said.

"Good luck with that. All that will do is harm U.S. trade with China," Emilio said. "How will President Tolley explain to American businesses that she's putting the interests of Chinese protesters over their ability to make a living?"

Tori ignored the barb and attempted to move on. "Until a few months ago, the citizens of Hong Kong still lived a mostly democratic society, and now they're getting shot in the streets by an oppressive regime for exercising their right to free speech. It will be interesting to see what actions the Tolley administration takes in response to China's aggression. This will be our first chance to get a glimpse into the new president's worldview on national security."

Emilio grimaced. "I don't expect this administration to take strong actions against China. Tolley will likely be even softer than Monroe was. How many times has China crossed a red line in the last six months?" He waved his hands in the air for effect. "The Chinese took over Hong Kong several months ago by sending its troops into the city streets. What did we do? Nothing. That failure is on President Monroe. But don't get me started on Tolley. She's been in bed with the Chinese for the past six months, getting all hippie with it on the environment. I just don't see her siding with the protesters and going against China on this one. Not that I support the U.S. getting involved in this mess. Because I don't. After all, China has already threatened retaliation if we get involved. And they did it on Twitter for the whole world to see!"

"There's some speculation on social media that the *China Xinhua News* handle may have been hacked," Tori said. "I've also read reports from some intelligence analysts suggesting that the tweets came from an individual not affiliated with the Chinese government."

"Well, isn't that convenient. You believe the videos of the massacre are real, but these tweets from the Chinese government, no... they must be fake," Emilio said, scrunching his face.

"Those are different issues, and you know it. Tensions are running high with China's planned war game, which is scheduled to start tomorrow," Tori said. "What if someone is trying to escalate a conflict between the U.S. and China? Plus, the tweets are way out of form for the Chinese government, don't you think?"

Emilio made another face. "Or maybe China is finally showing us its true nature? Look, when it comes to the protesters in Hong Kong, they're shit out of luck. It boils down to an issue of national sovereignty. Hong Kong belongs to China now. Even if China took Hong Kong back a bit early. What's done is done."

"You're saying we shouldn't care about the fate of protesters in Hong Kong?" Tori asked.

Emilio shrugged. "Don't get me wrong, I don't like seeing people die in the streets. But I think what happens inside China's borders is none of our business. Unless we're willing to go to war over it. But it's not in our national interest to take on a nuclear-armed country for running its internal affairs the way it sees fit. Frankly, I don't understand why everyone is surprised by this development. In recent years, China has become a bona fide surveillance state, oppressing its own population left and right, and no one did anything to stop it. Did everyone really not see the writing on the wall? And now we're supposed to fight for the people of Hong Kong?"

Through the glass, Tori glimpsed her executive producer signaling it was time for a commercial break.

Looking into the camera, Tori said, "Next up, we're speaking to one of the protesters with the Campaign Against Killer Robots. Stay tuned. We'll be back in a bit."

The cameraman counted down five seconds. "And we're off air," he said, relaxing his stance.

Tori turned to Emilio and shot him a fierce look. She clenched her fists. "I can't believe you implied the killing of protesters in the streets of Hong Kong is fake news. What the fuck were you thinking?"

He gave her a lopsided grin. "Hey, that's what I'm paid to do. Say terrible things and stir shit up. And I can't believe you wasted time interviewing that obnoxious kid this morning."

Tori returned Emilio a brilliant but fake smile. "The clip went viral within minutes of its posting. Now that's what *I'm* paid to do."

# [ 14 ]
## THE RUSSIA CONNECTION

MORGAN
0715
Situation Room
The White House

*Why did Tolley request my presence at this meeting?*

Over the past fifteen minutes, Morgan had listened carefully to every word of the heated back and forth between various cabinet members and wondered how she could possibly jump into the animated discussion.

*Am I expected to participate?*

If Morgan dared speak without an invitation, it would be like entering a boxing ring with the world's heaviest hitters in a fight to the death. Depending on how it went, she might not survive to see another day in her job, let alone her national security career. With a few well-placed social media posts by certain influencers, Morgan had witnessed carefully built reputations go up in flames in just a few hours.

She tugged on the edge of her beige skirt with clammy hands, trying to suppress her anxiety.

*Why would President Tolley call on me during a meeting of the National Security Council?*

Morgan stole a quick glance at President Tolley at the head of the table and admired her confidence.

Tolley's pale, freckled face was rather thin and long, which made her dainty features look larger. She wore a streamlined gray pantsuit with a black knit shirt. The color combination accentuated her shoulder-length reddish-brown hair and tawny brown eyes. For a woman in her mid-forties, Tolley was rather young-looking—that is, until she took control of a room full of power players and gave out commands to them. Then there was no mistaking her maturity or fierceness.

Morgan examined the other people in the room. Everyone who was anyone in national security was seated around the conference table in the Situation Room—the secretary of defense, the secretary of state, the chairman of the Joint Chiefs of Staff, the director of national intelligence, the director of the CIA, White House counsel, David McDonough, Morgan's boss and the national security advisor, and Tolley's chief of staff, Elise Russell.

The Situation Room was located in the West Wing of the White House and served as the primary spot for handling sensitive matters or dealing with a major crisis. The main conference room represented only a small part of the more-than-5,000-square-foot intelligence complex, which also housed the White House Watch Center that monitored world events around the clock. Morgan had been in the complex many times before in her six months at the White House, but rarely to attend a cabinet-level meeting. It was her boss's prerogative to decide whom to take with him, and he rarely chose her.

Morgan sat along the beige wall behind her boss's chair, the mahogany woodwork pressing into the back of her neck. From across the room, Luis, seated behind his own boss, tilted his head and grimaced at her. He attended such meetings on a regular basis as the chairman's plus-one. As his executive assistant, however, Luis would never be expected to participate.

*He's so lucky. Gets to be a fly on the wall without all the pressure.*

As the voices got louder, Morgan bit her lip.

"We can't just let the Chinese government slaughter people in the streets," Elizabeth Whitaker said, tossing her long, blonde hair behind her shoulder and shooting a death glare across the table at the secretary of defense. "Hong Kong was a democracy less than six months ago. Are you telling me that the United States is going to stand by and allow such bloodshed to take place with no response? If that's the case, then this is not the country I love anymore."

"What do you suggest we do about it, Beth?" Isaiah Burke asked, his tone gruff. "I don't mean hapless measures like your proposed resolution on economic sanctions at the UN Security Council, either. I mean real, tangible actions to stop the shootings from happening. We don't yet have satellite confirmation that the massacre is as terrible as it appears on social media. We can't afford to go to war with China over this. Especially not when they have two nuclear-armed submarines with missiles pointed at U.S. cities and parked God-knows-where off the fucking coast of Canada. Maybe we should talk about that situation before we worry about a few dead Chinese citizens."

Morgan suppressed a grimace.

*I can't believe he just said that.*

An uncomfortable silence descended upon the room. Apparently, no one else could either. Despite the star power around the table, no one wanted to get involved in the heated face-off between Elizabeth Whitaker—who had been Tolley's only pick for Monroe's cabinet and was a close friend of hers—and General Isaiah Burke, the first ever African American secretary of defense. He was a retired four-star general who had become a living legend during the cleanup of the Nightfall Incident.

Morgan had heard rumors of their mutual hatred in the news media, but this was the first time she'd had a chance to observe their bitter rivalry play out behind the scenes. Burke had vocally opposed Whitaker as Monroe's choice for the highest-ranking diplomat in the country. Ever since Whitaker's appointment at the beginning of President Monroe's term, he'd had an ax to grind with both Whitaker and Tolley. He also fumed over Tolley's clean energy deal with China, openly expressing his negative views in the news headlines. Burke viewed China as a dangerous competitor and potential enemy, an aggressive rival always seeking the upper hand in any form of collaboration.

Although they'd both led successful careers, Whitaker and Burke could not have come from more opposite worlds or held more different views.

Whitaker hailed from a wealthy family, attended Ivy League schools, and got her first job in Washington D.C. through her family's vast connections. Her career advanced quickly as a result of her powerful network, and she became known as a right-leaning Democrat, capable of working across the aisle.

Burke had grown up in the harsh streets of East Baltimore, paid his own way through college, and enlisted in the Army. After paying his dues as an infantry soldier, he attended Officer Candidate School and became a first lieutenant in the Army. Then he clawed his way up the military chain of command to reach four stars—a nearly impossible feat from such humble beginnings.

As a conservative Republican, Burke was a fierce defender of U.S. national security interests, but he defined them more narrowly than most. That was why he appealed especially to those on the far right and became Monroe's pick for SecDef. Monroe's political base liked the fact that Burke wasn't about to get the military wrapped up in another extended conflict overseas. Morgan had heard a rumor that Burke was gunning for the open VP position, which could explain Tolley's extreme caution around him.

Morgan was especially impressed that Whitaker had

managed to hold her ground against the notoriously cantankerous Burke.

*I'm not sure I would've fared half as well.*

The silence in the room was deafening. The demeanor of the meeting had gone from tense to exasperated, all within the first twenty minutes. In fact, it had gotten so quiet, Morgan could hear the wall clock ticking above her head.

*Tick. Tock. Tick. Tock.*

At the head of the table, President Tolley shuffled around a stack of papers, probably in an effort to delay her inevitable intervention for as long as possible. She placed her reading glasses on the table and turned to William Grayson, her director of national intelligence and one of her go-to advisors.

"Bill, you mentioned earlier this morning that your team was attempting to identify the true source of the tweets posted to the *China Xinhua News* handle. Have you had any luck?"

Morgan marveled at Tolley's ability to pretend as if a major blowout between her top two advisors hadn't even happened. With the president doggedly focused on the mission at hand, neither Whitaker nor Burke would dare return to bickering. At least for now.

*She's definitely a shrewd operator.*

Grayson cleared his throat and smiled as if he'd expected her to call on him. "Ma'am, we're still analyzing patterns in the post metadata from the IP address and haven't been able to confirm with absolute certainty where the tweets came from."

Sitting behind her boss, Morgan could tell David cringed internally. As the president's national security advisor, he'd felt slighted the past few days with President Tolley leaning so heavily on Grayson instead of him.

Earlier that morning, David had complained to Morgan about the director of national intelligence finding a way to steal his seat next to the president, a move that relegated David to the far end of the table. Lately, her boss had been acting deflated. It was as if his self-confidence had died with Monroe, and he didn't quite know how to find his bearings in a new administration. Morgan wondered if David would find the wherewithal to fight for his position of influence.

*I doubt it.*

David wasn't the aggressive sort. It was a miracle he'd reached such a powerful position in the government.

Tolley raised an eyebrow. "Absolute certainty? Bill, before you were certain the posts came from the Chinese government. Does that mean you have a new theory?"

"Actually, we received some intel from a Chinese counterpart in the Ministry of State Security about an hour ago, claiming their Twitter handle was hacked this morning," Grayson said. "They believe the user to be a Russian FSB agent."

Several mouths dropped around the table. Morgan frowned at the new development.

*Why would the Russian government hack China's official communication?*

"Are they sure?" Whitaker asked, her forehead creasing. "After many years of assisting China in bringing its nuclear triad online, Russia maintains a close relationship. Granted, they've had some tense moments over the U.S.-China clean energy deal in recent months. But I can't imagine the Russian government would attempt to infiltrate Chinese official communication channels in order to antagonize the United States. It doesn't make any sense. Remember that China still depends on Russia for technical expertise on their early warning systems. And Russia depends on China for its advanced military drones."

"Did they give you the identity of the agent?" Burke asked.

Grayson shook his head. "No."

"Well, that's convenient, now isn't it?" Burke said snidely. "Just blame it on the Russians. I bet if we asked the Chinese government through official channels about the tweets, they'll tell us absolutely nothing. They do love playing the blame game."

"Actually, we're inclined to agree the Russians are behind the posts as part of a disinformation campaign," Grayson said.

"But why would the Russians risk intensifying a conflict between us right now?" Whitaker asked, raising an eyebrow. "A nuclear exchange between China and the United States is definitely not in Russia's interest. Remember how other countries treated us and the Soviets during the Cold War? With kid gloves. The Russian government couldn't possibly expect to escape nuclear war between the U.S. and China unscathed. For that reason, they would never risk starting one."

Morgan's eyes widened. *Good point. What would be Russia's endgame here?*

"The Chinese source is not the only tangible reason for our suspicions," Grayson continued. "We've analyzed web activity at the IP address from which the tweets were posted. From that IP, the user posted on several other platforms as well. But we also found posts from the same profiles from IP addresses located just inside the Russian border, near the city of Vladivostok. It's only about two hundred miles from the Chinese city of Harbin to the Russian border and another hundred miles to Vladivostok."

"In other words, if a Russian agent found a way to sneak across the border, he or she could get in and out of China within several hours to upload the posts and make it look like they came from the Chinese government," David piped up from across the table.

Morgan cringed at his obvious desperation. David was trying to appear useful but had just failed miserably.

Grayson nodded. "That border area is mountainous and covered with thick forest. It wouldn't be hard to find a place to cross into China and back undetected."

Tolley leaned forward with her hands folded. "I'll be meeting with the Chinese ambassador for lunch today to discuss the unfortunate situation in Hong Kong as well as these posts. If we can assume for now that the tweets didn't come from the

Chinese government, why don't we move on to more pressing matters?"

Everyone around the table nodded in agreement.

"Bill, have we found any sign of those submarines?" Tolley asked.

Morgan suppressed a grimace. *We've lost track of China's submarines?*

Grayson shook his head. "No, ma'am, but we have as many eyes looking for them as possible. We've reached out to Canada with the help of Beth's staff at the State Department. The Canadian Navy is now on high alert and searching for them as well."

Morgan pressed her lips together.

*What are those submarines up to?*

# [ 15 ]
## AUTOPSY RESULTS

TORI
0720
Homeland Network News
Washington D.C.

The cameraman signaled to Tori that *The Counter View* was about to go back on the air. Just then, the executive producer rushed onto the set, slid a note across the news desk toward her, and then ran back off set. Tori glanced at it quickly, but didn't have time to read its full contents before looking up to face the camera.

"We're live in five... four... three... two... one." The cameraman pointed to Tori.

Smiling at the camera, Tori said, "A rowdy group of protesters were camped overnight outside the White House early this morning. They are hoping to sway President Tolley's decision to veto the autonomous weapons legislation—something they've named the Killer Robot Directive. I had the opportunity to speak with one of them about the dangers of killer robots. Let's see what message he had for the president." Tori cued the video footage, which played on the screen behind her.

A slight pang of guilt pierced Tori's gut when she thought of the editing hack job her executive producer had done to the footage. Tori had hoped to contribute to an important discussion with some of Drew's insights about the data problem for AI-enabled systems, but her producer insisted they stick to controversy—it was the bread and butter of *The Counter View*, after all.

The clip showed Drew looking into the camera, saying, "Today, President Tolley wants to authorize the Pentagon to unleash the Terminator. But we already know how those movies end. Humans die." The video footage ended abruptly.

"That was Drew Hudson, a graduate student at Georgetown University, expressing his views on the dangerous prospects of fully autonomous weapons," Tori said, suppressing a wince.

Emilio sighed heavily. "Yeah, yeah, yeah. Humans will die if we give autonomous machines the ability to make kill decisions. But I predict far more deaths if we don't field these weapon systems. If we fail to act now and deploy these systems, millions of Americans will die in a future war with China or Russia. If we allow other countries to gain the advantage of machine speed, it will be game over for us on the battlefield. Is that what these protesters want? To lie in their graves, forever comforted by their own morality?"

Tori nearly laughed out loud at his sarcasm but managed to keep her face slack. This time, he wasn't entirely wrong, but she would never admit it on air. "Well, we may not have to worry about that scenario," she said, pointing to her tablet. "The autonomous weapons bill just passed Senate about forty minutes ago, and it's expected to arrive on President Tolley's desk for her signature. Most experts believe the president will sign it without hesitation. Emilio, do you think the protesters have any shot at changing Tolley's mind?"

Emilio shook his head, pressing his lips together. "Oh, definitely not. There's a reason only a few hundred demonstrators showed up to protest against autonomous weapons systems."

Tori seized the opportunity to read the note from her executive producer, and her face blanched. She grabbed her tablet and began searching the news headlines. She didn't have to look very long. The breaking news was splashed across every news site and was spreading across the internet like wildfire.

"That's because most people understand the necessity," Emilio continued, unaware of the latest development. "We may not like the idea of robots killing humans, but we'd also prefer not to become slaves to China or Russia someday either. That's why the bill was so popular in Congress and generated unprecedented cooperation across the aisle. If Tolley knows what's good for her new administration, she'll just sign the bill."

Tori absorbed the headlines while listening for Emilio to finish talking. Suddenly, she perceived the awkward silence around her and looked up. "Of course, she'd also be honoring President Monroe's memory," she said, glancing at Emilio, who was now staring at the tablet in front of him, his eyes growing wide.

*He's seen it, too.*

"Some breaking news just came in over the wire," he said slowly, as if stunned. "There's been a new development in the investigation into President Monroe's death this morning. The medical examiner at the Bethesda Naval Hospital in Maryland just announced that she has completed the initial toxicology report. She remains unable to point to an exact cause of cardiac arrest but may have a potential lead from the president's blood panels. The toxicology report came back mostly normal, but Monroe had traces of chloroquine in his bloodstream."

"Chloroquine?" Tori asked. "Isn't that medicine used for the prevention of malaria?"

Emilio nodded. "The president's physician explained that Monroe was planning to travel to South Africa next week, where he would spend some time in areas with malaria present and was taking chloroquine as a precautionary measure."

Tori furrowed her brow as she recalled the side effects of malaria meds—the headaches and extreme fatigue. She'd experienced these when she traveled to Tanzania the previous year for a safari vacation. "Why is this relevant to his death?" she asked.

Looking back down at his tablet, Emilio said, "Apparently, chloroquine has a narrow therapeutic index."

"Can you translate what that means for our viewers?" Tori asked, narrowing her eyes.

Emilio nodded. "According to the medical examiner, it means that there is a small difference between a therapeutic and a lethal dose of the medicine. A lethal dose can cause immediate cardiac arrest in people with no history of heart problems."

"Are you suggesting the president might have died of an overdose of his malaria medicine?" Tori asked, the blood draining from her face.

Emilio shrugged. "Perhaps. The medical examiner said that there is no need for alarm at this time. Chloroquine is not usually detected on comprehensive toxicology screening. She ran the additional test because of the president's list of medications and screened him specifically for the presence of the chemical compound. She says they are looking closely at the levels of the compound throughout his organs to determine whether the medicine caused his heart attack."

From behind the glass, the executive producer signaled it was time to wrap things up. Tori breathed a sigh of relief. She never liked it when she and Emilio were compelled to cover breaking news without any prep. Especially news of such magnitude.

She turned her face back to the camera and faked a smile. "Stay with HNN for more breaking news on Hong Kong, President Tolley's decision on the autonomous weapons bill, and further news on the investigation of President Monroe's death. How does artificial intelligence help prevent nuclear war? Also, coming up, an in-depth analysis on the latest test of the Department of Defense's Autonomous Retaliatory Capability. Stay tuned, HNN Action News is next."

The executive producer came dashing out of the sound booth and gave them a thumbs-up. "Great work, you two. People are already tweeting about the suspicious circumstances behind President Monroe's death. This is going to blow up the internet."

Tori suppressed a sigh.

*That's great work?*

# [ 16 ]

## MUTUAL ASSURED DESTRUCTION

DREW
0755
Georgetown University
Washington D.C.

Drew dropped his green backpack on the floor, set his coffee cup on the table, and sank into a seat in the front row of his graduate class on the politics of national security. Somehow, he'd made it all the way to Georgetown's campus in Foggy Bottom a bit early, and the classroom was still empty.

He couldn't stop thinking about his conversation with the anti-nuclear protester. She had him wondering if the Campaign Against Killer Robots could ever effect positive change through demonstrations.

*Was she right about it all being useless? How come we haven't eliminated nuclear weapons yet?*

He thought about how she explained what she would have done differently had she known the results of her efforts in advance.

*But what else can I do?*

Drew had often thought an internship might be a better way to channel his passion against the development of autonomous weapons systems. But he wasn't sure he could fit yet another obligation into his already busy schedule. Most internships at think tanks in D.C. were unpaid, giving an unfair advantage to those possessing the financial means to work for free. Unlike many of his fellow students, Drew had to work nearly full time to support his graduate studies. The cost of living expenses inside the Beltway was out of control and weren't covered by student loans.

Between classes at Georgetown, mounds of homework, and daily shifts as a server at Octane Grill, an upscale restaurant located near the White House, he'd found it possible to slip in a demonstration here and there. It gave him the sense that he was doing something—even if it wasn't much in the grander scheme of things.

*But what if I'm not achieving anything tangible?*

Students filed into the classroom followed by the professor, who set his briefcase on the desk at the front of the room. He began writing on the whiteboard: "Does nuclear deterrence work?"

Drew smiled as his good friend Jay took the seat next to him. He still appeared to be wearing his clothes from the day before, and his ash blond dreads looked even more matted than usual.

Jay spent most of his time studying environmental science with the hope of becoming a marine biologist. He'd only taken the class on national security to check the box on his last social sciences core requirement. But mostly, he wanted to "see what all the fuss was about" after Drew wouldn't stop raving about the professor.

"Dude, you know you're famous right now, don't you?" Jay asked, clapping him on the back.

"What do you mean?" Drew asked.

"Your video clip went viral on social media this morning. It was featured on *The Counter View*. Didn't you see it?"

Drew sat in stunned silence for a moment.

"You interviewed with Tori Scott this morning? Here, take a look," Jay said, handing him the smartphone.

His hands trembling, Drew clasped the phone and pressed play. He blanched when he saw himself appear on the screen, his name in bold orange letters at the bottom. His light-brown hair was disheveled, and there were dark circles under his pale blue eyes from a terrible night of sleep. He sighed. At least the video camera added a few pounds to his lanky frame, making him seem less skinny for once.

*I'll never hear the end of this.*

The clip started out with him shouting, holding his protest sign, and walking toward the camera. Drew frowned.

*I didn't know Tori was taping that.*

In the next scene, Drew looked directly into the camera with a mic held to his face as he delivered his message to the president. His shoulders sank when he realized that *The Counter View* had only used the last thirty seconds of his interview.

*I should never have made that reference to pop culture!*

Drew could kick himself for being so stupid. Of course, he'd wanted his statement to go viral. And he sensed that Tori was specifically looking for something inflammatory to use as clickbait. He knew his complex arguments about data would be too obscure for most people so he sold out and mentioned the famous movie. But he wished he'd thought through the consequences.

"She cut out everything that came before that. The video gives the wrong impression. I actually meant to communicate the opposite." Drew's stomach clenched.

"What do you mean?" Jay asked.

"Well, I talked at length about the risks of data and autonomous weapons. I explained in detail why Tolley should reconsider America's future and the risks of integrating AI into weapons systems. Tori seemed to think it was all interesting. But apparently, she only cared about my answer to her last question. She even cut off the last bit of footage before I finished my point. I didn't end with 'humans die' like a crazy person, yelling at the president about the Terminator." Drew reached for his coffee and took a long drink, wishing it contained a shot of whiskey.

"Dude, I hate to break it to ya. But you are crazy, man." Jay smirked and tapped his temple. "Anyone who sleeps under an umbrella in the streets of D.C. and isn't homeless is certifiably insane. But you know what really makes you sound off your rocker?"

"What?" Drew asked, trying to signal with his dark expression that he was not in the mood for getting hassled.

"You thinking that Tori was going to make you sound intelligent or something." Jay laughed and slapped his knee. "Have you ever watched *The Counter View*?" he asked in a high-pitched tone. "Dude, it's like an entertainment news show featuring polarized analysis. Tori's from the left, and Emilio's from the right. The show exploits the extremes of any argument. They don't give two hoots about objectivity. What did you think would happen?"

Drew scowled and turned away from Jay.

"And aren't you taking a class with Professor Blake Tolley this semester? Not a smart move, bro," Jay added. "I heard his course is wicked hard. Hopefully, he doesn't come down hard on you for this."

*Shit.* In his excitement talking to Tori, he'd completely forgotten that the president's husband was one of his professors at Georgetown. Professor Tolley was responsible for inspiring his newfound passion for artificial intelligence, and he'd wanted to make a good impression. Drew swallowed hard.

*Hopefully, he'll understand.*

"Now if we're done celebrating our fifteen minutes of fame," a deep voice said, "I'd like to get started with class."

Drew looked up and saw Professor Johnstone remove his gray suit jacket and hang it on a chair. When they made eye contact, a knowing smirk spread across the professor's thickly bearded face. Suppressing a sigh, Drew closed his eyes for a moment and took a deep breath.

*Great. My professor has seen the video, too.*

"Good morning, everyone," Professor Richard Johnstone said, smoothing down his blue, striped dress shirt and navy-blue tie. He weaved his way around the desk toward the front row of students. "Today we're going to talk about nuclear deterrence, which continues to serve as a key cornerstone of U.S. national security strategy. As it has since the dawn of the nuclear age in 1945. But before we dig into substance, I want to start with some basics from the readings. Many of you have probably never thought about the threat posed by nuclear weapons. I know for a fact that some of you are a lot more concerned about autonomous weapons."

Professor Johnstone winked at Drew, and a ripple of laughter spread throughout the classroom.

*Awesome. They've all seen it.*

"Okay, I think it's important to understand the destructive power of nuclear weapons to set the context for our discussion," Johnstone said. "Let's say a nuclear weapon is detonated in a major U.S. city like Washington D.C." He turned and pointed at the quirky-looking girl in the front row. "Marie, you're working for a leading think tank focused on eliminating nuclear weapons this summer. What would happen if a city gets nuked?"

Marie smiled and took a deep breath before giving her answer. From her apparent lack of surprise, Drew assumed Professor Johnstone had given her some forewarning. Since many students already worked in the field at different organizations, the professor enjoyed leaning on the students' expertise to set up his lessons.

"Well, ultimately, it depends on the yield of the device," Marie said, repositioning her pink cat-eye glasses. "But a nuclear weapon wreaks unimaginable destruction in a single flash, no matter its size. Within a thousandth of a second, a sphere of plasma hotter than the sun grows into a fireball and instantly incinerates everything within a certain radius of ground zero. You'd be lucky if you're nearby because you'll die so fast you won't even know it happened. One second you exist, and life is normal, and less than a second later, you're gone. Obliterated. You don't exist anymore." She stopped to catch her breath before continuing. "Then, a bright flash of thermal energy burns everything within an even wider radius from ground zero. Anything that can catch fire within that circle, including human flesh, will do so. A few seconds later, the shockwave of high pressure and fast-moving air will reduce structures to rubble, causing buildings to collapse onto people. Any survivors will face radioactive fallout and die of radiation sickness if they're exposed to it. A massive area around ground zero will remain deathly toxic for some time to come and likely cost billions of dollars for decontamination."

"And just how many dead people are we talking about?" Johnstone asked grimly.

Marie nodded. "For a twenty-kiloton device detonating in downtown Washington, we're probably looking at about 80,000 dead within the first second after detonation and another 115,000 dead from severe injuries shortly thereafter. Those numbers do not include cases of cancer that develop much later."

Drew gasped out loud. *I had no idea.*

"Thanks for the graphic imagery, Marie," Johnstone said with a dark tone. Then he looked around the classroom at the shocked faces. "Folks, those are the casualties for a Hiroshima-size bomb. But that's a relatively small bomb these days. Since World War Two, we've developed nuclear bombs a thousand times more powerful. Today, your average nuclear bomb would destroy everything within a four-mile radius. Meanwhile, a fifteen-megaton thermonuclear bomb—the largest weapon ever tested by the United States—would annihilate every human and physical structure within the borders of the District of Columbia, including parts of Virginia."

*Holy crap.*

Drew craned his neck and saw a lot of bleak faces.

*Okay, they didn't know either.*

"The potential devastation of a nuclear weapon serves as the key starting point for U.S. nuclear deterrence strategy," Professor Johnstone said, walking back around the desk. "During the 1960s, nuclear experts began to realize that limited nuclear war was not possible and that such destructive forces must never be unleashed. For this reason, nuclear-armed countries have coexisted in what experts refer to as a state of 'mutual assured destruction'—that's the condition in which no country would use nuclear weapons against another for fear of massive retaliation. Therefore, an effective nuclear deterrence strategy makes the costs of using nuclear weapons so high that they will never be used in the first place." Johnstone went silent for a few moments, possibly to let the class absorb his grave points. Then he asked, "How many of you think nuclear deterrence succeeded as a strategy during the Cold War?"

A number of hands shot up, including Jay's. Still numb from the horrifying images of nuclear destruction swirling around in his head, Drew kept his hand down. But then he saw that it was more than half of the class, and he regretted his decision. When it came to his grad school classes, he didn't like being on the wrong side of the majority.

"Okay, what evidence can you offer to support your position?" Johnstone asked.

An attractive female student in the back of the room raised her hand. "It's pretty obvious that our nuclear deterrence strategy was a huge success during the Cold War. Not only did nuclear war never break out between the Soviet Union and the United States, there weren't even any conventional wars between the nuclear-armed powers."

"But is the absence of nuclear war a valid metric for

success?" a male student chimed in. "We came pretty close to using nuclear weapons during the Cuban Missile Crisis."

"Yeah, so what?" the woman retorted. "Common sense prevailed. The point is that Kennedy and Khrushchev didn't use nuclear weapons because they feared the horrible destruction that might take place. That's how deterrence works."

Drew furrowed his brow. *But what if common sense hadn't prevailed?*

"Okay, now how many of you think we just got lucky?" Johnstone asked.

Hesitating at first, Drew finally raised his hand. A number of other students followed suit with even less certainty.

Johnstone pointed to Drew. "Why do you think we got lucky?"

Drew swallowed hard. "Um, I'm not sure. It seems to me that deterrence depends on a lot more than mutual fear of destruction to function properly. For example, it assumes leaders on both sides of the deterrence equation are both rational and risk adverse. But if you look back on thousands of years of human history, that's a pretty big assumption to make. There are many examples of leaders who have tolerated significant risk, were not bound by moral limitations, and behaved recklessly to gain the military advantage. Because sometimes boldness pays off in war. Maybe even nuclear war."

"That's correct, Drew," Johnstone said. "Assessing the costs and benefits of using nuclear weapons depends on what leaders with the authority to push the nuclear button value and how they assign priorities to competing values. Since the adversary is dissuaded from taking undesirable actions, deterrence occurs in the minds of leaders—as long as nuclear weapons are not used, deterrence is perceived to work. However, deterrence failures can occur due to leader miscalculations, misperception, irrationality, high levels of risk tolerance, and even divergent value systems. Should we continue to assume that leaders accurately calculate and perceive the costs of nuclear war?"

*Probably not.* Then Drew realized something.

*Even if we succeeded in getting rid of Killer Robots here in the United States, leaders all over the world are approving them... what does that mean for the rest of us?*

Another revelation dawned on him.

*If nuclear weapons still exist and remain in use today, do we have any hope of preventing countries from fielding autonomous weapons systems?*

# [ 17 ]
## THE LOGIC OF DETERRENCE

MORGAN
0815
Situation Room
The White House

Morgan shifted her position in the chair, attempting to stimulate her circulation. She took a sip from her water bottle. Tolley's cabinet had deliberated for more than thirty minutes on how to pick up new signals from the two lost submarines. They debated back and forth about whether to ask the Russians for assistance or force the submarines to come to the surface by jamming their communications.

"Okay, I think we're decided, then," Tolley said. "At least for now, we won't ask the Russians to help us find them." She rustled the papers in front of her and turned to the secretary of defense. "General Burke, how serious is the threat from these submarines?" Her tone was stiff, as if compelled to engage him purely out of propriety.

"Ma'am?"

"Earlier, you asserted that China has two nuclear-armed

submarines with U.S. cities in their sights off the coast of Canada," Tolley said. "You seemed to indicate that they pose a critical threat to U.S. national security. Or did I misunderstand you before, sir?" Tolley stared down the table at him, her reading glasses sitting at the tip of her nose.

*Zing.*

Burke leaned forward, his mouth falling open for a moment as his eyes seemed to search the air for a good answer. "Ma'am," he said, after a too-long pause, "that was said in the heat of the moment. I apologize for misleading you."

Morgan suppressed a smirk and watched a satisfied look settle on Whitaker's face. Tolley definitely knew how to handle Burke in public. She'd waited for the perfect moment to make her point and put him in his place. Of course, he'd walked right into that trap. Morgan wondered if the win against Burke in the short-term would be worth it.

*I wouldn't want him as an enemy.*

Burke cleared his throat and continued, saying, "China is engaging in defensive moves that can be easily explained. Two weeks ago, China announced its new policy of forward deploying their submarines beyond the South China Sea. They're blaming our drone swarm surveillance and sonar sensor network near key choke points and waterways. They claim ocean transparency makes it hard for their submarines to travel undetected. I assure you that the deployment of submarines is part of China's planned war game tomorrow and nothing more."

"And you're certain of that?" Tolley asked, her forehead creasing.

Burke nodded. "I'm certain. It's part of the exercise. China wouldn't consider launching nuclear weapons at the U.S. from their submarines. It would defy the logic of deterrence."

*Logic?*

Morgan frowned. She never understood how senior leaders could simply forget about the essential starting point for deterrence whenever it was convenient to their argument.

*At its essence, deterrence is based on fear, not logic.*

Her thoughts drifted to her own theory about China's forward deployment of submarines that she'd proposed to the president shortly before his death. She suggested that China's new automated nuclear weapons system might have discovered a clever move to gain advantage in a nuclear conflict with the United States. She'd told him stories about the new moves discovered by DeepMind's AlphaZero in the games of chess and *Go* many years earlier. Unlike humans, deep neural networks were not tainted by bias regarding the theory of game play and often saw moves never before envisioned. But even she would admit her theory was a crazy idea.

"I disagree," Whitaker chimed in. "Even if the submarines are part of China's planned war game, they wouldn't separate from the flotilla and disappear for so long. Especially not the day before the exercise starts. Something feels terribly off about it."

"The strange circumstances do beg several questions for us to consider," Tolley said, turning her reading glasses over in her hands. "First, why did China add a nuclear component to its war game two weeks ago? Second, what role does China envision these submarines to play in that exercise? Third, are the Chinese exercising the first use of nuclear weapons against the United States, or are they exercising a retaliatory strike in response to our potential use of nuclear weapons? Fourth, why have two submarines gone missing and where are they?" Tolley paused for a moment, looking around the room. Her eyes stopped when she reached Morgan's face, making direct eye contact for a long moment.

*Oh God. She's not going to call on me, is she?*

Morgan slouched a bit in her chair, hiding her head behind her boss. Her heart pounded as if it might leap out of her chest. Then Tolley's eyes moved away from her as she turned toward the chairman. Morgan exhaled sharply.

"Admiral, you've been awfully quiet this morning. What's your assessment from a naval perspective?" Tolley asked.

Admiral Clarence Waller leaned forward in his leather chair. Despite his decorated military uniform and the four shiny stars on his shoulder, Waller's wrinkled face made him look more like a kind-hearted grandfather figure than a hardened military leader.

"Ma'am, submarine-launched ballistic missiles offer nuclear-armed countries a reliable second-strike retaliatory capability," he said. "It's the stealth of submarines that makes them such an effective means of retaliation. For example, if we were to use nuclear weapons on targets in China in a surprise first-strike attack and were able to take out their land-based intercontinental ballistic missiles, the Chinese would launch nuclear weapons from their submarines at U.S. targets in retaliation. And if we didn't manage to get all their land-based missiles in a first strike, they would hold their sea-based warheads in reserve for yet another move after first launching their remaining land-based missiles." The admiral stopped and waited for the president to respond.

*But why did the two submarines leave their flotilla? Wait a minute.*

A new theory popped into Morgan's head.

*What if the submarines are defecting?*

Morgan's heart began to pound at the notion, and she grabbed the thick arms of her chair.

*Would two submarines defect at the same time? What are the chances?*

She glanced around the room. Would someone else have the same thought?

*Not likely.*

The model of nuclear deterrence had become so ingrained in senior policymakers' worldviews over many decades that they rarely considered any alternatives. Plus, the scenario of two submarines defecting at the same time was an extreme outlier. Such incidents were considered black swans in international politics. They were rare, unexpected events with major cascading effects. No one would risk suggesting such an off-the-wall idea. Not in a high-caliber meeting, without tangible evidence. And if Morgan cared anything about her career, she wouldn't either.

"Ma'am, I share the admiral's views," David offered in another lame attempt to prove himself. "The Chinese are exercising a response to our use of nuclear weapons in the South China Sea, but we should still remain alert for other potential scenarios."

*Yes, other potential scenarios. Let's talk about those!*

Morgan hoped desperately they would explore the topic further, but she knew David raised it just for show. He was too worried about his career to propose any radical ideas.

Admiral Waller continued, "As far as the last-minute change from conventional to nuclear goes, the Chinese may have wanted to send us a strong signal not to intervene in the situation in Hong Kong. To remind us what's at stake, so to speak. But they may also be using the exercise to justify deploying their submarines away from the regional theater in the South China Sea, given our increased monitoring activities there. That could be why they announced it with such flourish. Otherwise, we might think they were up to something."

*Dammit. Think outside the box.*

Admiral Waller was softer spoken than Morgan expected from her boyfriend's work stories. Luis had described his boss as extraordinarily thoughtful and introspective. Unlike other more assertive military leaders, Waller withheld his opinions until they were extremely well-formed. In that same vein, he wasn't known to be a risk-taker. No, he would never raise the defection scenario. It was too risky.

"So you're also saying that China's deployment of submarines off the coast of Canada should be interpreted as a defensive move," Tolley said, appearing to confirm his statement. "According to the model of nuclear deterrence, that is."

*Please don't make me raise it.*

Morgan rubbed her hands together in anticipation. She knew

what she had to do. Her head throbbed, and each beat of her heart pulsated in her temples.

"Yes, ma'am," Admiral Waller said. "It wouldn't make sense for China to attack the United States with only two submarines. They don't carry enough warheads to take out our entire arsenal of land-based intercontinental ballistic missiles. If China were planning a first strike, they would want to reduce the amount of damage to Chinese territory when we retaliate. And as I said before, the Chinese would launch their land-based missiles first and save their sea-based missiles for their second or third moves."

When he stopped speaking, Morgan's pulse spiked. She opened her mouth, but nothing came out. Her chest tightened as she attempted to move her body out of her chair.

*It's now or never.*

Morgan rose slowly, clenching her fists to hide the trembling, and took a few steps toward the conference table. "Um... Madam President, I believe there's another possibility we haven't considered."

All heads around the table turned toward her in unison, some with wide eyes and others narrowed. Her boss, David, craned his neck and gave her a perplexed look. As she approached the table, the temperature in the room seemed to drop. Her hands were suddenly cold and clammy, and she struggled to keep her mind from turning into complete mush.

Morgan caught a slight scowl appear on Tolley's face, followed by a subtle nod.

"Yes, Dr. Shaw... please do enlighten the room with your theory." Tolley's tone was flat and emotionless.

*Welp. If this doesn't go over well, she may fire me for this.*

A heavy pit dropped in Morgan's stomach as she tried to find the right words—something that would make her idea sound more reasonable. But none came to mind. Only a simple but radical question rested on her lips. "What if the submarines are attempting to defect?" Her voice squeaked as she forced the words out.

The room went silent for what felt like an eternity. Unfriendly faces stared back at her as she waited for someone to say something. No one responded. The only sound was that of her heart pounding in her ears.

Morgan took a deep breath and said, "Okay. We have two missing submarines. As Dr. Whitaker pointed out earlier, it doesn't make sense that they would disappear the day before the war game is set to—"

"Let me get this straight," Burke said, his hand gestures bordering on dramatic as he continued. "You're proposing that two Chinese submarines operated by two different commanders may be attempting to defect from China to the United States or Canada? At the same time? I thought I'd heard plenty of nonsense this morning, but your ill-formed theory takes the cake."

In a panic, Morgan floundered for a rationale that didn't sound half-baked.

*Okay, maybe only one submarine is defecting?*

"Um... yes, sir," Morgan stammered. "Perhaps they aren't defecting at all but rather going rogue. What if one Chinese commander plans to start a conflict with an unauthorized launch of nuclear weapons? There are no technical barriers preventing naval commanders from launching their nuclear weapons. It's also possible that only one submarine is defecting, and the other is chasing it. I'm only suggesting these as possible scenarios for your consideration."

Burke's eyes bulged. "That's preposterous. The submarine commander can't launch nuclear weapons without help from the crew. Everyone on the boat would have to be in on it."

"Actually, it wouldn't take that many crew members to pull it off," Morgan said. "Maybe the captain and the executive officer. They have the keys to arm the—"

"Sweetheart, I'm afraid you've watched one too many

movies," Burke said. "It would require at least four crew members located in different parts of the submarine to launch the nuclear weapons. If just one of them refuses to participate, the launch would fail." He turned back to the president. "Plus, why would a submarine commander ever want to start a nuclear war? The choice would be a death sentence."

"But perhaps one submarine is defecting, and the other is giving chase?" Morgan asked, pressing forward in desperation.

Burke whipped his head back toward her, his lips curled. "Then how would you explain the behavior of the other attack submarines? They didn't even attempt to follow the others. If one of the submarines is attempting to defect, then why hasn't the commander communicated with us or with Canada about their intentions? And why hasn't the Chinese government said anything about this?" He turned back to the president. "Are we really going to waste our time listening to this?"

Morgan clenched her fists. The tension in the room was palpable. Whitaker looked like her face might explode. Grayson sat stiffly in his chair, shoulders hunched. Even Admiral Waller, the paragon of calm and collected, appeared piqued at her suggestion.

Not wanting to dig her grave any deeper, Morgan nodded deferentially, backed up a few steps, and then sank back into her chair. In that moment, she surrendered to all potential consequences of her foolish outburst. Her face burned hot, and she couldn't even steal a glance at Luis to confirm the impending disaster that was her career.

# [ 18 ]
## NORMAL ACCIDENT THEORY

DREW
0820
Georgetown University
Washington D.C.

Drew leaned his elbows on the table in front of him, his brow creased. The professor's voice droned on in the background about the many problems with U.S. nuclear deterrence strategy. But Drew couldn't shake his most troubling revelation. In his concern about autonomous weapons systems, he'd forgotten all about thousands of nuclear weapons pointed at U.S. cities and military targets.

In an era when autonomous weapons systems sped up the pace of warfare, what would that mean for nuclear deterrence? Would leaders of nuclear-armed countries be able to resist using nuclear weapons in a conflict taking place in mere nanoseconds?

Suddenly, Drew wasn't worried about robots on the next battlefield anymore.

*We might not even make it to see such a world.*

Staring in a thick daze at the whiteboard at the front of the classroom, he thought he heard his name called in the distance.

"Drew? Would you like to answer the question?" Professor Johnstone asked.

A rush of adrenaline shooting through his body, Drew's eyes opened wide, and he refocused on the professor's face like a laser. "Um, I didn't hear the question."

Johnstone threw his head back in a hearty chuckle. "Didn't get enough sleep last night?"

Drew's face flushed. "Yeah. Sorry. I was just thinking about everything you said earlier and got distracted."

"That's okay," Johnstone said. "I asked the class about other ways that nuclear deterrence can fail." He turned back to the class. "Even if nuclear deterrence 'succeeds' in preventing intentional nuclear war, we may still experience the massive destruction of a nuclear weapon one day because of nuclear accidents, false alarms, or unauthorized use. U.S. nuclear weapons are designed with redundant safety measures to prevent accidental detonation, but we've come close to disaster on a number of occasions. Can anyone talk about an example from the readings?"

Marie raised her hand. "In 1961, a B-52 bomber broke up midair and crashed into pieces on the ground in North Carolina. On the way down, two hydrogen bombs with megaton yields fell out of the plane. When the parachute on one bomb failed to deploy, it plummeted to the ground and broke into pieces. The parachute on the other bomb deployed, but the weapon nearly detonated on the ground after five of its six safety switches failed. That means the nuclear blast was stopped by a single safety switch."

"Thanks, Marie," Johnstone said. "That was a really close call. But it's not just accidents we need to worry about. Nuclear forces are designed for rapid action and can be ready for combat operations in mere minutes. Since the U.S. has planned to launch its nuclear weapons on warning of a nuclear attack, false alarms could lead to unintentional nuclear war. In your reading for today, did any of the past incidents hit a chord with you?"

Jay raised his hand. "I couldn't believe we nearly launched our entire stockpile of nuclear weapons against the Soviet Union in 1980 due to a janky computer chip."

Drew's jaw dropped. He must have missed that example in the readings.

Johnstone smiled. "Care to enlighten the rest of the class on the details of that incident?"

"Yeah, man," Jay said, pushing back a few dreads that had fallen forward. "We thought the Soviets were attacking, like for real. There was an official alert and everything. Brzezinski—he was the national security advisor, right?" The professor nodded, and Jay continued. "Well Brzezinski was about to wake up President Carter so the U.S. could drop nukes on the Soviets. But then the alert was called off a few minutes later. Turns out the whole thing was just a freak accident caused by a dollar-menu computer chip."

Drew sat back in his seat and let out a slow breath, shaking his head at hearing the account.

Johnstone clapped his hands. "Good. And that brings us to our key lesson for today. Has anyone heard of the normal accident theory?"

The classroom went dead silent, and Drew scratched his head, stealing a glance at the syllabus.

*Did I forget an assignment?*

Johnstone chuckled. "Don't worry, it's not a trick question. There weren't any readings on this topic. But does anyone want to guess what it is?"

More silence.

"Okay, has anyone heard of the Three Mile Island accident?" Johnstone asked.

Most of the class put up their hands, including Drew.

"Jay, want to give us a quick overview?" Johnstone asked.

"Sure," Jay said. "Some nuclear power plant in Pennsylvania

had a meltdown in 1979... I think it was because their cooling system was out of whack. Then the people working there made some mistakes, and radioactive gas leaked into the atmosphere. That's about the gist of it."

Johnstone nodded. "Yep. In the 1980s, Charles Perrow, a sociologist at Yale University, was trying to make sense of what happened at Three Mile Island. He developed some concepts that he called the normal accident theory, which argues that accidents are normal and nothing is failure proof. Perrow claimed that accidents are inevitable, especially when complex systems are tightly coupled."

Drew pinched his lips as a lightbulb went on in his head.

*Like nuclear weapons?*

"The biggest disasters start small and produce cascading effects," Johnstone continued. "In many cases, these disasters do not happen due to a major equipment malfunction but rather as a result of operator error and a lack of understanding of how the complex system functions."

Drew shot his hand in the air, causing Johnstone to stop talking and point at him. "I think I get the connection you're making," he said. "You're saying that nuclear weapons, with their many redundant safety features, are complex systems that are launched by other complex systems that control them. They are also delivered by complex systems such as bombers or ballistic missiles. So for nuclear weapons, we're not even talking about a single complex system, but rather multiple interconnected complex systems."

Johnstone nodded. "Yes, and the more tightly those complex systems are coupled together, the more likely we will see accidents in which the features of different complex systems interact in unexpected ways, leading to operator error and catastrophe. Small margins of error in each feature compounds as one thing leads to another."

"Is there any way to prevent normal accidents?" asked a male student in the back of the classroom.

Johnstone bobbed his head. "Perrow recommended that we reduce system complexity whenever possible and make sure that all systems designed to oversee complex processes can operate faster than a cascading incident."

"Wait a minute," Jay said, scratching his head. "Didn't the Department of Defense launch its new Autonomous Retaliatory Capability system several months ago?"

Drew shuddered at the thought of the system. The potential risks of ARC felt suddenly more real to him when he considered the destructiveness of a single nuclear weapon. He'd read about it a few times in his research but most of the information about ARC remained highly classified. Before Drew had perceived nuclear weapons and deterrence as abstract concepts compared to the more tangible idea of robots fighting wars on the battlefield.

*I wonder how many other Americans have no idea about any of this...*

Johnstone smiled broadly, showing his teeth. "Yes. The ARC system is designed to detect a nuclear attack, determine an appropriate nuclear response, and then give the retaliatory order without any human input."

"Wait, that thing can launch *nuclear* weapons?" Marie asked, her mouth dropping open. "I mean, I'd heard of it, but I thought autonomous weapons systems were illegal in our country."

Drew shook his head but held his tongue. He regretted not digging into the ARC system further and felt caught off guard by his own ignorance.

Johnstone crossed his arms and leaned against the desk. "Well, yes and no. ARC is a semi-autonomous system. Some of ARC's functions are carried out autonomously, but a human decision-maker can still intervene if necessary. It is also considered a defensives system rather than an offensive weapons system. In the press, the Department of Defense has justified ARC as a means of keeping us safe and considers it to be a semi-autonomous system capable of responding faster than humans."

"Keep us safe? That's so not cool, man," Jay said, his eyes

bulging. "ARC can launch the world's most destructive weapons and kill millions of people. I don't care what they want to call it to make us feel better. This thing is a doomsday device. Didn't anyone in our government stop to think how this could lead to an epic fail? As in, we're all dead like *that*." He snapped his fingers.

Johnstone nodded. "Congress held a number of hearings before authorizing the development of the ARC system more than a decade ago. And then it fell off the radar of the general public until recently. Experts argue that ARC will ensure credible nuclear deterrence in the event of a first-strike attack by one of our adversaries. If our enemies do not perceive the president to be able to retaliate with a massive nuclear attack, nuclear deterrence won't hold."

"But I thought the president has the sole authority to use nuclear weapons," Marie said. "Are you saying we just handed over that decision to a machine?"

"That's a good question, but no," Johnstone said. "ARC's designers took presidential authority into account. The president still has the sole authority to use nuclear weapons. But instead of giving the order to launch them, he or she must give the rescind order."

*Rescind order?*

Drew furrowed his brow. He considered the mere minutes it would take to launch U.S. intercontinental ballistic missiles from the many silos across the Western plain region. Once such missiles were airborne, they couldn't be called back. And that meant an all-out nuclear war would begin.

*But would the president have enough time to stop the attack?*

# [ 19 ]
## NUCLEAR OPTIONS

SUSAN
0830
Situation Room
The White House

*We're getting absolutely nowhere.*

After more than an hour, Susan still didn't have a clear path forward in the China crisis, and her team of advisors was more divided than ever. Susan stole a glance at the clock, trying not to wince as Burke and Beth went at each other's throats again. Of course, Morgan's harebrained proposal had not helped Susan maintain control of Burke's temper. Instead, it led him to hold sway over the majority opinion in the room while her advisors with outlier views cowered.

*I may have overestimated Morgan's potential for helping me with Burke.*

As he flapped his arms, Burke's strong, musky cologne wafted past Susan's nose, making her want to sneeze. It wasn't unpleasant, but it was overpowering, just like his personality. Susan could always detect when Burke was in the room, or even if he had been there recently, just by that scent. Sometimes, she'd pick up his residual aroma in the hallways of the White House when he was long gone.

She studied the room, still tuning out the cacophony of chatter. Susan wanted a decision in advance of her press briefing, but her advisors seemed to prefer starting another round of vicious back-and-forth insults. Beth insisted on a concerted response to the Mong Kok Massacre in defense of democratic principles. Meanwhile, Burke demanded they avoid any escalation that would lead to military action or war with China.

To them, the dead protesters and the lost submarines were opposite and incompatible sides of a political coin. The tense conflict with China also meant that Susan's hard work over the past six months to reach a clean energy deal hung in the balance.

*I need to talk to Ambassador Chen. Maybe we can dig ourselves out of this mess.*

In the midst of Burke's latest rant, Susan hesitated to intervene. It was way too early in her term as president to make enemies—especially one as powerful and dangerous as Burke. He enjoyed widespread support from President Monroe's base, and she did not. To get anything done within Congress, Susan would need to cultivate a cooperative relationship with him. But that didn't mean she had to like him or allow him to harass her allies.

She cleared her throat loudly, and her advisors finally stopped bickering for a moment. Beth mouthed the words, *I'm sorry.* Burke, on the other hand, wouldn't even look her straight in the eyes.

*Yeah, he's not sorry.*

Folding her hands together, Susan gazed at her cabinet members and said resolutely, "The State Department has issued a strong condemnation about the Mong Kok Massacre. We're also going to pursue economic sanctions at the UN Security Council and get independent confirmation from our intelligence services about the number of casualties in Hong Kong. But I'd like to table the discussion on further responses to the massacre for now."

She paused, and everyone around the table nodded.

"Have your staffs run through all the options this afternoon —diplomatic, economic, cyber, and military—and review any new intelligence that comes in over the wire today. We'll reconvene over secure videoconference in the early evening and come to a final decision. In the meantime, I'd like to discuss our nuclear options in the event of an escalating conflict with China."

"Ma'am?" Burke said, the muscles in his neck growing taut as he drew his eyebrows together and readjusted in his chair. "You can't possibly want to consider going nuclear."

*Stay calm. He's just trying to get a rise.*

Susan took a deep breath in an attempt to slow her heartbeat. "I was sworn into office four days ago. During my tenure as VP, I never expected to have the sole responsibility for launching a nuclear attack. While President Monroe was alive, he took the lead on national security issues. But now it's my responsibility, and I want to know my options." She paused to wait for head nods around the table. Then she leaned back in her chair and let her eyes meet the gaze of each person at the table. "For what it's worth, I don't think China wants a nuclear war with us. Especially not after we've worked for six months to achieve a historic clean energy agreement. That said, we have to consider the potential scenario in which the Chinese might be using this war game to put military assets into place. The last time we were distracted, China seized the advantage and took over Hong Kong. I don't want to get caught with our pants down again."

Everyone nodded in agreement.

"Ma'am, if I may begin the discussion," Admiral Waller said, leaning forward in his chair. "The U.S. maintains a nuclear triad with three different legs on land, at sea, and in the air. We currently deploy four hundred land-based intercontinental ballistic missiles stationed underground on high alert, ten nuclear ballistic missile submarines at sea, each carrying twenty missiles with multiple nuclear warheads, and sixty heavy bombers carrying gravity bombs and cruise missiles. That's a total of 1,550 nuclear warheads at our disposal. Our stockpile hasn't changed much since our arms control efforts with Russia fell apart a decade ago. But the same can't be said for China. Not only have they significantly expanded their nuclear arsenal over the years, they've invested a great deal into their sea-based delivery systems. They've deployed at least twenty new submarines in the past decade."

"But what's our plan for a nuclear conflict with China?" Susan asked.

Admiral Waller nodded and continued. "Until recently, we'd detailed our strategic nuclear war plan in Annex 25 of U.S. Strategic Command's Operations Plan 8010. The annex outlined a range of nuclear war fighting scenarios against different adversaries to deter and defeat a diverse set of targets."

Susan raised her eyebrow. "Until recently?"

"Ma'am, when we went live with ARC five months ago, we shifted from an approach involving pre-planned targeting and adaptive planning by U.S. Strategic Command staff to a new approach involving ARC's dynamic and autonomous planning in real time."

Susan frowned, wishing she'd given nuclear war more thought over the past six months. She was trying to make sense of the words *adaptive* and *dynamic*, but she didn't want to ask a dumb question—like what was the difference between the two concepts. She couldn't afford to come off as a complete amateur in front of Burke, but she also needed to understand her options.

*I never thought I'd be the one making these decisions.*

Admiral Waller continued, "Basically, we've trained ARC's deep neural network to assume command and control using all existing data on our nuclear forces and those of our adversaries. We've fed the network details from our nuclear war planning and targeting priorities over the past nine decades. During the training phase, ARC tweaked its algorithms until it produced reliable outcomes for many different types of nuclear war-fighting scenarios."

Susan frowned. "Please don't tell me you trained ARC to start and win nuclear wars," she said grimly. But she was only half-joking.

Admiral Waller's face blanched. Then he appeared to realize her sarcasm and chuckled. "Of course not, ma'am. Centoreum Tech used the nuclear deterrence model to train its deep neural network. The model provides the rules of the game, so to speak. The first rule of ARC's algorithms is to optimize its ability to retaliate after a nuclear attack. It is the most fundamental rule of the entire system. We made sure of it during the design phase in order to prevent the apocalyptic scenario you just suggested."

Susan exhaled. *Well, that's a relief.*

Admiral Waller continued, saying, "Moreover, to ensure ARC continues to function as expected and remains up to date, we run a test and evaluation each month. As you know, the fifth test is planned for this afternoon. This morning, ARC received another data infusion into its ISR component. During the test later today, we'll take ARC offline for a brief period, input a nuclear war scenario, run a simulation, produce synthetic data, and see how it performs. ARC will evaluate its ISR data and simulated nuclear attack data from the early warning system. Then it will devise a nuclear war fighting plan in real time. It delivers a custom nuclear retaliatory attack at a level appropriate to the provocation."

*Different levels of annihilation?*

Susan rubbed her chin. "In other words, you can't give me nuclear options until an attack is underway? Because ARC improvises in real time to provide flexible options based on the features of an actual attack?"

Admiral Waller nodded. "Ma'am, ARC offers a big improvement over the Cold War, when we had two basic choices. Back then, the president would have had to choose between an all-out retaliation—launching our entire arsenal at the adversary—or a controlled retaliation with limited nuclear attacks. Even so, many of us worried there was no such thing as a limited nuclear attack since a limited response would require nuance that just wasn't possible back then. The ARC system optimizes our chance of survival, so there are no better nuclear options than those recommended by ARC's deep neural network," he said with a smile. "You don't have to make a decision on how to use our nuclear weapons anymore. ARC does this for you."

*Now why doesn't that make me feel any better?*

"Today's scenario happens to involve a response to an escalating nuclear conflict with China," Admiral Waller said. "Once we have the results, we'll know better how ARC might respond in the current situation with China. If it's okay with you, ma'am, I propose we debrief you on the test results this evening. We can have a more productive discussion about possible nuclear options when we know the moves ARC recommends for today's exercise."

*Now I really need that technical briefing on ARC.*

Susan went silent for a few moments. She tried to remember the details of how ARC was supposed to function from her initial briefing, but her memories were blurry. "Let me make sure I understand correctly. Every month, we feed the ARC system new ISR data to keep it at the cutting edge of geopolitical and technological shifts. Then we take ARC offline and run a test scenario to make sure the system is functioning properly according to the model of nuclear deterrence. After that, we put ARC back online to monitor incoming sensor and intelligence data for emerging threats and nuclear attacks."

"Yes, ma'am, that's exactly how it works," Admiral Waller said.

"When the ARC system detects a nuclear attack via our early

warning radar and satellites, ARC plans an appropriate retalia-tory attack and gives the launch order," Susan added. "In this situation, I'll need to decide whether to issue the rescind order."

Admiral Waller nodded.

"And how long do I have to make that decision?" Susan asked.

"You'll have eight minutes and fifty-three seconds to rescind the launch order, ma'am."

*Eight minutes and fifty-three seconds?*

"That's it?" Susan asked, jerking her head. She hadn't really meant to speak her mind out loud.

*That's all the time I have to make a decision that will save or kill millions of people?*

"Yes, that's the maximum window of time for reaching a decision," Admiral Waller said. "We can't recall land-based intercontinental ballistic missiles once they're launched. And if we don't launch them before the first nuclear detonation hits U.S. soil, we might lose them in the first strike."

Susan furrowed her brow, imagining the total destruction that would ensue in a nuclear war.

*If the United States is hit with nuclear weapons, does it really matter if we can't launch our own in time? We'd all be dead…*

# [ 20 ]
## CHAIN OF COMMAND

GRACE
0840
E Ring, The Pentagon
Arlington, Virginia

Grace arrived early for the pre-brief meeting and stood outside the conference room, freshly showered and dressed in a clean uniform. Staring at the solid wood door, she wiped her sweaty hands on her navy trousers and took a few deep breaths. Since their morning meeting, she hadn't heard anything further from Colonel Martinez. For this reason, she expected her talking points must have made it into the read-ahead.

*I'm definitely going to have some explaining to do.*

Her thoughts drifted to the long series of texts from Zach she'd received the previous night. As expected, the tone had transitioned from legitimate worry to obnoxious irritation sometime around midnight and then finally arrogant anger by 3 a.m. His last text sounded particularly ominous and had stated rather bluntly, "We need to talk." Grace couldn't agree more. But she had other things to worry about so she didn't respond, knowing that might be enough to drive him over the edge. For a moment, she felt a prick of guilt.

*Maybe I should at least let him know I'm okay.*

Then she remembered how many times he'd done the same to her and given his extremely important job as an excuse. It was too late anyway. Her smartphone was already stashed in the lockbox, and she didn't want to pull it back out. Instead, she stared at the conference room door.

The Joint Chiefs of Staff conference room was located on the second floor in a Sensitive Compartmented Information Facility (SCIF) in the notorious E Ring of the Pentagon, which was home to more brass stars than she could count. As indicated on the plaque next to the door, the secure conference room was known as "The Tank" and used by the military's top leadership for discussing sensitive issues and wartime decisions.

Not daring to ring the bell and interrupt a high-level meeting, Grace decided to wait for someone with the code to the vault dial. She clenched her fists in anticipation. This was only her third time attending a meeting with the chairman, the most senior-ranking member of the U.S. Armed Forces and the principal military advisor to the president. If Colonel Martinez made good on his promise, she'd be giving the chairman part of his pre-brief for the morning test and evaluation of the ARC system.

*If only my father could see me now.*

Her father had never understood the importance of data and algorithms. She'd followed in his footsteps, attending the U.S. Air Force Academy in Colorado Springs and being commissioned as an officer. Instead of becoming a fighter pilot as her father had hoped, however, she'd majored in computer science and signed up for the Air Force's new data science career path. Her father worried she was making a terrible mistake, but Grace stood her ground. That said, she felt under constant pressure to prove she was right. Given her father's illustrious career as a fighter pilot, she had some big shoes to fill.

Down the hall, Grace spotted Arjun Sharma on the approach and pulled up her nose. The Pakistani-American was Centoreum Tech's onsite systems engineer for ARC and several years her junior. For a defense contractor, he was a smart engineer and seemed competent enough. Grace had really wanted to like him when they were assigned to the same team by her boss, Captain Dietz.

Sadly, Arjun had become her archnemesis after only a few months of working on the ARC system, and it was almost as if he wanted it that way. He constantly interfered with her ability to do her job. Time after time, whenever Grace put forward an objective analysis of ARC's weaknesses and potential problems to her senior leadership, Arjun would expertly counter her points one by one and then argue for its many strengths.

Even Captain Dietz would side with Arjun without question, ignoring any valid points she raised. But what Grace couldn't figure out was why her senior leadership would consistently disregard her analysis and then simply nod their heads whenever Arjun spoke.

*He's a defense contractor, not a high-ranking military officer.*

It was her primary responsibility to alert senior Pentagon leadership about any potential problems with ARC. She'd gone to Colonel Martinez precisely because none of them would listen to her.

Grace didn't take the decision to circumvent her boss or her boss's boss lightly. She knew she was putting her career on the line. But if she truly believed in her mission to protect the national security of the United States, she really didn't have a choice. It was a matter of life and death. The stakes were far more important than her career. She hoped her father would have agreed.

When he reached the door, Arjun gave her a smug smile and didn't bother to greet her properly. As usual, he was dressed to impress, wearing thick, black-framed glasses, a light blue suit and waistcoat, and a gray, floral-printed silk tie. With his flashy attire and diverse wardrobe, Grace was convinced Arjun must come from money.

*How else could he afford such clothes? Plus, who wears a vest during the summer?*

Grace returned Arjun's fake smile with a cold glare and rubbed her sweaty hands together. Feeling a bit plain, she glanced down at her Air Force blues—the starched light-blue blouse, a three-button navy jacket, matching trousers, and polished silver hardware. Her long, straight, black hair was tightly woven into a fresh French braid. She ran her fingertips along her hairline to make sure no loose strands were poking out. For a moment, she wondered if she should have worn the skirt and stockings this time; it was the only way she could elevate her image and comply with Air Force dress and appearance policy.

*I'm not going to let this kid stand in my way.*

Arjun tapped his pen against his binder and glanced at his watch. "By the way, I saw your comment about the *so-called* false positive you slipped into the chairman's read-ahead," he said, almost under his breath. "I'm surprised you went straight to Colonel Martinez without letting me clarify some things about the system design."

Grace said nothing. *No, you're not.*

"But hey, it's your career on the line, not mine." The corners of his lips turned upward into a self-satisfied grin.

Grace narrowed her eyes. "The ARC dashboard had a warning indicator. When I clicked on it, it stated that there is an emerging nuclear threat that requires a response in order to restore strategic stability. Specifically, ARC recommended an increase in the alert to DEFCON 3. The system has never done this before. When ARC doesn't function as expected, it's my job to bring this to the attention of Pentagon senior leadership. And I don't have to tell you about it first."

Arjun rubbed his chin. "Huh. Okay. But did you make

Captain Dietz aware of these issues before running to Colonel Martinez?"

Grace caught a knowing twinkle in his charcoal eyes and turned to avoid his gaze, her face flushing pink.

"Exactly what I thought," Arjun said.

"I don't know what you're talking about," Grace said, her voice wavering.

Arjun crossed his arms. "ARC is functioning exactly as expected, and you'd understand that if you would pay attention when I explain its design features. The system is supposed to identify anomalies in the ISR data and then recommend potential countermoves by U.S. nuclear forces. If ARC has recommended an increase in the readiness of the U.S. military, then we need to take it seriously."

"But that's exactly the point," Grace snapped. "It would be perfectly fine for ARC to provide recommendations if it were just designed to offer better situational awareness for U.S. military and political leadership. But there's much more to it than that, as you've just suggested. Both the early warning and command and control components of the system rely upon the threat context as determined by ARC's analysis of the ISR data. Thus, any anomaly in that analysis matters for determining the margin of error in ARC's recommendations for countermoves. The greater the margin of error, the greater chance of miscalculation, false alarms, or unintended nuclear war produced by the whole system."

"Grace, you're making a mountain out of a mole hill," Arjun said gruffly. "Do you really want to warn the chairman that the sky is falling when it's not?"

"Am I interrupting something?" A familiar voice boomed from down the hall behind Grace, causing her to swallow hard.

*Uh oh.*

Grace wished Martinez was there to defend her arguments, but he must be running late.

*Or maybe he's in the room for another meeting?*

Captain Trent Dietz was a former nuclear submarine commander in the Navy and the same rank as Martinez. Though he behaved and acted exactly the way Grace expected from the worst sort of O-6 officer—self-important, consumed by his own hubris, and nasty to the bone. There was something in her boss's tone that sent a chill down her spine.

"I take it you're discussing the points Major Lim sneaked into the read-ahead without talking to me first?"

Grace turned to see Dietz approach them. Instinctively, she saluted her boss with her right hand, as dictated by protocol. Dietz wore his Navy service uniform—khaki pants, short-sleeve khaki shirt, khaki belt, and black shoes. With his cap hanging from his belt, the sparse gray stubble on his bald head was visible. But Dietz's thick, black eyebrows were the most prominent feature on his face, and they were twisted into an angry scowl.

Dietz returned her salute and then shifted his attention to Arjun.

"Captain Dietz," Arjun said, stepping forward to shake his hand. "I'm just trying to rein in your data scientist before everyone in the Pentagon loses their shit."

*No name or rank? I'm just the crazy data scientist now.*

This was not the first time Arjun had paid respect to senior officers while stripping her of her title and dignity. Grace didn't understand what she'd done to garner such disdain. It wouldn't normally bother her, but Arjun's negative messaging had shaped how she was perceived in the office, and it affected her ability to do her job.

Dietz glanced at his watch and frowned deeply. "Major Lim, unfortunately I don't have time to lecture you about the chain of command or to help clean up the mess you've created for yourself." He paused for effect. "Instead, I've decided to let you sink or swim. If the chairman loses his shit for any reason," his lips curled, "and I mean for any reason at all, I'll hang you out to dry, and your career in the Air Force will be as good as over."

Grace gulped and nodded.

With that, Dietz swung around, walked toward the door, reached for the safe dial, and turned it back and forth, entering the secret combination. The door opened to a windowless room full of people, most of them in uniform. A large lump formed in her throat when she recognized many of the high-ranking military officers from the Joint Staff. Avoiding direct eye contact, Grace walked into the room as if she were treading on eggshells. She took a seat along the back wall behind her boss and surveyed the conference room.

Near the head of the golden oak table was Lieutenant General Richard Myers, a three-star general in the Army. He led the Joint Staff-6 Directorate for Command, Control, Communications & Computers/Cyber at the Pentagon where Grace, Arjun, and Dietz all worked. He was her boss's boss's boss's boss. Myers' deputy, Rear Admiral Thomas Trevino, a two-star admiral in the Navy, sat across from him. General Lawrence Hawkins, a three-star general in the Marine Corps and the director of the Joint Staff, sat at the opposite end of the table. A large entourage of junior officers, the plus-ones for the principals, was seated against the wall.

When Grace finished scanning the room, she froze for a moment. The chairman's seat at the middle of the table was empty, and there was no sign of Colonel Martinez anywhere along the back wall. The blood drained from her face.

"Let's go ahead and get started," Hawkins said gruffly. "Chairman Waller is running late. He got called to the White House this morning for an urgent meeting on China. I've heard from his military assistant that he was about to get in the car and head over to the Pentagon. Barring traffic, he should be here shortly. But I don't want to waste any time."

*Don't we need the chairman for this meeting?*

Panic settled in as Grace took her seat and realized Colonel Martinez would not provide any top cover for her as he'd promised.

*I'm screwed now.*

# [ 21 ]
## DECAPITATION STRIKE

SUSAN
0855
Situation Room
The White House

At least two things made Susan rather uncomfortable about the ARC system. In particular, she didn't like being in the dark about her nuclear options until a nuclear attack was underway. Depending on an autonomous system to devise and carry out launch orders also seemed like a disaster waiting to happen.

"What happens if ARC fails to respond to a nuclear attack?" Susan asked, shifting her legs under the table.

The question had been on the tip of her tongue for several minutes, but she'd hesitated to ask it. She recalled her heated discussion with Morgan, Jack, and Harrison in the Oval Office a week earlier. If Morgan was right about the rationale behind China's forward deployment of submarines, then the ARC system could be vulnerable to a surprise attack.

*I dismissed Morgan's theory out of hand then. But now it seems more plausible.*

"Ma'am, I don't know what you mean." Admiral Waller furrowed his brow. "Are you asking about a scenario in which ARC doesn't function properly? Because we test that every—"

Susan shook her head. "No, I'm asking about a scenario in which ARC is somehow taken offline, and the U.S. can't respond to an incoming nuclear attack. You just told me we've transferred all our nuclear planning, command, and control functions to ARC, essentially putting all of our eggs in one automated basket. That sounds like an awfully lucrative target to me." She paused for a moment to catch her breath. "What if our adversaries attempt to destroy the ARC system first? What if, for example, the Chinese are exercising a decapitation strike against the United States to take out our command and control system?"

*There. I said it.*

Several audible gasps rippled across the room, and eyes widened around the table. Admiral Waller jerked his head, Burke made a face, and Elizabeth moved around in her chair as if she was sitting on something hard. Susan was well aware of the political repercussions of challenging the concept of nuclear deterrence, which had practically become religion to many within the defense community. But she was sick and tired of her staff not thinking outside the box.

Even so, she worried about how Burke might respond to her radical question. A consummate Beltway operator, he wasn't the sort to criticize her to her face. He'd rather scheme behind her back in order to undermine her influence. Burke had to be the one behind the rumored suggestion that she didn't have what it took to be commander in chief. Susan suspected he was vying for the empty VP slot, and she didn't want to give him any more ammo.

Avoiding several incredulous glares from her cabinet members, Susan stared across the room, directly down the length of the table, at Morgan, who appeared to be shrinking into the back of her seat.

*Time to pass the buck.*

"Ma'am?" Admiral Waller said, his forehead creased more than usual.

"Actually, it's not my idea," Susan said with a smile. She sat up a bit straighter and then craned her neck to better see Morgan. She made direct eye contact and asked, "Dr. Shaw, wouldn't you like to enlighten the room with your China theory?"

"Gee, I hope this theory is as brilliant as the last one," Burke muttered under his breath. "Who is this Dr. Shaw, anyway? Your newly appointed good-idea fairy?" The sarcastic comment sent a cascade of nervous laughter around the room.

*Will she perform as I hope?*

Susan wasn't sure it was a good idea to invite Morgan to the meeting and allow her to participate. Given the intense power struggle between her and Burke, she didn't have many good options. But Morgan had already made one blunder with Burke, undermining her credibility. Would she be able to pull this one off?

*Maybe it doesn't matter.*

All eyes turned toward Morgan as they waited for her response. Susan found Morgan to be a rather attractive young woman but by no means stunning. She had long auburn hair tied back into a loose ponytail, youthful ivory skin, and a curvy figure. As her most striking feature, Morgan's hazel eyes seemed to change color depending on the light and the clothes she wore. The indoor lighting and her beige suit almost made them appear turquoise.

"Um..." Morgan said, looking rather uncertain and caught off guard.

"Don't be shy now, Dr. Shaw," Susan said, goading her lightly. "A week ago, before President Monroe's passing, you were in the Oval Office talking about the potential risks surrounding China's forward deployment of submarines. You thought it might mean something?"

"Yes, ma'am," Morgan said, her voice wavering. She rose from her chair and approached the conference table. "But it was just an abstract idea... I never meant to suggest—"

"That's okay, Dr. Shaw," Susan said. "I think we need to consider all possibilities."

Morgan nodded. "Yes, ma'am. Basically, I wondered about a scenario in which the Chinese might be toying with the notion of a preemptive strike against the ARC system. A decapitation strike, as you said, Madam President. If the Chinese could wipe out our early warning and command and control systems in one fell swoop, China would be free to take over Taiwan or anything else they're after while the U.S. reels from the consequences of a nuclear attack and is unable to retaliate."

"That's absurd," Burke said.

"Not really," Morgan said flatly, walking around the back of the room to face Burke directly. "The concept of deterrence is inherently based on the assumption that a nuclear war would be worth fighting under certain circumstances. At least that's how we've justified spending billions of dollars modernizing our nuclear arsenal over the past decade. We've claimed to the American public that we need to make nuclear war too costly for our adversaries to prevent them from wanton destruction. Thus, we need to protect our ability to retaliate against a nuclear attack. That logic also requires us to think about how our adversaries might tip the scale in their own favor. Strategically, it could make sense for China to neutralize our ability to use nuclear weapons against them in a war. Don't get me wrong, I'm not saying it's ever worth fighting a nuclear war, I'm just using your logic to illustrate possible scenarios."

*Impressive. The girl has audacity.*

Morgan tucked a loose hair behind her ear. "During the Cold War, we thought the Soviets could take out our leadership and command and control systems with only five nukes, removing our ability to retaliate. This exacerbated our worries about a surprise first-strike attack. We need to at least consider the possibility today. China's two missing submarines each carry twelve nuclear-armed missiles. If, as we suspect, China has equipped them with multiple independent reentry vehicles, then each missile carries up to four ninety-kiloton warheads. Each warhead is four times more powerful than the bombs dropped on Nagasaki and Hiroshima." She stared directly at Burke. "Sir, that's a total of forty-eight targets in the United States that could be hit with a massive weapon."

Susan inhaled a quick breath. *From only one submarine.*

"Dr. Shaw, you're punching way above your weight," Burke said. "And I promise it's not a good look for you."

Susan held her breath for a moment. *He's not one to make empty threats.*

"But sir, shouldn't we at least consider the potential for a decapitation strike?" Morgan asked. "What if the Chinese don't believe that U.S. nuclear retaliation is inevitable? What if China believes it can take out our command and control system from their submarines?"

"That's still far too few missiles to take on our four hundred land-based intercontinental ballistic missiles," Burke said confidently.

"Assuming we could still launch them," Morgan said quickly. "My point is that the nuclear firepower of these two submarines might be sufficient to wipe out ARC's command and control, thus eliminating our ability to retaliate and making a nuclear attack strategically profitable for China under certain circumstances. I think we need to consider a decapitation strike as a potential scenario."

"Wait a minute," Burke said. "First, you suggest the submarines might be defecting, or worse, that the submarine commanders might be planning an unauthorized use of nuclear weapons. Now you're proposing that China may be shifting its nuclear doctrine to an offensive strategy. Which one are you going to choose?"

Morgan shrugged nonchalantly. "Sir, I think we need to

consider all scenarios in the absence of tangible indicators in one direction or another. The defection idea came to me in the spur of the moment, but I've also been wondering about a decapitation strike for a while now. After an accelerated effort to develop a robust nuclear triad, China now has a total of twenty nuclear-armed submarines in service. Why so many? Seems like overkill for a pure second-strike capability."

Burke shrugged.

"Let's say the Chinese decide to deploy all twenty submarines to locations within reach of the United States," Morgan said. "That would add up quickly to about 960 nuclear weapons within reach of U.S. targets. That's enough weapons to take out all of our land-based ballistic missiles *and* target most major U.S. cities."

Burke scoffed at her. "The Julang-2 missile has a maximum range of about 4,500 miles. In order to do as you suggest, the Chinese would need to get their entire fleet of submarines out of their base at Hainan Island. They'd have to travel away from their safe coastal positions in the South China Sea, pass by our surveillance sensors and underwater drone swarms, and reach the open waters east of the Philippines. That's impossible to pull off without our detection. Plus, China usually protects its submarines with a fleet of surface warships and aircraft, making their movements easier to track." He paused for a moment. "There's no surprise attack brewing here. Maybe you should sit down, Dr. Shaw."

"I respectfully disagree with your level of certainty, sir." Her voice was elevated and wavered a bit. "The scenario I'm proposing has grown more plausible in recent months. Intelligence reporting suggests that China may be getting close to deploying the Julang-3 missile on its submarines. The new missile has a range of about 7,500 miles. That would allow China to hit targets within the U.S., even from its submarines sitting in the South China Sea."

Burke crossed his arms. "So what?"

Morgan began to slowly pace the length of the room. "If we are to assume that nuclear war is a viable option for our adversaries, then why wouldn't they consider launching attacks from submarines? For example, China could use such a move as a prelude to an all-out attack with land-based and air-delivered weapons. They could launch both attacks simultaneously. The submarine-launched ballistic missiles would take out Washington, the ARC system, and major coastal cities within less than fifteen minutes, impeding our ability to retaliate. Within thirty minutes, the land-based intercontinental missiles would destroy our silos and the rest of our population centers."

"And you're reading all of this into China's forward deployment of two nuclear-armed submarines?" Burke asked. He turned to Tolley, grimaced, and threw up his hands. "Where did you find this girl, anyway?"

Susan noticed Morgan cringe at the derogatory reference, but she didn't skip a beat.

Instead, Morgan turned to face Burke head on. "Perhaps this naval exercise is a prelude to China's grander strategy focused on submarines. Why do you think China has worked so hard to reclaim and fortify the Spratly Islands in the South China Sea despite the enormous operating costs caused by climate change?"

"Why don't you tell me? Since you clearly think you're the smartest person in the room," Burke said. Then he crossed his arms and scowled, indicating he wasn't going to play ball anymore. If he had anything to say about it, Morgan was a dead woman walking.

Susan suppressed a chuckle.

"Sir, it buys them more cover for their submarine patrols in coastal waters," Morgan said, answering her own question while continuing to pace.

"This is idiotic," Burke said, apparently unable to resist arguing with Morgan. "At best, the Chinese could only hope to blunt our command and control systems. A successful decapitation strike wouldn't be possible without launching a massive strike on our homeland. Even so, the targeting requirements would be extremely high without perfect intelligence on every communication node and command center. And that's not even taking our mobile command and control assets into account. If the Chinese were to miss just one of our command and control posts or communication links—and all it would take would be one—ARC would give the retaliatory order and launch a massive nuclear attack against China. Then the Chinese would face mass destruction of their own making. There is simply no rational incentive for the Chinese to initiate a first-strike attack with their submarines. Not unless they're prepared for an all-out nuclear war on their own territory, which is not in their interest." He slammed his hand on the table. "This cockamamie idea of yours defies the logic of deterrence."

*Exactly. Nuclear war is in no one's interest.*

"Sir, are you certain the Chinese know about ARC and understand how it works?" Morgan asked.

Burke sighed heavily. "The Department of Defense has broadcasted openly about ARC's development for several years. We publicly announced the launch of the system five months ago. I'm sure Chinese intelligence agencies have also been gathering plenty of information behind the scenes. How could they *not* know about it?"

"Even if the Chinese know about ARC, they still might make a terrible miscalculation," Morgan said. "As part of its information dominance strategy, China has leveraged its own AI-enabled systems to support its early warning and command and control systems for nuclear weapons. Unlike us, however, the Chinese remain highly insecure about their ability to detect a nuclear attack against them. For this reason, they are more concerned with false negatives."

"False negatives?" Susan asked, raising an eyebrow.

Morgan turned toward her. "Ma'am, a false negative occurs when a system fails to alert for a condition that exists. Due to perceived inadequacies in their early warning systems, the Chinese remain more vigilant toward the risk of surprise attacks than we do. They aren't confident in their ability to retaliate. The more worried they become about such scenarios, the more they'll pursue offensive strategies that favor a first-strike attack. If any of our actions heighten their fears, they may also suffer from an itchy trigger finger, causing them to launch before confirming the validity of an early warning."

Burke whipped his head toward Susan. "Madam President, this is absolutely ridiculous. I can't believe we're even entertaining this theory. For as long as nuclear-armed submarines have existed, they have served as a *defensive capability*, not an offensive one." He gazed down the table, making eye contact with Susan, and waited for a moment. "Ma'am, you can't possibly put any stock in this woman's implausible theories."

"General Burke, for the record, I also didn't find Dr. Shaw's theory that persuasive when she brought it up to the president last week, on entirely different grounds," Susan said. "I believe China will continue to abide by its traditional no-first-use policy on nuclear weapons even after the government finalizes its doctrinal review. And I share your views that China has deployed its submarines as part of its planned war game. However, the two lost submarines are a troubling development. I intend to clarify the situation with the Chinese ambassador later today." She paused for a moment to smile at Burke. "But one thing Dr. Shaw mentioned during our chat with the president last week did strike a chord with me."

"And what, pray tell, would that be?" Burke asked snidely.

"Dr. Shaw said that the Chinese have been tinkering with a fully automated nuclear weapons delivery system using a deep neural network. A bit like our ARC system, but it may be closer to being fully autonomous. Perhaps the network has learned a clever new move, one that we humans haven't considered before. And perhaps the Chinese are testing it out under the guise of this exercise. If autonomous systems are now part of the nuclear equation *for us*, then we must start considering how these systems would deter and defeat their opponents and whether that might diverge from how humans have done it in the past."

The room went silent for a few moments, as if everyone was stunned by the notion.

"Before we close, I have one final issue," Susan said, seizing the rare moment of silence. She looked over at Grayson expectantly. "Bill, do you foresee any problem if I decide to talk about the two submarines with Ambassador Chen at lunch today?"

Susan frowned when Grayson didn't respond immediately. He was staring at his secure smartphone with a troubled look on his face. He didn't appear to even hear the question.

"Ma'am, I don't think you should raise this issue with Ambassador Chen," Burke interjected. "We shouldn't let the Chinese know that we know about their submarines for now. It will reveal too much about our tracking capabilities."

*He's concerned about revealing our tracking capabilities?*

Looking up from his smartphone, Grayson said, enunciating each of his words, "I disagree with General Burke. The potential risk of escalation warrants clear communication about the submarines with the Chinese. The faster we can get this situation cleared up, the better. I think that's worth revealing something about our monitoring capabilities."

"Thanks, Bill. I will go ahead and raise the issue with the ambassador." Susan nodded briskly, putting her hands on the table and getting up to leave. "Okay, that's a wrap for now. Elise will send a meeting invite for the videoconference later today." As she turned toward the door and departed the room, a smile formed on her face.

*That went exactly as I'd hoped.*

# [ 22 ]
## THE OLIGARCH THEORY

MORGAN
0900
Eisenhower Executive Office Building
The White House

"Well, that was intense," Morgan said, sinking into her office chair and exhaling sharply. "Next time I complain about you not taking me to these meetings, please remind me of this experience."

She looked up at her boss. David hovered in the entrance of her cubicle with a deep frown on his pudgy, bearded face, but he said nothing. His navy suit jacket and tie were slung over one arm, and his pinstripe shirt tugged at his belly. The dark circles under his gray-blue eyes made him look rather cross.

*I hope he's not angry with me.*

Her adrenaline was still racing. In her head, she kept running through everything she'd said during the meeting and how Burke had responded, trying to determine how much damage control she'd have to do. She shook her head in disbelief. When she'd gone to breakfast with Luis that morning, the last thing she imagined happening that day was making a surprise splash at a cabinet-level meeting. It had been more like a typhoon—at least for her career.

*For better or worse, I'm on Burke's radar now.*

Morgan reached for her coffee cup and took a huge gulp, the lukewarm brew sloshing down her throat. She tried to collect her thoughts, but it was hard with her boss just standing there, staring at her.

"I wish you'd given me a heads up about your China theory," David said as if he'd finally gotten up the courage to confront her.

"You're not mad at me, are you?" Morgan asked, releasing a sigh. "Because you can get in a long line of people, after the president and the SecDef."

David ran his hand through his wavy brown hair. "No, I'm not mad. I just wish I'd known about it beforehand."

After over six months of working together as colleagues, David and Morgan had become fairly close. He'd often treated her as a confidante, running ideas by her before taking them to the president. Of course, Morgan was known as one of Harrison's favorites and having her support could go a long way in selling something to him. David had often used Morgan's connection to the president for his own benefit, and she'd allowed it to happen. Now that Tolley was the president, the flow of that arrangement would be disrupted. Morgan sensed she was reaching persona non grata status with President Tolley.

*I might actually be Tolley's least favorite person right now.*

Trying to shake off the irony, Morgan raised and lowered her shoulders. "Well, it wasn't an official theory. More like a random musing."

"A random musing that you just happened to share with President Monroe..."

*Oh c'mon.*

"David, you know I didn't try to go over your head. I was in the Oval Office with my Uncle Jack and President Monroe having a late-night drink after a long day. Tolley happened to come by the office before heading home and joined in our discussion. I never meant for her to overhear it. And I certainly didn't anticipate all the events that followed—particularly, President Monroe's death. I'm sorry if you feel slighted."

"Well, I can't give you any top cover when I'm in the dark," he said. There was a defensiveness to his tone she didn't like. She wondered for a moment how their working relationship might change under the new administration.

*This doesn't bode well.*

Morgan pinched her lips. "Give me a break, David. I wish I'd known Tolley was going to call on me. Weren't you wondering why the president wanted me to attend a cabinet-level meeting when Elise called you this morning? When she clearly doesn't like me..."

*Where was my heads up?*

"Yeah, that was a bit odd, wasn't it?" David said, his brow furrowing. "I'm now worried about the dangerous fallout that will be coming your way. You're the director of defense issues on the National Security Council staff. Knowing what I know about Burke, he's going to call for your removal when he gets back to the Pentagon this morning. I don't think anyone will be able to stop him."

*So... Tolley set me up with Burke.*

Morgan stuck out her chin. "Well, if Burke comes after you, feel free to duck down and send him my way. I can handle anything that bastard throws at me."

David broke eye contact and rubbed the back of his neck. "If you say so."

*Perhaps Tolley wants to get Burke to fire me. So she doesn't have to do it.*

"Now that I think of it," Morgan said, pursing her lips, "maybe Tolley wanted to raise the scenario herself, but she didn't want to deal with Burke's ridicule or the aftermath. So instead, she invites me to the meeting, waits to call on me until exactly the right time, and then trots me out there in front of everyone to make a controversial point for her."

*If I'm right, she's definitely a shrewd operator. More so than I thought.*

"You do serve at the pleasure of the president." David gave her a slight smirk. "Take it as a compliment. If that's true, she obviously thinks you're useful for fending off Burke."

Morgan grinned, flashing her teeth. "That's just great. It's my forever dream come true. To be the punching bag for the president's adversaries."

"What did you think about the Russia connection?" David asked, changing the subject.

Morgan's forehead creased. "I'm not sure if I buy the notion of the tweets coming from the Russian government. The Russian Federal Security Service is certainly not above engaging in dangerous shenanigans on social media. And they're highly skilled in designing effective global disinformation campaigns to achieve Russia's political ends. But I don't think the Russian government would risk instigating a conflict involving nuclear weapons."

David put his hand on his forehead. "Yeah, things have become far more precarious now that we have nuclear-capable hypersonic missiles deployed in several countries. When you've got delivery systems capable of hitting any target around the world in fifteen minutes or less, you have to think twice about engaging in any escalatory behavior. A single post on social media could go viral and lead a conflict to spin out of control, and then a few minutes later, everyone in the world is dead."

"Thanks for that uplifting image, Dr. Doom." Morgan grimaced at him, and he laughed. "Yeah, there's no way Russia would want to catalyze a nuclear exchange between the U.S. and China. Some of the radioactive fallout would likely reach into Far East Russia where the Russian Pacific Fleet is headquartered. That would be like shooting themselves in both feet and both hands and then swallowing a grenade."

David laughed out loud.

Morgan's adrenaline flowed freely. Discussing the worst-case scenarios in a matter-of-fact sort of way without breaking a sweat was what she loved most about her job in national security. It attracted her kind of people—they were nerdy, pragmatic, and somewhat twisted in the head.

She rubbed her chin as she considered a thought. "I do recall reading about Russia's belligerent opposition to the U.S.-China clean energy deal in the headlines a few months ago. At one point, the Russian president even threatened a precipitous decline in relations with both China and the U.S. if the deal went through. I assumed they were just blowing smoke. The Russians have plenty of other customers eager to buy their natural gas supplies. And then they didn't do anything when the deal was signed except huff and puff about it."

"Well, Russia's economy still depends on revenues from its oil and natural gas resources. With the Arctic opening up as a result of warmer temperatures, the Russians hope to capitalize on additional deposits formerly inaccessible under the ice. They were planning to sell their abundant supplies to China and other Asian customers as they've done for the past fifteen years."

"True," Morgan said.

Under the clean energy deal, China agreed to reduce the volume of its oil and natural gas purchases, replacing carbon-heavy sources with biofuels produced with sunlight and algae. They also agreed to add more capacity in nuclear, hydro, geothermal, wind, and solar energy. Morgan knew other countries would never be able to replace the huge volumes of natural gas Russia sold to China. The Russian government would be highly motivated to tank the deal.

A lightbulb went on in Morgan's head. "Okay, let's assume the U.S.-China clean energy deal has pissed off Russia enough to stir up trouble. Who in Russia stands to lose the most?"

"What do you mean?" David asked.

"What if the individual who hacked the *China Xinhua News*

handle and posted the tweets is indeed Russian, but not an agent of the Russian government?"

"Hmm, you might be on to something," David said, pausing to think for a moment. "How about a Russian oligarch with major interests in the oil and natural gas industry and strong ties to organized crime? That gives us motive and opportunity."

"Yeah," Morgan said, furrowing her brow. "Someone with major interests in oil and natural gas and a close relationship to the Russian president so that he's a trusted agent. But not too close, to offer plausible deniability. But also someone not afraid to orchestrate a rogue operation that might lead to the collapse of the clean energy deal. That would be of great benefit to the Russian government."

"Which Russian oligarchs fit the bill?" David asked.

"Off the top of my head, I'm not sure. But whoever it may be, they might not understand how dire the crisis between the U.S. and China has become. I'm pretty certain no oligarch in Russia would be looking for a nuclear war, but they might accidently stumble into one. Maybe we should ask Mike Palmer? As the senior director for European and Russian Affairs, he'd keep himself apprised of the activities of Russian oligarchs. He could probably narrow the list or at least point us in the right direction."

"Good idea," David said. "I'll let my assistant know we're going to pay him a visit."

# [ 23 ]
## THE READ-AHEAD

GRACE
0905
E Ring, The Pentagon
Arlington, Virginia

With one eye glued on the door, Grace listened intently as General Hawkins went over the detailed procedures for ARC's test and evaluation scheduled for later that day. She clasped her hands in her lap and tried to keep them from shaking. But her heart thumped so loudly she was certain Arjun, who was sitting next to her, could hear it.

Sooner or later, Hawkins would ask a question provoked by her comments in the read-ahead document. And without Martinez to come to her rescue, she envisioned a verbal bloodbath taking place with her as the main casualty.

"Focusing on our conflict with China over Hong Kong, the theme of today's simulation couldn't be more timely," Hawkins said. "Although it's been planned for two weeks, we've updated the simulation to take recent events into account." He paused for a moment while scanning the read-ahead. "What's this

155

about a false positive?" Hawkins asked, looking around the room at the blank faces at the table. He frowned when no one answered immediately. "Can anyone explain why this was flagged for the chairman's attention?"

*That's the issue he's worried about? Not ARC's recommendations?*

Stealing a glance at Arjun, she noticed a smug look on his face.

*Did Dietz get to Hawkins before the meeting?*

Captain Dietz cleared his throat. "Uh, sir, that note was apparently added to the read-ahead by Colonel Martinez at the behest of Major Lim."

Hawkins grunted and stared down his nose at Dietz. "Then I take it no one from the J6 senior leadership cleared the addition?"

"No, sir. We most certainly did not." He leaned forward to look at his boss.

Lieutenant General Myers nodded in agreement.

"Are you suggesting that the J6 is unable to manage its subordinates effectively?" Hawkins asked.

Dietz shrank back. "No, sir. I am not."

"Huh," Hawkins grunted. "Because mounting evidence suggests the contrary." His sarcasm was unmistakable. Then he turned to look at Grace, his steely gray eyes penetrating hers. "Major Lim, would you care to take a seat at the table and explain yourself?"

*Seat at the table?*

For a moment, Grace's body was paralyzed.

"Major, we don't have all day." Hawkins motioned impatiently for her to take the empty seat next to her boss.

She did so without further delay, an empty pit forming in her stomach. The feet of her leather swivel chair screeched against the floor as she pulled it forward. Before looking at Hawkins, she glanced down at her notes to recall the key points she'd wanted to raise with the chairman.

"Any day now…" Hawkins said.

Grace looked up from her notes and nodded tentatively, her face flushing pink. "Um, sir, the ARC system recommends that U.S. Strategic Command raise the alert of our nuclear forces to DEFCON 3. Moreover, the system recommends we undertake a countermove to restore strategic stability. I found this to be rather irregular."

Hawkins scrutinized the text in the read-ahead. "Ah, yes, I thought that was a rather interesting development as well. I see here that ARC recommends we disrupt low frequency communications between China's command and control satellite and its submarines. By jamming the frequencies available to submarines located deep underwater, we can force them to come to the surface in order to communicate." He grunted. "DEFCON 3 might be overkill, but the jamming sounds like a reasonable countermove. It would send a pretty clear message to China to get its submarines out of our coastal waters. What's the problem?"

Eyeing the door, Grace bit her lip. "Sir, the problem is that to function as expected, the model of nuclear deterrence requires the ARC system to interpret the forward deployment of China's submarines as a defensive move. But given the nature of ARC's recommendations, I believe it has assessed China to have a new offensive doctrine for its nuclear-armed submarine force."

"You're suggesting that ARC is not functioning properly?" Hawkins asked, his eyebrow raised.

"Yes, sir. That's exactly what I'm saying," Grace said. "We're using the model of deterrence as a failsafe to ensure that ARC continues to function as expected and doesn't learn new moves, in particular how to fight and win a nuclear war. I believe ARC has exceeded the parameters of the model. The recommendation to go to DEFCON 3 in response to defensive maneuvering by China deviates from the model of nuclear deterrence. The anomaly suggests the ARC system is no longer functioning as expected."

"And that's the false positive you've referenced in the read-ahead." Hawkins studied the paper.

"Yes, sir," Grace said.

His eyes moved slowly up and down as he read. "Okay, then please explain to me why ARC is producing such a recommendation. How do you know for sure that the system isn't functioning properly?"

Grace glanced at the door again, her lip quivering.

*Where's Colonel Martinez?*

"Sir, I don't know for sure. I can't explain it," she said.

Hawkins' eyes grew large, and his mouth fell open. "You don't know why? What do you mean you can't explain it?"

Her face flushing, Grace broke eye contact and stared at the table. "Sir, the design of the ARC system is too complex to explain causality in such a short timeframe. I need more time and a few additional analysts to run some in-depth diagnostics."

"How much time?" he asked.

"One or two days at—"

Hawkins cut her off before she could finish. "You're suggesting we cancel the planned test and evaluation? Do you understand how much is riding on it?"

"Yes, sir. I do, but—"

Hawkins interrupted her again. "In the absence of these diagnostics, you're making some rather big assumptions."

Grace nodded. "Sir, I'm assuming that the system is not functioning properly because ARC has never recommended a countermove before. And I don't have enough information to explain why. That's the problem."

Hawkins frowned. "I thought you said the problem was that ARC is interpreting China's deployment action as offensive. Now you're saying the problem is that you can't explain the reasons for the recommendation coming from ARC. Which is it?"

Grace cleared her throat. "Sir, it's both. Even with additional diagnostics, we may not be able to fully explain either issue. In rule-based systems of the past, programmers could trace outcomes or system behavior back to a rule or complex interactions among different rules. When a deep neural network learns from data, it tweaks its own algorithms to produce our desired outcomes. There are too many algorithmic layers and billions of interactions among them to make an accurate determination about what causes certain outcomes. This level of complexity allows ARC to solve complex problems, but it can also cause the system to fail or behave in unpredictable and complex ways. To put it simply, we can't understand how the deep neural network learns from the data we feed it—especially when new data diverges from the training data."

Hawkins furrowed his brow. "Okay, fine. Then if you can't explain why the ARC system produces a specific outcome, can you at least explain to me why I should care? I still haven't heard any reason why we shouldn't proceed with ARC's test and evaluation later today."

*Because ARC gives the order to launch nuclear weapons?*

"Yes, sir. The problem arises from the tight interlocking of the different components of ARC. As you know, the ISR component is directly linked to the early warning, command and control, targeting, and launch components. If the ISR component of ARC has misinterpreted the last round of data and deviates from the model of deterrence, the system could be recommending moves that are intended to defeat rather than deter an adversary. In short, ARC could be leading us down a path of nuclear escalation, but we can't be sure. For this reason, I think we should take the system offline until we can figure out why this is happening and make sure it doesn't unintentionally lead to further errors."

"Now you're suggesting we take ARC offline?" Hawkins said, his jaw tightening.

Dietz cleared his throat. "Sir, I think we're getting dangerously close to an overreaction here. My team's systems engineer from Centoreum Tech has explained to me that there is actually no false positive. The ARC system is functioning entirely as expected. Major Lim simply doesn't understand how the system functions and is dead wrong."

Her body tensed, and Grace looked at the door again.

*Still no sign of Colonel Martinez.*

Hawkins narrowed his eyes. "So, you're saying that there's nothing to worry about here?"

"Sir, that's correct," Dietz continued.

"What about the recommended move to DEFCON 3?" Hawkins asked. "Are you saying we should just do what ARC says and increase the readiness of our nuclear forces?"

Dietz shook his head. "Sir, that decision is above my pay grade. I'm saying we shouldn't get distracted by minor technicalities. Instead, we should calmly review the recommendations made by ARC. These recommendations come from Centoreum's proprietary technique for developing a 'dynamic' deep neural network. You may recall when the department put together the request for proposal, we specifically asked for a system that would be designed to learn continuously and remain up to date. We wanted to make sure the real-world environment would not evolve significantly beyond the algorithmic model generated by the training data. If that were to happen, the system would fail to operate in the real world. Obviously, this is something we needed to avoid—"

"But that's also the problem, sir," Grace said, interrupting her boss and making direct eye contact with Hawkins. "What if ARC's deep neural network has tweaked the algorithms to assume a greater likelihood of China's use of nuclear weapons than is actually the case? That will have effects on the other components in the—"

"Sir, the changes in the algorithm fall within acceptable parameters," Dietz said, his voice growing louder. "Centoreum Tech has developed a system to support our nuclear decision-making by detecting anomalies in behavior patterns of our nuclear adversaries. The fact that China has forward deployed two of its nuclear-armed submarines is an anomaly in its behavior, which may indicate a significant change in their doctrine and represent some form of escalatory signaling by the Chinese. Or it could mean exactly what the Chinese are claiming it means. It could simply be a defensive move in response to greater ocean transparency around key choke points."

Hawkins held up his hand. "Okay, I think I've heard enough." He glanced at his watch. "I'm afraid the chairman has gotten held up by traffic after all. I'll brief him when he gets in. Today's test will proceed as planned. If the ARC system functions as expected, we will put it back online and discuss implementing ARC's recommendations. General Myers and Captain Dietz, I'd like a word with you both, please. The rest of you are dismissed."

*Uh oh.*

Dietz shot Grace a death glare as he made his way toward the front of the room where General Hawkins stood. As Grace rose from the table, she glimpsed an I-told-you-so grimace on Arjun's face. Without giving him another glance, she grabbed her notepad and marched out of the room, her cheeks blazing from the heat of her embarrassment.

Outside the conference room, Grace pulled her smartphone from the lockbox and hurried down the corridor in search of a good signal. When she found two bars, she dialed Colonel Martinez's number. No answer.

Shaking her head in frustration, Grace typed out a text:

WHERE ARE YOU? WE NEED TO TALK RIGHT AWAY.

# [ 24 ]

## THE BENEFACTOR

MORGAN
0935
Eisenhower Executive Office Building
The White House

Morgan's high heels clacked on the black-and-white checkered marble floors as she strode through the long hallways of the Eisenhower Executive Office Building. Next to her, David shuffled along, struggling to keep up with her pace. Even more quiet and contemplative than usual, he appeared to be lost in another world.

To fill the void of silence, she caught herself looking down at her feet in search of the 400-million-year-old fossils visible in the polished stone floor tiles throughout the building. Even after six months of working at the White House, Morgan marveled at the building's beauty—the high ceilings and ornately decorated white woodwork, the mauve-painted columns and cream-colored walls, and the heavy, solid wood doors.

Her favorite elements were the cast-iron doorknobs, which

were embossed with old department symbols. They were historical markers of the early 1900s, during which the building housed the U.S. Departments of State, War, and the Navy.

Her smartphone buzzed with a text from Luis about the ARC system. Apparently, Grace was very worried about the system not functioning properly and was unable to convey her concerns to Pentagon leadership. Luis suggested that perhaps Morgan could bend the ear of the president and help them out.

*With what leverage?*

Morgan frowned at the new complication and wondered if she should pay the Pentagon a visit and learn about it herself. She'd have to know the details about the ARC system before bringing the matter to the president for her consideration.

*Not the best timing.*

David picked up his pace as he approached a tall wooden door. The plaque with a Presidential Seal notated the room number and the name of the office—European and Russian Affairs.

"Did you see the headline about the president's autopsy this morning?" David asked.

Morgan stopped in front of the door and stared at him wide-eyed, a hitch in her breath. "Uh, no, I didn't."

"The medical examiner found traces of chloroquine in his bloodstream," David said, biting his lip. "There's rampant speculation on social media that malaria medicine might be the cause of the president's sudden heart attack. Of course, the medical examiner has warned against jumping to such conclusions. The president was taking the med for his trip to South Africa. More tests are needed to confirm actual levels and to prove any connection to his death. But that's not stopping people on social media from claiming the president was assassinated."

*Holy shit.*

Morgan's pulse spiked, and the blood drained from her face.

*Was the president assassinated?*

She dreaded the answer to her questions. She looked at her watch.

*I need to talk to Jack.*

"Anyway, I thought you should know. I meant to tell you earlier," David said. "I guess there's never a right time for news like that. And I didn't want you off your game in front of the president this morning." David punched in his code on the electronic box.

The lock beeped as Morgan nodded, still reeling from the shock. David held the heavy door open for her as they entered the cluttered foyer. An administrative assistant looked up, her eyes widening at the sight of the National Security Advisor.

*Maybe we should have called ahead. Showing up unannounced might throw them off.*

Although he was her boss, Morgan sometimes forgot that David held the prestigious title and reported directly to the president.

"Dr. McDonough, how can I help you?" the administrative assistant asked, blinking rapidly, a look of awe on her face.

"Is Mike in his office?" David asked, pointing to the open door at the far end of the hallway.

The assistant nodded, glancing at her computer screen. "I think he's on the phone. But it's not important. I'm sure he won't mind the interruption." She gave him a sweet smile, and he nodded.

Morgan followed David down the hallway. As they got closer, she could hear Mike's voice. It sounded like he was talking to a good friend or perhaps his wife. David rapped softly on the doorframe, and they entered the office. Mike looked up at them, smiled, and held up his finger.

Morgan was certain Mike was in his mid-thirties, but his exact age was not apparent from his appearance. Though his face was mostly wrinkle-free, there was not a single stitch of hair on his shiny head. Unlike her boss, however, Mike was extremely fit and his athletic frame was visible under his checkered button-down shirt and navy pants.

"Babe, gotta go. The boss is here." Then he hung up and grinned from ear to ear. "What can I do for you, sir?"

Mike's office was quite expansive, fitting two large desks, a small table with chairs, several bookshelves, and even a sofa that looked like it had been worn in with some late nights. Mike sat at the desk facing them with his computer to his back.

"There's an extensive backstory, but I'll just get to the point," David said curtly, not bothering to have a seat. "Our intel folks think this morning's tweets from *China Xinhua News* may actually originate from a Russian agent who hacked the handle. Apparently, Chinese intelligence privately agrees with this assessment. But we're still trying to confirm the identity of the person who made the posts, so it's anybody's guess at this point."

Mike's eyes widened.

"Morgan and I think a direct connection to the Russian government sounds farfetched given the potential risks of nuclear escalation," David continued. "But perhaps a Russian oligarch with major interests in the oil and natural gas industry and a penchant for taking risks could be behind the mischief. Morgan and I were brainstorming if there are any Russian oligarchs who might like to mess with U.S.-China relations to ruin the clean energy deal."

"That could be any number of them," Mike said, staring up at the ceiling. He went silent for a moment. "Wait a minute... I may have something for you." His eyes lit up as he swung around to look at his computer. He opened up his file directory and began going through several news headlines he'd bookmarked. "Aha... yes, this is what I remembered reading about." He scanned the article on the screen. "During the peak of negotiations for the clean energy deal, two Russian oligarchs owning substantial natural gas deposits with interests in building pipelines to Russia made the news headlines with various threats against the United States."

"What sort of threats?" Morgan asked.

"They hinted about their connections to organized crime in Russia and claimed we would experience their retribution at a time, place, and means of their choosing. Something overly melodramatic like that." Mike gestured with his hands as he talked. "We've had our intel teams at the CIA and NSA tracking them for months, but nothing tangible has come in over the wire. Just a lot of chatter about organizing future cyberattacks against the United States—possibly targeting the electrical grid or the industrial control systems for nuclear power plants. We've had the FBI watching domestically for anything unusual to pop up. But nothing has happened."

"Okay, so who are these guys?" David asked.

"The two I'm thinking of are Igor Koslov and Viktor Pasternak," Mike said. "Both are self-made billionaires."

"And you think they're capable of hacking the handle and posting the fake tweets?" Morgan asked.

"Oh yeah," Mike said. "That and a helluva lot more. Of course, they hire people to do their dirty work. They have assets placed around the world and, as I said, connections to sinister types."

Morgan heard a door open, a woman's voice, and feet stomping down the hallway. Seconds later, Elise marched into Mike's office with her lips pinched together and her posture stiff.

"There you are," she said with her hands on her hips. "I have been looking everywhere for you two."

"I told my assistant where we were heading," David said, his tone slightly defensive.

"Well, she wasn't there," Elise said sharply. "I stood at her desk for five whole minutes, and she never turned up." She waved her hand around in agitation. "Anyway, the president wants to see both of you in the Oval Office right away. We've just received satellite confirmation that China has tested a ballistic missile in the South China Sea."

Morgan and David exchanged uneasy looks.

"Intel analysts are still examining the data to identify the missile type and ascertain the nature of the test," Elise continued. "The president wants to hold a press briefing in less than two hours and needs to be prepped." Elise motioned for them to follow her before they could respond. "Let's get going right now."

Elise left with the clear indication she expected them to follow. David thanked Mike for the information, and Morgan was about to follow him out of the office when Mike raised a hand.

"Before you go, let me just print out that article for you," Mike said.

David motioned to Morgan to wait for the printout and started down the hallway after Elise. Mike grabbed the papers off of the printer, stapled them, and handed them to her.

"Here you go," he said.

"Thanks," Morgan said, walking toward the door.

"Not a problem. Let me know if you guys need anything else, okay?"

Morgan nodded and quickly made her way out of the suite and down the hallway to the elevator. Elise and David were nowhere to be seen.

*They must have been really booking it.*

She sighed and pressed the button. Morgan glanced at the article as she waited for the elevator. Her heart nearly stopped when she saw the image on the front page that Mike had handed her.

*Holy shit.*

It was a picture of three men—the two Russian oligarchs mentioned by Mike were relaxing on a yacht with drinks in their hands. Morgan recognized the third man, who stood out next to the other awkwardly dressed pale-skinned and gray-haired men.

He was none other than Anton Vega, the famous American space technologist. His sepia skin and black hair glowed with a thin layer of sweat under the bright sun. Looking relaxed, Anton wore aviator sunglasses, a white linen embroidered shirt, and beige shorts. In the American news media, most reporters just called him Vega.

But Morgan knew him better as the Benefactor—the suspected financial sponsor behind the Nightfall Incident and a close friend and associate of her mother's.

Morgan's stomach roiled, and she felt like she might lose her breakfast.

*Is my mother somehow caught up in this mess?*

# [ 25 ]
## MISSILE TEST

SUSAN
1015
Oval Office
The White House

From her vantage point, Susan admired the exquisite carvings in the English oak wood of the *Resolute* desk. It stood in its full glory in front of the floor-to-ceiling windows which were wrapped by the classic light-blue curtains Harrison's wife had chosen for the Oval Office. The famous desk had been used by all of her predecessors over the past four decades. By now, it had practically become tradition for every president to use the desk.

Among other things, Elise had been bugging her about plans for redecorating the Executive Residence and Oval Office, but Susan hadn't decided yet what she wanted to do about any of it. Still reeling from Harrison's sudden death and overwhelmed with the China crisis, she barely had time to catch her breath, let alone think about furniture.

As her team filed into the Oval and took their places on the couches next to her chair across from the Resolute Desk,

Susan contemplated her preferences on what she felt to be a trivial matter. Despite a stab of guilt, she couldn't help indulging herself. There was a small part of her that yearned to focus on entirely inconsequential issues, even if for a moment.

*Should I just keep the desk to avoid further disruption?*

She rubbed her chin. To Susan, it seemed like the right thing to do given the circumstances. Or did she actually prefer the Theodore Roosevelt desk from her old office at the Eisenhower Executive Office Building? Though a few inches shorter than the *Resolute* desk, it provided a larger surface area for spreading out paperwork.

*I did like that desk.*

Of course, there were sentimental reasons to keep the *Resolute* desk in its place. Franklin D. Roosevelt had been one of many presidents to use the desk. It was a gift from Queen Victoria and was made from the timbers of the British Arctic exploration ship, the *HMS Resolute*. With the autonomous weapons legislation waiting for her signature and the presence of China's submarines in the Arctic's Northwest Passage, Susan felt a kinship with both Roosevelt and the desk. President Roosevelt had given the order to launch the Manhattan Project in 1942 from this very desk. She contemplated what must have gone through his head at the time.

*It's settled, then. I'll leave things the way they are.*

Susan turned her attention to her team and cleared her throat. "Bill, what can you tell me about the missile test?"

She considered each of the grim faces of the team Elise had gathered to analyze the latest development. Susan had kept the group intentionally small to avoid a repeat of the tense discussion between her cabinet members earlier that morning. On the couch to her right, Grayson clutched the latest intelligence on China's missile test, his wire-rim glasses riding down the tip of his nose. David and Morgan sat next to each other on the couch to her left, both appearing to be uncomfortable for some reason.

Elise hovered near one of the doors along the curved wall, ready to spring into action as usual.

"From the satellite infrared data, we know that China tested a modified Dong Feng-3 ballistic missile," Grayson said. "It's a two-stage, solid-fuel mobile rocket with a medium range. It was launched from a missile base near Harbin and carried a conventional payload—specifically, a kinetic kill warhead. The missile took a direct ascent as opposed to the standard ballistic trajectory."

*Direct ascent?*

Susan furrowed her brow as she pictured the launch in her head. "They were trying to shoot something in outer space?"

Grayson nodded. "Yes, ma'am, it appears the Chinese tested an anti-satellite weapon."

David grunted. "Okay, but how's this one different from the last anti-satellite test?" he asked, sitting on the edge of the couch. "Last time, China's anti-satellite reached low earth orbit and destroyed an aging weather satellite. We made a big deal about it, but did it really matter, beyond creating a bunch of space junk?"

Grayson's eyes narrowed. "Well, this one is quite significant," he said, his body movements jerky. "The Dong Feng-3 missile can reach into deep space and target our network of early warning satellites. The explosion of the nuclear weapon during the Nightfall Incident destroyed Constellation, our new layer of space sensors in low earth orbit that provided a continuous view of heat signatures on the entire earth's surface. For this reason, we now depend entirely on our early warning satellites for the detection of a nuclear attack."

"I still don't understand why this test is such a big deal," David said.

Grayson's posture tensed, his face reddening. "This test destroyed a broken satellite in highly elliptical orbit at an extremely high velocity in a head-on collision. Our sources claim the missile test was a stunning success."

Sensing Grayson's intense dislike of David, Susan leaned back in her leather armchair as if she was pondering the test's implications. Instead, she was thinking about how to manage the growing conflict between her two senior advisors. It was not at all like Grayson to treat a colleague so brusquely.

*There must be something going on between them.*

The last thing she needed was another egotistical showdown. Grayson had been pressuring her to consider a replacement for David from a list of several qualified candidates. To her, it was painfully obvious he was looking to fill the slot with someone more loyal to him—perhaps more submissive and agreeable. But Susan preferred to keep a competitive spirit among her senior advisors. That said, she did need to reduce internal strife in order to get things done.

Susan took a deep breath as she leaned forward. "Do you think this test is part of the *Prowling Tiger* war game?" She suppressed a frown when she thought about how Ambassador Chen had failed to inform her of the test in advance. Given their close friendship, that was not typical behavior for him. Perhaps he'd come clean with her at lunch.

"Ma'am, China gave us no prior warning of this test, so I'd assume it is just part of the scheduled war game," David said.

"And what do *you* suppose would be their war game objective for destroying one of our satellites?" Grayson asked, his tone skeptical.

"Actually, I may have a theory about that," Morgan said, jumping into the fray. Grayson stiffened further. Even David looked a bit piqued at her intervention.

Susan nodded and rubbed her forehead. *This woman has a theory about everything.*

Morgan leaned forward. "This test could be another indicator that China's war game has an offensive flavor to it. In most situations, nuclear-armed countries consider early warning assets for detecting nuclear attacks to be strictly off-limits to avoid increasing the risk of nuclear war. This is for the simple fact that our early warning satellites are the first layer of defense against a nuclear attack. Threatening such systems increases the risk of nuclear war. However, if the Chinese are exercising a decapitation strike as we were discussing earlier, they would definitely target these systems in order to prep the battlefield and gain the advantage."

Susan rubbed her chin and turned to her right. "Bill, what do you think?"

"Ma'am, I'm inclined to agree with Dr. Shaw this time," Grayson said with some hesitation. "With Constellation offline the past few months, we're now more vulnerable to a surprise attack, especially from hypersonic missiles. Of course, we still have infrared and optical sensors installed on a tight network of satellites. They are located in three different orbits to detect and track the launch of ballistic missiles during their boost phase."

Susan raised her eyebrow. "Boost phase?"

"Ma'am, that's the critical moment in the missile's trajectory that takes place immediately after lift-off," Morgan said.

"During the boost phase, the missile travels at a slower speed, making it easier to track," Grayson said, seizing control of the conversation. "The optical sensors capture the initial launch of the missile. Then the infrared sensors detect heat from the missile by picking up its booster plumes against the earth's background. These infrared sensors track the missile as it follows its path. As soon as a launch is detected, the data from all of these sensors is sent to earth and collected by the relay ground stations. Then the data is transmitted to the ARC early warning system where it is analyzed along with data from other ground-based radar systems to determine whether a nuclear attack has been launched. If we're under attack, ARC's command and control feature would take over from there."

Susan pressed her lips together and turned to her left. "David, you seem to disagree with Bill about the severity of the threat. How would you interpret China's missile test?"

David gave her a polite smile before answering. "Actually, I may be slowly coming around to Grayson's position. I hadn't fully absorbed the implications of our earlier discussion in the Situation Room. Morgan's theory about China's forward deployment of submarines provides some troubling context for this test."

Susan raised her eyebrow. She hadn't expected David to add support for Bill's points after their earlier friction. "How so?"

"Well, the concentration of our early warning capability into a small number of satellites in each orbit makes them lucrative targets," David said. "Each orbit—the geosynchronous equatorial orbit, the highly elliptical orbit, and the low earth orbit—plays a critical role in providing tactical warning of a nuclear attack. Our space-based early warning satellite system is designed to confirm that an attack is underway. From there, the ground and sea-based radar systems take over and detect specific signatures of the missiles and warheads and determine the nature of the attack, including its source, scale, and intended targets. That data is fed into ARC's command and control system. Without this data, we're essentially operating in the dark."

*Thoughtful answer.*

Susan had always liked David as a person and wasn't certain if she should replace him. He was one of the sharpest national security analysts she'd ever met. And surprisingly humble. Despite his education and prestigious career, David listened to everyone first before injecting his point of view. But Susan still wasn't sure she could trust him as her National Security Advisor. Out of the corner of her eye, she noticed Grayson crossing his arms and frowning deeply.

*Now what?*

"Ma'am, we also need to consider the potential threat from hypersonic missiles, which as I said before, makes this satellite test more significant," Grayson said. "Hypersonic missiles are maneuverable in flight, much like cruise missiles. They can navigate around our radar systems and evade other types of detection. Depending on the design and mission, they are capable of delivering conventional or nuclear weapons. They can travel undetected for certain periods, increasing the chance of a surprise attack. If our early warning satellites were to go dark, we wouldn't be able to detect the launch of such systems. And since our radars can't reliably pick them up, we might not know we're under attack until we're hit."

"Ma'am, I think Morgan may be right," David said with increased urgency. "With this test, the Chinese may have simulated an attack that damages our satellites in highly elliptical orbit to gain an advantage in a conflict with us."

Susan nodded, ignoring a large vein pop in Grayson's forehead. First, he'd appeared to be annoyed that David challenged his views. Now, he seemed frustrated that David was lending credence to them. This conflict was not at all like Grayson; it simply didn't fit with what she knew about his character.

*What is going on here?*

"Ma'am, there's something else interesting about the test," Morgan said, giving her a half smile. "Satellites located in highly elliptical orbit have a long dwell time. That means they sit over one part of the earth for a long time."

Susan returned her smile with a subtle nod. Morgan seemed to sense the growing friction between the two men and had intervened in part to reduce tension between them.

*She's rather perceptive.*

"This type of orbit is advantageous for keeping an eye on ground targets in the northern latitudes," Morgan said. "That makes this test an interesting coincidence. We believe the two missing submarines are located somewhere just north of Canada. If the Chinese were to take out one of our satellites in highly elliptical orbit, we wouldn't be able to detect any ballistic missile launches from the northernmost part of the U.S., most of Russia, Scandinavia, Canada, and Alaska, which are all located in high latitudes. At least not in the boost phase."

Susan's eyes opened wider. "The two lost submarines..." She

caught herself mumbling and closed her mouth. She hadn't meant to utter the comment out loud, but everyone nodded and returned bleak looks. "We wouldn't be able to detect launches of ballistic missiles from them," she said, finishing her thought.

"They could launch a surprise attack, and we wouldn't have any idea," David said, nodding in agreement.

"That's correct, ma'am," Grayson said, taking control of the discussion once again. By now, his face had become a dark pink. "Not until they come into range of our early warning radars."

Susan's forehead creased. *They're both agreeing with him. Why is Grayson only getting angrier?*

"But by that time, the decision-making window for retaliation is already closing fast," Morgan added.

Susan's mind drifted to the exact amount of time she had available to give the rescind order, and she shuddered.

*Eight minutes and fifty-three seconds.*

"Madam President, a single source of sensor data isn't reliable," Grayson said. "As a rule, we prefer to have confirmation of a nuclear attack from multiple data sources. This is to be absolutely certain there is no false alarm before launching our retaliatory attack and starting a nuclear war. That's why our early warning system consists of multiple radars and satellites in different orbits and locations. Our two satellites in highly elliptical orbit play an incredibly essential role in providing dual confirmation."

"If any of our satellites were to go offline for some reason, would the ARC system detect something like that?" Susan asked.

"Even better. I'd expect ARC to pick up advance signs of a looming attack against a satellite from its regular infusion of ISR data," Grayson said, "to prevent us from getting caught flat-footed. But even if we didn't get strategic warning of such an attack, the early warning component of ARC would immediately register the loss of a satellite. We'd know about it right away."

*I'd sure hope so.*

Across the room, Susan saw Elise point at her watch. Susan furrowed her brow, trying to recall the next item on her schedule. She could have sworn there was enough time to finish the meeting, but Elise gave her another urgent look.

Susan cleared her throat. "Thank you all for your analysis. I'll attempt to clarify the meaning of this test with Ambassador Chen at lunch today. Now, are there any other updates since our earlier meeting? Do we know who posted the tweets?" She glanced over at Grayson, giving him a hopeful look.

Grayson shook his head and started to stand up to leave. But David motioned with his hand to get Susan's attention, and Grayson sat back down with a dark scowl on his face.

"Ma'am, Morgan and I spent an hour pulling the thread on the potential Russian connection," he said. "She came up with an interesting theory."

Susan raised her eyebrow and gazed at Morgan. "Another theory?"

Morgan squirmed in her seat, her ears turning light pink. "Uh, yes, ma'am. David and I found it hard to believe that the Russian government would use social media posts to escalate a conflict between us and China. That got *us* to thinking that there are a number of private citizens, specifically wealthy oligarchs with interests in the oil and natural gas industry, who might be willing to engage in some risky behavior on behalf of their government. Remember how much fuss the Russians made about the clean energy deal with China?"

*What's with all this "we" and "us"? Did David put her up to this?*

"Oh, I remember, all right," Susan said under her breath. "I had the Russian ambassador in my ear, making all sorts of threats if we proceeded down the path with China."

"Ma'am, we talked to Mike Palmer just now," David said. "He dug up names for two Russian oligarchs. They made the news headlines at the peak of your negotiations with various threats against the United States. Specifically, they threatened to launch cyberattacks against us if we went through with the deal."

Susan frowned. "And you think they might have decided to hack China's official communications outlet?"

"Ma'am, it's just a possible theory at this point," Morgan said, shifting her position on the couch. "I wouldn't—"

"You said Mike dug up some names for us?" Susan asked, looking back at David, not hiding her impatience.

"Yes, ma'am. Igor Koslov and Viktor Pasternak."

Susan furrowed her brow.

"If you like, I can have my Russia team run this down for you," Grayson said quickly. "We can get you a dossier on both of them as soon as possible."

"That would be great, Bill," Susan said.

Across the room, Elise tapped her watch again. Susan rose from her chair, and the others followed suit.

"Put a rush on it if you can," Susan added to Grayson. "There's no time to lose. I also want a full report on the missile test as soon as you have more details. I'll need everything you've got before I hold my press briefing in about an hour. I expect to be fielding questions on the situation in Hong Kong and the autonomous weapons legislation. But now I'm sure someone will ask about the missile test."

"Yes, ma'am," Grayson said, moving toward the door.

Morgan and David followed closely behind him.

"One more thing," Susan said, clearing her throat. They all turned around to face her, their faces expectant. She shot a stern look at Grayson and then at David and pointed at the both of them. "Whatever this is going on between the two of you, I want it to stop. The mission has to come first." She paused for a moment to consider an idea that had just come to her. "Actually, why don't you two go to lunch today and figure it out. I expect a resolution by the end of the day."

The two men nodded grimly, their heads hanging a bit lower than before. Without another word, Grayson departed the Oval

Office. Morgan and David ducked out of the room after him, the door closing behind them.

Turning to Elise, Susan asked, "Why the sudden rush? Did something happen to the schedule?"

Elise nodded briskly. "FBI Director Laski is here to see you. He has some new information about Morgan Shaw and said it couldn't wait."

# REMITTANCE

ARJUN
1030
A Ring, The Pentagon
Arlington, Virginia

Arjun took a big bite of a dark chocolate candy bar with caramel-covered peanuts as he strode down the hallway toward the elevator. After the chairman's pre-brief, he'd gone down to the Pentagon's main food court to grab a coffee and a snack in the hope of alleviating the pounding in his head. He was headed back to his cubicle in the J6 suite to carry out some last-minute test preparations for the ARC system.

The morning had been far more stressful than anticipated. First there was the blindside from Grace in the chairman's read-ahead, forcing him to scramble to brief Captain Dietz in advance. Then the tense pre-brief with the Pentagon's top brass where Dietz got hammered for Grace's insubordination. And then an angry ambush by Dietz on the escalator.

Dietz must have spotted Arjun heading down to the cafeteria and followed him. Cornering him in the hallway, Dietz began demanding answers from Arjun about ARC's recommendations and the false positive. Grace had been the one to go rogue on her leadership in the J6, but Arjun was getting flack for it.

*But I told him all about it before the meeting. He just has his panties in a bundle.*

Arjun tried to recall the exact words he'd used with Dietz when he raised the issue earlier that morning. Of course, Arjun had downplayed the situation and countered all of Grace's points per direct orders from his CEO.

Although Arjun wasn't absolutely certain, he assumed the Navy captain was somehow on Mr. Warren's unofficial payroll. He'd found it rather strange when his CEO encouraged Arjun to keep Dietz apprised of any sensitive developments about ARC but never said why. He knew better than to ask questions.

However, Arjun sensed that Dietz might not be a true believer in what they were doing. Whenever any unexpected issues came up, Captain Dietz became rather agitated. This made Arjun wonder if there were certain lines the military officer would never cross—even for a large pile of cash.

The Navy captain was particularly furious about the verbal berating he'd received from General Hawkins. Grace had seen fit to bypass her chain of command with what appeared to be a serious and relevant issue, and the director of the Joint Staff wanted to know why. Even though Arjun agreed with Grace's concerns about the ARC system, he could never tell her that. His job was to reassure Pentagon leadership about the proper functioning of ARC.

The sugar from the chocolate and caramel rushed straight to his brain, giving him a momentary high. He shook his head and breathed in deeply for a moment as a sudden lightness filled his body. Arjun smacked his fist against the elevator button. Almost as soon as it lit up, the elevator dinged, and the door opened. He entered and pressed the button for the mezzanine floor.

The door was about to close when his smartphone buzzed. The number revealed the call was long distance from Islamabad,

Pakistan, his childhood hometown and the place where his parents still lived. His pulse spiked.

A sense of urgency surging in his chest, he accepted the call, but no sounds came across the line. Glancing at the screen, Arjun saw zero bars. He'd need a better signal in order to take the call, and the labyrinth of the Pentagon was a notorious dead zone. Quickly, he pressed the button to open the door, exited the elevator, and walked down the corridor toward the inner-most ring of the Pentagon as fast as he could without running. It was the only place in the building with a reliable signal.

"Hello? Dad?" Arjun said, his voice strained. "Can you hear me now?" He glanced at his watch and realized it was late evening in Pakistan.

*Why is my dad calling me now?*

There was still no answer.

Arjun sped up his pace, and the interior windows of the A Ring finally came into view.

"Dad, just one moment. I'm almost there," Arjun said as he reached the windows along the interior courtyard of the A Ring. Stopping next to a window, he pressed the phone to his ear and looked out into the courtyard below. "Can you hear me now?"

The sound on the speaker crackled from the poor connection.

"Yes, son. Yes, I hear you," his father said, his voice weary. "Listen. It's very late here. I'm calling about mom." He paused for a moment as if something were caught in his throat. "Your mother took a turn for the worse this morning. We had to go to the hospital right away."

"Are you with her now?" Arjun asked, his stomach sinking.

"Yes. Dadi and Nani are staying at home with your sisters," his father said.

Arjun's hands began to tremble, and his thoughts raced with questions. His mother had been diagnosed with stage four ovarian cancer several months prior. The doctors had performed an emergency surgical hysterectomy and then treated her with a full round of chemotherapy. She'd responded well, and the doctors were optimistically waiting to see if her cancer would go into remission. This was not the news he'd expected to hear.

"When will mom come home?" His voice cracked.

"I don't know," his father said. "They're running some more tests to see if the cancer has come back or spread. Your mother is not doing well."

There was some heavy breathing on the line and the sound of sniffles. Tears welled in Arjun's eyes.

"Dad, are you still there?" he asked.

"Yes. Son, I need to ask you a favor," his father said.

"Yes, anything. Do you need me to come home? I can see if there are any flights leaving later today," Arjun asked, his lip quivering.

"No, no. Too soon for that," his father said. "But that time may come more quickly than we'd hoped." He paused. "We received your remittance last week. Thank you so much for your love and devotion. We couldn't ask for a better son."

Arjun blanched as he anticipated his father's request. "But you need more money for the hospital bills."

"Yes," his father said, his tone tinged with shame. "I'm afraid so."

Arjun went silent for a moment. To cover his mother's medical bills, he'd been sending half of his paycheck home every month. With the high cost of living inside the Beltway, Arjun had needed to sell his car to make ends meet, but he couldn't bear to tell the truth to his father.

"Son, you know I wouldn't ask—"

"How much?" Arjun asked, his head throbbing hard. He could tell that a sugar crash lurked right around the corner, accelerated by the terrible news.

"We need one thousand dollars. That should carry us through this week. Son, I hate to ask so much—"

"It's okay, dad. I'll wire you the money after work." Arjun gulped. That was all he had left in his bank account.

"You're a good son, Arjun Sharma. The best... the best son any father could ask for. We're so proud of you."

A tear ran down Arjun's cheek, and he wiped it away. A quick look at his watch sent his pulse into action. "Dad, I'm sorry. But I have to get back to work now."

"Yes, yes. Of course. But did you get a chance to talk to your CEO? You know... about the ethical issues with your automated system? Because I still think it's the right thing to do."

"Dad, I tried to bring it up with him, but he wouldn't listen to me," Arjun said.

"You need to try again, son. When you reach the end of your life, you'll want to know you always did the right thing."

Arjun had tried to raise Grace's concerns with his company's CEO in the previous month, but to no avail. Dennis Warren had given him clear marching orders. Arjun was to ensure that the Pentagon leadership continued to support the ARC system, and he was to prevent Grace's voice from being heard at the highest levels.

His conscience gnawed at him again. When he'd first raised his moral quandaries about what they were doing, his CEO gave him a long speech about the trust gap for autonomous machines. Despite superior skillsets, humans found it difficult to have faith in machines if the smallest thing stopped working perfectly. That impossible standard meant they would need to keep some things about the ARC system under wraps to prevent the Pentagon leadership from taking it offline. Without the ARC system, the United States would face a greater risk of nuclear war. Or at least that's what Mr. Warren had told him to keep him in line.

Arjun dreaded his next conversation with Mr. Warren. He would have to fill in his CEO about the latest developments at some point. If the conversation didn't go well, it might be his last day at Centoreum Tech. He couldn't afford to lose his job, not when his family depended on him.

*Mr. Warren will get wind of it sooner or later.*

"Okay, dad. I'll do my best. I've got to go now. You'll kiss mom for me?"

"Yes. She sends all her love."

Arjun hung up the phone, rubbed his eyes, and made his way back to the elevator. Looking down at his other hand, he saw that the remainder of the chocolate bar had melted and smudged the sleeve of his suit jacket. He licked his finger and tried to rub off the chocolate, but the brown stain was stubborn.

*Shit.*

Now Arjun wanted to kick himself for splurging on a candy bar in the first place. On top of that, he'd also have to pay extra cleaning charges when he returned the suit from his monthly clothing subscription. Renting top-of-the-line suits from a small boutique in Alexandria was the only way he could afford to dress for success at the Pentagon.

Arjun contemplated his long list of to-do items before the ARC test and pressed the button for the elevator several times. When the door opened, an angry pair of dark brown eyes glared back at him. His chest tightened with a sudden burst of adrenaline, and he had to force himself to breathe.

"I've been looking everywhere for you," Mr. Warren said, snarling. He charged out of the elevator, grabbed Arjun's arm, and pulled him down the hallway. "We need to have a chat."

# [ 27 ]
## NIGHTFALL INCIDENT

MORGAN
1045
Eisenhower Executive Office Building
The White House


Morgan burst through the side door of the Eisenhower Executive Office Building, breathing heavily. She was greeted by the rush of thick, humid air, forcing her to put a hand over her mouth and cough a few times. The din of traffic gathering for the lunch hour, the loud honking of horns, and screeching of brakes made her wince. She rubbed her temples in an attempt to sooth her throbbing head.

Despite severe discomfort, being outside was much better than having the walls close in around her inside the White House. Her head still spun with the revelation about her mother's associate, Anton Vega, and his potential connection to the Russian oligarchs. China's anti-satellite missile test had raised some new questions, and she wondered if her crazy theory about Russia really did have legs to stand on.

*If they're shooting at satellites, there's definitely something going on with China.*

She desperately wanted to believe there wasn't any connection to Russia at all, an irony that tasted bitter in her mouth. Because a connection would mean... Morgan shook her head. No, she didn't want to think about it.

The implications of Russia's involvement in the Nightfall Incident terrified Morgan to her core. It meant she might not be able to keep the lid on her family's secrets much longer. It meant that her mother...

*It might just be a coincidence. Maybe China is up to something.*

After all, Morgan didn't even know if the Russian oligarchs were behind the fake tweets as she'd so boldly hypothesized to President Tolley. Before she could confirm the link, it was way too early to jump to wild conclusions. But she couldn't stop obsessing over the possibility. The more she thought about it, the tighter her chest became.

Morgan had decided to take a walk and shake it off—even if the hot, muggy weather wasn't cooperating with her need for fresh air. As she strode toward the street, the security guard noticed her badge and waved her through the gate. Turning left, she made her way down the sidewalk along 17th Street NW toward the National Mall.

Deep down in her gut, she knew the picture of Anton with the Russian oligarchs couldn't be a coincidence. In the past year, she'd discovered the world was a much smaller place than she ever imagined—especially among the world's elite and within wealthy circles. Everyone at the highest echelons of global society seemed to know each other, be in business with each other, or be colluding with each other in one way or another—sometimes on a grand scale and with widespread consequences.

She'd learned the lesson the hard way after moving to D.C. about a year ago—through her discovery about her own family's political activities and shady schemes. Like other elite families, the Shaws had long operated in the shadows of legitimate political institutions and channels. They were prone to corruption because they had sufficient power and money to circumvent the rules followed by ordinary people. It was human nature to seek the easiest path to achieve desired ends.

*Is this what President Monroe meant? When he said they are coming for us? Did he mean the Russians? Were they also involved in Nightfall?*

The intense morning sun beat down on her. The heat of its rays absorbed quickly into her suit and increased her body temperature. Within a few minutes, beads of sweat formed on her forehead, forcing her to wipe them away with her sleeve. Surprisingly, the heat didn't bother her that much. Being away from the entangled politics of the White House, even for just a moment, came as a huge relief.

*I really need to talk to Jack. He may know something.*

Morgan pulled out her smartphone and dialed his number. The phone rang a few times, but he didn't answer.

*C'mon, Jack. Pick up.*

The phone kept ringing. She stared at the screen for a moment in disbelief.

*Why isn't he answering?*

As his favorite niece, Jack always took her call—there were only a few exceptions. But he'd been unusually distant since Monroe's passing. At first, she'd chalked it up to grief. Now, she was wondering if that was the case. Her uncle wasn't the type of person to wallow for long. He was distancing himself from her, and she wanted to know why.

Her heart sank when she heard the familiar beep of his voicemail, and she fumbled with the phone to keep from dropping it. "Um, hi. It's Morgan. We need to talk. It's about what Harrison said to you... right before he died. Call me."

*That should get his attention.*

When Morgan hung up the phone and slipped it back in her jacket pocket, she saw something move behind a tree in the corner of her eye. She turned her head to see if someone was following her, but only a few tourists milled about the trees along 17$^{th}$ Street, taking photos of buildings.

*Great. Now I'm paranoid to boot.*

Ignoring the nagging in her stomach, Morgan walked briskly toward Ellipse Park and reviewed what she knew in her head about the Nightfall Incident. It wasn't all that much, but a bit more than most people knew.

As far as federal law enforcement authorities were concerned, a Sunni jihadist group based out of Lebanon and called *al Makhtar* had orchestrated the intricate plot behind Nightfall. The general public thought the group had stolen a nuclear weapon and detonated it from outer space to cause a massive power outage and the destruction of electronics across the entire U.S. Eastern Seaboard. The terrorist attack brought the United States to its knees for several months. As reported in the news, it represented an audacious bid by the jihadist offshoot to rival al Qaeda's achievements on the world stage.

At least, that's what everyone thought had happened. President Monroe and her uncle had somehow made sure of it. Few people knew that the late Kieran Callaghan, Jack's brother-in-law and the former director of the U.S. Secret Service, had led the operation for the Sons of Liberty—a far-right group of American radicals seeking to rise to power within the United States by co-opting the presidency with force. Or that the low-yield nuclear weapons used by the Sons of Liberty to blackmail the former president into resigning her office—cinching the election for Harrison—may have been developed by someone at Jack's company. Possibly right under his nose. Or that the plot was part of a larger conspiracy to steal and detonate a nuclear weapon in outer space in order to cripple the U.S. government after Harrison took office.

Morgan had never asked how her uncle and Harrison prevented the FBI special agents who had worked the case from speaking out about the gaps in the official cover story. Or how Jack could have missed the fact that someone at his company was producing highly enriched uranium and developing nuclear weapons. Her uncle denied any connection to the bomb.

Of course, everyone, including Morgan, had been duped by her mother, Faye Shaw. She'd turned out to be Kieran's partner in crime and the true ringleader of the operation. After Nightfall, her mother escaped detection and capture and went into hiding overseas, likely in Russia with Anton Vega's help.

The only other people alive who knew more than the cover story were her uncle, her father, Luis, the president before Harrison, and Morgan's former boss at the National Defense University. Morgan only knew bits and pieces of the story from Jack. But she'd always gotten the feeling they were only the ones he'd chosen to share with her.

*Jack knows far more than he claims.*

The circle of trust was an extremely small one, and Morgan cared deeply for most of the people in it. Thinking about the extent of her family's potential culpability for Nightfall made her sick to her stomach. Like her, Luis had been unknowingly dragged into the scheme. He'd also helped her keep the secret.

*This is why Luis always changes the subject.*

The day after Harrison's death, Jack decided to go back to heading his company, Innovative Neutronics Technology (INT), which sought to revolutionize the energy market through broad decentralization in electricity production. But her uncle's transition had been too seamless for Morgan's taste. She wondered what Jack might have done as Harrison's chief of staff to protect his firm from any fallout after the Nightfall Incident.

The Russian connection put a new spin on everything she'd known about the Nightfall Incident. Morgan had suspected Anton Vega to be the mysterious Benefactor behind the Sons of Liberty operation, given his close association with her mother. Without his financial backing, the use of a space rocket, and access to the International Space Station, the Sons of Liberty could never have detonated a nuclear weapon from such a high altitude. The group had pulled off a coup in more ways than one. And the American public had no idea.

The involvement of Russian oligarchs meant that the plot had likely not ended with Nightfall. If there was more to come, Morgan would have to come clean with law enforcement authorities. Protecting her family members after the fact was one thing. But she wouldn't allow herself or Luis to become accessories to any scheme that threatened U.S. national security. It was the main reason she'd taken the job at the White House—to keep an eye on her uncle and Harrison. To make sure they weren't up to anything.

As she thought about her theory, that Anton and her mother might be involved in whatever was happening with China, Morgan shuddered.

For once, she would do anything to be proven wrong.

# [ 28 ]
## CENTOREUM TECH

ARJUN
   1115
   Main Food Court, The Pentagon
   Arlington, Virginia

"Captain Dietz told me about the chairman's pre-brief," Mr. Warren said, pointing an angry finger in Arjun's face. "You let Grace make a powerful argument against the ARC system. How many times have I told you not to let that happen?"

*I didn't "let" her do anything. Where was Captain Dietz? Oh yeah. He was sitting right next to her.*

Arjun sat across from his boss in the main food court on the first floor of the Pentagon. The fifty-something billionaire CEO was dressed as if he'd just stepped out of a men's fashion magazine with his stylish glasses, a colorful silk tie, and a bespoke midnight-blue, double-breasted suit. His boss's attire was the main reason Arjun felt enormous pressure to dress for success. Mr. Warren was known for making critical comments on the appearance of his employees—something the CEO blamed on his fashion designer mother but spoke more to his extreme desire for perfection in all things.

Arjun just stared back at Mr. Warren as he continued to rail at him for his many shortcomings. There was no point to arguing with his notoriously ill-tempered boss. Arjun would let him calm down before saying anything—if he chose to say anything at all.

*What was I supposed to do? Get up in a room full of high-level military officers and argue my case as a defense contractor? Without being invited to do so by a Pentagon official? Yeah, I don't think so.*

"How did Grace get that talking point into the read-ahead in the first place?" Mr. Warren asked, spit flying from his teeth.

*I'm a systems engineer, not a babysitter. Grace is apparently much savvier than we thought.*

"What am I paying you for?" he added.

Arjun looked down at his empty coffee cup and said nothing. He knew his boss couldn't afford to fire him—definitely not moments before the monthly test of the ARC system. But that didn't mean the CEO wouldn't consider it at some point. He'd already threatened Arjun's job several times in the heat of the moment.

Given his boss's foul mood, Arjun suspected that Mr. Warren was mostly angry about President Tolley cancelling their lunch and was taking it out on him. During their long walk from the elevator to the cafeteria, Mr. Warren had railed against Tolley for her nerve and about how she owed him for everything. That meant the CEO would not be easily consoled no matter what Arjun said or did.

They sat in icy silence for a few minutes.

"Whatever happens, we can't have ARC going nuclear during the test this afternoon," Mr. Warren said, appearing to finally get a grip on his temper. "It would ruin everything we've worked so hard for. I sold the Pentagon leadership on the ARC system as a more reliable and predictable way to reinforce nuclear deterrence and reduce the chance of surprise attacks. ARC is supposed to be stabilizing. It's not supposed to increase the risk of nuclear war."

*Wait a minute… nuclear war? Why would ARC go nuclear?*

Arjun creased his forehead. "But we don't know for sure how ARC will respond to today's simulated scenario," he said tentatively. "It's possible that—"

Mr. Warren raised his hand to stop him mid-sentence "Look, I know exactly how ARC will respond to today's simulated scenario, given recent geopolitical developments. Today's test, it's a conflict with China, right?"

Arjun nodded, pressing his lips together. The details of the simulation were classified, but Dietz must have told him about it.

"Then at some point during the simulated conflict, ARC may recommend increasing escalation with China, possibly even the use of nuclear weapons," Mr. Warren said. "I need you to go back to your office right now and tweak the algorithms before the test. We need to rein ARC's recommendations back into more expected parameters. Once the test is over, we can switch everything back."

*Rein it in?*

Arjun furrowed his brow. "Sir, I don't understand. You've had me downplay ARC's recent recommendations as expected outcomes, occurring within acceptable parameters. Now you want me to bring the system back into line with a few tweaks?"

"There's nothing to understand," Mr. Warren said. "Today's test is a critical moment for ARC, and the simulated data matters for ARC's learning process for wartime operations. We don't have any relevant data to predict how ARC will behave in a real crisis. That's another reason why we need these monthly tests."

*Does the Pentagon leadership know anything about this?*

Arjun frowned. "But I thought—"

"Yes, you thought the model of nuclear deterrence would

serve as an obstacle to ARC's learning process," Mr. Warren said. "It doesn't, and I made sure of it."

*What?*

Arjun's eyes widened. He opened his mouth to say something, but no words came out.

*He's been lying to me. This whole time.*

Mr. Warren appeared to notice the stunned look on his face. "For the past few months, it was better you didn't know the truth."

"What don't I know?" Arjun asked.

"In the final stages of the system's development, I had my senior programmer tweak ARC to give it some more operating freedom from the Cold War's model of nuclear deterrence," Mr. Warren said. "I did so to ensure that ARC functions properly across a full spectrum of situations. However, I didn't anticipate a precipitous decline in U.S.-China relations to occur right before our fifth monthly test when the system's deep neural network remains somewhat in flux. We need about a year's worth of simulated crisis data to fully ensure ARC's effectiveness during a wartime scenario. When I heard about ARC's recommendation to go to DEFCON 3, I realized where the system was heading."

"And you need it to get back on course," Arjun said.

"Yes."

"But you've told the Pentagon that the ARC system will follow the rules of nuclear deterrence—whether we're in a crisis or not. If that's not how it works, shouldn't we just explain all of this to Pentagon leadership and—"

Mr. Warren chopped the air with his hands. "Have you completely lost your mind?"

*No, I'm finally coming to my senses.*

"Wouldn't it be better if they understood all the benefits *and* the risks of ARC?" Arjun asked. "It seems that the net impact is still a positive one." He was pressing his luck by trying to convince his boss to listen, but he at least had to try. Otherwise, he wouldn't be able to look his father in the eyes ever again.

Mr. Warren grimaced. "Do you know how long it took me to convince the Pentagon leadership to turn over any amount of control over nuclear weapons to a machine?" He paused for effect.

Arjun nodded quickly, not wanting to hear the speech again.

"It took years of persuading the general public with a multi-million-dollar ad campaign and then many more years of convincing policymakers and military leaders to do what's good for them," Mr. Warren said. "And now, finally, the ARC system is operational. Do you know what it would take for them to lose their confidence in ARC?"

Arjun shrugged even though he knew the answer. It was best to let his boss finish his rant without interruption.

"One fucking mistake," Mr. Warren said, slamming his fist on the table. "That's all it would take. Even the tiniest of errors would cause the Pentagon's leadership to lose complete confidence in the system. A single case of ARC being incorrect would destroy the trust we've built over the past decade. We never hold humans to that high standard."

"And you used the model of deterrence to build that trust," Arjun said, trying to move his boss along. "As long as everyone thinks ARC operates according to an accepted set of rules, it makes everyone feel comfortable."

Mr. Warren nodded. "Yes, we needed something to convince them to trust the system. Most of these folks continue to believe that nuclear deterrence will operate much as it did in the Cold War—despite rapidly changing technological and geopolitical circumstances. They don't just believe it works, they need to believe it. If they didn't believe it, they'd have to accept that nuclear weapons might actually increase the risk of nuclear war rather than prevent it."

"You didn't want ARC's deep neural network to become too hemmed in to that old mindset," Arjun said, understanding where his boss was going with his argumentation. "Otherwise it wouldn't function properly in novel situations or unpredictable environments."

"Exactly." Mr. Warren smiled broadly. "So, I relaxed the rules around ARC's interpretation of different actions and increased its freedom of maneuver."

"Grace was right... all this time," Arjun said, trying hard to suppress his disgust. "The ARC system interpreted China's forward deployment of its nuclear-armed submarines as an offensive move. She explained that this proves the system doesn't hold strictly to our accepted model of nuclear deterrence. She said it was possible that ARC has learned a new move to gain advantage over the other side."

"Yes and no," Mr. Warren said. "The tweaks to the algorithms account for ARC's interpretation of China's move as offensive. But the first rule still remains intact. As its first consideration, ARC is designed to optimize its ability to retaliate after a nuclear attack by an adversary."

"That means if ARC has recommended an increase in the alert status to DEFCON 3, the system has determined that its most fundamental rule is threatened."

Mr. Warren nodded. "Correct. An increase in our alert status reduces the vulnerability of our command and control system to a preemptive attack. ARC is protecting our ability to retaliate just as we trained it to do."

"But doesn't DEFCON 3 also increase our ability to conduct nuclear war if necessary?" Arjun asked. "Such a move could be misinterpreted by China and lead to unwanted escalation."

"That's why I'm asking you to tweak the algorithms. Just for today."

Arjun shook his head. "Sir, I don't think that's a good idea, at least not without telling Pentagon leadership. If they defer their judgment to a machine without questioning it, their trust will be blind. Then what happens when ARC makes a mistake or oversteps its boundaries? They won't detect the error or understand how it happened. And their ignorance and lack of critical thinking could lead to cascading human errors and potentially catastrophic results."

Mr. Warren shook his head. "In the absence of automation, the risk of catastrophe caused by human mistakes has a far higher probability. Such a scenario would be of far greater consequence than any of ARC's perceived shortcomings."

"But there's still some margin of error in ARC's code," Arjun said. "That means it's possible for ARC to propose a bad recommendation or, worse, to sound a false alarm."

"Let me ask you a question," Mr. Warren said. Arjun glimpsed an uncanny glint in his boss's eyes as they reflected the cafeteria lights from above. "If you knew with absolute certainty that a machine has superior skills to a human in performing all necessary functions, would you still want the human in control?"

Arjun jerked his head, surprised by the line of questioning from his boss. It took a moment for him to find his words. "Regardless of our fallibility, I believe humans should always have positive control over nuclear weapons. I don't think we should delegate such decisions to a machine no matter how effective it is."

"That's why we have the rescind order," Mr. Warren said. "The president essentially still holds the sole authority to launch nuclear weapons." He gave Arjun a knowing smile. "Despite its small margin of error, ARC outperforms humans in analytics, accuracy, and speed. Humans simply can't match a machine's ability to process large volumes of information—the judgements of a machine are based on significantly more data than a human mind can handle. The ARC system can identify threats in a rapidly changing and complex environment, improve situational awareness, and reduce the chance for false alarms in a crisis."

"But the ARC system still lacks common sense or human instincts," Arjun said. "More than once, the gut instincts of courageous humans have saved us from accidental nuclear war. And as a machine, ARC has no skin in the game. It will blindly carry out the outcomes derived from its calculations."

Mr. Warren furrowed his brow. "I'd choose computational models over human instincts any day. Once the Pentagon's leadership believes that ARC is more effective than humans, they'll have greater trust in the system and allow it to operate properly. In the meantime, we can't afford any uncertainty. When you get back to the office, I want you to tweak the algorithms. Once the test is done, you'll return things to the way they were."

"But sir—"

"No buts. This is for their own good," Mr. Warren said, pointing his finger toward the ceiling.

"What's for our own good?" a male voice called out from behind Arjun.

Mr. Warren looked up, smiled warmly, and rose from his chair. "Isaiah, it's so good to see you."

Arjun craned his neck to see that the man greeting his boss was none other than General Isaiah Burke, the secretary of defense.

"Dennis, likewise," Burke said. "I didn't realize you were in the building today. You weren't even going to stop by my office?" He didn't hide his disappointment.

Mr. Warren cleared his throat. "Sorry. Just here for a quick conversation with my systems engineer. To make sure he's all set for today's big test."

"Arjun Sharma, sir," Arjun said, stepping forward to shake Burke's hand. He gave direct eye contact and scrutinized the SecDef's face.

*Is he surprised to find Mr. Warren here? Or is it all a show for my benefit?*

Burke squeezed hard and then clapped the CEO on the back. "I assume ARC will pass the test with flying colors, just like the last four months."

Mr. Warren nodded.

"Good. Because I'm counting on it. By the way, my wife and I are looking forward to the annual Labor Day shindig at your place on the Chesapeake Bay," Burke said, smiling broadly. "Say, do you think you could rustle up an invitation for Admiral Waller and his wife?"

"That old fart?" Mr. Warren said, frowning.

"I think it could go a long way in smoothing over any of the rough edges for the ARC system," Burke said. "This will make him feel like he's one of us. It might be useful to bring him into the fold—just in case the president tries to take the ARC system offline."

"You think that's a real possibility?" Mr. Warren asked.

"I do," Burke said.

Arjun caught a stern look from Mr. Warren and took his cue to leave and carry out his boss's demand. His chest tight, he turned around and headed back to the office, his father's words about doing the right thing echoing in his mind.

# [ 29 ]
## THE FBI DIRECTOR

SUSAN
1050
Oval Office
The White House

Susan sat at the *Resolute* desk in the Oval Office with FBI Director Frank Laski standing next to her. Her body posture was stiff, and she was leaning awkwardly to one side, away from him. Despite a light woodsy cologne, she could detect his body odor, and it was an unpleasantly sour, musty smell. Every time he moved, she got a stronger whiff that made her want to gag.

Frank was in his early sixties and looked his age. He was also an unusually tall and thin man, and his frame cast a large shadow on her desk. His squinty eyes sunk into his face, overpowered by angular cheekbones, a pair of thick lenses, and silver, bushy eyebrows. Susan found it difficult to trust a man when she couldn't see what was going on in his eyes. She couldn't quite put her finger on the reason, but his presence made her skin crawl.

She cringed at the thought of being left alone with Frank to discuss sensitive issues, especially pertaining to someone on her staff. Thankfully, Elise was still in the room, even if she was preoccupied with her tablet.

Susan wasn't the only one who sometimes referred to him as Director Lackey instead of Laski behind his back. The man seemed to have no spine when it came to dealing with Harrison, and Susan suspected that Harrison had taken advantage on occasion. When the previous FBI director resigned one month into the Monroe administration, Harrison had selected Laski as the replacement over Susan's strong objections. She expected more fortitude and objectivity from a director of the nation's leading law enforcement agency.

Susan looked up to confirm Elise planned to join them, but her chief of staff pointed to her smartphone, shook her head, and ducked out of the Oval Office. Suppressing a sigh, Susan nodded at Frank to begin.

The director placed a file on her desk and flipped it open to the front page. Putting on her reading glasses, Susan swallowed hard as she anticipated the worst, but a lump remained stubbornly lodged in her throat. Her eyes widened when she saw the image on the first page.

The file was a dossier for a striking woman in her sixties with long, wavy blonde hair and piercing blue eyes. There was something strangely familiar about her. Then she noticed the woman's name at the top of the sheet—Faye Shaw.

"Is this woman Morgan's mother?" she asked, her pulse spiking.

"Yes, ma'am," Frank said grimly.

"That would also make her Jack's sister-in-law," Susan said, a pit forming in her stomach. She looked up at Frank for answers with her eyebrow raised. His dull face was expressionless, and his small eyes hid behind his thick glasses, betraying no information. "Why are you showing this to me?"

"Ma'am, Grayson asked me to look into any connection

between Morgan and Nightfall. He said you requested the information?"

*Grayson initiated the investigation?*

Susan nodded, trying to hide her surprise.

"Ms. Shaw entered the country a week ago," Frank said. "She traveled from Lebanon under the assumed name of Maria Koslova with a false Russian passport. At immigration, Faye claimed she was an executive working for Nesti Oil and Gas, and she didn't raise any flags upon entry. We have video footage from TSA confirming her arrival last Tuesday through customs and immigration at Dulles airport."

*Koslova... now why does that name ring a bell?*

"If Ms. Shaw didn't raise any flags upon entry, how did you figure out who she really was?" Susan asked.

Frank nodded as if he expected the question. "Ma'am, we ID'd Ms. Shaw through cellphone communications in which one of her contacts slipped up and used her real last name. After that, it wasn't hard to discover her true identity by tracking her smartphone signals."

"But why were you listening to her communications? Is Ms. Shaw already under official investigation for something?"

"No, ma'am. Recordings of several phone calls between Ms. Shaw and possible Russian foreign intelligence operatives came in from the NSA's signals collection as part of an investigation in the FBI's counterintelligence division. We're tracking a number of Russian citizens in the country believed to be working for Russia's Federal Security Service. We think these individuals are actively engaging in gray zone operations—"

"Isn't Ms. Shaw an American citizen?" Susan interrupted. "I sure hope you haven't exceeded your authority here."

"Ma'am, under our mandate, any American citizens with direct ties to suspected Russian agents are fair game. But as of this morning, we've requested a court order for more comprehensive surveillance of Ms. Shaw's activities. Anyway, there's a direct connection to Morgan Shaw on your staff at the National

Security Council. I mentioned it to Grayson right away. He told me you wanted me to dig further. And that's why I'm here."

"Have you found anything interesting?" Susan asked, flipping through the contents of the file. There was nothing terribly compelling in the folder as far as she could tell. At least not enough to raise suspicions about Morgan's loyalties to the United States or its Constitution.

"Ma'am, interesting isn't the word I'd use for what we found," Frank said, a dark look descending on his face.

"What word would you use, then?" she asked, taking another look at the thin file. She was stumped about what he could be referring to.

"I guess if I had to choose just one word for it, I'd say it's a sockdolager."

"A what?" Susan's face tightened. She wasn't in the mood for any levity and certainly not from Frank.

"Sorry, ma'am." Frank gave her a shy smile. "It's an old-fashioned term. To put it more plainly, what I've found is a decisive blow to everything our country stands for."

Susan jerked her head, her pulse quickening. "Please explain."

"As I said before, we began digging into Morgan Shaw at Grayson's behest. This morning, we discovered a single reference to her mother's name within FBI case files in connection with the Nightfall Incident. Naturally, that caught my attention, and I asked for more information. But that's when we hit a brick wall, and I decided it was necessary to inform you immediately."

"What sort of brick wall?" Susan asked.

"Ma'am, I'm not sure how to tell you this."

"Go on," she said, crossing her arms.

"President Monroe sealed the early investigation files leading up to the Nightfall Incident and then later halted the investigation of Nightfall before it was fully complete. Of course, this was all before my time as director. My predecessor signed off on everything."

Susan's eyes nearly popped out of their sockets. "Harrison did what?"

"Ma'am. Apparently, the president demanded we seal all files on *al Makhtar* shortly after his inauguration. It was one of his first acts in office. He called the former FBI director's office himself and ordered the physical destruction of all existing hard copy files. He also sealed any electronic files with the highest level of encryption. President Monroe insisted that no one have access without his authorization, including the FBI director himself. Since the president has passed on, I've had my IT guys trying to crack open the files all day. They'll keep trying to break the code with brute force, but it's really no use. The files have been encrypted using the most advanced algorithms, and only the president held the key to break it."

Susan turned her head slowly back and forth as she thought through the implications, and then she gasped out loud when it hit her. "The president's request to seal those files was illegal."

*Is that why the FBI director resigned?*

"Ma'am, it was highly illegal," Frank said.

"Why would the president actively prevent the FBI from gaining access to possible intelligence leads before the Nightfall Incident occurred?"

*Unless the investigation would implicate him?*

Frank cleared his throat. "Ma'am, I don't think the president anticipated the Nightfall Incident. I had an opportunity to speak to the former FBI director about it. He wouldn't say much, but he did explain what he knew about the president's rationale. When Monroe requested the files be sealed, he claimed he didn't want to destabilize the country with the information that would come to light through further investigation. He said uncovering the depth of the conspiracy behind *al Makhtar* would undermine trust in the U.S. government since the group had direct ties to a massive network of American citizens in positions of power across the country."

"And the former FBI director just believed him?"

"He said he had no choice. Monroe was not only the president, he was also close friends with his boss, the attorney general. Apparently, he didn't want to lose his job."

*There has to be more to it than that.*

"But he resigned anyway," Susan said, her mouth hanging open slightly.

"Yes. And he wouldn't say why," Frank said, his bushy eyebrows squished together.

Susan's mouth remained open, but she was unable to find words. Her boss and good friend was not the man she thought he was. Her heart sank at the realization of how far Harrison had strayed from the ideals of the Constitution.

*I can't believe Harrison would do something like this.*

"There's more. As I hinted at earlier, the president went a step further after sealing the files on *al Makhtar*. He also interfered in the investigation into Nightfall," Frank said. "In fact, he halted it prematurely when questions began to surface about the files and what might be in them. That's when the FBI director made the announcement about the responsibility for Nightfall. Of course, the Islamic jihadist cover story conformed to the expectations of American citizens. Claiming *al Makhtar* had sole responsibility for the Nightfall Incident was an easy sell to the general public."

"I always wondered if there was more to it," Susan said. "The official document trail was spotty, and there were gaping holes in the investigation's findings. When I read through the report, it felt as if we'd only uncovered the first layer of the conspiracy. But I figured the president would dig deeper if he deemed it necessary."

*I was wrong.*

"Ma'am, I now believe the official story about the Nightfall Incident to be a well-orchestrated cover by the president and his top officials. And I will not shirk my responsibility in finding the truth. I want to make this right, if you'll let me do so."

Susan looked up at Frank and nodded solemnly. Her arms

went limp at her sides, and a bitter taste filled her mouth. In her shock over the president's betrayal, she'd bitten her cheek.

*Perhaps I misjudged Frank as well.*

"Have you spoken to any of the agents who were investigating *al Makhtar* before Nightfall?" she asked.

Frank bobbed his head. "I tried talking to them today, but haven't had any success in getting more information. One is dead. Another is working overseas as a legal attaché in Denmark and hasn't returned my calls. The one with a bad reputation is willing to talk, but as the FBI's resident conspiracy theorist, she'll be of no real help. That leaves us with one young female special agent hired specifically to work the *al Makhtar* case around the time that the files were sealed. But she came to the FBI from the Treasury Department with background knowledge about the financial trail of the group."

"Did she talk?"

"I met with her this morning, but unfortunately, she's too afraid to say anything. Apparently, the president threatened her career at the FBI if she didn't keep silent."

"And Harrison's death isn't enough to remove the threat?" Susan asked.

Frank shook his head. "Ma'am, we need to reopen those files and figure out who is all involved in this."

"You said they were encrypted. What do I need to do to unseal them?"

"Ma'am, all I need is your consent and that encryption key."

Susan stared back at Frank, her jaw clenched. "I don't know of any encryption key." She paused for a moment to think. "What if the key died with President Monroe? Is it just a password?"

"My IT guys said it would be a small USB drive with software and a password to unlock the encryption code. Is it possible that President Monroe gave it to any of his confidantes?"

"You mean to Jack?"

Frank nodded. "Possibly to Morgan?"

"You think she knows about all of this?" Susan asked, a deep frown forming on her face.

She'd been on the fence about Morgan since she was sworn into office. Her first inclination had been to fire her along with Jack. But out-of-the-box thinking about the threats posed by nuclear weapons was so rare inside the Beltway and her own administration, Susan had decided to wait and see about her fate. Earlier that morning, Morgan had proven herself useful for poking at Burke, making Susan want to keep her around. But if what the FBI learned about Morgan was true, she could also be a liability for Susan.

Frank shrugged. "How could she not? Jack's her uncle, Faye's her mother, and Monroe was a longtime family friend."

"But you have nothing directly linking Morgan to *al Makhtar*, to the Russians, or to the sealed files?" Susan asked.

"That's correct, ma'am," Frank said. "I have no tangible evidence of any wrongdoing on Morgan's part. On the contrary. As you know, she was instrumental in navigating the fallout after the Nightfall Incident. Some might still call her a hero."

"Then what should I do about all of this?" Susan asked, suppressing the sinking feeling in her gut. She recalled Morgan's theory about the Russian connection, and her stomach roiled.

*How did Morgan come up with that idea? Was it a coincidence?*

Now Susan wished desperately that Elise had stayed for the conversation so she could consult her for advice. Looking up at Frank, she asked tentatively, "Do I fire her?"

Frank shook his head. "Ma'am, if I were in your shoes, I'd keep her close for now. But not too close, just in case she has ties to the Russians. We've put two FBI special agents on her to track her movements. We're also working to get a court order for her communications. Until we know more, I'd keep her around but severely limit her access."

"And what about Jack?" Susan asked.

"We have him under surveillance as well. But if he's communicating with Faye or the Russians, I doubt we'll get wind of it from him. Since the president's death, he's gone mostly underground. If he's involved in this scheme, Jack is not an amateur at subterfuge."

"What more do we know about Faye Shaw?" Susan asked.

"We haven't had a chance to learn much since she came up on our radar. But we do know she departed the U.S. yesterday, this time using her U.S. passport."

"Where did she go?" Susan asked.

"She got on a flight leaving for Moscow."

Just then, Elise burst into the office. "Ma'am, sorry to interrupt, but we need to get ready for the press briefing."

Susan frowned. "But you've already briefed me on everything."

"There have been some new developments. You know those videos of the massacre in Hong Kong on social media?"

Susan nodded.

"It looks like they're deep fakes," Elise said, her forehead creased.

"So, there's no massacre?"

Elise made a face. "Not sure. Our intel analysts are poring over satellite images as we speak to get a better sense of what's happening. But the press and social media are both spinning out of control with conspiracy theories."

"Fake tweets, deep fakes, what's next?" Susan asked, shaking her head.

*I probably don't want to know.*

## [ 30 ]
### DEEP FAKES

MORGAN
1100
Washington Monument
The National Mall

Morgan took a deep breath and tried to admire the pristine view of the Washington Monument from the Ellipse, but she was too distracted to take it in. She stood holding her smartphone in the oval-shaped park located just south of the White House. She dialed Jack's number again. It rang twice with no answer. Then he finally picked up.

"This is Jack," a weary voice answered.

"Why didn't you pick up the phone before?" Morgan asked.

"I was busy." His voice was unusually cold.

"Did you get my voicemail message?"

"I did."

"And you didn't call me back?"

"Well, I was rather confused by your message. I don't know what you were referring to."

*What's he playing at?*

"You don't remember calling me just after Harrison died on the golf course?" Morgan asked.

"No."

*Why is he doing this?*

Morgan frowned, contemplating her uncle's possible motivations for playing cat and mouse with her. Then she realized something.

*Maybe he thinks someone is listening in?*

"What did you think about the autopsy results?" Morgan asked, testing the waters.

"Well, I wouldn't say we have *results* just yet," Jack said. "The medical examiner has not finished her analysis. I'd rather not talk any further. I'm being investigated by the FBI and the Secret Service at—"

Her eyes widened. She hadn't expected him to come out and say it. "Wait a minute. Investigators think *you* may have had something to do with the president's chloroquine dosage?"

He sighed. "Not sure what they think. They claim they're following due diligence on the investigation. And since I was with Harrison most of the day, I'm a person of interest for now. Is this why you're calling me, because if so—"

"Jack, please don't hang up," Morgan said urgently. "I called to discuss something important. And it may help your case."

"I'm listening."

Morgan took a deep breath. "Do you know how Anton Vega might be connected to Russian oligarchs named Igor Koslov and Viktor Pasternak? I found a picture of them partying on a yacht and started wondering if there was something more to it."

"Hmm… Those names sound familiar," Jack said. "Don't they have ties to Russia's natural gas and oil industry? Weren't they angry at the Monroe administration for the U.S.-China clean energy deal?"

"Yes, those are the ones."

"Well, it wouldn't be all that strange for Vega to hang out with fellow billionaires, would it?" Jack said. "Especially those with similar interests. Given Vega's plans to normalize consumer space travel in the next few years, he's invested heavily in sources of energy, including oil and natural gas. I'm sure Russia would be a lucrative supplier for him. But I don't know of any specific business he'd have with Koslov and Pasternak."

"Do you think the Russians were somehow involved in Nightfall?" Morgan asked.

"Harrison and I looked into it. We didn't find a direct link to the Russians, but we also didn't look too hard. I think you know what I mean." He paused for a moment. "Why are you asking? Has something happened?"

*Besides the president's sudden death?*

"I assume you heard about China's aggressive tweets earlier this morning?" Morgan asked.

"Yes, I've been following the situation in China all day," Jack said.

"Well, we don't think the tweets came from the Chinese government. There's evidence that someone from Russia might be behind the posts, attempting to stir up trouble between the U.S. and China during the escalating conflict in Hong Kong. Maybe one of these oligarchs is behind it."

"And you think these tweets are part of some nefarious plot?" Jack asked, his tone skeptical. "There must be more going on than a few posts on social media."

Morgan took a deep breath. "Well, there's two nuclear-armed Chinese submarines traveling just off the coast of Canada, supposedly for the scheduled war game tomorrow. They separated from their flotilla, and we've lost track of them."

Jack grunted. "Huh. That's an odd development, even for a war game. I'm sure China's missile test this morning and the government's crackdown on protesters in Hong Kong has everyone on edge. With the deep fake videos that have surfaced on social media, it's become impossible to tell what's really happening."

"Deep fake videos?" Morgan's mouth fell open. She hadn't had time to check the internet all day.

"The videos are spreading quickly. It appears that most of the footage came from a major outbreak of violence that occurred several years ago between protesters and Hong Kong police. Someone has pasted pieces of the footage together and released the videos to make it appear like it's happening today. Whoever did it is a real pro. On the surface, the videos look one hundred percent authentic. However, the reputable Truthbusters website ran deep forensic analysis on the videos and determined them to be fake."

"Somehow, I missed that."

"If you haven't been following the situation in real time, you wouldn't have heard about it yet," Jack said. "Truthbusters made the announcement about twenty minutes ago."

"Are you saying the Mong Kok Massacre isn't actually happening?" Morgan asked, her mind racing to make connections between the tweets and the deep fakes.

"Something is definitely happening in Hong Kong, but not what's being advertised," Jack said. "The faked videos have helped to distort the situation and inflate casualty tallies by reporters. Social media posts coming out of Hong Kong are all over the place. Many posts claiming extreme violence have been found to be bots."

"Bots?" Morgan asked, scratching her nose. "That would mean someone wants to make it look like the Chinese government is killing protesters in the streets. Just like the aggressive tweets this morning, this could be part of a digital disinformation campaign to mess with our perception of reality. But what would be the motivation?"

"The disinformation campaign appears to be targeted at the United States," Jack said. "Perhaps they're attempting to get us to intervene in Chinese domestic affairs and start a military conflict."

"But what would be the end game?" Morgan asked. "Who would benefit from war between the U.S. and China?"

"If I had to put money on it, I'd say Russia has the most to gain," Jack said. "A wedge between the U.S. and China pushes the Chinese closer to Russia. Plus, a falling out might lead to the collapse of the clean energy deal, freeing up China to purchase Russia's oil and natural gas again."

"Do you think the disinformation operation could be about more than oil and natural gas? Maybe it's bigger than we think."

"What do you mean by bigger?" Jack asked.

"What if someone got to Harrison? What if he was assassinated? What if his death is related to Nightfall?" Her stomach sizzled as she uttered the dreaded questions for the first time. They had been on her chest since the news about the autopsy report.

Jack was silent for a few moments before answering. "I'd be careful throwing such insinuations around. We don't know enough about what caused Harrison's death." He took a deep breath. "However, if the Russians were working with Vega to carry out the Nightfall Incident, then the disinformation campaign could be a follow-on to further destabilize our country. If that's the case, then I'd be on the lookout for more to come. But those are some big ifs, Morgan. Complete speculation."

"Yeah, you're right."

"Maybe you should check in with the Cyberthreat Intelligence Integration Center for any unusual cyber activity," Jack said. "Before you take any of this to the president, you'll need to know the full range of cyberattacks going on at the moment. Grayson should be able to get you access. Perhaps his people have identified other threats related to the tweets and deep fakes."

"Yeah, that's a good idea," Morgan said, glancing at her watch. "I'll head over there right now. I don't think we can afford to ignore the 'what ifs' until we know for sure."

"Morgan, one more thing," Jack said.

"Yes?"

"Watch out for Grayson, okay?"

"What do you mean by that?" Morgan asked, her brow furrowed.

There was silence on the other end of the call. She glanced at her screen and saw that Jack had hung up.

## [ 31 ]

## THE PRESS BRIEFING

SUSAN
1120
James S. Brady Press Briefing Room
The White House

Susan took a deep breath, leaned against the podium for some extra support, and looked out into the eager audience of reporters raising their hands. Thus far, the White House Press Corps had not gone easy on her. They'd fired one hard question after another about the suspicious circumstances surrounding the president's death. But before the press briefing, she'd strategized with Elise about how to answer all of them. So far, so good. As long as she stuck to the script, she'd be fine.

Susan pointed at Bernie Hale, a reporter from Atlas Cable News (ACN). Hale had often been critical of the Monroe administration, and she expected a pointed interrogation from him.

"Madam President, does your delay in responding to the Mong Kok Massacre have something to do with China's submarines traveling through the Northern Sea Route?"

Susan shook her head, taking a large breath of air. "The presence of China's submarines did not influence our decision-making."

She didn't like giving half-truths to the press, but Elise had advised that it was necessary to signal to China that the United States would not back down even under pressure of a nuclear conflict.

"We responded immediately to the unrest in the streets of Hong Kong earlier this morning," Susan continued, following the script. "The State Department issued a statement condemning violence against protesters, and we explored the possibility of imposing economic sanctions on China. However, we have since discovered that reports of the massacre were significantly overblown as a result of deep fake videos spreading around the internet. While the U.S. intelligence community gathers more information to get a clear picture of the situation in Hong Kong, I'm planning to meet with the Chinese ambassador this afternoon to discuss the matter."

"Ma'am, but how does your administration plan to deal with the incursion of China's submarines into our coastal waters?" Bernie pressed.

"China's flotilla of submarines in the Northern Sea Route poses no immediate threat to the United States, as it is intended to strengthen nuclear deterrence," Susan said. "The submarines will play a defensive role in China's *Prowling Tiger* war game scheduled to take place in a few hours."

"But didn't China just threaten to use nuclear weapons in its flurry of aggressive posts this morning?" Bernie asked. "Has China abandoned its no-first-use nuclear policy?"

"Not yet. We don't believe the Chinese government meant to threaten the United States with nuclear weapons on social media. We are currently looking into the true origin of the posts from the *Xinhua News* handle," Susan said, going off script. Out of the corner of her eye, she noticed Elise's stiffening posture as she threw Susan a brief, stern glare.

During their strategy session, they'd disagreed on whether

she should disclose the uncertain origins of the social media posts. Susan had argued for transparency, hoping it would open the door for the Chinese government to admit the cyberattack. But Elise had warned her that the press briefing might not go well if she went there. Now they would see who got it right.

One of her favorite correspondents, Joan King from HNN, raised her hand, and Susan eagerly pointed at her, hoping to shift the discussion in a more favorable direction.

"Madam President, are you suggesting that the tweets did not come from the Chinese government?" Joan asked, tilting her head.

Susan nodded, feeling some unexpected heat behind her ears. "Yes, that's exactly what I'm suggesting."

"If the Chinese government was not behind the posts, then who was it?" Joan asked.

"We can't offer a definitive answer yet," Susan said, glancing at Elise, whose lips were pressed into a thin, tight line, her facial muscles tense. Susan recognized her old friend's attempt at glossing over her disapproval for the sake of public unity. "The director of national intelligence has undertaken comprehensive analysis to identify the source of the posts, especially in light of the deep fake videos. Once we have that, we'll let you know right away."

"Why do you think the Chinese government has remained silent about the source of the tweets and deep fake videos?" Joan asked, wrinkling her forehead.

"That's not clear," Susan said, her mouth suddenly dry. "I'm hoping to clarify China's official position on today's events during my lunch with the Chinese ambassador."

Paul Wright from the Global Broadcasting Service raised his hand, and Susan called on him next.

"Madam President, you said earlier that China's submarines pose no immediate threat to the United States. Are you suggesting that these submarines are unable to launch their nuclear weapons at our cities?"

Susan shot a sideways glance at Elise, who returned a curt nod.

"That's not at all what I'm saying," Susan said. "Nuclear-armed submarines are a defensive capability and used for retaliatory attacks. It wouldn't be in China's interest to start a nuclear war since the U.S. retaliation would be massive and swift."

"Then how does China's ballistic missile test fit into all of this?" Paul asked. "A source of mine said the missile was an anti-satellite weapon. Do you see this test as further evidence of China's aggressive stance on the world stage?"

Susan shook her head. "We consider China's missile test to be part of its planned war game and thus not part of a major policy shift on the part of the Chinese government. This is not the first time it has tested an anti-satellite weapon."

Bernie's hand popped up again, and Susan reluctantly pointed at him.

"Ma'am, a student from Georgetown University on *The Counter View* this morning claimed that if you sign the autonomous weapons legislation, you'll be responsible for unleashing the Terminator," he said. "How would you respond to this allegation?"

Susan's eyes widened, the question catching her off guard. Truthfully, that very thought had haunted her ever since Harrison died and Congress began moving swiftly to pass the legislation. She swallowed hard at the notion of fully autonomous robots taking to the battlefield as foreseen by *The Terminator*. A tingle swept up the back of her neck and across her face.

With the twists and turns in the China crisis that morning, neither she nor Elise had the chance to peruse the news headlines for inflammatory statements. Susan also didn't have enough time to consider her final decision on the legislation, and she still remained on the fence about it. Coming into the press briefing, she'd planned to take Elise's advice and announce her intention to sign the legislation. It made the most sense and would allow her to hit the ground running with her presidency. But all of a sudden she wasn't sure anymore.

"U.S. autonomous weapons systems already exist in different countries around the world," Susan said, her hand trembling. "This bill merely authorizes the Department of Defense to activate them for use on the battlefield." She didn't believe her own words. It was an awkward attempt to dodge the student's statement while suppressing the doubts rising in her chest.

"Are you planning to sign the bill, then?" Bernie asked. "Since it's apparently meaningless?"

"We are currently focused on the situation with China at the moment," Susan said, sensing her rapid pulse. "Once that is resolved, I'll review the legislation and make my decision."

Paul's hand shot in the air, and she called on him.

"Ma'am, I'm a bit confused," he said, holding his notepad ready. "What's so dire about the situation with China that you've been unable to reach a decision on President Monroe's hard-won legislation? Didn't you just say that the posts did not originate from the Chinese government, that the Mong Kok massacre didn't occur as advertised, that the submarines don't pose an immediate threat, and that the missile test was part of China's war game?"

*Shit.*

Susan cleared her throat. "As I said earlier, we've been responding to each new development with China as it occurred, and we're still working to confirm a final resolution to all of them. I expect to have better answers *after* my lunch meeting with the Chinese ambassador."

"Are you concerned about how the ARC system might misinterpret these developments and cause unwanted nuclear escalation?" Paul asked, his eyebrow raised. "I have a source at the Pentagon who expressed uncertainty about today's test. Something about a false positive?"

*Where did that question come from?*

She stole a glimpse at Elise before answering. Her chief of staff's jaw was tense, and her body language betrayed growing unease.

"The ARC system already passed its four monthly test and evaluations with high scores," Susan said. "I expect today's test to be another success."

"With all due respect, ma'am, you said you're undecided about the autonomous weapons legislation, but tout the wonders of the ARC system," Bernie interjected. "How can you have zero problems with ARC while denying President Monroe his legacy?"

*I never touted its wonders.*

"ARC is a semi-autonomous defensive system," Susan said, stumbling slightly. "And the final decision to launch nuclear weapons remains in the hands of the president. That's why it doesn't fall under the current legislation."

"Actually ma'am, that's incorrect," Bernie said. "The ARC system gives the launch order. While you do have the authority to rescind the order, the ARC system initiates the kill decision."

Elise strode out onto the stage and put her hand on the mic. "That's all for now, folks. The president has a busy schedule and has to get back to work." She put her hand on Susan's back and guided her out of the briefing room.

Susan's cheeks burned when she saw Blake waiting for her in the wings, a pained expression on his face. She turned toward Elise, who followed closely behind her. "Was I that bad?"

"It wasn't your finest hour," Elise said. "I thought we'd decided to sign the legislation. What happened?"

Susan looked at Elise and then at Blake, shook her head, and lifted her shoulders. "I don't know. I guess I had a crisis of conscience."

"I wish you'd had it about thirty minutes ago," Elise said grimly. "The headlines are not likely to be kind to you. And it's not the best time for a public relations crisis."

"How do we fix this?" Susan asked, staring at her feet.

Elise shrugged her shoulders.

"That kid is a student of mine at Georgetown," Blake said tentatively. "I can talk to him if you want."

Susan narrowed her eyes at him and then shook her head. "No, that will only make things worse. I can just see that head-lines now: 'President Bullies a Graduate Student into Submission.'"

"How about this..." Elise said, rubbing her temple. "Let's invite him to the Oval Office for a little chat this evening."

Blake cocked his head and gave her a skeptical look. "Sounds like a publicity stunt to me," he said, not hiding his sarcasm.

"Well, that's what it is," Elise said. "But it's a brilliant one. This kid has become the face of the opposition. By talking to him directly, we'll neutralize the opposition and have a shot at reversing the negative headlines from today's press briefing."

Susan nodded quickly, now understanding precisely where her chief of staff was going with the scheme. "I'll say I took the time to consider opposing views, discussed them with this kid, and then signed the bill anyway." She felt a bit of her energy return.

"Because that's what President Monroe would have wanted," Blake said, finally catching on to their plan.

"Exactly," Susan said.

"You should have Tori Scott moderate the discussion between you and Drew," Blake said.

"Oh, you're just looking for an excuse to meet your news crush," Susan said, nudging him playfully.

"Whatever works," Blake said, grinning back at her.

# [ 32 ]
## THE LIVE INTERVIEW

DREW
1140
Homeland Network News
Washington D.C.

*How did I get here?*

Drew wanted to pinch himself, to make sure he was actually standing in the studio of *The Counter View*. He fidgeted with his hands as he waited to go on air with Tori Scott and Emilio Valdes.

When he left his Georgetown class earlier that morning, he'd received an unexpected call from the show's executive producer. Since the internet was still abuzz with his video clip, *The Counter View* hosts wanted him to reprise his role as an emerging antagonist to the president on the issue of autonomous weapons. He'd said yes without hesitation.

*This is my chance to do something. To make a difference.*

But now, standing in the studio near all the bright lights and cameras, he was having second thoughts. He was about to make his debut on national television, and he didn't want to waste the opportunity. If he pulled it off, the interview might change his life.

*What if I mess this up?*

Drew blinked rapidly, trying to control his bodily functions, all of which were running haywire. To avoid making a fool of himself, he'd have to overcome his growing anxiety and zero in on what he needed to say, all whilst sitting under bright lights and facing the camera. It was a tall order for an amateur.

*I'm not sure I can do it.*

Rubbing the back of his sweaty neck, he stood behind the cameraman, watching as Tori and Emilio bantered back and forth about what they'd just seen on live television. Both of them were as stunned by the development as he was.

President Tolley's press briefing was thrown into disarray when reporters began challenging her intentions regarding the autonomous weapons legislation. Tolley wouldn't say yet if she was going to sign or veto the bill. The reporters actually quoted Drew, mentioned his video clip, and asked Tolley if it was her plan to unleash the Terminator on humanity.

When things got out of hand, the president's chief of staff cut things short.

*That was because of me.*

Drew smiled to himself. His viral video clip had somehow hijacked the news headlines despite major developments in China. His head felt like it was floating in the air, high above his body, in a foggy dreamworld. Another surge of adrenaline intensified the nerves in his stomach to remind him of what was coming—a live interview on national television.

A makeup artist appeared next to him, going to work on his sweaty face with some tinted powder. As soon as she touched up his face, beads of sweat reappeared, causing her to frown. A few moments later, she grimaced and then apparently gave up.

Drew's hands started to shake, and he clutched them together. To distract himself, he took quick breaths and tried to listen to Tori and Emilio's newscast.

"We just heard from the president," Tori said. "And it's clear that Tolley has no idea what she's going to do about the legislation sitting on her desk, waiting for her signature." Tori shook her head, apparently still stunned by what had happened. "I can't believe she wasn't prepared for that line of questioning. Hasn't anyone in the White House been following social media this morning? Are they asleep at the wheel?"

"Apparently." Emilio smacked the desk with his hand, a huge smile spreading across his face. "It made my entire year to see Tolley get hammered by those reporters and come off as a complete amateur. Someone in the White House should get fired for this." He pinched himself multiple times. "This is like the best day ever. Tell me, is it Christmas?" Emilio was almost giddy.

Tori rolled her eyes at his theatrics. "Well, in her defense, Tolley might have been a tad preoccupied by the situation with China. The missile test. The aggressive tweets. And don't forget, a few hours ago, we thought thousands of protesters were dying in the streets of Hong Kong. Anyone would be distracted under those circumstances."

"Huh." Emilio grunted. "I'm not sure what you mean by *we*. I, for one, didn't think thousands of protesters were dying. I don't want to come off as smug, but I called it on the deep fakes. I just knew something wasn't right."

*Yeah, right.*

Drew smirked as he observed the contortions on Tori's face. He caught her rolling her eyes at her co-host for a second time.

Emilio waved his hands. "But now that we know the massacre is fake, you'd think Tolley could catch up on the most important piece of legislation of this decade." He furrowed his brow. "Or maybe she can't handle being commander in chief. If she can't hack it, I bet General Burke is willing to step up to the plate."

Drew raised his eyebrow.

*Isn't Burke the secretary of defense?*

225

Then he remembered seeing a headline about Burke wanting the empty VP slot.

The makeup artist returned to comb Drew's hair and dab his face one more time with powder and disappeared again. Seconds later, a producer showed up next to him, gave him a nudge, and handed him a notecard. Realizing he was about to go onstage in a few minutes, Drew's heart began pounding like a bass drum.

"Look, Tolley has had her hands full this morning. China conducted a missile test of an anti-satellite weapon," Tori said, defending Tolley. "All things considered, that's a pretty provocative move. Maybe there are things going on behind the scenes that we don't know about."

Emilio's eyes bulged, and he slapped the desk again. "But that's what the damn press briefing was for! To let the American people know what's going on. To help us understand why her administration appears to be flailing about without any sense of direction. To give us something to chew on. And what did we get? Nothing. I don't know of anyone with credibility making a big deal about that missile test. Why not? Because it's obviously part of the scheduled war game tomorrow. Are we gonna freak out every time China blows something up over the next few days? Don't we have the most powerful military in the world?"

Tori shrugged nonchalantly. "For once, I don't disagree with you. She did fall short of what I expect from a president."

"Well then, there's a first time for everything," Emilio said, grinning at her and then directly into the camera. "Folks, here's your soundbite for today. Tolley completely missed the boat on the most important issue for the American people—the question of authorizing the Department of Defense to field fully autonomous weapons systems on the battlefield. I don't know of a more important issue at the moment."

Tori turned her body toward the camera and smiled. "And that's why we're thrilled to have Drew Hudson back here with us to talk about the risks posed by autonomous weapons systems after the break. Stay tuned for more."

"And we're off air," the cameraman said. Everyone exhaled and began moving about the set. A stage assistant rolled a third chair up onto the stage and situated it between the other two chairs.

Emilio scowled and crossed his arms, glaring at Drew and then at Tori. "Since when do we invite a single guest, representing only one side of the issue?" he asked, pointing a finger at Drew.

"You don't think you can handle debating both of us?" Tori asked, poking fun at him.

A pit formed in Drew's stomach. *I'm not going to have to argue with Emilio, am I?*

"That's not the point," Emilio said. "If we're going to interview Terminator Boy, shouldn't we also feature a guest who favors the development of autonomous weapons systems? Doesn't our show always present both sides of the issue and let the audience decide?"

Drew shrank back, avoiding eye contact with Emilio. His pulse spiked.

*Terminator Boy?*

"We couldn't find someone on such short notice," Tori said. "We didn't expect the video clip to have such a huge impact on social media. The executive producer decided it was a useful target of opportunity. It's not my fault."

"The executive producer, my ass," Emilio said, throwing up his hands. "You're the one who set this up, Tori. You might end up regretting this."

Drew blanched. He'd assumed the interview would be a friendly affair. But now he got the impression he was being offered up as bait by Tori to one of the world's most famous conservative commentators. If that was the case, Emilio would have him for lunch and then some.

# [ 33 ]
## THE DOSSIER

MORGAN
1200
Liberty Crossing Intelligence Campus
McLean, Virginia

Morgan pushed open the glass door and strode into the modern-looking suite of the National Intelligence Council. She flashed her White House badge at the receptionist, who nodded at her. Then Morgan followed the signs on the wall, making her way directly to the cubicle belonging to the national intelligence officer for Russia and Eurasia. This would only be her first stop at the Office of the Director of National Intelligence. Before learning more about potential cyberthreats, she needed to dig deeper on the Russian connection.

Rounding the corner, she saw a familiar face in the gray cubicle. Mike sat in an office chair across from two young intelligence analysts.

"Mike, what are *you* doing here?" Morgan asked.

Mike's eyes widened when he saw her. He jumped up and approached her with his usual gusto. "Doing a deep dive on the

Russian oligarchs. Since I managed to get a few minutes on the president's schedule later this afternoon, I figured I'd better get up to speed on potential threats coming from Russia. You had the same idea?"

"Yeah." Morgan nodded and glanced at the intelligence analysts in the cubicle, who were staring up at her.

"Does Grayson know you're here?" Mike asked.

"Uh, yeah. When David and I brought the issue to the president, Grayson suggested I come by to see if his analysts could uncover any leads on the Russian connection," Morgan lied.

After her uncle gave her a strange warning about Grayson, she'd decided not to ask him for access. Given the antagonistic relationship between him and her boss, Grayson wouldn't probably want her anywhere near his staff. But the intelligence analysts didn't need to know that. Mike turned and walked back toward the cubicle and initiated the necessary introductions.

"This is my colleague, Dr. Morgan Shaw, director for defense issues at the NSC," he said.

The petite Asian-American woman stood up, her long, straight black hair falling forward as she shook Morgan's hand. "Niko Takahashi, national intelligence officer for East Asia. I think we've met before when I had the opportunity to tag along on the president's Daily Brief."

Morgan's face lit up. "Yeah, great to see you again." She pulled over an empty chair from another cubicle and sat down next to Mike.

The male analyst reached over for a quick handshake. "Ma'am, I'm Wyatt Evans, national intelligence officer for Russia and Eurasia." The skinny black-haired kid looked like he was fresh out of graduate school. "By the way, that was a stroke of genius to think of Russian oligarchs as being involved in this scheme. Without your suggestion, we would never have gotten as far as we have on our analysis."

Morgan suppressed a frown, eager to get the pleasantries out of the way and down to business. "Okay. Between the tweets and fake video footage, I get the sense that there's something more going on here. But this doesn't feel like the prototypical Russian disinformation campaign. Things are moving way too fast for their usual strategic approach. I'm worried this morning's mischief could be the prelude to something bigger."

Mike bobbed his head. "Actually, we were just discussing exactly that theory, but you're missing one major element."

"I am?" Morgan asked, searching her mind for the one thing she was forgetting. She leaned forward in her chair.

"Brace yourself for a bombshell," Mike said with a grim look. "The NSA has just picked up some chatter among Russian agents about some Top Secret space rocket launches scheduled to take place from a site in Siberia in the next few days."

"What?" Morgan's mouth fell open, and she shrank back. "The Russian government is planning to launch rockets without telling anyone about it? That's extremely reckless. Have you informed Grayson or the president?"

Mike shook his head. "Not yet. For one, we're not sure the Russian government is directly involved. It looks like the space activity might be coming out of the private sector. The NSA is still verifying the veracity of the information. But if the rumors are true, it changes everything."

"I can't imagine a private sector company launching space rockets without authorization from the Russian government," Morgan said, sliding into a daze. Her thoughts drifted to Anton Vega and his grandiose plans for space travel.

*Could Vega be behind all of this? Why the extreme secrecy around the space launches?*

"But why bother with the bogus tweets and deep fake videos?" Wyatt asked, his face aghast. "How does that help with the space launches?"

*Someone wants the United States and China distracted...*

"Do we know where the tweets came from yet?" Morgan asked, snapping herself back from her internal thoughts to focus on the task at hand.

"We had our cyber specialists at the Cyberthreat Intelligence Integration Center take a look at the hack of the news handle. They found a known hacker's signature."

"The hacker left a signature?" Morgan asked.

"Yes, the hack was signed N0V4, or Nova as the hacker is known by name. Hackers like to sign their masterpieces, which also allows us to track their work online," Wyatt said. "However, they're also skilled at hiding their true identity."

Morgan leaned back in her chair and crossed her arms. "Okay, someone wants to toy with our perception of China's intentions."

"Yes," Wyatt said. "We've also identified the individual who actually posted the tweets to the *China Xinhua News* handle. Thanks to some video footage of him leaving the building located next to the state news agency headquarters in Harbin, China. That's the building linked to the IP address where the posts were uploaded. We also have infrared confirmation that no one else was in the building at the time. The man's name is Dimitri Molotov."

Morgan smirked at the irony. *Molotov as in the explosive cocktail?*

"Molotov is a former Russian FSB agent and now a well-known rogue operator for hire by organized criminals—and sometimes by the Russian government," Wyatt said. "But he's an equal opportunity thug who will work for anyone who pays in suitcases full of cash."

"How in the world did you get your hands on that video footage and infrared data?" Morgan asked, giving them a blank stare.

"From our counterparts at the Chinese Ministry of State Security," Niko said. "Didn't Grayson mention our informal back channel with Chinese intelligence analysts this morning?"

Morgan shook her head, trying to recall his exact words.

"Well, I wasn't at the meeting," Niko said, "but I definitely put a note in Grayson's talking points. Didn't he bring it up?"

Morgan nodded. "Yeah, Grayson said Chinese intelligence admitted the Twitter handle was hacked and claimed the hacker was a Russian FSB agent. I guess they got it partially right. He's Russian and former FSB."

Niko gave her a slight smile. "Even if the Chinese government won't make any official statements, they seem rather determined to clear up the misunderstandings behind the scenes."

"But that doesn't help us on the world stage," Morgan said, furrowing her brow. "Or inspire much confidence. How do we know the Chinese intelligence analysts are telling us the truth? Maybe they're just feeding us a line to keep us confused. Do you think this Molotov character was also behind the deep fakes?"

"We don't know for sure," Wyatt said. "NSA analysts have traced the source of the video footage from the deep fakes to an IP address within Russia, but we haven't confirmed the identity of the individual who posted them."

"What was the time lag between the tweets and the deep fakes?" Morgan asked.

"Huh. I hadn't thought about that angle," Wyatt said, glancing down at a piece of paper and pointing to the information. "The tweets were posted between 3 a.m. and 4 a.m. this morning in Harbin, China. The videos went live around 6 a.m. from an IP address in Vladivostok, Russia. Wait a minute. I know why you're asking. Molotov didn't have enough time to make the long drive to do both. He must have been working with someone else, perhaps this notorious hacker."

"Exactly," Morgan said. "Do we know who hired Molotov?"

"Actually, we do," Wyatt said. "It's quite a coincidence. We've known for a long time that Molotov works on occasion for Igor Koslov, one of the two oligarchs Mike named for you. Interestingly, Koslov happens to be in New York City at the moment."

Morgan's eyes widened. "Koslov is here in the country? And he's hired Molotov to mess with our relationship with China?"

Wyatt nodded. "We know this because the FBI has been surveilling a number of suspicious Russian citizens in our country and listening to their communications. Anyway, we picked up several conversations between Igor and his contacts in Russia, including Molotov. They were talking in code, using popular cocktail names. We believe they are playing up the irony of Molotov's surname. Or they know we're listening, and they're just screwing with us."

"What sorts of things have they said?"

Wyatt grabbed a classified folder from his desk, flipped it open, and read from the document. "In the first conversation, Igor told his Russian contact he was out with Maria at a Mexican place drinking both a piña colada and a daiquiri, but that the night ended with a blue lagoon."

Morgan furrowed her brow. "What in the world does that mean?"

Wyatt shrugged. "No idea. We think Molotov could be the person on the other line. The phone is a burner so we're not one hundred percent certain. In the second conversation, Igor said Maria finished an Americano and plans to take a Moscow mule. And the last conversation was about a white Russian, black Russian, and a side car."

"Huh," Morgan said, rubbing her chin. "Maria must be a person, perhaps a female friend of Koslov."

"Yup," Wyatt said. "We're still waiting on further information from the FBI about her. They're pretty sure they know who she is. Once we have her identity, we might be able to get further in our investigation."

Morgan squished her brows together, still thinking about the cocktail names. "The first three drinks mentioned… maybe they have something in common that offers a clue to their meaning? Piña coladas and daiquiris both have rum?"

"But the blue lagoon has vodka in it," Mike said, shaking his head.

Morgan's shoulders sank for a moment. Then a new idea came to her. "Okay, but don't they all have ice in them?"

"Nope. A daiquiri is served straight up," Mike said, sighing.

"But they're fruit drinks," Morgan said. "All three are served chilled."

"Look, we've already spent too much time trying to decode the messages," Mike said. "Koslov is probably trolling the NSA. He has to know he's being monitored. I think we're wasting our time attempting to figure out what these messages mean."

"Sorry. You're probably right," Morgan said. She turned to Wyatt. "What do you know about Igor Koslov?"

"Not much," Wyatt said. "But we've only had an hour or so to gather the dossier together after Grayson came back from the White House. Koslov was born in Vladivostok and grew up dirt poor. His parents died when he was a child, and he spent many years at an orphanage. Somehow, he mustered up the funds to attend the state university in Vladivostok where he studied engineering. In his early twenties, he moved to Moscow for graduate school on a full scholarship at Lomonosov Moscow State University and became an engineer for the oil and natural gas industry upon graduation—"

"Wyatt, this is all very interesting background," Morgan interrupted, not hiding her irritation. "Did you find anything pertinent to the disinformation campaign?"

"Not really," Wyatt said, his shoulders sinking. "Koslov has been traveling on business for the past few weeks for Nesti Oil and Gas, one of his many energy-related companies. He paid a few visits to some tech companies in Palo Alto. But on the surface, everything appears legit."

"Have you thought at all about what their next moves might be?" Morgan asked.

Mike, Wyatt, and Niko looked at each other with blank faces and shrugged.

"C'mon, guys," Morgan said. "Think like a bad guy. If you

were trying to erode relations between the U.S. and China, what would you do next?"

All three of them said nothing.

Morgan sighed. "Okay, let's start with what we know. The tweets mess with our communication with China. If we believe they're real, we think China is signaling the possibility for aggression. Next, the deep fakes make it look like the Chinese police are carrying out a massacre, a direct challenge to our core values—democracy and the right to free speech. This alters our perception of Chinese intentions and may spur us to action." Her mind began to race with possibilities. "The next logical step might be to shut down our communications."

Niko's face lit up. "Yes, they'd want us in the dark. Like Nightfall."

Morgan's pulse spiked.

The thumping of feet sounded down the hallway. A red-faced man appeared in the cubicle entrance, his armpits drenched in sweat. He frantically looked between those gathered, zeroing in on the analysts. "Niko, Wyatt, you're needed in the Cyberthreat Intelligence Integration Center right away. And bring that dossier you were working on."

Wyatt blanched, and Niko looked worried as they got up to follow the man.

"What's happened?" Mike asked, standing up to follow them.

"We've lost communications with one of our satellites," the man answered.

# [ 34 ]
## USE OR LOSE

DREW
1215
Homeland Network News
Washington D.C.

Drew gulped when *The Counter View*'s executive producer signaled the show was about to go back on the air.

Tori walked over to him. "Are you ready for this?" she asked, craning her neck as she walked up the stairs and motioned for him to take his seat on the stage next to her.

Drew faked a big smile and followed her up the stairs. "Ready as I'll ever be." Feeling numb, he moved toward his chair, but it was like he was walking through a vat of molasses. With each labored step, his heart thudded hard in his chest.

"Just be yourself," she said, sitting down in her chair and flashing her white teeth. "Like you were this morning after you warmed up."

Drew gave her a nervous smile and sat down next to her. To his left, Emilio grunted, read his news tablet, and paid him no attention. Behind the glass, the executive producer pointed to her watch.

Tori lowered her head and whispered, "We're going on air in a few moments. Take a deep breath and relax."

Drew's body seized as he tried to think about what he wanted to say in the interview. His thoughts suddenly turned to mush, and his knowledge of artificial intelligence seemed to evaporate into thin air. He couldn't even remember how he defined it as a concept. His chest tightened, and he found it difficult to breathe.

"We're ready in five... four... three... two... one," the cameraman said, pointing to Tori, who began to speak and welcome viewers back to the show.

Only a few seconds under the hot lights, and his armpits were already moist. Drew could barely hear Tori speak against the sound of his heart thrashing in his ears. Her voice sounded strangely distorted and deep, like a recording playing back on slow speed. It was as if time came to a stop, except for his racing pulse. In the distance, he picked up someone saying something about the video clip that had gone viral. Clenching his jaw, he tried to pull himself back to reality.

*Need. To. Get. A. Grip.*

"Drew, did you hear my question?" Tori asked, leaning forward to see his face.

After a jolt of adrenaline, the focus of Drew's eyes went from blurry to laser-sharp. Squinting under the glaring lights, he looked out into the studio and winced at the lenses of the cameras. He was distracted by black spots in his vision. Just then, he realized he was holding his breath and not taking in any air. He exhaled sharply and breathed deeply.

*In. Out. In. Out.*

Inside the sound booth, Drew could see the executive producer making something that looked like a cut signal with her hands.

"Uh, sorry, I might have missed the question," he said awkwardly, his voice rasping.

There was an audible sigh to his left.

"That's okay, Drew," Tori said gently. "I just apologized for cutting your video footage from this morning. I told our viewers about the fascinating conversation we had on the critical role of data for the algorithms that power autonomous weapons systems. I wanted you to know that we'll be airing the full interview on our website after our discussion."

Drew felt the blood return to his face and the clarity of his surroundings returned. "Uh, thanks... That's great."

Tori studied him with some uncertainty, but he smiled back to let her know that his stage hysteria had passed.

"Earlier today, we promised viewers a discussion about artificial intelligence and nuclear war," she said. "I was hoping you might help us understand this complex topic in light of today's test of the Autonomous Retaliatory Capability by the Department of Defense."

"Yeah, sure." Drew had been obsessing about the ARC system ever since his morning class and felt like he might have something to say.

"Great, I'll start with the obvious question," Tori said. "How does artificial intelligence help prevent nuclear war?"

"Um, I'm not sure it does," Drew said, furrowing his brow. For a moment, he wondered if he'd heard the question correctly.

"But that's not what ARC's developer, Centoreum Tech, claims," Tori said. "The fifth test of ARC is due to take place today. Meanwhile, Centoreum Tech's shares are up by twenty percent. For the sake of discussion, can you try to envision the rationale for integrating AI into nuclear weapons systems?"

*But I don't see any rationale.*

Drew hesitated to respond, blinking rapidly. His mouth opened, but nothing came out.

Emilio cleared his throat. "Thanks as always for ensuring we cover both sides of the issue, Tori," he said sarcastically. "I'm more than happy to answer this question while our guest figures out if he has anything to say."

Drew held his breath for a moment as he realized what was happening. *She's setting me up to debate Emilio...*

Emilio smiled at the camera. "There are many significant benefits of AI for nuclear weapons, which is why Congress authorized the development of the ARC system and why the Department of Defense decided to launch the system five months ago. The most obvious advantage of AI-enabled systems is to save precious time. When you're facing an incoming nuclear attack, every extra second counts to ensure the survival of a nation. Because AI has been integrated into our daily lives, commercial systems, and soon, into our military systems, almost every part of the world now moves at machine speed. We can't afford to have our nuclear weapons systems function as slowly as they did in the past. The only way to buy more time is to leverage AI-enabled systems, supplanting humans who require way too much time to analyze data and reach decisions."

"Thanks Emilio," Tori said before turning to Drew. "You're a well-known opponent of autonomous systems and have warned us about the risks of something like Skynet from *The Terminator*. If time is of the essence in nuclear war, what arguments would you make against the ARC system?"

Drew pinched his lips. "As you know, I'm a graduate student at Georgetown. In class this morning, we were discussing the risks posed by nuclear weapons, which we've tolerated for almost a century. At any moment, due to miscalculations, false alarms, accidents, or unauthorized use, the world could stumble into a nuclear war that kills millions of people. AI-enabled systems will speed up the process of using nuclear weapons and reduce such decisions to mere nanoseconds. This leads to a fundamental question... Once a nuclear attack is detected, do you honestly think leaders of nuclear-armed countries will be able to resist an all-out nuclear war? If anything, I'd hope that world leaders would come to their senses and try to reduce the speed of such decisions and leave AI out of it."

Emilio chuckled. "You should probably keep studying at that school of yours. Because it's obvious you don't understand a thing about nuclear deterrence."

"Your problem is that you think you know too much," Drew said. "You're so wedded to past concepts of nuclear deterrence that you're unable to see how they could fail. I only recently started learning about the risks posed by nuclear weapons. Actually, I received my first introduction to the nuclear deterrence theory this morning. But it didn't take me that long to see through all of it—the logic of first and second strikes, the need for a nuclear triad, missile defense, etcetera. For most of the Cold War, decision-makers had at most thirty minutes to launch nuclear weapons in the event of a nuclear attack. Thirty minutes to launch missiles that would kill millions of people. Today, that timeframe has shrunk to around eight minutes. Maybe less."

"See, you've just proved my point," Emilio sneered at him. "If we don't launch U.S. intercontinental ballistic missiles from their silos before the first nuclear-armed missiles hit our soil, we'll lose them. The ARC system will help ensure that decision-makers launch our retaliatory attack before this happens."

Drew nodded. "So I hear. Is that how the ARC system is going to *help* us? By making sure our adversary suffers more annihilation than we do? Because I'm not sure that's a good solution. If we're really so afraid of this 'use or lose' situation, then why don't we just eliminate all of our intercontinental ballistic missiles in the first place? I mean, don't we have enough submarine-launched ballistic missiles to retaliate on a massive scale within a short timeframe?"

Emilio's eyes bulged. "If we get rid of our land-based missiles, our adversaries will target our cities instead of silos. We need to keep these missiles operational to absorb an initial nuclear attack and spare the lives of innocent civilians."

"Really? You think we're going to spare lives?" Drew

smirked. "Once our land-based missiles are airborne, they can't be called back. That means an all-out nuclear war will begin shortly after our missiles are launched at their targets. And I'm pretty sure if an adversary starts a nuclear war, they'll want to make sure they cripple our country so that we can't fight back. Land-based ballistic missiles won't spare U.S. cities from destruction. Given economic interdependence, a nuclear attack against any of the great powers would end life as we know it for everyone around the world. If we eliminate land-based ballistic missiles, then time no longer has to be of the essence. If we slow down nuclear decision-making enough, everyone might be able to come to their senses."

Emilio's mouth hung open slightly for a moment as if he were stunned. "Um... You're forgetting the other advantage of machines. The ASR system can analyze millions of data points in seconds and provide better situational awareness for nuclear decision-makers than we've ever had before. Rather than rely upon our early warning systems for detection of nuclear attacks, now we have strategic warning or long-term indicators prior to the launch of that attack. I'd say that's a net benefit from the ARC system."

"Actually, I agree with you. Better situational awareness is a good thing," Drew said. "But—"

Emilio grinned and pointed at him. "The kid just proved me right again."

Drew shook his head emphatically. "Not really. That's only true if the dataset is of high quality, broadly representative, and fits the problem you're trying to solve or the outcome you're trying to produce. If the data is garbage to start, then the AI-enabled system's outcomes will also be garbage. In that case, I'd prefer slow humans analyzing less data over machines analyzing garbage at a high speed."

Tori smiled at him. "Drew, you mentioned this morning that there is often not enough data to solve complex national security problems. In light of this, how confident are you that the

ARC system would respond effectively to a nuclear threat, or worse, a nuclear attack?"

"I have zero confidence in the ARC system," Drew said.

"None whatsoever?" Tori asked.

"We have yet to experience a conflict in which nuclear weapons were used against a nuclear adversary," Drew said.

Tori jerked her head, apparently surprised by the statement. "World War Two?"

"The use of nuclear weapons on Nagasaki and Hiroshima doesn't count because Japan didn't have nuclear weapons with which to retaliate," Drew said.

Tori frowned. "Then, I guess we don't have the data."

Drew half-smiled. "That's why I doubt we're training the ARC system to operate reliably in the event of a nuclear attack. There's almost no data on nuclear crises, with the exception of the Cuban Missile Crisis. Generally, we can track wartime mobilization, but the nuclear signals of our adversaries remain fairly hidden. That means we don't have reliable indicators for a nuclear attack and won't have the so-called strategic warning Emilio mentioned as an advantage of the ARC system. Which means we'll rely on early warning systems as we always have… except this time, they're directly linked to our command and control and nuclear launch systems. And ARC can give the order to launch U.S. nuclear weapons all on its own."

"Well, that's all we have time for, folks," Tori said. "Drew, thank you so much for joining us for a fascinating conversation this morning. Stay tuned for HNN news. We'll see you all again tomorrow on *The Counter View.*"

The cameraman signaled that they were off air. Emilio remained seated in angry silence.

Tori turned to Drew and said, "That was amazing! You did great. I admit I was worried at first, but then you came alive."

"Yeah, I did, didn't I?" Drew felt rejuvenated and energized, almost like he was about to jump out of his own skin.

The executive producer approached the desk to shake Drew's

hand. "Well done. And it looks like someone else wants to talk to you. This just came by messenger." She handed him a folded note.

His hands shaking, Drew opened the note. His eyes widened when he realized it was on White House letterhead.

"What is it?" Tori asked, looking over his shoulder.

"Um... it's an invitation to speak with the president at the Oval Office this evening," Drew said. "And she wants you to facilitate the interview between us."

"Wow, that's quite an honor," Tori said, her face flushing.

# THE CHINESE AMBASSADOR

SUSAN
1220
Yellow Oval Room
The White House

For several minutes, Susan and Donghai Chen—her longtime friend and the Chinese ambassador—ate in silence, exchanging the occasional small talk about their families and shared pastimes. Neither of them had broached the fact that the U.S. and China were edging toward a nuclear conflict.

Susan stared out the window at the Washington Monument and took a deep breath. For her part, she'd already been through a war zone and back and didn't feel up to serious conversation, even with a dear friend. After her disaster of a press briefing, Susan could think of nothing else. Her cheeks burned when she thought about her catastrophic performance, instigated by a young Georgetown student and his incendiary statement about unleashing the Terminator.

*I didn't see that coming.*

Now, Susan dabbed her mouth with her cloth napkin and

smiled at Donghai, who was still finishing off his last few bites of lunch. "We should get the kids together again soon for a play-date," she said, still trying to break through the thick wall of ice between them.

Donghai nodded and smiled, revealing several crow's feet around his eyes. "Yes, yes. That is a fine idea, Susan. We should do that very soon."

"Do you think Nianzhen would like to come play with Lucy at the White House?" Susan asked. "That would be the easiest option for us these days."

"It would be our greatest honor," Donghai said, bowing his head.

Donghai had aged only slightly since they had first met fifteen years ago in graduate school at the Fletcher School of Law and Diplomacy in Medford, Massachusetts. The forty-some-thing Chinese man had a broad, flat face with high cheekbones, pin-straight black hair, and the kindest dark-brown eyes she'd ever seen. Despite coming from different sides of the world, the intellectual connection between them had been instant, and they became study partners and fast friends in grad school.

Sitting across from her old friend, she recalled fond memories of their many study hours in the Reading Room of the Ginn Library. Back then, neither of them could envision reaching the lofty positions they now held.

This was not the first time she'd dined with Donghai in the Yellow Oval Room, the yellow-painted room mostly used for receptions of foreign dignitaries before State dinners. Harrison had allowed Susan to invite Donghai to lunch there once before when they'd celebrated his appointment to Chinese ambassador to the United States. Donghai had become a major player in the Communist Party of China and happened to be a close friend of the Chinese president. If something strange were going on with China, Susan assumed he would know about it.

After chewing his last bite, Donghai set down his knife and fork on his plate, signaling that he was finished.

"Well, we have a lot to cover today. Shall we get down to business?" Susan asked, her voice stilted with formality.

Donghai nodded. "Yes, indeed. We have much to discuss. But before you raise the first agenda item, if I may, I would like to deliver an official message from Beijing."

Susan gave him a warm smile. "Of course. But you know this discussion is just between you and me today. I was hoping for a more informal conversation between friends to clear up some important misunderstandings."

"If you would please indulge me for a moment," Donghai said, glancing down at his notecard. "The Chinese president wishes to offer you his warmest greetings and express his sincerest hope that China and the United States will continue to collaborate on key issues of concern to both of our countries as we have recently done on the clean energy deal. The basis of such cooperation has always been a mutual respect for national sovereignty. On that note, we ask that the United States refrain from meddling in the internal affairs of Hong Kong." He stopped reading and gave Susan an apologetic look. "Forgive me, I had to read the message per my orders from Beijing."

"Donghai, that's perfectly fine. I do understand your position. Now that we have your president's official statement out of the way, I'm wondering if we might resolve some important issues. Can we start by discussing the tweets from the *China Xinhua News* handle this morning?" Susan waited for her friend to nod in acknowledgement. "Our intelligence analysts have been attempting to discover the origin of the posts. We don't think they came from your government. Perhaps you're able to shed some new light?"

Donghai's forehead creased, and his body tensed. "The true origin is *China Xinhua News*."

Susan furrowed her brow. She hadn't expected Donghai to deny the strange circumstances surrounding the posts. Especially given the information her people had received through back channels with Chinese intelligence analysts. "Then you're saying the posts amount to official communication from the Chinese government?"

*Maybe the analysts weren't authorized to communicate with us.*

He nodded but avoided eye contact.

"No one hacked the handle of your state news agency and uploaded the tweets to stir up trouble between us?" Susan asked, pressing the issue a bit further.

Donghai shook his head. "The posts reflect the current policy of the Chinese government."

*Why are the Chinese so sensitive about this hack? Is there something else going on?*

Susan shrank back, her gaze clouding for a moment. This didn't sound like her old friend talking candidly as he had in previous months. Not one bit. There was only one possible explanation. Donghai must have been given strict orders from Beijing to keep silent and wasn't able to deviate from the official message for some reason.

*But why?*

"In other words, the Chinese government intends to threaten the use of nuclear weapons against the United States?" Susan asked, trying one more time to get through to him.

He nodded stiffly.

"Donghai, it's just the two of us here," Susan said, giving him direct eye contact. "I can't possibly imagine your government would want to antagonize us. Please speak as freely as you can. Whatever you say will remain private between us, for the sake of reducing our countries' strained relations."

"That is all I can say on this matter," Donghai said curtly and pressed his lips together. "My leadership was not pleased with your statements at the press briefing earlier today. You implied we've lost control over our internal affairs. That is simply not the case."

"Donghai, any suggestion that the posts did not come from the Chinese government was intended to decrease tensions. I'm trying to defuse a conflict between our countries and prevent certain constituencies within the United States from calling for decisive action in response to the Hong Kong situation."

"That is not how we see it."

Susan's heart sank with a thud. The issue of the rogue tweets was by far the easiest item on her agenda. And for some reason, her friend was stonewalling her, possibly to cover up a cyberattack interfering with Chinese official communications.

*Did we get it completely wrong? Are the Chinese shifting to a more aggressive policy?*

# [ 36 ]
## BLACK BOX

ARJUN
1230
National Military Command Center
The Pentagon
Arlington, Virginia

Arjun's fingers raced across the keyboard as he typed a few more lines of code. His suit jacket hung on the back of his chair, and his shirtsleeves were rolled up. He tried to ignore the beads of sweat gathering on his forehead, but the heat was starting to get to him. It felt as if someone had cranked up the temperature by ten degrees.

For the past hour, Arjun had been working diligently to carry out his CEO's onerous demands. Not only was time extremely limited, but he had to make sure to keep his work a secret from everyone. He'd just finished tweaking the last of ARC's algorithms.

Taking a momentary break, he wiped sweat from his brow with his sleeve and glanced over his shoulder, making sure he was still alone. Then he looked up at the wall clock overhead.

Each tick seemed to thud against his chest, reminding him there wasn't much time before ARC's big test was scheduled to take place.

So far, Arjun had been extremely lucky that everyone was either at lunch or in some big meeting before the test. But if he couldn't finish the last few tasks to cover up the changes he made, his luck would be out. To his relief, he was almost done. A few more touch-ups, and no one would know the difference.

A crisis of conscience nagged at him since his conversation with Warren. Although he'd often questioned his CEO's lack of transparency, Arjun assumed he knew everything there was to know about ARC. His stomach roiled, thinking about how he had been deceived.

*This isn't right.*

Per his boss's orders, Arjun had reprogramed the ARC system to behave within expected parameters for the monthly test. This would prevent Pentagon leadership from taking it offline when ARC did something unexpected. But he wasn't sure if he bought into Warren's excuse for the subterfuge. Even if the adaptable ARC system would improve its performance over time, justifying the interim deception, Arjun believed that full transparency was a better policy. Unlike his boss, Arjun believed Pentagon leadership would give the ARC system a fair shot and not completely lose trust if they knew its limitations. Sadly, the decision was way above his pay grade.

Arjun's thoughts drifted to the autonomous weapons legislation he'd read about in the news earlier that morning. The integration of any AI-enabled system into military operations would face the same challenges—the so-called black box of a deep neural network. No one truly understood how they worked or the full range of what they could do. The complex network of algorithms and the interactions among them were often too complicated to grasp for skilled mathematicians and computer programmers, let alone senior-level leaders. For that reason, he'd never envied Grace's position where she was expected to explain the network to them.

*And I haven't made things any easier for her.*

Although it caused him serious heartburn on each occasion, he'd been able to dance circles around Grace's attempts to tell her bosses about ARC's weaknesses. All Arjun had to do was speak a few incoherent technical sentences that appeared to refute her valid points. Then he would dazzle the senior leaders with the amazing features offered by the ARC system.

It helped that Pentagon leadership desperately wanted to believe that ARC effectively solved a critical problem with nuclear deterrence—that it mitigated the shrinking time window for making nuclear decisions.

*This is no different than anything else I've done.*

Arjun had operated in an ethical gray zone ever since he'd accepted the lucrative job with Centoreum Tech, just out of grad school. When he first started, they'd promised him the opportunity to make history and help program one of the most important defense systems of the 21$^{st}$ century. But it wasn't long before he learned about some major issues with ARC. Of course, by then, he'd signed a nondisclosure agreement, any breach of which would cost him his job and potentially much more.

In the end, Arjun justified his actions based upon his family's survival. He'd made his deal with the devil long ago, sacrificing his morality to save the people he loved. He couldn't turn back now.

*Or could he?*

His father's words rang in his ears. Arjun swallowed hard and tried to refocus on the task at hand. Before proceeding, he checked his work several times. Everything looked good to him on the surface. But this was not a time when he could afford to make any errors. He began reviewing his changes one last time.

When he was finally satisfied with his work, Arjun reread

the detailed instructions his boss had given him to recalibrate the ARC system and verified the final steps.

*Just a few more things, and I'm done.*

"What do you think you're doing?" Grace asked in a stern tone, coming up behind him.

Arjun caught his breath and froze for a moment. Unfortunately, he'd missed his chance to delete evidence of his changes in the system's event log. Somehow, he hadn't heard her open the door to the office suite. Taking a deep breath, he spun around to face her with a big smile.

"I'm just prepping the ARC system for the test," he said, mustering up as much confidence as he could.

Grace moved to look over his shoulder and read his screen. "No, you're not."

Arjun stood up to block her view, but she shoved him to the side. He thought about pushing Grace back but realized that more people would be arriving shortly. He couldn't afford to have anyone catch him in a physical tussle. That would be grounds for his immediate dismissal. Grace sat down in his chair and stared at the screen intently.

"Grace, please get up," Arjun said. "C'mon, I need to finish what I was doing."

"I don't think so," Grace said, her eyes still glued to the screen. She moved the cursor, opened up the system's event log, and began scanning a list of recent processes and events. A few moments later, she looked up at him, her dark-brown eyes wide and full of anger. "You're making changes to ARC's algorithms. Why?"

"It's not what you think," Arjun said. "I'm making some minor corrections."

"Bullshit," Grace said, a dark scowl forming on her face. "You're making sure the Pentagon's leadership doesn't realize I was right. You're covering up your own incompetence... or worse, your company's corruption."

"That's not true. I'm making a few corrections, that's all,"

Arjun said. He tried once more to force her out of his seat, but she resisted. Then, without warning, Grace got up quickly from his chair and moved toward the door. "Hey, where are you going?" he asked, his heart racing and a lump forming in his throat.

Grace put her hands on her hips. "I'm going to tell Colonel Martinez about what you've done and stop the test this afternoon. Then I'm going to report you to the J6 and get security to haul your ass out of here."

Arjun leapt up from his chair, lunged toward her, and grabbed her arm, stopping her from exiting the room.

"Let go of me," she shouted, struggling to break free.

"Grace, please. Don't go. Please. If you stay, I'll tell you everything. Please, listen to me. I beg you. I can't lose this job. You don't understand... my whole family depends on this job." A tear rolled down his cheek. "My mom is in the hospital. She's very ill. If I get fired, she won't receive the necessary medical care to save her life."

She pulled her arm away and glared at him, her eyes bright with rage. But she must have seen the look of terror on his face and noticed his tears because her features softened.

"Fine," Grace said. "I'll hear you out, but I can't promise not to report you."

SUSAN
1240
Yellow Oval Room
The White House

Susan shook her head at Donghai and stared down at her sheet of talking points Elise had prepared for her. Her attempt to clarify things with the Chinese ambassador had not gone as planned. His refusal to cooperate with her was baffling.

"Okay, let's turn to the situation in Hong Kong," she said. "Initially, we received reports of massive casualties caused by Chinese police against the protesters. News reporters called the incident a massacre on the scale of Tiananmen Square. But after Truthbusters, a global nonprofit think tank, ran deep forensic analysis on the videos from social media, they claimed that much of the footage was faked." She stopped for a moment to see if he might respond.

When Donghai said nothing, she continued, "For this reason, we had our intelligence community collect and analyze all the satellite imagery available for Hong Kong. Although we have detected some protester casualties resulting from police violence, we have confirmed there was no massacre. That means someone is actively working to distort the events occurring in Hong Kong. Specifically, we believe the deep fakes were created by Russian agents as part of a disinformation campaign. Do you know anything about this?"

"I know nothing about any deep fakes," Donghai said, his face expressionless. "All we ask is that the United States refrain from interfering in the situation in Hong Kong."

Susan clenched her jaw, looking directly at her friend. "Donghai, what's going on? I invited you here for lunch today to resolve escalating tensions between our two countries. I've brought some troubling information to your attention in the hopes we can get to the bottom of this together. We need identify who might be attempting to cause a conflict between us. But if you deny everything and refuse to go public, then our two countries will come closer to the risk of nuclear war. Is that what you want?"

Donghai crossed his arms and leaned back in his chair. "I'm sorry I do not have answers that are pleasing to you."

Susan straightened her posture in response to the chilly distance between them. She didn't understand what had changed in their friendship. Her only thought was that Donghai had to be under some sort of unrelenting pressure from his government in Beijing.

*Did they threaten him somehow?*

"Can you at least explain the anti-satellite missile test that took place this morning?" Susan asked, squishing her brow together.

Donghai nodded and gave her a half smile. "Yes. That's a rather simple issue. The test was part of our scheduled war game."

Susan sighed. "Donghai, we've always kept our lines of communication open on these matters. The missile test was rather provocative. It destroyed a satellite in a highly elliptical orbit. Surely, you must know what sort of signal that sends. I don't think China wants to threaten our early warning systems. Why didn't you warn us in advance to prevent any misinterpretation?"

He gave her a blank look. "My government felt there was no need for an additional warning. Two weeks ago, we announced a war game with a nuclear component. As you know, satellites assume an important role in nuclear conflicts. The missile test was part of our naval exercise scheduled to begin in a few hours."

Susan fell silent for several moments, unsure of where to go next in the conversation. She hadn't even raised the most important issue—the presence of China's submarines lurking under the surface of the ocean, somewhere off the coast of Canada.

She took a deep breath and gave Donghai direct eye contact once more. "I have brought these issues to your attention for urgent clarification. If I am to interpret today's incidents to be intentional expressions of China's official policy, then my national security team would be compelled to view your country as engaging in nuclear brinkmanship. We would have to act accordingly to defend our interests." She paused to watch her words register in Donghai's eyes, which she noticed, for the first time, were a bit red and unusually moist. For a moment, she thought he might want to say something, but he remained stubbornly silent.

Seeing no other way out of the situation, Susan folded her linen napkin neatly and set it on the dining table in front of her. She rose slowly from her chair, and Donghai followed suit.

Then she turned toward him, handing him a piece of paper, and said, "You will please deliver this message to your government as official communication from the United States."

He took the paper and nodded in acknowledgement.

"It says that we know that two of your submarines have separated from their flotilla and traveled into the Northwest

Passage near the coast of Canada," Susan said flatly. She watched his expression like a hawk, trying to decipher if he knew about the submarines. But Donghai's face remained blank, except for a faint flicker in his eyes. She continued. "We believe they are now located somewhere in the Beaufort Sea. You will bring these two submarines to the surface immediately and redirect them through the Northeast Passage instead. If China refuses to take these measures to indicate their peaceful intentions, we will have no choice but to take actions to remove the threat against us."

Donghai nodded solemnly but said nothing. For a moment, Susan thought his face had turned a shade paler, but she couldn't be sure in the bright midday light. Susan led him to the door. Before opening it, she turned to him and gave him a firm handshake.

"I had sincerely hoped, given our history as friends, we could make some sense of all of this and back away from the risk of intensifying the conflict between our countries," she said. "If you change your mind and wish to contact me, please feel free to use my direct number."

"Thank you for a delightful lunch, Susan," Donghai said, smiling. "I will pass your message to my government and let you know of any response."

Susan watched him stride down the hallway, a pit forming in her stomach. Suddenly, she felt as if she would be sick and hurried to the closest bathroom.

# [ 38 ]
## OCTANE GRILL

DREW
1300
Octane Grill
Washington D.C.

Pulling a hand-sized tablet from his apron pocket, Drew approached his newly assigned table where two men were deeply engaged in a conversation. They didn't seem to notice his arrival and kept talking. The two men wore the standard business attire, but they dressed a bit too drab to come from the private sector.

*They must be in politics.*

Drew fidgeted with his tablet and tried his best not to listen in, but the heated discussion tugged at his attention.

"I don't think freezing her out is the right call," the younger man said. "Even if she is caught up in something nefarious, it's better to keep our eyes on her."

"Thankfully, that's not for you to decide," the older man said, not hiding his disdain. "The president has made her decision, and I don't think you'll convince her otherwise. Her building access has already been revoked."

*The president?* Drew's eyes widened. *They must work at the White House. And someone is about to get fired.*

Located on Pennsylvania Ave NW, just a few steps from the White House, the Octane Grill was a favorite lunch spot for many political operators. After working there for more than a year, Drew was accustomed to serving some of the Beltway's most elite, and he often overheard tidbits of sensitive conversation. He'd learned to feign ignorance while doing his job, and he never mentioned anything he overheard to anyone.

He didn't initially recognize either of them. The older man wore a blue, dotted tie and a black suit that had seen better days. His hair was gray and thinning, and wire-framed glasses stood out on his wrinkled face. He looked as if he'd weathered more political battles than he could count. The younger, more timid-looking man was noticeably overweight, had neatly coiffed brown hair, and wore a newer navy suit, a pinstripe shirt, and a navy tie. Though he had far fewer wrinkles, the younger man had dark shadows under his eyes.

Suddenly, Drew recognized the younger man and gulped.

*Wait a minute... That's David McDonough, the national security advisor.*

His heartrate rising, Drew smoothed his black apron, held his tablet ready, and waited another moment for their attention.

"For the record, I think the president is acting in haste. Dr. Shaw is her top nuclear weapons expert. This is about the worst possible day to give her the boot. But you're not thinking about U.S. national security, now are you?"

"So, you'll deliver the news?" the older man asked gruffly, ignoring the barb.

McDonough nodded grimly. "Tell me. Are you gunning for me next?"

"Excuse me?" the older man said, his eyes bulging.

"Don't play dumb. You know exactly what I'm insinuating," McDonough said.

"You're gonna have to spell it out for me."

"Fine," McDonough said. "I think you know that I know something about what you, Jack, and President Monroe covered up about Nightfall. You're worried Jack might grow a conscience now that he's been kicked out of the White House and tell me or Morgan the truth. That's why you want me gone as well."

Drew cleared his throat and wiped his free hand on his apron.

McDonough nodded grimly and then turned to face Drew.

"Welcome to the Octane Grill. My name is Drew, and I'll be serving you this afternoon. Can I get you both anything to drink?"

The older man frowned deeply, possibly realizing that Drew had caught the end of their conversation. "Just some black coffee for me, thanks."

"I'll just have ice water," McDonough said, "but I think we're ready to order, if you don't mind."

"Of course, I'm happy to take your order now," Drew said, looking down at the screen to make sure the voice recognition software had registered the drink orders.

"Great, I'll have the cornmeal-crusted cauliflower," McDonough said, folding his menu and handing it to Drew. "I assume that's gluten-free?"

"Yes, sir." Drew nodded.

"Did you actually just order a plate of veggies for twenty-five bucks?" the older man asked snidely, still studying his menu. "Life is too short for ordering that shit."

Drew glanced over at McDonough, who didn't answer the rhetorical question. McDonough's intense stare met his gaze, causing Drew to shrink back.

Without missing a beat, the older man said, "I'll have the eight-ounce filet mignon, rare. And if you wouldn't mind, could you talk to the chef personally and make sure it's bloody and pink this time? I don't have time for another do-over today."

Drew nodded and was about to head to the kitchen to deliver the message when McDonough said, "Hey, I recognize you. Aren't you that kid from *The Counter View* clip this morning?"

*Crap.*

"Oh... no, sir. I don't know what you're talking about." Drew fidgeted with the tablet. The lie came off his tongue more smoothly than he expected, but the rush of adrenaline surging through his body made him tremble. He hoped desperately that McDonough wouldn't figure out the truth. He couldn't afford any trouble at work.

The manager of Octane Grill had expressly forbidden staff from discussing politics in the workplace to protect against any damaging conflicts between the restaurant and their high-powered customers. As far as Drew knew, there were no exceptions to this rule. Not even if the customers started the conversation in the first place.

"Yes, you are that kid," McDonough said, touching his forehead. "His name was Drew Hudson. And that's *your* name." He pointed to the name tag on Drew's black vest. He stared up at Drew's face in disbelief for a moment and frowned. "I found your statement about autonomous weapons to be hyperbolic and oversimplified."

*He must have missed my live interview.*

Drew's chest tightened, his frustration growing about the cut video footage and how the brief clip on social media had misrepresented his views. Tori had released the remainder of their discussion, but most people only saw the clip. Drew nearly opened his mouth to say something but then thought better of it and held his tongue.

"But what's new? You people don't understand what's at stake," McDonough said. "And this is why your movement won't succeed at achieving anything meaningful."

Feeling his ears burn with heat, Drew tried to shrug it off.

"Sir, I'll go talk to the chef to make sure your steak is cooked to perfection." He smiled politely at both men, turned on his heel, and marched toward the kitchen, hoping smoke wasn't blowing out of his ears.

Pushing the door open, Drew poked his head in the kitchen and asked one of the assistants, "Can you tell Benny I'm sending him a special steak order for a VIP? He claims he ordered it rare last time, but it wasn't bloody enough."

The kitchen assistant nodded.

A ding alert sounded on his tablet, signaling he'd been assigned to a new table. When he saw it was a table of ten customers, Drew sighed heavily. The extra work of managing such a table at lunchtime was never worth the tip in most circumstances. Approaching the table, he smiled, introduced himself, and took drink orders. As he stepped away and walked across his section to check on a previous table, Gordon Stemper, the restaurant manager, intercepted him.

"I need to talk to you," Gordon said, motioning for him to step to the side and out of hearing distance of their customers. Just like all the servers, his manager wore a white shirt, black vest, black trousers, and a black bowtie.

Drew furrowed his brow. It was highly unusual for a manager to interrupt a service shift.

"Don't worry. Jennifer will cover your tables." Gordon gave him a stern look. "I stopped by your section to see if our customers are enjoying their experience at the Octane Grill. And something interesting happened. A VIP customer said that he recognized you from TV. Do you have anything you want to tell me?"

Drew's heart began to race. He knew he couldn't wiggle out of this one with a fib. His boss could quickly verify that it was him in the video or on the subsequent interview. "Uh... I was, um... at a protest this morning and was interviewed by a reporter. The clip went viral on social media. Apparently, the

VIP customer saw it and asked if it was me. I said no, but he didn't believe me."

Gordon frowned. "Let me get this straight. You lied to the national security advisor of the United States?"

Drew shuffled his feet. "Sir, you said that we should never talk about politics, even when customers engage us in conversation. I thought it was better to deny it and avoid a discussion that would go against the rules."

"But I never told you to lie to VIP customers either," Gordon said.

Drew's stomach sank. He'd only meant to dodge the issue and refrain from a political discussion. "Sir, I'm very sorry. It was the wrong call. It won't happen again."

Gordon waved off his apology. "The lie isn't the issue. I watched the video—"

"Sir, the reporter cut out twenty minutes of—"

"The impromptu video footage was one thing, but then you decided to go on *The Counter View* for a follow-up interview," Gordon said, his nostrils flaring. "And now I have to hear from our VIP customer that you've finagled yourself a one-on-one with the president."

Drew's mouth ran dry. He didn't know his impending meeting with the president was widely known. He'd honestly pushed the thought of it away for his shift, trying to focus on his job and *not* freak out about it.

"We don't run political campaigns out of my restaurant," Gordon said. "The Octane Grill can't afford to take sides. If we do, we lose half our clientele and our business." He made a large sweeping gesture, snapping Drew out of his daze.

"But sir—" Drew said.

Gordon's eyes protruded, and he chopped his hands through the air. "I'm surprised you didn't think about how such public, controversial statements directed at the president might affect your job here at the Octane Grill. After more than a year on staff, you must know our business depends on serving an elite political clientele. The last thing we need is for that crude news show or people on social media to make a connection between your political views and our establishment. Which is something one VIP customer has already done. For this reason, I'm sorry, but I have to let you go."

"You're firing me?" Drew's lip quivered.

Gordon's face softened. "You've been a great server, always reliable and professional until now. I really hate doing this. But you've left me no choice. I can't have you damage the Octane Grill's longstanding bipartisan reputation with your political views."

"But..." Drew said, reeling from the shock of what was happening.

"To honor your good work for the past year or so, we'll give you one week's severance pay to make up for the short notice," Gordon said. "But for now, please hand over your tablet and apron."

Glimpsing sympathetic looks from other servers, Drew undid his apron and handed over his tablet to Gordon. Without saying another word, he turned and stumbled toward the front door.

# [ 39 ]
## TRANSFER LEARNING

GRACE
1300
National Military Command Center
The Pentagon
Arlington, Virginia

Grace sat stiffly in front of Arjun's terminal, studying the changes he'd made to the code of ARC's algorithms. Although she understood the impact of each change separately, she couldn't foresee how the revised code might interact with each other and produce unexpected outcomes.

Her stomach tightened at the notion of going into the monthly test and evaluation with senior Pentagon leadership, not knowing exactly what might happen. But she didn't have enough time to compare and analyze the two versions side by side. Although Arjun's story about his sick mother in the hospital and his financial sacrifice had moved her, there was only one viable option—to return everything to the way it was before Arjun messed with it. That way, the test would demonstrate the problems with ARC. Maybe then, her bosses would finally listen to her.

"I need you to reverse the changes," she said over her shoulder with a stern tone.

Arjun grimaced and shook his head. "I can't do that. If I reverse my changes, ARC will most likely start a nuclear war during the simulation this afternoon. Then the Pentagon leadership will lose their confidence in the ARC system. And they'll take the system offline."

"Like I care what happens to your precious software," Grace said as she started to get up from the chair. "If the ARC system really is that fragile, then maybe it should stay offline."

"You don't understand," Arjun said, grabbing her arm and pinching hard.

"Let go of me," Grace snapped, wincing from the tightness of his grip. She glared at him as she sat back down.

"Grace, there's more at stake than just my company's software. It's way too late to reconsider this kind of automation for nuclear weapons systems. Without ARC, the United States will be exposed to the threat of an attack by nuclear-armed countries with their own automated command and control systems. We won't be able to credibly deter our adversaries anymore, and they might be tempted to initiate a first-strike nuclear attack. We need ARC online to prevent nuclear war from happening."

*Why do these guys think everyone wants a nuclear war?*

Grace raised her eyebrow. "Alternatively, if we don't take ARC offline now, the United States will face the risk of nuclear war anyway as a result of escalation. The system will continue to misinterpret actions by other countries as aggressive." She stopped to look at him for a moment. "Arjun, you do know that's where the ARC system was heading—down a slippery slope toward recommending nuclear war with China. That's why your CEO had you make these changes prior to the test. This morning, the ARC system recommended we go to DEFCON 3 and take action against China's two missing submarines. Do you want to find out what the system will recommend at the next stage of the conflict?"

Arjun shook his head but pointed up at the wall clock. "Look, even if I wanted to revert the ARC system back to its previous state, I don't have enough time before the scheduled test."

Grace shook her head. "Well then, that leaves me no choice. I can't just let you make major changes to the ARC system without reporting them to my leadership. It's my job to make sure ARC is functioning properly. And obviously, there are some serious problems with the system if you're recoding the algorithms to cheat on a congressionally mandated test."

She started to get up from her chair again, but Arjun grabbed her arm once more, causing her body to tense. "Before you do something you regret, there's something I haven't told you," he said.

Grace whipped her head around and raised her fist to punch him. "Touch me again, and you'll regret it."

He shrank back in his chair.

Grace narrowed her eyes, scowled at him, and remained seated. "You've been lying to everyone since your first day on the job. Not to mention screwing me over. Why should I believe anything you say now?"

Arjun winced. "I'm sorry. It was never my intention to mislead or screw you over. Whatever I've done, I did on the orders of my CEO. If my company finds out I'm telling you this now, I'll be fired." He swallowed hard, waiting for her response as he furled and unfurled his fingers.

Grace crossed her arms and tapped her foot on the floor. "We don't have all day, you know."

Arjun initiated direct eye contact. "So... you'll keep this between us?"

She frowned. "You know I can't make that promise. But if you don't tell me right now what else you're hiding, I'll have no choice but to report what you've done to Pentagon leadership."

The more she threatened to report him, the less confident Grace felt about it. At first, she was carried away by her moral impulse to do the right thing. But every time she imagined how it would go down when she informed Pentagon leadership, she shuddered. Someone would have to take the fall for what happened. And she worried it would be her head on the chopping block.

"Okay, okay," Arjun said, throwing up his hands. "Look, the changes I made today... they actually reverted the ARC system back to its original version."

"Original version?" Grace's eyes popped, and she blinked at him several times. "You're saying this is how ARC was set up when the system was first launched five months ago?"

"Yes."

"But then... how?" Grace stared at him dumbfounded for a moment. "You've altered the algorithms before today?"

Arjun shook his head vigorously. "No, it wasn't me. I didn't know any of this until today. I swear."

Grace tilted her head. "You're the onsite systems engineer for ARC. If it wasn't you, then who did it?"

"It was my CEO, Dennis Warren," Arjun said, lowering his head and whispering.

Grace gasped, covering her mouth. "Your CEO made the changes himself?"

"Well, not directly. He ordered his senior programmer to make them using an invisible back door to the program."

*Invisible back door?*

Grace blinked rapidly. She was at a complete loss for words.

"I know it's hard to believe," Arjun said. "After ARC's first test passed with flying colors, a senior engineer working directly for Warren accessed the system remotely through the back door and secretly tinkered with the algorithms."

"But why would Warren do that, if the ARC system was such a success?" Grace asked.

"Warren said without the changes, the ARC system would

quickly become outdated and useless for providing strategic warning of a nuclear attack."

Grace furrowed her brow. "But I thought your boss sold ARC to the Pentagon on the basis that it could adapt to changing technological and geopolitical circumstances. Isn't that the point of the monthly data infusions and simulations—to keep the ARC system up to date?"

Arjun cleared his throat. "That was definitely Centoreum Tech's pitch to the Department of Defense in its response to the request for proposal, and we did build the system to include such capabilities. To give the system the ability to adapt to changing circumstances, we integrated several deep neural networks into ARC using different learning methods. But when all was said and done, my boss didn't think your leadership would accept ARC if we launched the system with its full functionality."

"You only launched part of the ARC system five months ago?" she asked.

Arjun nodded. "The first iteration of the ARC system was based on a supervised learning technique. Basically, we trained ARC on all existing data for conflict behavior across history and integrated the model of nuclear deterrence into the algorithmic structure."

Grace wrinkled her nose. "But there's not much relevant data on nuclear conflict. And whatever data we do have is heavily biased toward the Cold War time period and the specific conflict between the U.S. and the Soviet Union. Plus, most existing conflict data involves the use of conventional weapons to win wars. With nuclear weapons, countries need to avoid wars, not win them."

Arjun nodded. "We used a process called multi-targeted transfer learning to overcome the problems with the small dataset," he said.

Grace gave him a blank look.

"It's our proprietary technique. First, we trained ARC's

network to analyze billions of data points about conventional war and conflict. Then we trained the last few layers of the network on the smaller dataset that exists for nuclear conflict. The network first learns the fundamentals of conventional war and conflict. Then it learns how nuclear war and conflict are different. This way, the deep neural network is able to transfer its vast body of knowledge about conventional conflict to predict outcomes in nuclear conflict. Finally, we used the model of nuclear deterrence to tweak the code until we produced expected outcomes."

"Okay, that explains why the Pentagon's leadership thinks the ARC system won't deviate from our model of nuclear deterrence," Grace said. "But this morning, after the latest data infusion, it did."

Arjun bobbed his head. "Last month, my boss added more functionality to the ARC system using the back door. To enhance the system's adaptability, we built in another deep neural network trained with unsupervised learning methods. That's the ISR component that provides policymakers with strategic warning. It has a powerful ability to identify anomalies that don't fit previous patterns and have no known signatures."

"That's the component which interpreted China's forward deployment of submarines as offensive?" Grace asked, her forehead creased.

"Yes and no," Arjun said. "That result was produced by both parts of the ARC system working together to generate the final interpretation. But the model of nuclear deterrence was supposed to act as a failsafe. Or at least that's what I expected until today."

Grace raised her eyebrow. "Okay. Then what changed?"

"My boss apparently made adjustments to the system's rigid adherence to the longstanding model of nuclear deterrence. The changes allowed the ARC system more flexibility to deal with today's technological and geopolitical parameters. Once set free, the ARC system must have learned a better way to achieve a credible deterrent under current circumstances."

"A better way?"

"Remember the system is designed to optimize its ability to retaliate?" Arjun asked.

Grace nodded.

"ARC recommended the U.S. raise the alert on nuclear forces to DEFCON 3 this morning because it perceived a threat to the first rule of the system," he said. "ARC wants us to take actions to protect the U.S.'s ability to retaliate after a nuclear attack."

Suddenly, it dawned on Grace. "And that's why you assume ARC won't play by our rules of nuclear deterrence during the test today. Because it's already deviating from our expectations and proposing moves we haven't considered before."

"Exactly," Arjun said, exhaling sharply. "Whenever we beta-tested the ARC system with any amount of adaptability, it would quickly deviate from the accepted model of deterrence. My boss worried that the ARC system might learn too much, adapt its algorithms too quickly, and end up behaving in ways too radical to be understood or accepted by the Pentagon's leadership. For this reason, he wanted ARC to perform as expected for several tests in order to build up confidence that the system was working properly. Then Warren planned to gradually alter the algorithms to allow the ARC system to learn new moves and evolve into the adaptive system originally promised by Centoreum Tech."

"I was right all along," Grace said numbly.

"Yes, you were," Arjun said. "ARC started learning too rapidly for my boss's liking. Of course, he didn't anticipate the worsening situation with China. So today, he asked me to revert ARC to its original version to prevent your leadership from freaking out and turning it off. There's a great deal at risk if ARC goes offline. Without the time advantage provided by ARC, the U.S. will face dire consequences for its national security and possibly even its survival in the event of a nuclear attack."

Grace remained silent and stared at the terminal for a few moments, running through all of her options.

"Are you going to report this?" Arjun asked with a downcast expression.

"I have to report it," Grace said glumly, a deep frown forming on her face. "I don't have a choice. It's my job." She didn't want Arjun to lose his own job in the process, especially given the situation with his family. But she couldn't imagine another viable way out of the situation.

"But do you have to report it *right now?*" Arjun asked, pressing his lips tight. "Would it be possible to wait until after the test today?"

*Timing is important.*

Grace continued to stare at the terminal as she considered the pros and cons for reporting the problem immediately or delaying until a later point. It would be much easier for her to break the news about the ARC system after the widely publicized test. Even if she reported it now, she wasn't even sure if anything she told them would dissuade them from going through with it. Waiting would allow everyone to save face.

"Grace, everyone is counting on its success," Arjun said, pleading. "Think about it. The entire senior leadership of the Pentagon will be embarrassed if the test gets cancelled and the ARC system is taken offline. Less than an hour ago, the SecDef himself told my boss how important the test was for him."

She remained silent. Her thoughts shifted back to Arjun's earlier arguments about the dangers of taking the ARC system offline. Without further data, she couldn't determine whether leaving ARC online or taking it offline would be worse for national security. Whatever happened, she didn't want Pentagon leadership to act in haste. If they learned what she knew about ARC in one fell swoop, they were likely to have a knee-jerk reaction, and it might not be the right one.

"Wouldn't it be better if we tell them afterwards?" Arjun asked. "That way they can handle the situation more quietly, away from the glare of the media and congressional monitoring."

*Maybe it would be better to tell them later. When everything is calmer.*

A tense silence descended between them for a few moments.

"Okay. I'm not going to report you today," Grace said, taking a deep breath.

Arjun heaved his chest.

"On one condition," Grace added, a sharpness to her tone.

"Whatever it is, I'll do it." Arjun nodded quickly, his eyes full of eagerness.

"I need you to promise that you'll help me explain this to my leadership as soon as the time is right. First, we'll go to Captain Dietz. Then we'll run it all the way up my chain to the chairman and the secretary of defense. And this time, you won't counter each of my points with a load of crap about how awesome ARC is. Instead, you'll come clean about the ARC system and support me. You'll tell them everything. You got that?" She glowered at him.

Arjun gulped and nodded.

Grace narrowed her eyes. "Even if the truth gets you fired," she added.

He nodded again.

# [ 40 ]
## SATCOM

MORGAN
1315
Cyberthreat Intelligence Integration Center
Liberty Crossing Intelligence Campus
McLean, Virginia

Morgan huddled with several others around a classified terminal belonging to Eric Zieman, a cyber specialist responsible for monitoring threats to U.S. military space assets. He'd just spent more than thirty minutes explaining a long list of potential causes for the loss of communications with the Polaris satellite. It was located in highly elliptical orbit and represented a critical component of the U.S. space-based early warning system.

Morgan shifted her weight back and forth and fidgeted with her hands, politely waiting for Eric to get to the bottom line. Mike was behaving far less patiently. He put his hands on his hips and huffed every few minutes.

*What's on his mind?*

Morgan scratched her head as she stared at Eric's computer, trying to decipher the words on his screen. But the code flashing across the display remained a mystery. Odin, the artificial intelligence system for the U.S. intelligence community, scanned through trillions of bytes of historical data to ascertain the source of the satellite disruption. And although the computer moved at an impressive speed, it would take a few hours to go through everything.

Morgan glanced at the advanced equipment situated around the room. The amount of computing power humming in the space was impressive. The round-shaped room resembled other operations centers she'd visited at the FBI and the NSA. It was dimly lit and contained several curved rows of computers manned by IT experts, cybersecurity specialists, and intelligence analysts. The teams were situated in front of a massive wall of flat screens displaying various data analytics, real-time sensor information, and 3D maps.

The center's primary mission was to oversee Odin, which integrated information on cyberthreats coming in from all sixteen agencies of the intelligence community and various partners in the private sector. Based on Odin's analysis, the intelligence team provided actionable recommendations to William Grayson, the director of national intelligence.

"You're telling me you don't actually *know* what happened to disrupt the communication link?" Mike asked, a deep frown on his face.

His anxiety was contagious and sent a tingle down Morgan's spine.

Eric rotated his chair to face the group, his expression grave. "Odin failed to detect any intrusion signals to the Polaris satellite prior to loss of communication. Thus far, it hasn't been able to produce a clear answer about what happened to cause the link to shut down. We can't exactly send up a technician into space to check it out. That makes it difficult to know what happened. We have to rely upon delayed data signals we receive here on earth. Without active signals, all Odin can do is analyze the historical data we've received from the satellite before we lost communication."

"What are we doing to recover communications with Polaris?" Mike asked, stuffing his hands in his pockets.

"Space Force Command is currently trying to re-establish the communication link through our satellite network, but they've told me we're completely shut out of the system at the moment," Eric said. "It's like the satellite doesn't even exist up there right now."

"What's the worst case?" Morgan asked.

"That would be a cyberattack designed to seize control of the satellite," Eric said. "But I suspect it has just malfunctioned. Satellites are protected against jamming with advanced encryption, frequency hoppers, and AI-enabled cyber defense systems. They're also hardened against electromagnetic interference. But hacking a satellite is not as difficult as you might think. At least not for a determined hacker with the requisite resources and skill sets. At the end of the day, satellites are no more than advanced computers running some specialized software built for an austere environment. They are vulnerable to the same cyber-attacks as your computer."

"Do you think something crashed into it?" Morgan asked. "Like a meteor or another satellite?"

"If we were talking about a satellite in low earth orbit," Eric said, "I'd say a collision with another object would be a high probability scenario. The traffic in LEO these days is worse than rush hour on the Beltway in a rainstorm."

Wyatt and Niko chuckled out loud at Eric's joke. But when Mike glared at them, they stopped giggling and their faces went slack.

"What about highly elliptical orbit?" Morgan asked.

"HEO is a different story," Eric said. "Several advanced countries involved in space exploration have one or two satellites in HEO. But that's about it. The distant orbit remains out of reach for all but the most advanced countries and biggest companies.

Less traffic means less chance of collision. That said, there's still the risk of collision with meteors and other space objects. But we would receive a warning about an approaching object, and Odin didn't detect anything out of the ordinary."

Morgan furrowed her brow. "What are the chances there's something wrong with Odin? Is it possible a hacker corrupted Odin's analysis?"

Eric frowned. "That's an extremely remote possibility."

"But still possible?" Morgan pressed.

Eric tilted his head back and forth. "Yes. All AI-enabled systems are as vulnerable as any other system connected to a network. But there is one important difference."

"What's that?" Morgan asked.

"AI-enabled systems are also vulnerable to the introduction of adversarial data. A capable adversary could manipulate the input data transmitted into Odin, compromising its analytic outputs. It's possible that a hacker could first mess with Odin's deep neural network and trick us into thinking Polaris was operating properly. All the while, the hacker could have seized control over the satellite. But to do this, the hacker would have to defeat multiple layers of our best AI cyber defenses. That's next to impossible."

"If someone did manage to defeat all of our defenses," Morgan said with her finger on her chin, "they would have to have access to some of the best cyber offensive systems in the world. Not to mention the financial and technical resources equal to an advanced country."

Eric nodded. "Yup. A cyberattack of Polaris would require enormous resources. That's why I asked you guys for help."

Mike put his hands on his hips. "If *you* don't know what is happening up there," he said, pointing to the TV screen on the wall which displayed real-time footage of outer space in the vicinity of Polaris, "how do you possibly think we can help *you?*"

Eric grimaced. "Well, I heard you guys are exploring the perpetrators of the cyberthreats coming out of China and Russia today. I thought you might be able to help me narrow down the list of potential scenarios. I expect Grayson to come back into the office and demand answers shortly."

"This HEO satellite... isn't it one that belongs to the ARC system?" Morgan asked as an idea popped into her head.

*Is this connected to China's submarines?*

Eric nodded. "Yes, it's the one dwelling above the Arctic region at the moment. Polaris scans the earth's surface every ten seconds, searching for infrared activity."

"In other words, we're now blinded to any launches from northern latitudes," Morgan said.

"Only until our ground radars pick them up," Mike said. "But yes, there would be a delay in detection."

"See, it all kind of adds up," Eric said. "China has a nuclear-themed war game scheduled for tomorrow."

Morgan glanced at her watch and hitched a breath. "Actually, with the time difference, it will kick off in just a few hours."

Eric nodded and said, "The tweets and the deep fakes have put us on edge and compromised our ability to communicate effectively with the Chinese. The missing submarines and the anti-satellite missile test raise the specter of an offensive nuclear attack. And now we've experienced the loss of communications with an early warning satellite. Possibly at the hands of an expert hacker."

Morgan bobbed her head in agreement. "Either someone is trying to start a nuclear conflict between China and the United States, or they're engaging in some extremely risky diversionary tactics."

Everyone nodded in agreement.

"What would it take to pull off a cyberattack against this Polaris?" Mike asked, biting his lip.

Eric gave him a curt nod as if he expected the question. "It would require access to a specialized ground antenna. These antennae used to be extremely expensive, but have dropped significantly in cost, lowering the barrier to such attacks.

Reaching a satellite in HEO still remains difficult, if not impossible, for most non-state actors. The hacker would have to wait for the satellite to pass overhead before sending it commands."

"I assume that means the hacker would have to be located somewhere in the northern latitudes?" Morgan asked.

"That would mean Canada, Russia, Scandinavia, Alaska, or somewhere in the Arctic," Mike added. Then he held up his finger. "I knew it! This has to come from Russia. I bet Nova, Molotov's hacker, is behind this."

*So, it's likely not China.*

Eric nodded. "The hacker would need to connect to the satellite's antenna from the ground, crack the encryption, defeat Odin's cyber defensive systems, and leverage weaknesses in the satellite's software in order to seize control of the unit. From there, the hacker would be able to disrupt, intercept, or modify all communications that pass through the antenna. The hacker might also decide to destroy the satellite with a cyber-physical attack."

"A cyber-physical attack?" Mike asked, pulling up his nose.

"Such attacks exploit both physical and digital components," Eric said. "Satellites run on solar power provided by physical systems like panels, electronics, batteries, etcetera. Once a hacker seizes control of the satellite, they could adjust the solar panels using digital controls to increase the power levels, blow out the batteries, and fry the satellite's electronics. But this scenario is the least of my worries at this point."

Morgan's eyes widened. "What could possibly be worse than that?"

"Well, if a hacker can gain control over one of our satellites in a network, they can access other devices in the same satellite network," Eric said. "And then they could make everything go dark."

Morgan's mouth fell open. "Wait a minute. Are you saying that a hacker could gain access to anything else connected to the Polaris satellite? Including other early warning systems?"

"In principle, yes," Eric said.

Morgan swallowed hard as a new threat picture formed in her head. She wasn't sure if Anton Vega's company operated a satellite in HEO. At this point, nothing would surprise her.

"You talked about hacking a satellite from the ground. But could a hacker access Polaris from another satellite in the same orbit?" Morgan asked, clenching her fists to keep them from trembling.

*What if Anton Vega supplied the resources for these hacks?*

"That's definitely possible," Eric said. "Do you know any hackers with access to major resources? What about this Molotov character you mentioned?" He turned to look at Mike, who nodded.

"We think a hacker that goes by the screenname Nova is working for Molotov, a former FSB Agent," Mike said, his forehead wrinkled. "And they appear to have access to unlimited resources through Igor Koslov."

Morgan avoided eye contact. She had a specific scenario in mind—one that conveniently linked several pieces of the puzzle together. But if she was right, it could put her, Jack, and Luis in some hot water.

A loud beeping from Eric's terminal startled the group. Morgan jerked her head up and stared at the screen.

"What's happening?" Mike asked, his eyes bulging.

Eric turned to look at the screen, and his mouth fell open. He shook his head in disbelief. "The Polaris satellite is back online. Downlink transmissions have been restored. We're receiving signals again."

*Saved by the beep?*

Everyone exhaled sharply.

"Just like that?" Morgan asked, her forehead creased.

"Apparently," Eric said, his jaw still slack.

"How long will it take to resume sending information to the satellite?" Mike asked.

"It may be a few hours yet before we can ping the satellite

for its status, given the usual signal delays. Odin will have to spend some time running diagnostics and testing Polaris to make sure everything is in working order," Eric said with a slight smile. "But this is really good news."

*Maybe.*

Morgan furrowed her brow. "Don't you think it's odd that Polaris went offline for a while and just came back on without any prompting?"

Eric shrugged. "Not really. Polaris must have experienced some sort of malfunction. It must have shut itself down and then restarted. We'll know for sure after Odin completes the diagnostic tests."

"What's going on here?" a familiar voice boomed behind them, causing Morgan to jump.

Everyone turned their heads. Grayson marched into the operations center with a tense look on his face and his fists clenched. His steely gaze told her everything she needed to know. Morgan felt her blood run cold.

*I'm not supposed to be here...*

Eric jumped up from his chair. "Sir, the Polaris satellite experienced a brief communications outage, but it's back online again. Odin's already running diagnostics to determine the cause."

Grayson nodded and then said gruffly, "Dr. Shaw, a word?"

"Of course, sir," Morgan said. As she got up out of her chair and passed by him, she caught a whiff of bourbon float by her nose. Following Grayson to the far corner of the room, sweat broke out on her forehead as her mouth ran dry. "Um, sir, I'm sorry I didn't tell you I was here. I stopped by to follow up on the Russian connection for the president."

Grayson stared down his nose at her, the wire-rimmed glasses near its edge. "Have you talked to your boss recently?"

Morgan's eyes widened. "No, not since our meeting at the Oval. Has something happened?"

*Has Burke managed to get me fired?*

Grayson grunted and stuck his hands in his pockets. "Dammit. He was the one who was supposed to tell you."

"Tell me what?" Morgan asked, getting another strong smell of liquor. She pulled her head back. "Sir, have you been drinking?" She uttered the question before thinking.

Grayson's face turned bright red, and he looked like he might explode. "I'm going to have to ask you to leave."

"But, sir, I was just—"

"Leave. Now." Grayson pointed to the door. The others gave her strange looks.

"What was my boss supposed to tell me?" Morgan asked.

Grayson glared at her, following close on her heels. "You'll have to ask him." Then he grabbed her arm, pinching hard, and began leading her out of the operations center.

"Sir, what's going on?" Morgan asked, struggling to break free of his grip.

"Talk to your boss," he said, his eyes going hard and cold. He clamped his jaw shut and refused to look at her as he dragged her out of the suite and left her outside in the lobby, completely bewildered and utterly shaken.

*What just happened?*

# [ 41 ]
## TEST AND EVALUATION

GRACE
1425
National Military Command Center
The Pentagon
Arlington, Virginia

Grace watched the last move of the simulation play out on the massive video screen at the front of the auditorium-style room in the National Military Command Center. She tried to breathe normally but couldn't stop thinking about everything she knew. Glancing over her shoulder, she glimpsed Arjun sitting one row up next to Captain Dietz. They looked a bit too cozy for her comfort, and it made her wonder whether she'd done the right thing.

*Arjun better hold up his part of the deal.*

She surveyed the star-studded room and shuddered at the chaos that might have ensued if she'd reported Arjun. Her career might have likely unraveled in that single moment.

The room was packed to the brim with senior military officers and policymakers, including Chairman Waller, SecDef

Burke, director of the Joint Staff General Hawkins, the vice chairman, and the entire senior leadership of the J6 Cyber Directorate and the J3 Operations Directorate. The Commanders of the U.S. Strategic Forces Command, Global Strike Command, and the North American Aerospace Defense Command (NORAD) also participated in the test and evaluation over secure video conference.

Surrounded by so many powerful men, Grace realized how little influence she held and how few allies she had. One by one, she studied their relaxed faces and postures, and with each, her frown deepened. They all looked eager to celebrate another victory, as if the success of the test was a foregone conclusion. Even though the exact details of the test were classified as Top Secret, the event was rather high-profile. If ARC's test were to be cancelled for any reason, the press would have a field day. And Congress would be up in arms about the Department of Defense not fulfilling its legislative requirement.

She swallowed hard, thinking of how close she'd come to turning it all upside down. Every time Grace ran through the cancellation scenario in her head, she ended up becoming the unfortunate patsy blamed for ARC's dismal failure. She probably wouldn't have even gotten the chance to convince anyone about ARC's problems before she was booted out of the room, relieved of her duty assignment, and reassigned out of the Pentagon to somewhere extremely remote and unimportant— the worst sort of dead end for her military career. No one at the senior level would ever be held accountable, and life would carry on much as it had before. Except for hers.

*No, I did the right thing.*

Colonel Martinez stood at the podium to narrate the automated simulation, but mostly to make sure the A/V system functioned properly. The large meeting space was used to support the National Command Authority and was officially called the Emergency Conference Room. But most Pentagon insiders fondly called it the war room, invoking scenes from the classic film *Dr. Strangelove*. In the past, Emergency Action Messages would be sent to U.S. nuclear forces from the war room to give the launch order during a nuclear crisis. The room now hosted one of several servers for the ARC system that were scattered across the country. Although the room sounded impressive to outsiders, it didn't look much different than the typical conference room at the Pentagon.

At the base of the stage, there stood a long table with a bank of built-in computers manned by operations officers, each of whom monitored the reactions of the ARC system in real time. The test and evaluation process involved taking ARC offline, inputting data about a potential nuclear conflict, and running the simulation to see how the ARC system would perform.

Grace took a few short breaths. She just needed to get through the test. Then she could ask Colonel Martinez and Morgan for help navigating the minefield for disclosing the truth about ARC. Unlike Grace, her friends held influential positions and could use their personal relationships to persuade their bosses to do the right thing about the ARC system.

*This will be better handled behind the scenes.*

"And that's a wrap," Martinez said over the microphone, causing Grace to exhale sharply. "The escalating threat of nuclear war has forced the U.S. and China to the negotiating table where both countries have agreed to a new set of measures to protect the stealth of submarines."

A loud round of applause rose from the auditorium as everyone got up and gave each other handshakes and nodding smiles. Grace watched as Arjun followed Captain Dietz down the aisle toward the front of the room where the SecDef and the chairman were chatting. Grace walked down the aisle toward Martinez, who was tidying up a stack of papers on the podium.

Captain Dietz leaned over to Burke and whispered a few words, which caused the SecDef to break into a broad smile.

*Well, they seem friendly.*

Grace raised an eyebrow as Burke clapped Arjun on the back.

Captain Dietz stood next to Arjun, beaming proudly. She slowed her pace toward the front of the room, straining her ears to eavesdrop on the conversation.

"How does it feel? Working for a company that strives to make our country safer?" Burke said to Arjun who shook his hand and gave him an embarrassed smile.

"Thank you, sir." Arjun grinned from ear to ear. "It's an honor to work on such an important project."

*Ugh. He's practically gushing.*

Grace's stomach lurched. A sour taste entered her mouth with fears that she'd been played by Arjun. She approached the podium as Chairman Waller stepped forward to shake Arjun's hand and smiled warmly. "A job well done," he said.

"It's a pleasure to meet you, sir," Arjun said, a grin spreading across his face.

"Likewise," Waller said, his face breaking into a wide smile. "Your boss called me right before the test."

"Oh really?" Arjun's face paled slightly when he spotted Grace watching him.

"Mr. Warren invited me and my wife to his annual Labor Day party on the Chesapeake Bay. Please thank him for the kind invitation. It will be such a treat for Linda to go for a ride on their yacht with the ladies while us men enjoy the good life, partaking in the finest bourbon and cigars. I expect you'll be there?"

Arjun nodded slowly, not breaking eye contact with Grace. She wanted to hit herself in the forehead.

*Of course. Centoreum Tech is in bed with Pentagon leadership.*

As bile rose up the back of her throat, Grace thought she was going to be sick. The world spun around her. Suddenly, everything was clear to her. Arjun's magical touch with Pentagon leadership had nothing to do with his superior argumentation or even his gender. It had to do with the fact that his CEO was tight with the SecDef. And soon he'd be buddy-buddy with the chairman as well. Her hopes of warning them about the ARC system were sinking fast.

Grace pressed her lips together, and she turned to look at Martinez, who gave her a grim smile.

"Oh, you didn't know about that?" Martinez asked, pointing to Burke and then to Arjun. Not only had the colonel seen her coming, he'd apparently witnessed her reaction and read her thoughts.

Grace sighed dejectedly, feeling the energy drain from her limbs. "No, but it explains an awful lot. Too much, actually." Guilt rose in her chest for not telling Martinez about her most recent findings. She'd wanted to inform him before the test but worried that he might have the same impulse to cancel it.

Martinez gave her another smile. "Chin up, Grace. It's all part of the politics game. If you want to win, you've just got to learn how to play."

*And what if I don't play the game? Then I lose?*

Suddenly, Martinez shifted his attention away from her, his eyes widening. "Sir, is there something I can help you with?" he asked.

Grace turned to see Admiral Waller on the approach, with Burke and Hawkins tailing behind him. She gulped.

Admiral Waller cleared his throat. "I just learned the president requested we debrief her on the ARC test. She's moved up the timeline for the meeting—"

"Wasn't Tolley supposed to have lunch with the Chinese ambassador to clear up this whole mess with China?" Burke interrupted with a smirk. "I guess it didn't go as planned." He chuckled, but no one joined him.

Admiral Waller frowned and looked at Martinez. "Anyway, we'll need to head over to the White House at 1500. Can you call the motor pool?"

"Of course, sir," Martinez said. He looked at the chairman, who remained silent for a moment. "Something on your mind, sir?"

Admiral Waller wrinkled his forehead. "Actually, yes. I'm still uncertain about one thing... maybe it's because I missed the discussion at the pre-brief this morning. Or maybe it's because the test went off without a hitch. But didn't you flag something for my attention about a false positive in the ARC system?"

Grace nearly choked on her own saliva. She gave Arjun a panicked look, but he just shrugged at her before ducking out of sight.

*Is he wimping out on me?*

"Yes, sir." Martinez turned toward Grace. "It was Major Lim who brought it to my attention. We talked about it at length this morning." He put his hand on her back and nudged her forward. She took a few reluctant steps toward the chairman and eyed Burke nervously.

*This is not the right time. Not here. Not like this.*

Burke's eyes narrowed as if he was giving her a warning look.

*Does the SecDef already know?*

"Um, sir... yes, I did ask Colonel Martinez to put it in the read-ahead as a precautionary measure," Grace said. "But um... since the test was a success, perhaps I overreacted. I'm terribly sorry for the confusion."

Martinez's eyes bulged, and his face reddened.

"Not a problem, Major," Admiral Waller said. "It's always good to be cautious in matters of national security. Colonel, pick me up in thirty minutes?"

"Yes, sir," Martinez said, his voice strained.

Admiral Waller walked up the aisle, Burke and the others following behind him. Without saying a word, Martinez turned on his heel and marched up the aisle after them.

"Colonel Martinez. Wait! I need to talk to you," Grace said, running after him. "Wait!"

If Martinez had heard her calling after him, he certainly didn't indicate it. Instead, he picked up his pace.

*Crap.*

# [ 42 ]
## WILD THEORIES

MORGAN
1445
The Pentagon
Arlington, Virginia

Morgan headed down the hallway toward the elevator to reach the underground floor of the Pentagon where the National Military Command Center was located. That's where she expected Luis to be holed up without access to his smartphone. If things were running on time, the test and evaluation of the ARC system should have just ended. Hopefully, she could catch Luis before he made it back to his office or disappeared into another Top Secret meeting.

She pressed the elevator button a few times and waited for it to arrive. Ever since Grayson tossed her out of the Cyberthreat Intelligence Integration Center, Morgan had been moving about in a daze. Unable to decipher Grayson's codespeak, she'd called David to get some answers. But her boss didn't pick up. And, for some reason, the email service on her work phone was down. Morgan had a strange inkling that returning to her office at the White House wasn't an option. In her mind, that left only one choice—to head over to the Pentagon. She needed to see Luis and follow up with Grace about the ARC system.

As she waited, her stomach released a long, angry growl. Morgan glanced at her watch again and realized she'd missed lunch. The adrenaline rush from losing communications with a critical early warning satellite followed by a tense interaction with Grayson had caused her to completely forget her hunger. But now, an intense pang of starvation reared its ugly head, making her legs weak and her head dizzy.

When the elevator door finally opened, Morgan glimpsed Luis with a dark scowl on his handsome face. She smiled at him, warmth filling her chest. But before she got a chance to say anything, he barreled out of the elevator and made a sharp right. Apparently too lost in his own thoughts to recognize her, he began heading down the corridor at an impressive clip.

"Luis," Morgan called out after him. "Babe. Stop!"

He didn't appear to hear her calling, so she ran after him, dodging several junior officers in the hallway.

"Colonel Martinez! Sir!" Morgan shouted. "Slow down for a minute."

Tilting his head, Luis stopped and turned around slowly to look at her. A half smile crept onto his otherwise cross face as he approached. "Morgan. What on earth are you doing here?"

Morgan suppressed the moisture forming in her eyes. She didn't quite know how to respond to what felt like a loaded question. The day had started on the wrong foot and had gone steeply downhill from there. Her instincts had brought her to the Pentagon for some reason. It felt like the place she needed to be. Seeing him standing there confirmed her intuition. She desperately needed to see a friendly face.

Without answering his question, she threw her arms around his neck and hugged him tightly. She rested in his strong embrace for a few moments, breathing slowly, and then pulled away.

Luis brushed a hair from her face and gazed into her eyes. "What's wrong?"

"Um, nothing," Morgan said, somewhat fumbling her lie. She'd meant to follow up on his texts urging her to talk to Grace about the ARC system. But if she was honest, Morgan really just wanted to see Luis, to feel his kind eyes on her face and the comfort of his embrace. If Morgan told him the truth, that she really just needed a hug from her boyfriend, she might burst into tears and fall apart. There was no time for a meltdown. She had to focus on answering a growing list of questions and bring answers back to the president.

*That is, if she'll still hear what I have to say.*

"You said this morning I should talk to Grace about the ARC system, remember?" Morgan asked, raising her eyebrow. "And then you texted me later about a major problem with it?"

Luis frowned. "Oh. You're here to see Grace." The warm light in his brown eyes dimmed. "Well, I don't know where your friend is right now." His tone was suddenly gruff.

*Your friend? Was that displeasure?*

"But I did come to find you first," Morgan said, trying to assuage his obvious irritation. She smiled at him, pausing for a moment to gather her thoughts. "This has been a really weird day."

"Tell me about it," he said, cracking a bit of a grin. "You just called me colonel... and sir? I don't know how I can possibly carry on."

Morgan laughed, her body relaxing slightly. "It was all I could do to get your attention in that angry huff of yours. You nearly ran me over coming out of that elevator. What happened? Did something go wrong with the ARC test?"

Luis shook his head, his face becoming slack. "No, the test went fine, minus some unnecessary drama I'd rather not talk about. Has the president fired you yet?" He gave her a playful smirk.

Morgan swallowed hard, the blood draining from her face.

Luis winced. "Oh no. It was just a joke. I never thought…"

She brushed it off with a crooked smile. "The truth is I don't really know for sure. You saw the president humiliate me this morning in a cabinet meeting, putting me directly in Burke's crosshairs. Well, something else seems to have happened, but I don't know what it is." Morgan moved in closer and lowered her voice. "Jack was behaving super cagey on the phone this morning, like the FBI might be investigating him in connection to Monroe's death. And just now, Grayson threw me out of Liberty Crossing, demanding I talk to David about something. But I can't reach my boss, and my work email isn't working."

"You spoke to Jack?" Luis asked, his eyebrows squishing together. She really didn't like the disapproval in his tone.

Morgan pulled Luis to the side of the hallway where they could talk more privately. "I've made a possible connection between the Russian agent we think is responsible for the tweets and Anton Vega." She paused to study his face for comprehension. "And you know what that means."

Luis blanched. "You think the Russians might be connected to Nightfall?"

Morgan rubbed the back of her neck. "It sure looks that way. But I don't have tangible proof. Just another wild theory at this point. But things seem to be adding up. And when I was at Liberty Crossing, we lost contact with the Polaris satellite for about an hour."

Luis clenched his jaw. "What? How?"

Morgan shook her head. "They don't have the faintest clue. There wasn't any evidence of a cyberattack. At least not from earth. They're assuming it was a system malfunction and are running diagnostics now. Of course, I couldn't help thinking about how Anton's company might operate a satellite in that orbit. Maybe he used it to seize control of our early warning system?"

"To do what?"

Morgan shrugged. "I dunno. Cause mayhem? More destabilization? War with China? If Anton was willing to produce an EMP with a nuke delivered from the International Space Station, I'd say the sky is the limit, don't you?"

He pursed his lips, not hiding his skepticism.

"Like I said, it's a wild theory," Morgan said. "But I just can't shake the feeling that everything is connected."

"Okay, let's say you're right," Luis said. "Does that mean your mother is involved somehow?"

Morgan took a step back and stared at his worried face. She was surprised by the direct question. Usually, Luis preferred to dodge her personal connection to one of the worst disasters ever faced by the United States. "That would be my worst nightmare," she said.

"There you are," a female voice called out from behind them.

Morgan jumped, and Luis's body tensed.

"Colonel, I've been looking everywhere for you," Grace said. When she finally registered Morgan's presence, she stopped in her tracks, her eyes growing wide. "Morgan, what are *you* doing here?"

"Well, I came to see you about the ARC system," Morgan said. "Luis texted me about a problem you found this morning."

Grace nodded quickly and turned to Luis. "I'm really sorry about what happened before with the chairman. I felt like I had to downplay the issue with the SecDef standing there."

Luis let out a frustrated sigh and threw up his hands. "Grace, by backtracking with Admiral Waller just now, you've made it really difficult for me to approach him about this again." He shook his head. "First you tell me you need to flag something in his read-ahead this morning. So, I go through the trouble of getting your talking point inserted. And then you deny there was ever a problem to the chairman's face. And now you want me to tell him you were lying? I don't think so."

Grace's face flushed. "No, that's not what I'm saying. It's just... um, I... well, you missed the read-ahead meeting this morning," she blurted.

"I didn't miss it. I was at the White House for a Cabinet-level meeting with the chairman," Luis said deadpan.

*C'mon babe. Don't be a jerk.*

Morgan glared at him and poked him with her elbow.

Grace took a deep breath. "I know, I know. I just wish you'd been there. Then you'd know that I defended my talking points as best as I could. But Captain Dietz intervened, and I lost the argument. And then just before the test..." Her face paled slightly, and she looked uncertain.

"What happened?" Luis asked, leaning closer.

"Well, I promised I wouldn't tell anyone today," Grace said, scratching her nose.

Luis pinched his lips and crossed his arms. "Look, I don't know what you want from us. You say you need our help. But now you can't tell us why."

"Okay, I'll tell you," Grace said, "but we need to be extremely careful how we carry this information up the chain. I don't know how many senior leaders are involved in the conspiracy. That's why I think you both should talk directly to the president and the chairman."

Morgan's eyes widened. "You've uncovered a conspiracy?"

"I'm not sure, but there's definitely evidence of corruption," Grace said. She turned to Luis. "That's why I was so afraid to tell you before... with the SecDef standing right there. For all I know, he's up to his neck in it."

Morgan looked over at Luis, and he gave her a pained expression.

"It's okay, Grace. Tell us what you know, and we'll do what we can," she said.

"Okay. I caught Arjun tweaking ARC's algorithms right before the test. He made the changes to prevent the simulation from spiraling out of control. He was worried the ARC system would recommend nuclear war against China, leading Pentagon leadership to shut it down."

Luis shrank back, speechless for several moments. Then he

began pacing in a tight circle and rubbing his chin. "You're saying Arjun changed ARC's software to cheat on the test?"

Grace bobbed her head. "When I confronted him about it, Arjun claimed his boss, the CEO of Centoreum Tech, demanded he make the changes if he wanted to keep his job. Arjun said the changes would return the ARC system to its original state when it was first launched. I'm sorry I didn't tell you. I didn't know. What. To. Do." Grace's voice hitched, and tears welled in her eyes.

"Wait a minute," Luis said. "That means someone has tweaked the ARC system before this point?"

Grace nodded.

Luis creased his forehead, a deep frown on his face. "What do you want us to do?"

Morgan frowned at his annoyed tone, but it didn't seem to bother Grace.

Grace looked back and forth between them. "Morgan, you need to warn the president about the dangers of the ARC system." Then she turned to Luis. "You have to warn the chairman. If we don't take the system offline now, I'm worried about what could happen with China."

Luis glanced at his watch and frowned. "Crap. This is really serious. I wish I could help with this now... but I have to get the chairman over to the White House for a meeting."

Morgan snapped her attention back to Luis. "There's another meeting at the White House?" She stole a glance at her work phone. No missed calls or texts. And still nothing from her boss. The silence from her boss was deafening.

Luis gave them both an apologetic look and turned to walk down the hallway. "The president wants to be debriefed on ARC's test and evaluation and decide what to do next with regard to China."

*I should be at that meeting.*

For a moment, Morgan felt paralyzed.

*Am I fired?*

"Luis… If I don't make it to that meeting for some reason…" Morgan said, "find a way to warn the president for me." She knew what she was asking would be difficult for him. As a plus-one, Luis didn't have an easy way to participate in a Cabinet-level meeting.

Luis gave her a pained look. "I'll do what I can, okay?" Without another word, he hurried down the hallway.

SUSAN
1500
Executive Residence
The White House

Susan entered the West Sitting Hall and found Blake relaxing in his easy chair, reading the news on his tablet. Penny leapt up from her spot, raced over to her, and sat obediently at her feet. Susan reached down to scratch Penny's ears. Then she straightened up slowly, walked over to Blake, and sank into a chair next to him.

A sudden weariness came over her. Since she'd run from one crisis to the next, she'd barely gotten a chance to talk to Blake except for the short conversation after her disaster of a press briefing. She desperately wished she could have a do-over, especially for the lunch with Donghai. But then, she wasn't sure if it would have gone any differently, no matter what she had said.

Blake looked up from his tablet and smiled. "How was your lunch with Donghai?"

Susan grimaced, recalling how she'd lost her meal after the

failed attempt to clear up political misunderstandings and the awkward parting with her old friend. "It was terrible."

"Oh?"

"Donghai is obviously under great pressure from Beijing at the moment," Susan said. "He wouldn't break face once throughout the lunch. That's not like him at all. Even when things get tense between our countries, Donghai has always been able to let go of the politics and talk to me like an old friend. But not this time. Frankly, I've been rather spooked by it ever since."

Blake raised his eyebrow. "What do you think is going on?"

"I don't know, but it's gotta be pretty big," Susan said. "It feels like the Chinese government is trying to hide something from us. I told Donghai we know about the two nuclear-armed submarines in the Northwest Passage, and he didn't even flinch. I don't know what to make of it. Anyway, I've delivered a strong warning to the Chinese government, and we'll see how they react. If they don't bring those submarines to the surface immediately and redirect them through the Northeast Passage, we'll have to up our game. Because if we don't, the Chinese may interpret that as a lack of resolve."

Blake's forehead creased. "If the Chinese fail to yield to your demands, we'll have to take aggressive action to demonstrate our political will. And then, depending on how China responds, we may be walking into a nuclear conflict we don't even want. So basically, we're going to play a game of chicken with nuclear weapons."

"That's my fear," Susan said. "In a few minutes, I'm headed to another Cabinet meeting to get debriefed about the test and evaluation of the ARC system. Elise gave me a sneak preview, and there's something about a recommendation to raise the alert of U.S. nuclear forces to DEFCON 3."

Blake's jaw fell open. "What? Things are that bad?" He fumbled with his tablet before setting it down on the table next to him.

"The complete stonewalling by the Chinese government in the midst of rising tensions has me quite worried." Susan massaged her temples. "The DEFCON 3 recommendation comes from the ARC system, not from my defense advisors. I'm not sure what I'm going to do. I suppose I'll hear them out and then make my decision."

"Speaking of decisions, have you decided if you're going to sign the legislation?" Blake asked cautiously.

"Why are you asking that again?" Susan shot him an irritated glare. "Didn't we decide that I would sign? Remember our conversation before the press briefing?"

"I know, Susi," Blake said, reaching for her hand. "It's just that you didn't seem too enthused with the decision and that showed during your press briefing. You need to do what you think is best... and not what will satisfy everyone else. You're the president now. This morning you told me the decision will cost you something either way. I want to make sure whatever costs you will bear are worth it, and you'll have no regrets."

Susan smiled and let him stroke her hand for a moment. "Obviously, I haven't had much time to think it through. I've had more pressing issues on my mind. The bill would allow the Department of Defense to flip the switch and take humans out of the loop on the battlefield. Of course, I don't like that idea at all."

"I do recall you warning Harrison repeatedly about the risks of giving robots control over kill decisions on the battlefield," Blake said.

"Yep, to no avail. His mind was dead set on them. Harrison was convinced it would be the only way for us to prevail in the great power competition with China and Russia—if our adversaries have such systems, so must we. I was pretty certain I was going to sign the bill today until that viral video from one of *your* students. Now I'm not sure."

"Drew is a smart kid," Blake said, a flicker of pride in his eyes. "One my best students, actually... He's the only student I gave an A+ on the opinion editorial assignment last semester. You know… Drew gave a really thoughtful follow-up interview on *The Counter View* after your press briefing. If you get a chance today, you should watch it. But whatever you do, don't let social media sway your decision-making," he said, furrowing his brow.

"But isn't it an indicator of popular views?" Susan asked.

"Viral posts don't necessarily mean anything," Blake said. "They represent a momentary whim of a narrow slice of the population. For all we know, more than half of the accounts retweeting the video are bots. Who benefits the most if you veto the legislation?"

Susan scrunched her face. "China and Russia."

"Exactly."

Susan sighed heavily. "I'm not sure I have a choice on whether or not to sign the bill. At least not politically. Not if I want to continue to get things done. The power players in U.S. Congress want me to sign it. The majority of my administration wants me to sign it. Hell, I'm sure Harrison would want me to sign it."

"Then why don't you just sign the bill and get it over with?" Blake asked.

Susan shrugged. "I don't know. The idea of greenlighting automated killing machines gives me a bad feeling."

"Don't tell me what Drew said got under your skin," Blake said.

"Well, he does have a point. Maybe I'll feel different after my interview with him. Plus, what if I can convince Drew to change his mind? That would give the press and social media something to chew on." She gave him a mischievous smile.

Blake chuckled.

Susan narrowed her eyes. "What's so funny?"

"Susi, you haven't even made up your own mind," Blake said, still chuckling at her. "What if Drew convinces you to veto the bill? He's quite persuasive, you know."

She shrugged off his point. "Where's Lucy?" she asked, changing the subject.

Blake raised an eyebrow. "She's reading a book with the sitter."

"That book you gave her?" Susan asked, wincing as soon as the words passed her lips.

"No, not that book," Blake said flatly, his face darkening.

She turned to look Blake directly in the eyes. "Babe, I'm really sorry for yelling at you this morning. You were right. Lucy overhears things, and we need to help her understand them."

"It's okay. I know the enormous pressure you're under. I'm sorry I didn't tell you beforehand."

Susan smiled warmly. "I don't know if I've told you this lately... but you amaze me. And I don't know how I got so lucky."

"Right back at ya," Blake said, grinning at her.

His tablet buzzed on the table, and he glanced down at it quickly. As he scanned the HNN news headline, his eyes widened. "You need to see this," he said, reaching for the remote and turning on the TV.

Susan turned toward the screen, read the headline at the bottom of the screen several times, and then stared speechless at Blake as the reporter went into further detail.

MEDICAL EXAMINER DETERMINES PRESIDENT MONROE
INGESTED A TOXIC DOSE OF CHLOROQUINE
THE FBI INVESTIGATES POSSIBLE ASSASSINATION

# [ 44 ]
## THE FIRST RULE

MORGAN
1515
National Military Command Center
The Pentagon
Arlington, Virginia

Morgan perched on the edge of her seat beside Grace in front of a computer terminal. She couldn't stop clenching and unclenching her fists, and her whole body felt cold.

Grace had already filled her in on the clandestine tinkering by Centoreum's CEO, the changes Arjun made to the software, and details about ARC's latest test and evaluation. The more she learned about the ARC system, the more concerned she became, especially about the Pentagon leadership's false sense of security. Their overconfidence in the ARC system had the potential to lead to grave mistakes in a crisis situation—especially a conflict plagued with as many misunderstandings as the one with China.

Every muscle felt tight and strained. She couldn't stop obsessing over the meeting at the White House. Or rather the lack of an invitation. The morning meeting in the Situation Room and her dramatic showdown with Burke gnawed at her.

*Why isn't David telling me what's going on? Did Burke succeed in getting me fired?*

Morgan's gaze shifted back to the screen. Grace was still studying results from ARC's simulation with China.

"Did you check if Arjun reversed the changes?" Morgan asked.

"You mean the ones he made right before the test?"

Morgan nodded.

A look of dread flashed across Grace's face before she turned back toward the terminal. "Arjun promised he wouldn't touch the ARC system again. At least until we had a chance to talk to Captain Dietz and other senior leaders within the J6."

"And you trust him to do the right thing this time?" Morgan asked, scrunching her nose.

"I'd assumed Arjun wouldn't have had the time to reverse everything after the test finished. But just to be sure... let me check." Grace typed several commands into the computer. Seconds later, a diagnostic screen appeared with information on the latest version of ARC. Grace studied it for a moment. Then she exhaled sharply, closed her eyes, and covered her face with her hands.

Fearing the worst, Morgan glanced at the computer screen and tried to read the text. But none of it made sense to her. "Did he reverse the changes or not?"

Grace removed her hands from her face. Her expression was grim. "Apparently, Arjun saved his changes as a single software update. After the test concluded, he only had to enter a single command to revert the ARC system back to the previous version of the software. He must have planned this all along..." The dullness in her eyes suggested she might be losing hope.

Morgan took a deep breath. "But didn't you say that the CEO of Centoreum Tech accessed the ARC system remotely?"

Grace nodded and bit her lip. "Yeah. He built himself an invisible back door."

"Then can you check the system event log to see if it was Arjun who reversed the changes?" Morgan asked.

Grace's face lit up. "If Warren did it, we wouldn't be able to detect any evidence of the changes. I'm sure he must have figured out a way to hide any of his tinkering. But Arjun would have to access the ARC system from the front door at the Pentagon. That means his actions would show up on the event log." She began typing quickly.

The event log screen opened up with the long list of incidents coded in a shorthand Morgan couldn't decipher. Grace stared intently at the screen, her eyes moving from the most recent incidents at the top down toward the bottom.

Then she turned to Morgan with a slow smile and let out a huge breath. "It wasn't Arjun. He didn't betray me. He kept his word."

Morgan put her hand on Grace's shoulder. "Now that we have that part figured out, let's focus on fixing this."

Grace bobbed her head.

"As my first question, I'm wondering why Warren thought ARC would recommend nuclear war with China during the test," Morgan said.

Grace frowned. "Warren relaxed the system's adherence to the model of nuclear deterrence, which prescribes avoiding war and relying instead upon retaliation."

"Yes, but didn't you say the most important rule of the ARC system is to optimize its ability to retaliate?" Morgan asked.

Grace nodded. "Yeah, we call it the first rule. When I learned that Warren relaxed the deterrence framework, I assumed that would mean the ARC system would produce a wider range of outcomes than we normally would. But I didn't consider the implications."

Morgan nodded quickly, an idea forming in her head. "Over the course of history, humans have made many assumptions about how deterrence operates, but a machine is not limited by bias or experience. It is possible that ARC has discovered another move to optimize the U.S.'s ability to retaliate against a nuclear attack. What if the first rule leads the ARC system to prioritize its own survival?"

Grace gave her a funny look.

A surge of adrenaline filled Morgan's body. "No, that makes complete sense. Listen, if the first rule of ARC is to optimize our ability to retaliate, and ARC considers itself as the fulcrum of that ability, then it would likely prioritize actions to protect itself. Then the critical question becomes this: what if ARC perceives a decreasing ability to retaliate?"

"What do you mean?" Grace asked.

"Well, if the ability of ARC to retaliate is threatened, the system may shift its posture from a defensive one to recommend offensive actions. For example, a disarming first strike against an adversary might become more attractive under certain conditions." Morgan paused to study Grace's face.

"Are you saying the ARC system might recommend preemptive nuclear war to protect itself?" Grace asked.

Morgan nodded. "I assume the ARC system recommended a countermove this morning?"

Grace's expression suddenly became bleak. "ARC recommended an increase in alert status to DEFCON 3 as well as actions to force China's submarines to the surface."

*Holy shit.*

Morgan's eyes widened. "If ARC detected an increased potential for a decapitation strike scenario, then its recommendation to go to DEFCON 3 makes sense. On the surface, the move could be perceived as defensive, that is, designed to restore strategic stability. But it could also serve to prepare for a nuclear attack... Maybe the first rule is *the* problem."

"How so?"

"Think about it," Morgan said. "We're asking the ARC system to optimize its ability to retaliate above all else. ARC may not be acting to prevent nuclear war, but rather to defend its survival. If I'm on to something, the ARC system might drag us into a nuclear war simply to keep itself functioning properly."

"If you're right," Grace said, "then we need to tell the president."

*Yeah, before it's too late.*

She glanced at her smartphone and was surprised to see an email from her boss sent to her personal account. Her hand trembling, she clicked on it.

MORGAN,

PRESIDENT TOLLEY HAS SUSPENDED YOUR ACCESS TO CLASSIFIED INFORMATION FOR THE TIME BEING. YOU ARE NO LONGER ALLOWED IN THE EISENHOWER EXECUTIVE OFFICE BUILDING, AT THE WHITE HOUSE, OR IN OTHER SENSITIVE SPACES WITHOUT PRIOR APPROVAL AND AN OFFICIAL ESCORT. I'M VERY SORRY TO DELIVER THE BAD NEWS. I'LL LET YOU KNOW IF OR WHEN ANYTHING CHANGES. TAKE CARE.

BEST,

DAVID

"What happened?" Grace asked.

Morgan stared at the message, rereading it to make sure she'd understood it properly. "I think I just got fired."

# [ 45 ]
## DEFCON 3

SUSAN
1530
Situation Room
The White House

Susan massaged her temples in an attempt to alleviate a migraine. The rhythmic pounding started when she first learned of Harrison's overdose of chloroquine. The terrible news felt like it should be a tipping point for some major revelation, but she had no clue what that should be. Even as the troubles with China continued to mount, she could think of nothing else. There were so many unanswered questions.

*Was Harrison assassinated? Was his death somehow related to Nightfall? Were the Russians involved? Why did Faye Shaw come up on the FBI's radar?*

For a moment, Susan regretted shutting Morgan out of the White House, even if it was temporary. It may have been smarter to find out what Morgan learned about the Russian connection. But for all Susan knew, Morgan represented the common link across many strange puzzle pieces that led to

Nightfall, Harrison's death, and the disinformation campaign against China. And that meant she was a threat to Susan's presidency and, more importantly, to national security.

*No, it's better to keep her out for now. Until we know more.*

Regardless, Susan could definitely use some of Morgan's creative thinking in this meeting.

"Ma'am, are you sure you made our demands clear to the Chinese ambassador?" Burke asked.

A flush of anger crept across her cheeks. Susan ruffled at his suggestion that China's lack of a response might be her fault. Though she'd promised to resolve the misunderstandings with China and had failed to deliver.

*He won't let me forget it.*

She glared at him. "Yes. I delivered the message exactly as we discussed. I demanded the Chinese government bring the two submarines to the surface immediately and redirect them through the Northeast Passage. I couldn't have been clearer."

After lunch, she'd hoped Donghai might call her with news from Beijing or at least acknowledge that her message had been received by his government. The eerie silence nagged at her.

Her head throbbing, she glanced at her watch. China's war game was scheduled to begin in about thirty minutes—it would start during the early morning hours on the other side of the world.

*Perhaps we'll get some answers soon.*

"And we have no indication that they've taken any actions to meet our demands?" Burke asked, turning to Grayson.

Grayson shook his head. "We've been unable to pick up any sign of the submarines. There has also been no backchannel communication that the Chinese intend to comply with our demands."

"Then they've called our bluff," Burke said with a matter-of-fact tone, leaning back in his chair with flourish. "China thinks we're weak. They assume we'll do nothing about their incursion into our coastal waters. If we fail to act now, they will seize the advantage again. Just like they did several months ago." He leaned forward again to give Susan direct eye contact. "We should send out a force of attack submarines to track the missing subs and jam their signals. That will compel them to come to the surface. We need to send China a clear signal of determination, or they won't take us seriously—not now or in the future. Madam President, this is imperative to ensure effective nuclear deterrence. I can't emphasize that enough."

"Your recommendation is duly noted, General Burke," Susan said curtly. "Before we go after China with our guns blazing, I want to consider why the Chinese refuse to respond or say anything about what is going on."

Elizabeth sat up a bit straighter. "Ma'am, do you think Dr. Shaw's defection scenario might have merit in light of these new circumstances? That could certainly explain the silence of the Chinese government. They would want to get the situation under control before telling us anything about it."

Burke waved his hand around and shook his head emphatically. "Not this again. If the Chinese are silent, then they're planning to do something we won't like. We can test the waters by going after the two submarines in the Northwest Passage. Then, if they take further aggressive actions in response, we'll have our answer."

"Ma'am, I agree with Elizabeth. There's something strange afoot, even for China," Grayson said. "We've now confirmed that the *China Xinhua News* handle was hacked by a cyber thug—a Russian citizen working for a wealthy oligarch with major ties to oil and natural gas. But the Chinese government continues to act like the tweets constitute official communication. I just don't think we should interpret their behavior as aggression toward us."

Susan nodded. Although she agreed with Elizabeth and Grayson, she couldn't let that be known until they finished the discussion. "I called this meeting to review ARC's test and evaluation and discuss the merits of *both* recommendations—the countermove against China's submarines and the decision to raise the alert status to DEFCON 3. Before taking any actions proposed by ARC, however, I'd prefer to discuss all options on the table with my human advisors."

"I couldn't agree more," Burke said through his teeth. Then he flashed a smile that failed to hide his growing frustration. "ARC passed its fifth test with flying colors today, but this one holds by far the most significance. During a heightened conflict with China, the ARC system took actions that successfully deescalated the crisis and avoided nuclear war. For this reason, I have utmost confidence in ARC for providing us with the best possible response to China. We should implement both of ARC's recommendations without further delay."

Elizabeth cleared her throat. "Madam President, I disagree. I don't think we should be so hasty. ARC has zero operational experience during a real conflict," she said, wrapping a loose blonde hair behind her ear. "The only nuclear crisis in U.S. history where we've deviated from peacetime routines was the Cuban Missile Crisis. That means there's no real-world nuclear conflict data on which ARC can train. As a result, we simply don't know how the ARC system will behave as we approach the brink of war. I don't trust it."

"And that's why we run the monthly tests," Burke said, practically spitting at her. "Each month we generate significant volumes of synthetic data from advanced simulations about combat procedures and wartime operations. We feed that data into ARC along with a real-world data infusion from its ISR component. Both data streams help the system learn about the realities of nuclear conflict."

"Oh, now I understand," Elizabeth said, her tone laced with sarcasm. "You guys shore up ARC's lack of real-world knowledge about nuclear war with *synthetic* data about nuclear war. Yeah, I feel so much better now." She paused for effect and then glanced at each of the faces around the table. "Look, these simulations are abstractions of the real world and nothing more. The synthetic data will not help the ARC system understand how to operate in a real-world crisis involving nuclear weapons or grasp the stakes for humanity. I predict it will drag us into a nuclear war of its own choosing. I, for one, vote that we dispense with ARC's recommendations, do some critical thinking for ourselves, and come up with our own response options."

*Critical thinking about nuclear deterrence in this crowd?*

Burke's facial muscles tightened. With a few veins popping in his forehead, it appeared like his head might explode.

"Madam President, for my part, I recommend we increase the alert of U.S. nuclear forces to DEFCON 3, at a minimum," Admiral Waller said, the boom of his deep voice cutting through the tension.

Susan breathed a sigh of relief at his timely intervention. She didn't think the spat between Burke and Elizabeth would help ease the headache that was pounding on the inside of her skull like a jackhammer.

"At DEFCON 3, the ARC system would receive another data infusion from the ISR component and improve its situation awareness," he continued. "New data about the fake tweets and the deep fakes could clear up some potential misinterpretations about China's actions today. Our command and control network would also become less vulnerable to the threat of a decapitation strike. And we're also more ready for combat if the Chinese are indeed mobilizing for war. Ma'am, consider it a precautionary measure."

Susan nodded.

"But the Chinese could see moving up a rung on the alert ladder as escalatory if we don't provide them any reassurance," Elizabeth retorted, gesturing as she spoke. "As you've noted, going to DEFCON 3 would shift us from peacetime to preparation for combat. Whatever we decide today, I think we should deescalate the situation with China and avoid increasing tensions. We need to get more information about the real purpose of China's submarines in the Northwest Passage. We're not going to achieve that by poking them in the eye."

*But I tried diplomacy and failed.*

"Ma'am, I'm inclined to agree with Admiral Waller," David said from the other end of the table. "At DEFCON 3, we have a better shot at detecting any incoming nuclear strikes since additional ground radars are switched over to the early warning mission. Moreover, we improve the redundancy of communications and further disperse our bombers and command and control units, both of which enhance our ability to retaliate after an attack."

"They're both correct," Burke said, regaining control of the discussion. "We would render any chance of a surprise first strike moot." He paused to give her a crooked, knowing smile. "That means we would eliminate the decapitation strike scenario you were so worried about this morning."

Susan suppressed a frown, ignoring Burke's jab. She was about to say something, but Burke continued to speak.

"Since we're thinking beyond ARC's recommendations, I might even propose raising the alert to DEFCON 2 to let China know we're very serious," he said nonchalantly. "If we did that, we would eliminate most of the vulnerabilities in our command and control systems."

*DEFCON 2?*

"Are you fucking mad?" Elizabeth blurted, her eyes bulging at Burke. "You might as well tell the Chinese we're preparing for nuclear war. Because that's how they'll see the mobilization activities. Especially if they're dealing with some internal crisis they can't tell us about."

Just then, Elise jumped out of her chair, her face pale. She stared at the screen of her secure work phone and moved quickly toward the exit. She gave Susan an odd look, pointed at the door, and then left the room.

*Where the hell is she going?*

Her stomach tingling, Susan leaned forward in her chair and

looked directly at the admiral. "Just a hypothetical question... How much warning would we receive if China is using the war game to prepare for a nuclear attack?"

"Ma'am, the ARC system is designed to provide strategic warning of any nuclear-related preparations, which is as good as it gets for anticipating a nuclear attack," Admiral Waller said. "In my view, I believe the ARC system has already detected aggressive changes in China's nuclear posture that require us to restore strategic stability. We need to reduce the vulnerability of command and control systems that exists during peacetime operations by increasing the alert status. We also need to directly counter the threat posed by China's submarines in the Northwest Passage by raising them to the surface. We'll have a better understanding of Chinese intentions based on how they respond to these actions."

*Exactly what ARC recommends. Another true believer.*

"One thing we haven't done yet is reach out to Russia to see if they have any information on the two submarines," Elizabeth said. "I'm sure they must be as curious as we are about their presence in the Northwest Passage."

Susan shook her head. "No, let's keep Russia out of this for now. I don't want to have to decipher their agenda on top of everything else. Figuring out China's endgame is complicated enough as it is."

She inhaled a deep breath. In that moment, she recalled Blake's grim comment about accidentally sliding into a nuclear conflict that neither the U.S. nor the Chinese wanted.

"Thank you all for your recommendations," she said. "I need to think for a bit and will give you my answer—"

The door flung open, and Elise burst into the room. "Ma'am, there's been another development. Fishermen near the coastal waters of the Philippines have flooded social media with posts in the last five minutes, claiming they've spotted UFOs in the South China Sea. They have posted images of flying objects with long, white tails of smoke in the sky. It looks like they could be submarine-launched missiles."

Susan blanched.

*Is this how it begins?*

"That's impossible," Burke said. "Our satellites would have detected the infrared heat signatures immediately and relayed the signals through the ARC system to NORAD. Within less than a few minutes, we would have received an alert about the missile trajectories and estimated targets. Not to mention NORAD would have already informed us if the missiles posed a threat to targets in the United States or any of our space assets."

"That's exactly what I thought," Elise said, shooting Burke an annoyed look. "So, I gave NORAD a call. They confirmed there are no indicators of missile launches coming from the ARC system. Our early warning satellites have not detected any bursts of infrared activity coming from the South China Sea."

"Then these alleged missile launches must be another hoax gone viral, just like the deep fake videos of the massacre," Burke said dismissively.

Grayson cleared his throat. "Madam President, I didn't think to raise this before, but we did experience a minor communication issue with the Polaris satellite that resolved itself about an hour ago."

Susan jerked her head toward Grayson in irritation. "You're picking a fine time to bring this up. Do we know why we lost communication?" She rarely addressed him with harsh rebuke, but it felt necessary.

Grayson winced. "The satellite was offline for about forty-five minutes. We think the communication link broke as a result of a malfunction. After the satellite rebooted itself, it came back online and then restored its communication links. We're still running diagnostics, but there were no signs of any cyber intrusion."

"We're certain no one hacked into Polaris?" Susan asked.

Grayson nodded. "We've detected no foreign signals from

the ground and are ninety-nine percent certain there was no cyberattack."

Susan rubbed her forehead, took a deep breath, and pressed on. "Let's consider the one percent chance for a moment. What's the worst-case scenario?"

Grayson sighed heavily. "Ma'am, you know I don't like worst cases. They often tell—"

"Just humor me," Susan said sternly. Her reserves of patience had nearly depleted. "Let's say someone was able to hack our satellite. What's the worst possible thing that could happen?"

"Ma'am, the worst-case scenario would be a hacker gaining control of Polaris's software," Grayson said. "The hacker could ensure the satellite would send us normal signals so that we wouldn't know anything was wrong with it. Once the hacker had full control over the satellite, they would have several options, including making the satellite go completely dark."

Susan pressed her lips together. "In other words, we would have no eyes in the northern latitudes. The hacker could prevent an alert from being sent by Polaris to the ARC system at NORAD."

Grayson nodded. "Yes. The hacker could also exploit control over Polaris to gain access to the other satellites in our early warning system."

"Are you saying they could control our entire early warning system?" Susan asked.

"In principle, yes… but it's highly unlikely," Grayson said.

"Madam President, why would anyone attempt such a feat?" Burke asked snidely. "Think of the resources involved. And what would the hacker gain from this expensive shenanigan?"

"Well, we wouldn't be able to see an incoming nuclear attack," Susan said, frowning.

Burke grimaced. "Only for a short time during the boost phase. So what? Our ground radars would detect and track the ballistic missiles as soon as they're flying above the horizon.

Why would someone go through the trouble of messing with our satellites? Especially when the risk of doing so could mean nuclear war?"

"There's one possible reason," David said. "If we lost our early warning satellites, we wouldn't be able to detect the launch of hypersonic missiles either. And our radars wouldn't be much use then. Ma'am, if someone went through the effort to shut down our entire satellite network, it would make the most sense to use hypersonic missiles in a surprise attack."

"But the use of hypersonic missiles wouldn't explain the failed detection of the launches from the South China Sea, assuming the images on social media aren't fake," Grayson said. "We only had a small problem with Polaris. The rest of the network is working fine."

"If China really launched hypersonic missiles at any targets we care about, we would know by now," Burke said grimly. "They would have reached their targets in just a few minutes."

"It's already been more than five minutes since the social media posts," Elise said.

"And that's assuming the fisherman posted them immediately after they snapped their images," Burke said. "Ma'am, this is just another hoax."

Susan nodded and turned to Grayson. "Find out who is behind these social media posts. Also, I want a full diagnostic report for Polaris as soon as possible." Turning to face the room, she rose from her chair and said, "I'll make my decision about next steps with China by the end of the day."

Admiral Waller jumped out of his chair, nearly stumbling over his feet. "Madam President, if you have a moment."

When she saw the anxious look on his face, Susan motioned for him to follow her.

## [ 46 ]
## ACCESS DENIED

MORGAN
  1615
  The Grind Cafe
  Washington, D.C.

Morgan pressed her nose over the edge of her coffee mug, took in a strong whiff of her mocha-java brew, and exhaled slowly. It was all she could manage for now. With her stomach tied in knots, she couldn't bring herself to take a sip. But it was probably better that way. She didn't really need another spike of caffeine to go with her already frayed nerves. She'd only purchased the coffee to justify occupying a choice spot in the cafe.

Under the table, Morgan's foot tapped a mile a minute as she deliberated on how to warn the president about the ARC system. From her window seat, she had a clear view of the Eisenhower Executive Office Building. She closed her eyes for a moment, wishing she could just teleport herself into her office.

Her options were becoming extremely limited. Both Luis and David weren't responding to her texts. David was probably stuck in the same meeting as Luis in the Situation Room. She tried calling several of her other colleagues on the National Security Council staff, but no one picked up.

When everything else failed, she tried entering the building, only to be denied access by the same security guard who'd seen her leave and go for a walk earlier. Not only had he refused to succumb to her sweet talk, he'd confiscated her badge and reprimanded her for trying to get past security without the right credentials. Nearing her wits' end, Morgan retreated to the cafe to regroup and sent an SOS call to her uncle. Maybe Jack could find another way to get through to President Tolley.

A shadow appeared above her table. Morgan jumped slightly and then looked up to see her uncle staring down at her, a deep frown on his angular, worn face. As usual, Jack looked well put-together. With a fortune to spend on clothes, it wasn't all that hard. He wore a bespoke suit made from ultralight cashmere fabric. The dark gray color matched his thick, silver hair and goatee.

Despite the fancy threads and neat appearance, Jack looked rather disheveled. His bloodshot eyes darted back and forth. He took a seat across from her, without offering any greeting. Instead, he took a long sip of his drink and placed the cup on the table. The fresh scent of mint tea wafted toward Morgan, followed by a surprise—the fruity smell of rum.

*I guess it's almost five o' clock.*

She leaned forward to say something to him, but he held out his hand for her to keep silent. Jack glanced nervously over his shoulder and around the cafe as if he were looking for someone. Then he studied the sidewalk and street outside for a few minutes.

When he was finished inspecting their surroundings, he turned to her and breathed a sigh of relief. "Good. I've managed to lose them for now." He kept his voice low. "Do you have your phone on you?"

Morgan nodded.

318

"Turn it off," Jack said.

"But I'm waiting for some important phone calls."

"Turn it off," Jack repeated, this time his voice gruff.

Morgan sighed, pressing the power button on her smartphone until the screen went black. Then she powered down her work phone. Looking up, she asked, "Who's following you?"

Jack put his finger to his mouth and whispered, "The FBI? U.S. Secret Service? Probably both."

"But why?"

He leaned in closer. "I'm being framed for the president's assassination."

Morgan's eyes widened. "What?"

"Well, I was the only one with Harrison all day on that golf course, even though we were surrounded by Secret Service. Since I'm the only 'outside' person who had access to him, I'm the key person of interest. Secret Service has already questioned me three times. But it's only a matter of time before they take me into custody. An old friend told me the evidence against me is mounting."

"That's ridiculous," Morgan said. "If you could poison the president, so could each one of the Secret Service agents. How do they think Harrison overdosed on his malaria med?"

"The president drank a bottle of water from one of those refreshment carts pushed around by a pretty girl in a short skirt," Jack said. "The water bottle was sealed, and Secret Service checked it before he drank. They think the lethal dose of chloroquine came from that bottle."

"And they think *you* had something to do with that?" Morgan asked. "What about the girl with the cart? Are they looking into her?"

Jack nodded. "She disappeared into thin air. Apparently, she was a new cart girl, hired two weeks ago under a false name. Her prints and DNA aren't in the FBI's database, but they did find something interesting during the search. That's why they came back around to interrogate me a few more times. They now suspect my involvement."

Morgan raised her eyebrow. "I'm confused. Why would they suspect you of being involved if this girl took a job under a false name? She's the one who operated the cart with the poisoned water. How did she know the president was golfing that day?"

"Well, it's no secret that the president golfed at that course on a regular basis. Someone knew about the planned outing, but it wasn't through me. And although the girl's DNA wasn't in the system, the DNA of someone to whom she's closely related was…"

Morgan blinked at him several times. She wasn't getting Jack's hint and needed more information. "Whose DNA?" She leaned forward in anticipation, her hand clasping the coffee cup tightly.

"Your mother's."

The words thudded in her head like a heavy weight hitting the floor. Morgan's mouth fell open, and she sat in stunned silence for a few moments as she put all the horrible details together. Then she gulped and stared wide-eyed at her uncle.

"Oh, it's far worse than that. The DNA from your mother came from a hair sample. The girl shares mitochondrial DNA with your mother," Jack said.

"What does that mean?" Morgan asked, her brow furrowed.

"That means that the golf cart girl was your sister. And—"

Morgan did a double take, and her mouth went slack. "I have a sister? And she's working with my mother?" Her words sounded distant, and there was suddenly a high-pitched ringing in her ears.

"Apparently," Jack said grimly. "Yet another thing Faye kept from us. Morgan, listen, this is important for you to understand. The FBI got the DNA test results back about an hour ago. This could explain why you've been shut out of the White House…"

Morgan sat up straighter, still reeling from the shock of finding out about her newfound sibling. "But why?"

"Your mitochondrial DNA would be identical to your sister's," Jack said. "But they will think it belongs to you. They'll arrest you."

It took several moments for the information to sink in. And when it did, Morgan's stomach dropped. "That means the evidence in Harrison's death... will point to me... I mean us... They'll think we..."

Jack nodded glumly. "Your mother set us up. I've been doing some digging with the help of an old friend at the FBI. Apparently, your mother was in the country last week, traveling under the name of Maria Koslova on business for Nesti Oil and Natural Gas. She must have really been here to oversee the operation to remove Harrison and frame both of us in the process."

Morgan's hand flew to her chest as a sudden coldness hit at her core. Faye's alias was familiar, but so was the name of the business. Then she remembered the strange coded messages received by the NSA. "That's Igor Koslov's company. You think Faye's in bed with him?" Knowing her mother's tendencies, she meant it both literally and figuratively.

Jack nodded again.

Morgan's thoughts raced as she connected the dots between her mother, Anton Vega, Igor Koslov, Harrison's assassination, and the disinformation campaign. If they had colluded to bring about the Nightfall Incident, then there was a Russian connection to that attack. Morgan concluded that the same players must also be involved in the disinformation campaign, the hacking, and the president's assassination.

*But why?*

"Are they trying to catalyze a nuclear conflict between China and the United States?"

"Possibly," Jack said.

"I don't get it," Morgan said, contemplating what possible endgame would require bringing two countries closer to nuclear war.

"It doesn't make sense to me either," Jack said. "Parts of Russia would experience severe destruction if nuclear war were to break out between the United States and China. I can't imagine that Vladivostok in Russia's Far East would survive the fallout. Plus, that's where the Russian Pacific Fleet is located."

"They must not understand the instability of the ARC system," Morgan said, "because the stuff they're doing to stir up trouble has the United States and China dangling precariously from a nuclear cliff."

"It's that bad?" Jack asked, his forehead creasing.

"Don't get me started. Apparently, the ARC system has learned how to best protect itself and that plan doesn't look good for humanity." Morgan paused for a moment and then perked up. "Wait a minute..." She glanced at her uncle with a new energy and lowered her voice to a whisper. "It's all starting to add up now. The tweets were posted by Molotov in the Chinese city of Harbin, a few hundred miles away from Vladivostok. Intelligence analysts believe a hacker working for Molotov and Koslov produced the deep fake videos, making it look like the Chinese state police were engaging in a massacre. And while I was over at Liberty Crossing trying to get to the bottom of all of this, we lost communication with the Polaris satellite."

Jack winced.

Morgan pressed her lips together. "The explanation for the brief outage didn't sit well with me. The others were convinced no one hacked the satellite because there were no signals from the ground. But I kept thinking about the possibility that Anton might own a satellite in the same orbit and have people capable of hacking Polaris. If I'm right, all the other stuff is a distraction, convincing us to focus on China."

Jack's eyes lit up for a moment. "You're definitely onto something. Before his death, Harrison and I were investigating Anton Vega's assets to get a better sense of his involvement with Nightfall and to understand his ultimate endgame. Just last week, before the president's death, we discovered that his company operates a satellite in highly elliptical orbit."

Morgan's mouth fell open as she absorbed the new information. Then she glared at her uncle. "But before, you acted like there was no connection between Anton Vega and the Russians. You told me my theories were complete speculation."

"I'm sorry I couldn't tell you this before," Jack said, rubbing his forehead. "I was afraid someone might overhear us when we talked on the phone."

"But how did Anton get it into outer space without anyone knowing?" Morgan asked, forgetting her irritation.

"That's the same question Harrison and I had," Jack said. "Based on Space Command's annual survey of space objects, the satellite is quite new. It must have been launched into space sometime within the last six months. We've studied all of the space launches in that time period, and we suspect the Russians might have sent it up there for him shortly after Nightfall. Either that or it was Vega's own rocket launched under Russian auspices."

"Morgan, at the time, they were attempting to seize the advantage in space." Jack said, averting his gaze. "And they still are. We don't have tangible evidence that Vega is working with the Russians. Yet."

"If our suspicions are correct, both China and the U.S. are being played by Anton Vega, a corrupt Russian oligarch, and their stooges to carry out some secret agenda." She paused for a moment and then said, "We need to warn the president."

"She does need to know about everything." His tone was unusually dull.

"Unfortunately, I've been locked out of my building and stripped of my ID," Morgan said, ignoring the sudden dip in his demeanor. "And no one will answer my emails or calls. Do you have any way to get back into the White House?"

Her uncle laughed out loud. "The Secret Service is practically breathing down my neck. If you really want to get back into the

White House, you're going to have to find a way in on your own. But I was secretly hoping you'd consider another option."

"What other option?" Morgan asked, her eyebrow raised.

Jack leaned in and said in a low voice, "My jet is standing ready on the tarmac at Dulles. I want you to come with me."

Morgan heaved a breath. "You're fleeing the country."

He nodded. "Secret Service will be coming for you soon. But it's not too late if you come with me now."

Morgan shrank back. "If I run, I'll look guilty... and I've done nothing wrong." Her thinking blurred for a moment, followed by a sudden moment of clarity.

"That won't stop them from interrogating you and putting you through hell on my account," Jack said.

Morgan took a deep breath and shook her head. "I'm staying. I have to warn the president about Anton Vega and the Russians."

Jack sighed. "I was afraid you'd say that." He pulled something out of his pocket and pressed it into her hand. "This might be helpful. It won't comfortably get you through the front door of the White House, but it will get President Tolley's attention once you're inside."

It was a small USB drive. Morgan turned it over in her hands several times and gave her uncle a quizzical look. "What is it?"

"It would be better if you didn't know. Otherwise you'd have to lie to the president. I expect Tolley will be looking for this very soon," he said. "You should give it to her. Say you got it from me and don't know what it is. Tell her Harrison gave it to me right before he died. Tell her Grayson has a copy."

Morgan blinked a few times.

*Grayson has one too?*

"Will this get you in trouble?" she asked, holding up the thumb drive.

"I'm already in trouble. But it should get you out of it since it points blame in the right direction."

Morgan frowned. She didn't like it when her uncle spoke to her in code.

Jack's eyes became moist. "Whatever happens... I want you to know that I've always loved you like a daughter. I've made some big mistakes. But everything I did was in the interest of the United States. No matter what the evidence says, you have to believe that I'm innocent."

Morgan nodded briskly. "I believe you." She knew better than to ask where her uncle was going or when she'd see him again. He wouldn't want to put her in a tough position by telling her.

Jack rose from the table. "Good. Because I'm going to need your help to clear my name." He leaned over and kissed her on the forehead. Then he headed out of the café and didn't look back.

Morgan watched him walk down the street and disappear around the corner. Her eyes darted back to her office building where the same guard secured the side entrance.

*I have to find a way to get back in.*

# [ 47 ]
## COMMAND AND CONTROL

SUSAN
1630
Oval Office
The White House

"Admiral, why didn't you raise this issue during the meeting?" Susan asked with a deep frown. She squinted at him, trying to hide the extreme discomfort of her headache. Susan stood in a huddle with Admiral Waller and Colonel Martinez just inside the door of the Oval Office. Her arms were crossed, and she tapped her foot impatiently.

Admiral Waller cringed. "I'm sorry, Madam President. The notion began nagging at me when Grayson mentioned the loss of communication with Polaris toward the end of the meeting. I don't have any tangible evidence to support my gut instinct, so I didn't bring it up. But I'm compelled to tell you now. Between the tweets, the deep fakes, and now, this missile launch hoax… it feels more and more like someone wants us to focus on the conflict with China. Maybe so that we're too distracted to notice something else?" He shuffled his feet, apparently uncomfortable with any form of speculation.

"You mean like a red herring?" Susan asked. "You think the Russians might be up to something? And they want us to keep our eyes on China?"

Admiral Waller nodded. "Ma'am, the issue with Polaris is particularly troubling without Constellation. The Department of Defense is desperately trying to replace the layer of space sensors as we speak. But until we do, we're rather vulnerable to a surprise attack with hypersonic missiles because they can evade our radar systems. And if we don't have operational satellites with infrared sensors, we can't even detect their launches."

Susan stared down at the edge of the oval carpet at her feet, biting her lip. "You're saying that if our early warning satellites go dark, the ARC system can't see hypersonic missiles coming toward us at all."

"We would be operating blind," Admiral Waller said. "At least until hypersonic missiles hit their targets."

"Madam President, if I may." Colonel Martinez took a small step toward her and blinked rapidly. "On that note, there's another issue you should be aware of." He looked a bit peaked, and he rubbed the back of his neck as if he were uncertain about speaking up.

Admiral Waller snapped his head toward Martinez, apparently surprised by the intervention. Even so, there was no flicker of irritation on his wrinkled face. Susan had always been impressed by his ability to remain calm no matter what the circumstances. It was for this reason that she found the admiral's uncertainty about the U.S. early warning system especially upsetting.

Susan's skin tingled. She was unaccustomed to seeing a high-ranking U.S. Marine display any obvious signs of distress.

*What could possibly be more important than the detection of missile launches?*

"What is it, Colonel?" Susan asked, giving Martinez an encouraging smile.

"I'm concerned that ARC may be misreading signals from China as aggression," Martinez said, avoiding direct eye contact. "That means—"

Admiral Waller raised his eyebrow and interjected, "What are you trying to say, Colonel?" There was a hint of strain in his voice now, and he widened his stance. "You attended the same test with me today, and ARC performed better than we both could have imagined during a conflict with China. Afterwards, you reassured me there was nothing to worry about."

"That's the thing, sir. After we spoke, I learned something new—"

"Madam President!" Elise came running through the door, her face dotted with red blotchy spots and her eyes as round as saucers. "Ma'am, I need you to come to the Situation Room right away." Then she noticed the admiral. "You too, sir."

"What now?" Susan said, putting her hand on her forehead. She desperately needed to take some pills for her headache.

Elise waved urgently at them to follow her. "NORAD has confirmed missile launches from China's submarines in the South China Sea."

Susan held her breath. "What? But I thought... missile launches?" She stopped in her tracks, froze, and stared at Elise's face. "Wait, why didn't NORAD detect them before?"

*Are these the same missiles from social media?*

"Ma'am, I don't know the details, but there's no time to lose," Elise said, holding the door and motioning for them to hurry. "C'mon. We need to move. Now."

* * *

Susan marched into the Situation Room to find her advisors sitting stiffly at the conference table. When they noticed her arrival, a chilly tension filled the air, causing the hair on her arms to stand on end. Everyone rose from their chairs as dictated by protocol, but she urged them to quickly take their seats again. Admiral Waller and Colonel Martinez filed into the room after her and found their seats.

Everyone turned to look at her expectantly. The stark silence among the country's top civilian and military leaders felt like a vacuum, sucking up every bit of hope she had left. Her body tensed, and time seemed to slow way down. A burst of adrenaline caused her head to throb even harder than before.

Susan paused for a moment before sitting down to survey the new features in the room. A panel had opened up at the center of the table to reveal one of the ARC system's servers and a small projector, which shone light from its lens. A blue and white hologram of the ARC dashboard hovered above the table. A small number keypad sat on the table near her chair.

Her advisors around the table seemed entranced by the red blinking lights on the dashboard. Her eyes darted to several white flashing missile markers located on the world map. From a quick glance, it appeared that several missiles were emanating from the South China Sea.

Susan had only seen the hologram dashboard once before when she'd received her initial technical briefing on the ARC system. Even as a demo, the notion of watching nuclear war unfold in real time had haunted her imagination for several weeks.

This was it, the point of no return. Susan had the feeling she was about to face the biggest nuclear crisis of her generation, maybe even the worst in world history. And it was her job to navigate a clean way out of the mess. It was up to her to save millions of lives and perhaps even life on the planet itself. As if doubling the force of the Earth's gravity, the burden of that responsibility pulled on every muscle in her tired body.

From the head of the table, she nodded at her advisors around the room and then at the large divided video screen on the wall on which the commanders of NORAD, Strategic Command (STRAT-

COM), and Indo-Pacific Command tuned in over secure video conference. The screen next to it broadcasted video footage live from the National Military Command Center where a gaggle of sober-looking Pentagon senior leaders gathered in the war room.

Susan took a deep breath and then raised her eyebrow. Everyone was present except for one notable figure. "Where's General Burke?" she asked, turning to Elise as she sank into her chair.

Elise shook her head. "Ma'am, we weren't able to catch him in time. He headed straight back to the Pentagon right after the last meeting concluded. He will tune in from there shortly."

"No," Susan said quickly. "Call him now. Have him go directly to Andrews Air Force Base."

"But ma'am," Elise said. "This isn't... um... is it?"

Susan knew the question her chief of staff was asking, but she couldn't afford to fathom the possible answers. Not now. Even if Susan might be living through her last few minutes before the start of a nuclear war, she couldn't acknowledge that fact yet. No, Susan had to pretend there was a small chance she could figure out a way to prevent a nuclear war from happening.

"Just do it," Susan said. "Burke can call into the meeting from Air Force One. But I want him in the air and on the way to Raven Rock in less than thirty minutes. Do you hear?" Susan grabbed Elise's arm and pulled her closer. Now whispering in her ear, she said, "Have Secret Service collect Blake, Lucy, and Penny and bring them to the bunker. I'll be able to think more clearly if they're down there." She ignored the painful stab in her gut at the thought she might never see her family again.

Elise nodded quickly and departed the room to make the calls.

Susan swallowed hard and swiveled her chair around to face the room again. The irony of Burke surviving an initial nuclear attack while all of them perished deliberating in a conference room tasted bitter in her mouth. But she couldn't worry about that and needed to focus on the task at hand. Susan turned to her military commanders on the screen with a sense of haste. "Sirs, please fill me in on the situation."

"Madam President, our early warning satellite network has gone completely offline," the NORAD Commander said on the video screen. "That's why we failed to detect three nuclear-capable hypersonic missiles launched from China's submarines in the South China Sea."

"These are the same ones reported on social media by the fishermen?" Susan asked, holding back a scowl since she already suspected the answer.

"Yes, ma'am. We picked them up on our sea-based radar for only a few seconds, but long enough to get some data. They were traveling near the coastal waters of the Philippines, but we lost them again. Without Constellation, it's extremely difficult to track them."

Susan glanced at her watch. "But that was more than ten minutes ago now. I assume they would have reached their targets by now."

"You are correct, ma'am," the NORAD Commander said. "We believe the test launches were part of China's war game. We assume the missiles armed with conventional warheads must have landed in the ocean somewhere nearby, but we couldn't see them without our eyes in the sky."

Susan exhaled a breath of relief and relaxed her shoulders. Then her brow furrowed as she absorbed the bad news. "Do we know why our early warning satellite system has gone offline? Does it have anything to do with the loss of Polaris communications earlier?" She looked at Grayson for answers.

Grayson dipped his head before speaking up. "Ma'am, I haven't had time to confirm the details. But it would appear that a hacker has gained control over Polaris and used it to corrupt our entire early warning satellite network, as well as other military intelligence satellites—"

Susan wrinkled her forehead. "Other military satellites? Are you saying we can't see anything overhead at the moment?"

"Ma'am, we lost so many of our space assets during Nightfall that we temporarily networked many of the remaining ones with other satellite networks," Grayson said. "We also doubled up our sensors on each satellite to compensate for the loss in our capabilities. But that made our network of networks more vulnerable to cyberthreats, especially in the event that one satellite was compromised. As far as detecting any nuclear missile launches goes, it looks like we are now operating in the dark. At least until our radars pick up signals from ballistic missiles after the boost phase."

Susan's eyes darted to Elizabeth, who was unusually quiet without her arch nemesis in the room. "Have we heard anything from the Chinese?"

Elizabeth shook her head. "No, ma'am. They've not said anything on official or unofficial channels. But whatever we do, I believe reassuring the Chinese of our peaceful intentions must be the first step in any response plan. I think we should call the Chinese ambassador to clarify our position... before it's too late."

Susan looked at the ARC dashboard again. The blinking white missile indicators nagged at her. "Why hasn't ARC updated the status of the three missiles launched from the South China Sea? I thought we decided they landed in the ocean somewhere." She pointed to the hologram dashboard and then stared at her military commanders on the video screen.

"Ma'am, that's because ARC doesn't have any information to verify the status of those missiles," the STRATCOM commander said.

Susan nearly laughed out loud but caught herself just in time. *The system has no common sense.*

The STRATCOM commander paused for a moment, giving her a strange look on the video screen as if he were trying to see better. When she said nothing, he continued. "ARC relies upon the data it receives from our early warning satellites, radar systems, and other sensors to reach its conclusions. Because ARC currently can't detect the launch of the missiles, determine what type of missiles they are, or see the missiles land in the ocean at the moment, it can't update the status. The ARC system is waiting for some sort of definitive signal before drawing a final conclusion."

*Are you fucking serious?*

Susan recoiled. "But can't ARC derive their status from the lack of radiation or electromagnetic pulse? Doesn't the complete absence of signals suggest the obvious outcome?"

"Ma'am, the hypersonic missiles were nuclear-capable, and we're assuming they were armed with conventional warheads in the absence of either indicator," the STRATCOM commander said. "Since explosions caused by conventional warheads don't produce easily detectable signatures like nuclear weapons, ARC doesn't have the necessary data to update the missile status."

Admiral Waller leaned forward. "Ma'am, if I may suggest something."

She nodded.

"We discussed increasing the alert status to DEFCON 3 earlier, and you were going to take time to consider your decision," he said. "Unfortunately, I think that time has come sooner than you'd hoped. If we increase the alert status of U.S. nuclear forces, we would unlock the barrier between ARC's ISR component and the rest of the system. This allows the ARC system to receive a data infusion just like it does in advance of its monthly tests. That would improve the fidelity of our situation awareness which, I think, has become critical given the complete lack of data from our satellites."

Susan scratched her head as she wondered what other shocking limitations ARC would demonstrate in a crisis situation. Before she could formulate her next question, Elise jumped out of her seat and whispered something in her ear.

Susan held up her finger to signal a pause in the meeting,

and her advisors began discussing the situation among themselves.

"Ma'am, I just learned that Secret Service have taken Morgan Shaw into custody," Elise whispered. "Apparently, she tried to break into the White House in order to speak to you."

Susan held back a smirk of respect. *Well, I didn't see that one coming.*

Elise continued, "The agent who interrogated her said Morgan has information that's critical to national security. She's demanding to speak to you now."

Susan sighed heavily. "Go find out what she wants."

Elise nodded and moved toward the door.

Susan craned her neck. "But don't stay away too long, okay? I need you here."

Elise bobbed her head and ducked out of the room.

Turning back to the meeting, Susan looked at the admiral and smiled. "Thank you for your advice. Although I recognize the importance of additional information, I would like to avoid any escalatory moves if possible." Then she turned back to the STRATCOM commander on the video screen and tried to remember the question she'd wanted to ask before. "Okay, back to the ARC dashboard. What do the red lights mean?"

"ARC appears to be spinning up some nuclear retaliatory options," the STRATCOM commander said.

Susan gasped out loud. "What?" Now she understood why her advisors had been so entranced by the red lights earlier. "But I thought... Doesn't ARC produce options *after* it detects a nuclear attack? This is *not* the time for nuclear escalation."

"Yes, ma'am. This is just a preliminary planning stage in ARC's phased approach," he said.

"Do we know what caused ARC to start preliminary work on nuclear options?" Susan asked, scanning the dashboard for answers but receiving none. "We've determined the detected missile launches to be part of China's war game, but the ARC system doesn't register that. Does it still consider those missiles to be a threat?"

"Ma'am, the user interface on the ARC dashboard provides high-level information to avoid confusion during tight decision-making windows," the STRATCOM commander said. "It doesn't tell us how ARC reaches its conclusions or why certain indicators occur. The system designers simplified the dashboard to prevent humans from second-guessing the system and wanting access to more information."

"Then what does the dashboard indicate?" Susan asked abruptly. There was an uncomfortable tingle in her chest, and her breathing felt suddenly restricted.

"One blinking red light indicates an emerging threat," the STRATCOM commander said. "Two blinking red lights indicates that ARC has devised some preliminary nuclear options. That reflects the current situation."

"And what do the third and fourth red lights mean... should they start blinking?" Susan asked, flinching in anticipation of the answer.

"When the third light illuminates, the ARC system has selected a nuclear option and is ready to give the launch order," the STRATCOM commander said. "And the fourth red light indicates that ARC has transmitted a launch order for a retaliatory attack."

"No," Susan said, slapping her hand on the table, surprising even herself. Everyone else in the room jumped a little in their chairs. "I'm the commander in chief. I should be the one to evaluate nuclear options and give the order to launch. This ARC machine does not grasp the nuances in our circumstances with China or apparently possess any common sense. There's no reason to seriously consider nuclear options at this time. There is no nuclear attack under way."

"But ma'am, that's not how our command and control system works anymore," the STRATCOM commander said. "Once an imminent attack is detected, ARC begins functioning autonomously and improvises to provide the best possible nuclear options. The system is designed to act quickly rather than wait things out. Once things start to happen, we have an incredibly finite window in which to make a decision. If ARC detects a nuclear attack, it gives the order to launch nuclear weapons and you give—"

"I know full well how our system works," Susan said, her voice raised with a slight tremble. "And it's fucking wrong," she said, her nostrils flaring. "Look, we've just established that the ARC system doesn't have the data it needs to detect missile launches and discriminate between different missile types, warheads, and decoys. How can we expect it to devise effective nuclear options under such conditions?"

"Ma'am, the ARC system builds nuclear options based on sensor data it had before the loss of satellite communications," the STRATCOM commander said. "Granted, it's not one hundred percent perfect, and it would function much better at DEFCON 3. But given its ability to process massive volumes of data in seconds, I'd still trust ARC's conclusions over ours any day."

*And over mine as well, apparently.*

Heat rose behind her eyes as she glared at her advisors. She didn't doubt they were true patriots, each of them making sacrifices to serve their country. But many of them belonged to the nuclear priesthood; they had been blinded for decades by deterrence doctrine from the Cold War and now by the perceived superiority of machines. And here they all were. On the brink of nuclear war. At the mercy of a semi-autonomous system that needed its data fix in order to make an informed decision.

*How could we let this happen?*

For a few moments, Susan closed her eyes. Then an apocalyptic vision took shape in her mind. She saw an accidental nuclear war between the United States and China unfold in a series of horrific images—the terrible destruction of the first strike, followed by complete annihilation of the second and third strikes. People were burned alive, cities were destroyed, and civilizations ended in a flash. Hundreds of millions were dead in less than thirty minutes. The scourge of nuclear fallout would destroy millions of square miles of land, killing everything that lived and breathed. And nuclear winter would shroud the world in darkness. Tears welled in her eyes, and she opened them. Gazing out at the people around the table, she enunciated every word. "Shut. It. Down."

The faces around the table blanched. On the video screen, junior military officers scrambled to and fro behind their frazzled-looking commanders. The Situation Room turned into a cacophony of raised voices, her advisors arguing with each other.

Susan pointed to the military commanders at the video screen and said over the din. "You heard me. Take the damn thing offline right now."

# [ 48 ]
## CUSTODY

MORGAN
1640
West Wing
The White House

Morgan sat in complete darkness, her tail bone pressing into the hard, metal folding chair. Zip ties tightly bound her hands behind the chair so that she could barely move. She now questioned the wisdom of her crazy plan to get a message to the president. She recalled how she'd jumped over the turnstiles at the first security checkpoint for the Eisenhower Executive Office Building and made a mad dash toward the second one. Less than a minute later, she was tackled by two agents who were accompanied by a tenacious German Shepherd.

Five minutes later, Secret Service realized she was an employee on the National Security Staff who had had her access revoked earlier that day. After a brief interrogation, the agents seemed to understand the gravity of the information Morgan possessed and said they would check in with the president's staff.

As the agents were hauling Morgan down the hallway, presumably to have a word with the chief of staff, she'd stolen a glimpse of several other agents ushering the president's husband and daughter down the stairs to the bunker in the basement. Then the agents hastily stashed her in an empty broom closet in the West Wing and closed the door.

*Something has happened.*

Morgan's heart pounded as she raced through the possibilities in her head.

*The conflict is escalating with China. Or is it with the Russians?*

For all she knew, the president's advisors had no idea how Molotov, Koslov, and Vega were connected to the situation and were incorrectly pinning everything on the Chinese government.

*Are nuclear-armed missiles on the way?*

Just then, Morgan heard agents talking loudly over their comms, and heavy footsteps pounded down the hallway.

"Hey!" she shouted at the top of her lungs. "Are you going to leave me in here?" She kicked violently with her legs, and her chair moved forward a few inches. She now doubted the agents passed along her message to the president.

*I have to warn her.*

Then an idea came to her. She kicked with her legs again, and the chair moved forward. And again. A few more inches. She kept doing it until she came within inches of where the doorknob should have been located. She leaned forward slowly, feeling about in the dark for the knob with her chin, but she was still too far away.

*Dammit, can't reach.*

She kicked her feet one more time and moved another inch. Now she could reach the doorknob with her chin. Pressing hard against the cold metal, she turned her head slowly to the right. To her surprise, the knob moved with the touch of her chin.

*It's not locked!*

Morgan took a deep breath and moved the knob a bit further. When she reached a forty-five-degree angle, she thrust her chin in a quick downward movement in an attempt to unhook the latch. A soft click sounded, and the door opened inward a tiny crack, letting in a stream of light.

Unfortunately, Morgan was too close to the door to open it any further. She began to rock back and forth in her chair to slide it backwards. Once she was about two feet away, she reached out with her leg and hooked her foot around the edge of the door, pulling it wide open.

*I did it!*

The doorway looked out into a hallway on the first floor of the West Wing. She recognized her location from the 19th century oil painting hanging on the wall across from the door. Although she wasn't that far from the Situation Room, getting all the way there tied up in her chair would take forever. And someone was bound to notice her soon.

*I've already come this far.*

Morgan kicked with her feet again, inching the chair forward. But when she reached the edge of the doorway, the feet of her chair got caught on the hallway carpeting and wouldn't budge any further. She gave it another hard kick. Still no luck.

Just then, the president's chief of staff rounded the corner. Elise's eyes grew large when she spotted Morgan tied to the chair, lingering in the doorway, but she didn't seem surprised to see her there.

"What are you doing?" Elise asked.

"I need to speak to the president," Morgan said, a rush of adrenaline coursing through her body.

"So I hear."

"Take me to her," Morgan said, out of breath from her struggle. "Please."

"She's busy at the moment."

"Is the ARC system escalating a nuclear crisis with China?" Morgan asked. "Because that's what it's programmed to do."

Elise blanched and took a step back. "No, the ARC system is programmed to prevent nuclear war."

"You're wrong. I just came from the Pentagon where I spoke to Major Grace Lim, ARC's chief data scientist," Morgan said. "She caught Centoreum Tech's system engineer reprogramming the algorithms right before the test this afternoon. It was done at the company CEO's direction."

Elise's mouth fell open. "But why would he do that?"

"So that ARC would pass its test today," Morgan said. "The systems engineer was worried ARC would go nuclear during the simulation. And then apparently, it was switched back after the test by someone at Centoreum Tech. Given its programming, ARC may overreact to incoming data and recommend nuclear escalation."

Elise scratched her head. "But I thought that ARC was designed to protect our ability to retaliate above all else. That was supposed to prevent something terrible from going wrong with it."

Morgan nodded. "Exactly. And that's the problem. Major Lim and I figured out that ARC might consider protecting *itself* to be the most vital strategy for ensuring effective retaliation. But that's not the same thing as preventing nuclear war."

"You're saying that ARC might start a nuclear war to protect itself?" Elise asked.

"That's my theory. But I don't have any proof. It's just a gut instinct."

Elise frowned. "That doesn't make any sense." She went silent for a few moments. "What's your message for the president?"

"You won't take me to her?" Morgan asked.

"No. But I will give her a message."

"Fine. Tell President Tolley to listen to whatever Grace Lim says we need to do to resolve the issue. She's ARC's data scientist and works at the National Military Command Center. If you're in the middle of a nuclear crisis in the Situation Room, my bet is Grace is sitting along the back wall in the war room. She knows what's wrong with ARC and probably has a way to fix it. She's the only one who can save us from the end of the world if the ARC system runs amok."

Morgan hoped she wasn't overselling her friend's capabilities. But she couldn't imagine anyone else having sufficient agility of mind or critical thinking skills to find the solution to the problems of the ARC system. Not in the middle of a nuclear crisis.

*If Grace can't find a way, we're doomed to face our demise.*

Elise nodded and turned to go.

"Wait," Morgan said. "One more thing."

"What is it?" Elise asked curtly.

"I have something for the president. It's a drive from Jack. I don't know what's on it, but President Tolley is probably looking for it."

Elise looked at her expectantly. "Okay, where is it?"

"Um. It's stuffed in my bra. Sorry." Morgan's face flushed slightly, and then she shrugged helplessly. "It was the only place I knew Secret Service wouldn't look, in a quick search at least."

Elise moved her hand toward Morgan's blouse, but hesitated.

Morgan nodded, urging her onward. "Just take it. Oh, and tell the president that Grayson has a copy."

Elise shook her head in disbelief as she reached into Morgan's shirt and then into her bra. Her hands were clammy against her skin. When Elise found the drive, she pulled out her hand, turned, and walked back down the hallway.

"You're just going to leave me here like this?" Morgan asked, her voice raised.

Elise, still walking away, looked over her shoulder and shrugged.

# [ 49 ]
## RETALIATION ORDER

SUSAN
1650
Situation Room
The White House

With a deep sense of foreboding, Susan watched as an intense bustle played out in the Situation Room in response to her drastic order. Her stomach growled angrily, reminding her that she'd not kept anything down since breakfast. Hoping to tame the hunger, she took a long drink of cold water from the glass in front of her.

The commotion among her advisors and military commanders had mushroomed into complete chaos. And it quickly became clear to her that they were fearfully debating the long list of risks of her decision to shut down the ARC system. They didn't appear to be considering the risks of the alternative—the inevitability of nuclear war if they failed to stop ARC's automated escalation. No one dared to follow through with her orders, and no one questioned the dangers of not doing so.

ARC's server continued to purr unabated, and the projector displayed the hologram with the red blinking lights.

*They lack the necessary courage.*

Or perhaps it was a lack of faith in her leadership and discernment as commander in chief. The reasons didn't matter.

Susan leaned forward, opening her mouth to speak out again, but then stopped herself when Elise came rushing into the room with a frantic expression. Her body relaxed slightly at the sight of her chief of staff. She turned her chair in anticipation of the news from Morgan. "What did Dr. Shaw have to say for herself?"

"Actually, she shared some rather worrisome things about the ARC system," Elise said.

"I just ordered them to shut it down," Susan said bleakly, pointing to her advisors and military commanders. "No one will listen to me. They think I've gone mad."

Elise's eyes widened. "Ma'am, you're not going mad. Morgan said the Centoreum Tech systems engineer reprogrammed the algorithms to cheat on today's test. Otherwise ARC would have likely escalated to nuclear war in order to protect itself and its ability to retaliate. And then someone changed it back again after the test concluded."

Susan's jaw dropped. The news confirmed the worst of her fears—that the ARC system was fatally corrupted and would not help them stop a nuclear war. But because they found themselves in a tense nuclear crisis with China, her advisors would argue they had no choice but to rely upon the autonomous system in order to maintain effective nuclear deterrence. And if Susan let ARC make all the decisions for them, the machine would drag them into a nuclear war of its own choosing.

"She also gave me this," Elise said, handing her a small USB drive. "Morgan said Jack gave it to her, and you would know what it is. Apparently, Grayson has a copy as well."

*Is this the encryption key?*

Her brow furrowed, Susan stole a glimpse at Grayson and

turned the drive over in her hand a few times. She remembered what FBI Director Laski had told her about the encryption key. He said it was a small drive containing the key and a software program that would unseal the FBI files about Nightfall.

*Why wouldn't Grayson have told me about it?*

She stuffed it in her pants pocket. Grayson had lied to her. He'd been drinking. He'd removed Morgan and attempted to get rid of David. And now this.

*I may have misjudged Morgan. And Grayson.*

"Ma'am, one more thing."

Susan looked at Elise expectantly.

"Major Grace Lim is ARC's lead data scientist at the Pentagon. She's the one who caught the Centoreum Tech systems engineer making the changes. Morgan said she'd know how to fix the problem with the ARC system if things spin out of control."

"But how do we find her?" Susan asked, wrinkling her forehead.

"Actually, she should already be here. Morgan said she'd probably be sitting in the war room along the back wall," Elise said, glancing at the live broadcast on the video screen.

Susan cast her eyes along the wall, searching the back for a young woman in uniform, but couldn't spot her.

*She must be off camera.*

Just then, Admiral Waller leaned forward in his chair and cleared his throat. "Ma'am, we can't just turn off ARC in the middle of a nuclear crisis," he said, his deep voice cutting through the din. "If we do, we'll lose our command and control and won't be able to launch our nuclear weapons. You see, everything is currently linked to the ARC system. If we take ARC offline and shut it down, we won't be able to retaliate at all. Then we'll open ourselves up to a first-strike attack. Ma'am, I've told U.S. Strategic Command to stand down until we have more time to discuss our options." He jutted out his chin. "We simply can't afford to implement your order."

*I could fire them both for this.*

A loud crackle followed by a familiar voice resonated from the telephone speaker on the table. "Madam President, this is Isaiah. I'm on Air Force One as we speak," Burke said. "I just overheard the admiral's intervention, and I couldn't agree more. With China's lurking near the coast of Canada, we must prepare for the potential risk of nuclear war. The ARC system needs to remain online."

*Oh, so now the submarines do pose a risk.*

Susan grimaced at the pervasive insubordination of her senior advisors, her vision clouding and ears pounding. She clenched and unclenched her hands as she tried to get a hold of her temper.

She'd expected this kind of response from General Burke, but not from the admiral or her other military commanders. In the back of her mind, she wondered if President Monroe would have ever experienced such open defiance in response to a clear order. She pushed such thoughts away for the moment.

She got up out of her chair, inhaling a long breath. "If we want to prevent the worst from happening, we have to stop thinking like this." Susan began pacing the room back and forth, everyone's eyes following her every move. "We've been stuck in this rigid frame of mind all day." She stopped at the head of the table to face them and held out her hands. "I need you all to think long and hard about the consequences of holding steadfastly to your biases." She glared at each of the solemn faces around the table.

She raised her hands in the air. "For example, why do we assume China would want a nuclear war? Because they can catch us with our pants down? Because they can inflict more damage on us if they act first? Because our nuclear deterrence strategy has failed to deter them? Tell me in real terms. What could possibly be worth fighting a nuclear war, from China's perspective? Or from any country's perspective for that matter? If someone can tell me one good reason to fight a nuclear war and bring wanton destruction upon innocent people, then I'll reconsider my decision to shut down the ARC system."

An unsettled silence descended upon the room. Her advisors fidgeted with their hands, stared down at the table, and shuffled their feet.

"No one can offer a good reason why China would want to take us into a nuclear war?" Susan asked, still walking about the room.

"Ma'am, we can speculate endlessly about China's intentions," Burke said over the speakerphone, "but at the end of the day, we have to proceed on the basis of their aggressive actions to ensure deterrence holds. And we have no more powerful tool at our disposal to analyze all the available data than the ARC system. But I know you have a *special* relationship with the Chinese and *feel* close to them. And so, I urge you to also consider your own biases, Madam President."

Audible gasps of dismay rippled around the room at his suggestion. Several mouths remained open for a few moments. Unlike Susan, they were apparently shocked by Burke's latest testing of his boundaries with her authority.

But she was ready for him this time, thanks to Morgan. Deep down, Susan wondered if the SecDef knew the truth about the ARC system from his good friend and was in on it. Her new suspicions made her wish she could look the general directly in the eyes when she said, "And what about your *special* relationship with the CEO of Centoreum Tech? What about your cozy weekends at his family home on the Chesapeake Bay? Are those things clouding your analysis about the functioning of the ARC system?" Out of the corner of her eye, Susan thought she caught a flinch from Admiral Waller.

"Of course not," Burke said, his voice notably gruffer than before. But he appeared unable or unwilling to refute her points.

Susan walked to the other side of the room and gazed steadily at the speakerphone as if it were Burke. "Would it surprise you to learn that your good buddy has been cheating on the ARC tests this whole time, to fool you into blindly trusting the system?" She paused to wait for his response, but there was dead silence on the phone.

Before she could challenge him further, the ARC dashboard began beeping loudly, causing everyone to direct their gazes toward the center of the room. Susan froze in place and gaped at the hologram. Three new white-colored missile indicators appeared on the map over Siberia.

"What's happening?" Susan asked. Her eyes opened wide and her hand flew to her chest.

"Ma'am, it appears that the ARC system has detected the launch of three unidentified objects from a base inside Siberia," the NORAD commander said.

"But how?" Susan asked, her posture stiffening. She returned to her seat at the head of the table with her fists clenched. "I thought we didn't have satellite coverage?"

"ARC just received radar data from a nearby U.S. icebreaker ship in the Arctic, confirming the launches coming out of Russia, ma'am," the NORAD commander said. "But ARC can't reliably identify them since we lack other sensor data, and the icebreaker's radar is not designed to provide that information."

"What do we know about this Siberian missile base, then?" Susan asked, looking at Grayson, who was busy typing on his computer.

He nodded, still staring at his screen, raised his finger, and said, "It's owned by a private space tech company called Green Dragon Pioneers. We started noticing some construction activity around the area about two years ago. We've been tracking it as part of the CIA's regular collection on space activities. Our satellite imagery from the last few days shows the existence of three launch pads. They seem to have come out of nowhere, which leads us to believe they were constructed underground. They must have recently moved to the surface in preparation, presumably for today's launch. My staff informed me about it about an hour ago."

"What are the space pads for?" Susan asked.

"Ma'am, they're most likely space rockets for launching microsatellites into low earth orbit," David said.

"From a secret base in the middle of Siberia?" Elizabeth asked, narrowing his eyes. "And without announcing the launches in advance?" She shook her head. "All private companies in the space launch industry know better than that. No one wants to inadvertently cause nuclear war as a result of a false alarm."

"And why would a private company need three separate launchers to send a bunch of microsatellites into space?" Susan asked, her eyebrows raised. "That's a ton of tiny satellites."

"Ma'am, that's a good question," David said, rubbing his chin. "I read an intelligence report last month that suggested Russia plans to contest our supremacy in space. Maybe Russia has contracted with the private company to install its own space sensor layer to detect hypersonic missiles," he said, pressing his lips into a fine line. "That could also explain the secrecy about the launch. Maybe the Russian government plans to beat us in rebuilding—"

Before David could finish his sentence, a third red light on ARC's dashboard began to blink ominously, and everyone stared at it, dumbfounded for a moment.

Susan jabbed a shaky finger at it. "What does that light mean again?"

"Ma'am, the third blinking light means ARC has produced several nuclear options matching its threat assessment. It will soon select one and initiate launch procedures for a retaliatory attack," the STRATCOM commander said.

"But we don't know yet if we're under attack," Susan said, her voice raspy. "How could ARC know this if it can't get access to sensor data from our satellites? Can we stop it?"

"Ma'am, the command and control component of the ARC system is fully automated except for the rescind order. We can't stop it until after a launch order is given," the STRATCOM commander said.

Susan held up her hand. "You're saying that *this system* has the ability to launch our entire nuclear arsenal, and we have no way to stop it from doing so, prior to me issuing the rescind order? Surely, there's some sort of kill switch to prevent the accidental annihilation of millions of people in case I'm unable to do so?"

"No, ma'am. That would defeat the purpose of the ARC system."

*Defeat the purpose?*

Susan's eyes popped.

"Ma'am, the system is designed to operate in extremely tight time windows for nuclear retaliation," the STRATCOM commander said. "Any hesitation would not only reduce the credibility of our deterrent, it might also invite a first-strike attack by our adversaries."

Susan shook her head in utter disbelief and spoke her thoughts out loud. "In other words, you're telling me we've justified this calamity based on the sole assumption that the leaders of every nuclear-armed country secretly hunger for the desolation of a nuclear winter."

An awkward silence hung in the air as the harsh reality of their situation settled into the minds of her advisors. They weren't playing games anymore. This was not a simulation. The ARC system was about to launch a nuclear attack, and all they could do was sit in their chairs in the Situation Room and watch the horror unfold—at least until Susan could issue the rescind order.

"How long do we have until ARC transmits the nuclear launch order?" Elizabeth said, her face now white as a sheet.

There were many other pale faces around the table, and no one wanted to offer an answer.

"Ma'am, we've never come this far in a crisis with ARC before, not even in the monthly tests. We're not entirely sure what happens next," the STRATCOM commander said. "But for some reason, ARC has detected the threat of a nuclear attack and is responding accordingly."

"You're telling me we don't know when the countdown clock starts for the launch of our nuclear weapons?" Susan's eyes bulged. "Surely, that's written down in a software manual somewhere. Anyone care to look it up?"

Admiral Waller cleared his throat. "Ma'am, the ARC system will give the launch order upon detecting a nuclear attack. The dashboard will indicate this by displaying the detected missiles in red instead of white. The only way to potentially change ARC's planned course of action now might be to increase the alert status to DEFCON 3 as was recommended this morning. The ARC system will then receive a new data infusion from its ISR component and be able to provide better situational awareness. Perhaps it will learn that no attack is underway after all and stand down."

"And what if ARC misreads the new data, overreacts, and continues down its path toward nuclear escalation?" Susan asked.

"Ma'am, that's definitely a risk we need to consider," Admiral Waller said. "However, I'd point out that at DEFCON 4 our command and control system remains quite vulnerable to a first-strike attack. If ARC perceives a threat to its ability to retaliate, moving to DEFCON 3 should ease the situation. Once the ARC system registers enhanced deterrence against a first-strike attack, we might be able to persuade it to shift back into a defensive mode."

Susan mulled over her options for a moment. And then she realized she had none—that is, if she wanted any shot at reversing ARC's escalation.

"Fine. Proceed to DEFCON 3," Susan said, sighing heavily.

"Copy that, ma'am," the STRATCOM commander said. "We're raising the alert to DEFCON 3 now. We should see the effects of the data infusion into ARC within a few seconds. Also, our command and control units will begin dispersing immediately. More radars will be transferred to the early warning mission. Although the data infusion will be nearly instantaneous, full combat readiness under DEFCON 3 will take a few hours to fully activate."

Susan stared at ARC's dashboard in a daze, trying not to blink for fear she'd miss any change in its status. Her eyes darted back and forth between the red blinking lights and the white missile indicators. But nothing happened for what felt like an eternity.

Then, in an instant, the ARC dashboard lit up like a Christmas tree with two more white missile indicators appearing on the map in the Northwest Passage.

Now there were a total of three sets of indicators for missiles on ARC's dashboard. The new pair of missile indicators, presumably from the submarine flotilla as part of China's war game. The earlier ones in the South China Sea that were unresolved but must have reached their end destination. And the three missile indicators over Siberia they assumed were heading into space.

*Oh, thank God. They're all white.*

Susan exhaled sharply and rubbed her forehead. Her eyes darted to the red blinking lights on the launch panel.

*But will ARC stand down?*

A loud beeping sound emanated from the ARC computer, startling everyone. A second later, three missile indicators over Russia blinked several times and then turned red. Susan gulped as the fourth red light on the launch panel started blinking.

"What's happening?" Susan asked.

Admiral Waller blanched.

Another loud beeping sound alerted. Then the missile indicators over the South China Sea and the Northwest Passage flickered a few times. Then they turned from white to red as well.

Susan's jaw dropped, and her heart sank.

A ticker announced ARC's launch order in some text at the bottom of the dashboard, but Susan's eyes were too blurry to read it.

Then an airy, computerized female voice announced:

ARC HAS TRANSMITTED THE LAUNCH ORDER FOR AN ALL-OUT NUCLEAR WAR AGAINST RUSSIA AND CHINA

THE FIRST STRIKE WILL TAKE OUT THEIR COMMAND AND CONTROL SYSTEMS AND LIMIT DAMAGE FROM ANY FOLLOW-ON STRIKE AGAINST THE UNITED STATES

A NUCLEAR ATTACK WILL BEGIN IN T-MINUS TEN MINUTES

THE RESCIND ORDER MUST BE INITIATED IN EIGHT MINUTES AND FIFTY-THREE SECONDS TO CANCEL THE LAUNCH

A countdown clock appeared on the dashboard and began ticking down, second by second. Each second felt like a sickening thud in Susan's head.

She closed her eyes for a moment. Her mind drifted to her last minutes with Lucy and Blake, and her stomach knotted. The memories already seemed distant and hazy in her mind. An empty dullness filled her chest.

# [ 50 ]
## RESCIND ORDER


SUSAN
1700
Situation Room
The White House


Susan's eyes fluttered open less than a second later, sensing the ticking clock. It now read seven minutes and forty seconds. Adrenaline began coursing through her body, sending a gush of energy to her limbs. Straightening her posture, she searched the faces of her team of advisors and military commanders, expecting their input. But they all sat in stunned silence as if they were frozen in time, locked in a hypnotic trance.

"What's the procedure for giving the rescind order?" Her voice wavered while her eyes remained stubbornly glued to the dashboard. Her hands trembled as minutes and seconds seem to slip through her fingers like grains of sand.

More silence.

"Anyone?"

When no answer came, she looked down the table at Admiral Waller and threw her hands up in the air.

"Um, sorry," he said, clearing his throat. "Ma'am, you need to enter your 24-digit rescind order code from your nuclear code card into the keypad in front of you. That will cancel the launch order."

Elise rushed over to her and placed a small black case on the table in front of her. Susan pressed her finger on the scanner to allow for biometric authentication. The case lock released with a hiss and a click. She opened it and pulled out the nuclear code card and saw the 24-digit rescind order code. Without hesitation, she reached for the keypad and placed her finger over the first number.

"Um, ma'am, shouldn't we discuss the situation before you give the rescind order?" The STRATCOM commander asked, looking visibly flustered on the screen.

Susan gave him an incredulous look. "What more is there to discuss?"

"Ma'am, sorry. The ARC system has detected a nuclear attack from Russia and China. Shouldn't we confirm that this is a false alarm before we rescind the order?" he asked. "If we don't launch our weapons right away, we will lose our land-based intercontinental ballistic missiles when we absorb the first hit."

"Do you honestly think the Russians and the Chinese have just started a nuclear war with us?" Susan asked.

"Ma'am?"

"I'm asking a serious question."

"Ma'am, the ARC system—"

"I'm not asking you what the ARC system thinks. I don't fucking care what it thinks. I want to know, given your vast military expertise leading the U.S. Strategic Forces Command, whether you think it likely that Russia and China have launched a nuclear attack."

"Ma'am, it doesn't seem to make sense, but—"

"Have any missiles shown up on our radar yet?" Susan directed her steely gaze at the NORAD commander for a moment before returning to the countdown clock. It read six minutes and ten seconds.

"Not yet, ma'am. Our radars detect ballistic missile launches as soon as they're above the horizon," the NORAD commander said. "The phased-array antenna allows us to track missiles from multiple directions at the same time."

A weary voice sounded over the phone. "I think we need to take ARC's findings seriously," Burke said, breaking his long silence. "The lack of radar detection is not definitive for a few reasons. For one, Russia and China could have launched nuclear-armed hypersonic missiles which cannot be reliably detected by our radar. Second, radar systems are not infallible. That's why we use dual confirmation from satellites to detect nuclear attacks. And then there's the issue with someone taking our satellite early warning system offline. Wouldn't they also attempt to interfere with our radars? There is a chance that the ARC system knows something we don't. I'd rather not bet against it in favor of your gut feeling, Madam President."

Susan took a deep breath as heat flushed through her body. A few of her advisors and military commanders nodded in agreement. She couldn't fathom how they could have more trust in a machine than their own common sense.

She cleared her throat. "What do we know about the missiles?"

"Ma'am, the three unidentified objects launched from Siberia took off about four minutes ago and are above the horizon," the NORAD commander said. "From our sea-based X-band radar sensor data, their signatures suggest that they are space rockets rather than ballistic missiles. The rockets appear to be on a direct ascent pathway into low earth orbit at the moment."

"You're saying the three so-called missiles from Russia currently displayed in red on ARC's dashboard are actually rockets travelling into space?" Susan asked.

"Yes, ma'am," the NORAD commander said.

"That appears to confirm my theory," David said. "These rockets are sending microsatellites into space for Russia."

"Then why does ARC view these launches as threats?" Susan asked, scrunching her face.

No one answered. Because no one had the answer. None of her advisors truly understood what went on inside the deep neural network. And yet, they would rather place their trust in that thing than in her leadership.

"What about the red missile indicators over the Northwest Passage?" Burke asked over the phone. "We spent much of this morning discussing our concerns about China's two lost submarines. Granted, the ARC system seems a bit off, but it has detected a nuclear attack. What if it has misread the threat posed by the Russian missiles but gotten the threat of the Chinese missiles right?"

"Sir, we're not picking up any signals on our radars for those missiles," the NORAD commander said.

"So, we're not certain where they are headed," Burke said.

"They're probably part of China's war game," David said. "Just like the three earlier launches."

"I'm not sure I feel comfortable making such blind assumptions," Burke said.

"Why would China first launch three hypersonic missiles as part of its war game to put us on alert and then launch a surprise nuclear attack from its concealed submarines?" Elizabeth asked.

No one spoke up with an answer. Because it didn't make any sense.

"Ma'am, should we give the Chinese ambassador a call?" Elizabeth asked. "Maybe if Chen understands the situation, he could give us a straight answer about what's going on."

Susan eyed the clock again. Five minutes and twelve seconds. "No. We don't have time for a phone call. By the time you get him on the phone and explain the situation, the clock will have run out."

"It's possible that China noticed our increase in alert status to DEFCON 3," Burke said. "That could explain their changing course of action."

"Or what if Morgan was right about the defection scenario this morning?" David blurted.

Susan swung her head in his direction, her eyes wider than before.

"You're suggesting a rogue submarine commander might have launched nuclear weapons at us?" Elizabeth asked.

"It's possible," David said. "And it could explain why the ARC system has gone completely haywire."

"But we have still detected no missiles approaching our airspace," Elizabeth said, her eyes round and pupils dilated. "Ma'am, I'm worried this is a false alarm."

Out of the corner of her eye, the clock now read four minutes and fifty-one seconds.

"Does any of this really matter?" Susan asked briskly. "We need to make a decision. Here. Now. With the limited information we have on hand." She paused to take a deep breath. "The ARC system has issued a launch order for an all-out nuclear attack against Russia and China. If, as I suspect, the ARC system is wrong, and we allow the launch to proceed, then we will have accidentally killed millions of innocent people. We will also have started a nuclear war, which will lead to a retaliatory strike, devastating U.S. cities. If the ARC system is right, then we will absorb an initial blow from Russia and/or China, and our ability to retaliate may be compromised. Either millions of Americans will die. Issuing the rescind order is the only scenario that has the potential to avoid such a catastrophe altogether."

There was silence in the room. Most of her advisors stared pale-faced at the clock, which read four minutes and five seconds. Susan glanced at Elise, who gave her a grim nod.

Susan reached for the keypad, grabbed the nuclear code card, and entered the 24-digit number for the rescind order. Before pressing the enter key, she compared the entry screen to the number on her card to confirm she'd entered the right number. She inhaled deeply and pressed the button. Then she turned her attention to the ARC dashboard, the sound of her heart pounding in her ears.

The ticker at the bottom of the hologram dashboard announced that the rescind order had been received and acknowledged by the ARC system. Exhaling sharply, Susan leaned back in her chair and stared numbly at the table, wondering if she had mere minutes to live. Her eyes flickered back to the countdown clock, and she was jolted out of her seat.

The clock continued its countdown, second by second.

*Three minutes and fifty-eight seconds.*

# [ 51 ]

## COUNTDOWN

GRACE
1703
National Military Command Center
The Pentagon
Arlington, Virginia

*Did the president make the right call?*

Grace breathed steadily, consciously moving air in and out of her lungs in an attempt to calm her nerves. Her muscles remained tense, and she sat stiffly along the back wall of the war room. To her left, Arjun cowered in the corner with his face scrunched up. Grace wasn't sure if he was more horrified of what might come or that he'd helped to bring it about.

General Hawkins stood in front of the videoconference screen in the National Military Command Center, awaiting the president's next order. In the absence of the SecDef and chairman, he'd taken charge of operations in the war room. Surrounded by senior civilian and military leaders of the Pentagon, his eyes remained stubbornly stuck on the countdown clock. Grace suspected that General Hawkins, like everyone else, was waiting to learn the answer to her question.

*Did the president make the right call?*

Grace jerked her head toward the clock when she thought she saw the number of seconds change. She blinked her eyes a few times just to be sure. There were three minutes and fifty-eight seconds left. Then, three minutes and fifty-seven seconds. Three minutes and fifty-six seconds. She tilted her head and frowned.

*Wait. Isn't the countdown clock supposed to stop now?*

The ticker at the bottom of ARC's dashboard revealed an ominous announcement, followed by the same airy, female voice from before.

ARC HAS CANCELED THE RESCIND ORDER ISSUED BY THE PRESIDENT

IN THREE MINUTES AND FIFTY-FIVE SECONDS, ARC WILL TRANSMIT THE LAUNCH ORDER TO U.S. NUCLEAR FORCES

THE NUCLEAR ATTACK WILL COMMENCE AS PLANNED

A few people gasped audibly. Others looked to be in a state of shock. There were terrified faces everywhere she looked. The room felt as if it had dropped a few degrees in temperature. Even General Hawkins appeared visibly shaken by the news.

No one had seen this coming. No one had anticipated that the autonomous system would learn how to strip its designers of their autonomy. If someone had any inkling at all that something like this were possible with ARC, the Department of Defense would never have launched the system.

Grace sat stunned for a moment, trying to grasp the terrible truth.

*The rescind order has been rescinded. We're going to start a nuclear war.*

"Ma'am," General Hawkins said, "should we initiate emergency procedures for devolution and delegation of authority to ensure the line succession in the—"

"No," Tolley said. "General Burke will be arriving at Raven Rock shortly and will fill in for us if need be."

*We're probably going to die here if we don't stop ARC.*

Grace sank into her chair, leaned forward, and rested her face in her hands. She started going back through everything she knew about ARC's code in her head. But every time she followed a potential line of reasoning, she came to the same dead end.

*There's no way out of this.*

"Let's focus on stopping the ARC system from carrying out the launch," Tolley said on the video screen. "General Hawkins, I want to shut it down now."

"Ma'am, that's no longer possible," General Hawkins said, his chin dipping.

"What do you mean, no longer possible?" Tolley asked.

"Once the ARC system gives the launch order, the option to shut it down is disabled," he said. "The system engineers designed it this way for our own protection. The rescind order is the only way to stop ARC from carrying out the launch. And..." General Hawkins went oddly silent.

*For our own protection?*

Grace shook her head in disgust and glanced at the clock.

*Four minutes and ten seconds.*

Adrenaline pumping through her veins, she searched her mind frantically for a possible way out.

*Could Arjun tweak the algorithms again?*

"That has worked out really well for us, hasn't it?" Tolley seemed to finish the general's thought for him and then shook her head in apparent disbelief. When the president looked up again, she appeared to be looking intently at the screen as if she were looking for someone or something. "Where is Major Lim?"

Grace snapped her head up, her heart pounding even harder than before. She furrowed her brow.

*The president is asking for me?*

"Ma'am?" General Hawkins asked.

"I'm looking for Major Grace Lim," Tolley said. "Is she in the room with you or not?"

General Hawkins nodded and turned his head toward Grace, his hardened eyes landing squarely on her face. With an eyebrow raised, he motioned for her to hurry up and join him at the center of the room.

While the rest of the senior Pentagon leadership stared at her in surprise, Grace pushed her heavy legs forward as fast as she could toward him. When she came into view of the camera, the president gave her a half smile.

"Ma'am, how can I be of help?" Grace asked, her voice shaking. She stole another glance at the clock and gulped.

*Three minutes and fifty seconds.*

"Morgan mentioned you might know a way to get us out of this mess. She said you understand what's happening with ARC?"

*She did? But why would she say that?*

Grace's mind searched desperately for the reason. With everything that had happened, her conversation with Morgan felt so long ago. Then it came to her like a bolt out of the blue. She remembered Morgan's theory about ARC and quickly realized how that might explain their current predicament.

"Ma'am, ARC has overridden the rescind order because it defies the first rule of the system," Grace said.

"The first rule?" Tolley asked.

"Yes, ma'am, as its first rule, ARC is designed to optimize its ability to retaliate after a nuclear attack. The system engineers designed it that way because we believe the fear of retaliation has prevented nuclear war for decades."

Tolley rubbed her chin for a moment and said, "Then ARC must have perceived a severe threat to its ability to retaliate. Otherwise, it would not have launched this attack."

Grace nodded. "Yes, ma'am, that's what I'm thinking. It's possible that ARC encountered new technological and geopolitical developments for which there was no matching training data to guide its interpretations within the model of deterrence. As a result, ARC has improvised in order to uphold its first rule and adopted an offensive posture. If ARC is able to take out the nuclear arsenals of our adversaries with a massive first strike, it will be better positioned to retaliate in the next moves."

Tolley nodded eagerly. "ARC might not have to retaliate at all because Russia and China will be rendered incapable of launching a massive counterstrike. This would be the optimal situation from ARC's perspective."

"Exactly," Grace said. "But not so optimal for us."

"Then how do we fix this?" Tolley asked. "Is there a way to adjust ARC's programming?" She paused for a moment. "General Hawkins, you said we can no longer shut ARC down. Are we also unable to make changes?"

General Hawkins cleared his throat. "Ma'am, unfortunately, now that ARC has given the launch order, we are completely shut out of the system until the order is carried out."

"Actually, I may have an idea to get around that," Grace said tentatively. She turned to look at Arjun, who was now sitting up straight in his chair and appeared to be on alert. The urgent look on his face suggested he'd just had exactly the same thought she did. Turning back to the president, Grace said, "Ma'am, Centoreum Tech created an invisible back door to the ARC system to make changes to the algorithms. By invisible, I mean that it's undetectable to us at the Pentagon, but also to the ARC system itself. We could try using this back door to somehow modify the first rule of the system."

"You think that would convince ARC to back down and rescind its own launch order?" Tolley asked.

Grace nodded. "If we change the first rule of ARC from optimizing its ability to retaliate to something like preventing nuclear war instead, I believe it would cancel the launch and retreat into a defensive stance."

"Do it," Tolley said firmly.

Grace peeked at the clock and shuddered. *Three minutes and two seconds.*

"Um, ma'am. Unfortunately, I can't do it myself. I need help from Centoreum Tech's systems engineer. And he's right here in the room with us."

Tolley glared at the video screen, her face muscles tightening. "Is this the same engineer who cheated on ARC's tests?"

Grace grimaced. She craned her neck and saw Arjun squirming uncomfortably. "Yes, ma'am, but we don't have time to worry about his mistakes right now. Please... he's the only one who intimately knows his way around ARC's code."

*Two minutes and fifty seconds.*

"Fine."

Grace and Arjun hurried over to a terminal. From a standing position, she typed in her login, password, and authorization code to open a non-classified connection to the internet. Then Arjun sat down in front of the computer, and Grace hovered behind him. General Hawkins came up behind them, his arms crossed, a scowl on his face. Arjun began typing quickly. The other civilian and military leaders formed a tight huddle around them.

"I first need to get through the backdoor without being detected by ARC," Arjun said.

"But I thought ARC couldn't detect the back door," Grace said.

"We've now entered wartime operations, and ARC is programmed to prevent any type of intrusion," Arjun said. "With the front door disabled, it will be easier for ARC to detect us if we're not careful." He typed so fast, she couldn't keep track of what he was doing.

Grace glanced at the clock.

*Two minutes and twenty-eight seconds.*

"You need to hurry up," she said. "We have less than three minutes left."

"I'm going as fast as I can," Arjun said, wiping sweat from his brow. His fingers raced across the keys for several seconds. "There. I've entered the ARC system through the backdoor." He looked up at the hologram dashboard.

"What are you looking for?" Grace asked.

"I'm just checking for an alert message from ARC about a possible intrusion, but it looks like we're good."

When Grace glimpsed the countdown clock, she put her hands on her cheeks and bit her lip.

*One minute and forty seconds.*

"Now I need to find the right location in ARC's source code," Arjun said, staring back at the screen full of computer code. His eyes darted back and forth as he read each line.

Grace closed her eyes and focused on her breathing.

"Found it," Arjun said. "I found the code for the first rule."

Her eyes fluttered open. "Do you know how to change it?" Grace asked.

"Not sure," Arjun said. "I need to think for a moment. I'm not sure how to express a new first rule."

"Don't think for too long," Grace said. She stared at the screen and tried to make sense of the code. "If there's a first rule, wouldn't there also be a second rule? Maybe we could just cancel the first one."

"Yes, but it's not that simple. ARC's system is based on the model of deterrence, which consists of a number of rules that are considered together in order to prevent nuclear war. And the notion of preventing nuclear war might be too vague to change anything. The ARC system already thinks it's preventing nuclear war by removing the capability of our adversaries to fight nuclear war in the first place."

Grace wrinkled her brow. "Is there a way to limit ARC's use

of nuclear weapons?" Her eyes darted to the clock, and her heart sank. "What if we code the first rule to prohibit ARC from using nuclear weapons except after getting hit by a nuclear attack?"

*Fifty-five seconds.*

"Arjun, we're running out of time," Grace said. "Think."

"You mean like China's no-first-use nuclear policy?" Arjun asked.

Grace nodded urgently. "Instead of launch on warning, can we change the code to launch on attack?"

Arjun squinted at the screen, a bead of sweat running down his face. His fingers floated over the keys, moving as if he were designing code in his head, but he wasn't typing yet. Then his fingers touched the keyboard and began moving quickly, compelling lines of code to appear on the screen. Grace followed along but couldn't understand his logic.

Grace peeked at the clock again.

*Twenty seconds.*

Arjun pressed the enter key and exited the back door to the ARC system. He exhaled sharply and leaned back in his chair, his face blotchy with sweat. "I did what I could," he said. "I changed the first rule as you suggested. But I don't know if it will work."

Arjun and Grace turned to watch the clock. Grace held her breath and prepared her mind for the worst.

*Ten. Nine. Eight. Seven. Six. Five. Four. Three.*

The clock stopped at three. Grace's eyes opened wide.

*Did it work?*

All eyes in the war room locked onto the hologram dashboard. They waited in tense silence for a message from the ARC system. And then it came.

ARC HAS RESCINDED THE ORDER TO LAUNCH NUCLEAR WEAPONS

The war room erupted in loud cheers, whoops, and shouts of

relief. On the video screen, Grace saw President Tolley stand up and clap. For a moment, a rush of happiness filled her. But then she remembered. Grace glanced up at the hologram dashboard once more. The clock had stopped, but the missile indicators were still red.

*Wait.*

Grace cringed.

*Are we about to get nuked by China and Russia?*

## [ 52 ]
## ACCIDENTAL NUCLEAR WAR

SUSAN
1707
Situation Room
The White House

Susan exhaled sharply, her heart still pounding from the intensity of the last few minutes. But the celebration over shutting down ARC's nuclear launch ended quickly, and the silence in the Situation Room was deafening. Susan watched as the horrible realization spread across the faces of her senior advisors.

*This isn't over yet.*

Although they successfully prevented the United States from starting a nuclear war, an attack still might be underway by China or Russia. And they had no way of knowing for sure without access to the early warning satellite network—at least until ARC's radars picked up incoming missiles, or the ground underneath them shuddered from a detonation.

Susan's eyes darted to the red missile indicators on the ARC dashboard, and she tried to decipher the potential threat.

Three sets of indicators over the South China Sea, Siberia, and the Northwest Passage were still red. She was pretty certain the missiles over the South China Sea did not represent a threat. They were likely test launches by China and had presumably landed in the ocean more than an hour before. But it made no sense that ARC had switched them from white to red after being unable to resolve their final status. This unnerved her.

*Another issue to investigate when this is all over.*

NORAD had provided some minimal information about the missile indicators over Siberia. The details were scanty, but given their trajectory, it seemed they were most likely unannounced launches of space rockets from Russia. That left the unexplained missile indicators over the Northwest Passage where the submarines lurked deep underneath the surface of the ocean.

*But only two missiles?*

Recalling the earlier discussion about a decapitation strike, she'd counted up twenty-four missiles between the two submarines. Susan pressed her lips together and inhaled through her nose. In the unlikely event that China launched a first strike from its submarines, it would not be a limited one.

*It wouldn't make any sense.*

She cleared her throat and looked at her military commanders on the video screen. "Have we picked up any incoming missiles on our radars?"

"No, ma'am," the NORAD commander said. "And given the location of the launch in the Northwest Passage, we should have detected them within a few minutes or less, that is if they were heading for actual targets in the United States."

Susan furrowed her brow. "Commander, do you think these were test launches by the Chinese?"

"Our radars appear to be in working order, ma'am," the NORAD commander said. "I think we can safely assume these were test launches that are part of China's war game."

"What about the indicators over Siberia?" Susan asked, her eyes trained on the video screen again.

"Ma'am, without access to our satellite network, we don't have any further information about those launches at this time," the NORAD commander said.

"Might I suggest we reach out to our European colleagues," David said. "They might have been able to pick up the launches from their satellites and have more information."

"Get them on the phone," Susan said.

David reached for the conference phone in the middle of the table and began dialing the number. But before he could complete the call, a loud beeping began emanating from the ARC system, sending gasps around the room. The hologram dashboard at the center of the table flickered a few times, but all of the indicators remained the same.

"What's happening?" Susan asked, her pulse surging. On the video screen, her military commanders appeared to be scrambling to understand the latest development.

Then an airy female voice sounded from the computer.

ALL MISSILE THREATS ARE NULLIFIED

THERE ARE ZERO INBOUND MISSILES HEADING FOR
TARGETS IN THE UNITED STATES

On the ARC dashboard, all the missile indicators disappeared suddenly from the hologram, and the system's threat status decreased to a lower level.

"Is it over?" Susan asked, staring at the blank faces around the room.

No one answered, but stared in stunned silence at the ARC dashboard.

"Why did ARC change the status of the missiles?" Susan asked.

"Ma'am, our satellite network appears to be back online

again," the STRATCOM commander said, his voice shaky. "That could by why."

Susan's mouth fell open. "Is it fully functioning?"

"It seems so," he said. "We have to run some diagnostics to be certain, but ARC now appears to be receiving real-time data from our satellite sensors."

"Do we have a final status on all of the missiles ARC detected?" Susan asked, feeling some discomfort about their sudden good fortune.

"Ma'am, I just ran a full data query from our satellite network," the NORAD commander said. "There are no missiles over the South China Sea or the Northwest Passage. The launches from Siberia were three Russian spaceships, as we thought. Given the course of their trajectory and speed, they appear to be headed for the moon."

"The moon?" Susan asked. "How did we not see this coming?" She looked over at Grayson, who fumbled with a stack of papers. Her stomach gave a sudden loud growl, reminding her of the time and her basic needs.

"Ma'am, I'll get a team together right away to gather all existing intelligence on Russia's plans for their space mission on the moon," Grayson said.

"Thank you, Bill, that sounds good," Susan said curtly, folding her hands together. Then she turned toward the video broadcasting from the National Military Command Center. "General Hawkins?"

"Yes, ma'am?" he said.

"I want you to shut the ARC system down immediately," Susan said. "I think we've had one too many close calls with the system today, and I'd prefer to get some sleep tonight." Several of her advisors and military commanders tensed their bodies at the order. But this time, no one dared speak out against her. "Can you do that from the Pentagon?"

"Yes, ma'am," General Hawkins said. "We'll get on that right away."

"Great." Then Susan shifted her eyes to the video screen with her military commanders. "I want NORAD to decouple our early warning satellite systems from ARC. How long will that take?"

There was a long pause while a junior officer whispered into the NORAD commander's ear. "Uh, ma'am... we think it can be done within an hour," he said.

"Good." Susan now looked at the STRATCOM commander. "How long will it take for you to revert back to our old command and control systems?"

"Ma'am, we've kept our old systems in place for the sake of redundancy," he said. "We can have them up and running as soon as ARC goes offline."

"Excellent." Susan surveyed the room, looking each of her advisors in the face. "It's been quite a tense day, and we should all head home to spend time with our loved ones. Tomorrow, we'll get back to work. As our first action, we will launch full investigations into the ARC system and Centoreum Tech." She took a breath and continued. "I'd like to thank each and every one of you for allowing cooler heads to prevail. This has been to the great benefit of our government, the American people, and the entire world. Together, we prevented an accidental nuclear war from occurring. Although few people will ever know of your bravery and public service, they will be forever indebted to you. Goodnight everyone. Now go hug your families."

The meeting began to break up, and Susan nodded to Elise, who immediately understood her signal. Then she rose slowly from her chair, and a sudden sense of urgency filled her chest. But her body felt unusually heavy, and she could barely move. Her most recent surge of adrenaline had worn off, and the previous tingles underneath her skin had turned to aches of fatigue.

*I need to see Lucy and Blake.*

"Madam President, do you have a quick moment?"

Susan froze in her place, closing her eyes.

*Now what does he want?*

She'd wanted to avoid speaking to Grayson until she was ready for a confrontation. She wanted to ask him about the drive Harrison had given to him and his apparent vendetta against Morgan.

*Did he lie to me? Betray me?*

Or was there even more to it than that? Before turning around, she sighed heavily, took a deep breath, and opened her eyes.

When she looked at him, Grayson's face twisted up with tension. He leaned in closer to her, apparently not wanting anyone to overhear him. His eyes were bloodshot. But a strong whiff from his woodsy cologne drowned out any scents of alcohol she'd picked up earlier.

"Ma'am, I just received an email from FBI Director Laski," he said. "There's an urgent development. We need to alert Secret Service about Morgan Shaw and have them take her into custody right away." His gray eyes seemed to have recovered a bit of their usual brightness.

*He desperately wants her out of the way.*

"What does the FBI have on her?" Susan asked, her ears pricking up. She felt around for the USB drive in her pants pocket.

"Jack Shaw has fled the country on his private jet, and the FBI fears that Morgan may have escaped with him."

"Really?" Susan asked, feigning as much surprise as possible and avoiding direct eye contact.

*He doesn't know where she is.*

Grayson crossed his arms. "They've found DNA evidence that places Morgan Shaw at the golf course on the day that President Monroe died. They consider her the primary suspect for his assassination. Ma'am, she's the one who gave him the bottled wat—"

"Madam President, I beg your apology for the rude interruption," David said, eyeing Grayson with extreme distaste. "But I overheard you talking about Morgan and the president's death, and I want to set the record straight."

Susan motioned for David to continue over Grayson's visible objections, fingering the drive in her pocket.

"Morgan could not have possibly been at the golf course that day," David said. "I know this because she was in the office working all day, and we met several times to discuss various issues. If you don't want to take my word for it, you can check her badge swipes if you need to. Plus, I'm sure there's video footage of her comings and goings."

Grayson's eyes bulged in response to David's intervention. He opened his mouth to speak, but Susan held out her hand.

Giving Grayson direct eye contact, Susan said, "Morgan was taken into custody by Secret Service earlier this afternoon." She watched Grayson's face carefully and detected a slight relaxation in his jaw muscles at the news of Morgan's arrest.

"But ma'am..." David said, a look of panic on his face.

Susan held out her hand to stop him, turned to Grayson, and showed him the encryption key drive. "Whilst in custody, Morgan gave me this. Do you recognize it?"

Grayson flinched slightly. "Not at all," he said firmly. But the look on his face signaled dread.

*Strike one.*

"Well, that's interesting," Susan said. "Because Morgan said you possess an identical drive. Are you sure you don't know what it is?"

"No. How did she... but you were in the..." he stammered.

*Strike two.*

Susan nodded quickly as her chief of staff stepped back into the Situation Room. Their eyes met briefly, and Susan received the confirmation she was looking for. Turning to Grayson, she said, "Elise ducked out to talk to Morgan about an hour ago... in the middle of our nuclear crisis. Apparently, Morgan attempted to break into the White House, desperate to deliver some important information to me about the ARC system." She paused for a moment to catch her breath. "Bill, you're the one who convinced me to strip Morgan of her credentials and deny her access to the White House. Without her insights, we might not be standing here right now... the whole world might have gone up in a cloud of nuclear dust. You've had it in for her since Harrison died... why?"

"Ma'am, the FBI director..."

"Don't FBI director me, Bill," Susan said. "I know what you did. You had Laski look into Morgan because you wanted her out of the White House. Apparently at any cost. And I want to know why. Tell me what is on this drive that you don't want me to know about."

"I don't know," he said.

*Strike three.*

Susan gave Elise a subtle nod.

Grayson took a few steps backward as two dark figures entered the room. He stared at Susan in stunned silence as two Secret Service agents approached him, handcuffs at the ready.

# BOURBON

GRACE
1800
E Ring, The Pentagon
Arlington, Virginia

Grace took a small sip from her tumbler, the lukewarm liquor tingling the back of her throat as she swallowed. Standing in a sitting room outside the chairman's office, she huddled in a tight circle with Admiral Waller, General Hawkins, Colonel Martinez, Arjun and several others. Captain Dietz was notably absent.

Everyone except Arjun held a glass with two fingers of the finest bourbon from the chairman's hometown in Kentucky. Admiral Waller said he kept the bottle in his office for special occasions.

"I'd like to make a toast to our two young heroes," Admiral Waller said. "Because of their quick thinking and courage under heavy fire, they saved us all from our worst nightmare." He lifted his glass and nodded at Grace and then at Arjun. "Today, I tip my hat to Major Lim and Mr. Sharma."

Grace's face flushed. Arjun dropped his chin to his chest and attempted to smile.

"Hear, hear," General Hawkins said, a broad grin on his usually stern face. It was the first time she'd ever seen him smile. For an old guy, she'd admit he was quite handsome.

Arjun lifted his glass of water as the rest of them lifted their bourbons, enjoying a long sip of whiskey in silence. Then the chairman pulled General Hawkins aside for what appeared to be a private conversation.

Someone nudged her in the arm from behind, and Grace turned to see Colonel Martinez smiling at her.

"I can't seem to get a hold of Morgan," Martinez said.

"Me neither."

"She must still be at the White House," Martinez said. "Otherwise the President—"

"—would never have called on me in the middle of a national security crisis?" Grace said, finishing his sentence. She still wasn't sure how she felt about Morgan thrusting her into the spotlight.

"Hey, you did good," Martinez said, appearing to read her doubt. "Morgan obviously knew you could do it or she would have never told the president to ask for you."

The heat in Grace's cheeks intensified. "But it was Morgan's theory about the ARC system that saved the day."

"No, that was all you," Martinez said quickly. "Morgan planted the idea, but you thought at the right time and came up with a workable solution. And of course, Arjun's swift translation of your idea into code was critical." He nodded at Arjun, who was standing awkwardly off to the side.

Arjun shuffled over to them, a shy look on his face.

"Any word on your mother?" Grace asked, trying not to sound cold. Even if Arjun had helped her save the world, she'd not forgotten everything he'd done to sabotage her job for the past several months.

Arjun nodded. "I got a text from my dad. The doctors think

my mom's symptoms are caused by a bacterial infection from her surgery last week. She's still in the hospital receiving fluids and antibiotics, but her cancer is most likely in remission. We don't know for sure. They're still running some tests."

Grace half-smiled at him. "That sounds like good news, all things considered." She paused, taking another sip of her whiskey.

Arjun turned to her and grabbed her arm, an urgent look in his moist eyes. "Grace, I swear it wasn't me who reverted ARC back to its previous version," he said, his voice choked with emotion. "I meant what I said. I want to help you warn Pentagon leadership about the problems with ARC. I promise I didn't go back on my word."

"I know," Grace said firmly.

Arjun's eyes widened. "You know I didn't do it?"

Grace nodded. "Well, Morgan and I checked the event log. We know you didn't do it because you'd need a Fed to authorize access to a non-classified internet connection to use the backdoor. It must have been your CEO or someone working for him who reverted the ARC system. I assume Mr. Warren gave you instructions to put all the changes into a single update?"

Arjun nodded sheepishly. "If only I had..."

Martinez clapped him on the back. "Arjun, you were operating under the orders of your CEO. Anyone in military service would understand the extreme pressure you faced. And despite that, you decided to do the right thing. That took enormous courage. I'll make sure the chairman becomes aware of your actions when the investigation begins. And I'm sure Major Lim will back you up as well."

Grace nodded, inhaling slowly. Arjun had come through in a major way. Not just anyone would have been able to write code with the threat of nuclear war hanging over their head.

*Just as long as Dietz gets what's coming to him.*

"What are you going to do about your boss when he finds out?" she asked.

Arjun flinched. "I'm pretty sure Mr. Warren will be too distracted by his own trouble to bother with me. Also, he's no longer my boss."

"You quit?" Grace asked.

"I should have done it a long time ago," Arjun said, his face falling.

"Don't worry, Arjun," Martinez said, giving him an encouraging smile. "Once the dust settles on the investigation, you'll get snapped up by another contractor in no time."

Grace's smartphone buzzed. She looked down to see a text from Zach and nearly jumped out of her skin.

*Crap. I forgot to call him back.*

Then she read the latest text, and the blood drained from her face.

THIS ISN'T WORKING FOR ME ANYMORE

I'VE PACKED UP YOUR THINGS AND SET THEM IN THE HALLWAY

PLEASE LEAVE YOUR KEY AT THE FRONT DESK

Grace stared at the words for several moments, trying to absorb the development. She frowned briefly at the thought of being homeless and shrugged. There wasn't much that could bother her after a brief flirtation with the end of the world.

"What happened?" Arjun asked.

"Oh, my boyfriend just broke up with me. On a text." The corners of Grace's mouth turned upwards as a huge wave of relief filled her chest.

## [ 54 ]

## REUNITED


SUSAN
1815
Executive Residence
The White House


Susan lay sprawled across the couch in the West Sitting Room with her eyes closed, the weight of her body sinking deep into the cushions. She focused on her breathing and tried to release the tension from the day. Penny had nestled herself in between Susan's legs, providing a comforting warmth. She couldn't remember a day when she'd felt more spent and aware of every bone in her body.

*Today, we almost started a nuclear war for no reason.*

"Are you finally going to tell me what happened?" Blake asked tentatively.

Right after the crisis had passed, Susan rushed down to the bunker to collect her family. After several rounds of bear hugs from Blake and her daughter, Lucy went up to her bedroom for a much-needed nap. Blake had asked her this question then, but she was unable to answer him. She wasn't ready to process everything that had happened.

With Lucy tucked into her bed, Susan and Blake had headed down to the White House kitchen to grab a small bite for dinner. Despite her extreme hunger, she was unable to down a thing. While she sipped some hot mint tea, Blake had regaled her with stories about his harrowing experience in the bunker. Apparently, he'd fielded hundreds of questions about the Yooks and the Zooks and their eclectic arsenal of weaponry.

In retrospect, Susan was rather glad that he had a special language to explain to Lucy what was happening in a way she could understand. She had half a mind to force her advisors and military commanders to read the Dr. Seuss book and report back their findings. They might learn a thing or two.

Now back in the West Sitting Room, Susan's eyes fluttered open, and she turned her head to gaze at her husband's handsome face. She smiled faintly and said, "Well, we almost launched our entire nuclear arsenal at Russia and China today. So, there's that."

Hearing the words pass through her lips made the entire experience feel surreal. Perhaps she'd endured a horrible nightmare and had just woken up on the couch. Or maybe she'd gone through the most intense trial of her political life. Either way, the terrible moments she'd spent in the Situation Room, looking down the shafts of hundreds of ballistic missiles, seemed a million miles away.

Blake furrowed his brow. "But I thought we were in a conflict with China."

"It turns out we were in a conflict with no one but ourselves," Susan said wryly. Recalling the last few moments when she thought a nuclear war would be starting shortly, she took several deep, calming breaths. "NORAD confirmed there were zero inbound missiles heading for targets in the U.S.," she added grimly. "And then our early warning satellite system came back on... just like that. Our blind faith in a machine nearly led us into nuclear war. There's really no other way to say it."

Her thoughts about the ARC system and everything that had gone wrong kept going round and round in her head. Until now, she'd not fully understood the true implications of maintaining the ability to retaliate against a nuclear attack. For better or for worse, keeping that capability conceded some value to fighting a nuclear war. Because if all countries decided it would never be worth fighting such a war in the first place, no country would need the ability to retaliate.

*There's nothing worth fighting a nuclear war.*

A strong sense of determination rose in her chest. Someone desperately needed to break the chain of such thinking before it was too late. When she became VP, she never imagined herself playing an important role in solving questions about nuclear weapons. That was understood to be Harrison's territory. Here and now, she resolved to use the remainder of her presidency to focus on ridding the world of such a dangerous scourge. But first, she had a big mess to clean up with Nightfall, the ARC system, and Harrison's assassination.

"I took the ARC system offline today," Susan said wearily.

Blake raised his eyebrow. "Oh really?"

"Yep," she said, sighing heavily. Now she regretted bringing it up because she didn't have the energy to tell him the reasons for her decision. "I also ordered a full investigation into Centoreum Tech and fired General Burke."

Blake sat up straighter and stared at her with round eyes. "You fired Burke? How did he take it?"

Susan grinned broadly. "Not well, as you can probably imagine. This whole time, he's been vying for the VP slot and undermining my leadership behind the scenes. I called him right after the crisis was over, and he berated me for my decision-making in the Situation Room and taking the ARC system offline... I couldn't believe it. If it were up to him, we'd have started a nuclear war. And for what? I realized in that moment that in order to do this job right, I need to clean house."

"Do you think it's wise to create such a forceful enemy on the outside of your administration?" Blake asked, his forehead wrinkling.

"I know the saying... keep your enemies closer. But it's harder for Burke to put a knife in my back if he's farther away from me." She grinned at Blake. "Plus, I plan to surround myself with stellar people who are capable of protecting the agenda I want to set for my presidency."

Blake nodded.

"You know, if it weren't for some super smart women on my staff, we'd all be nuclear toast by now."

"Promote them all," Blake said, giving her a playful smirk. "They've definitely earned their paycheck today."

*That and much more.*

She went silent for a moment, thinking again about what she should do about Morgan. The woman had surprised Susan with her loyalty. Clearly, there was more to Morgan than Susan initially thought. She'd asked the Secret Service to keep Morgan in custody until she got a chance to talk to her. But now it was getting late, and it was unfair to torture the woman any longer. Reaching into her pocket, she felt for the encryption key drive and turned it over in her hand a few times.

*If this is what I think it is...*

There was a soft knock at the door, and Elise stuck her head in. "Madam President?"

"What now?" Susan asked a bit too sharply.

Elise's face twisted up slightly. "Sorry to interrupt, ma'am... the Chinese ambassador is here to see you."

"Donghai?" Susan perked up right away, coming to a seated position on the couch.

"I figured after everything that happened today, you'd want to speak to him," Elise said.

"Yes, of course," Susan said, getting up off the couch. "You were right to bother me. I'll speak to him in the Oval Office in a few minutes."

Elise nodded and closed the door.

"What do you suppose he wants to talk about?" Blake asked, frowning.

Susan paused in front of the wall mirror to straighten her hair. "Not sure. Maybe he finally has permission to speak freely about those pesky submarines that started this whole mess."

Blake got up out of his chair and walked over to her, his eyes twinkling. Before she could resist him, he grabbed her into his arms as if they were dancing. He dipped her gracefully and kissed her deeply.

Then he lifted her gently back up, caressed her face, and pushed a stray hair behind her ear. "I don't know if I've told you this lately... but you amaze me. And I don't know how I got so lucky."

Susan pressed her lips together and kissed him, moisture filling her eyes. "Right back at you, babe."

# [ 55 ]
## DISCLOSURE

SUSAN
1830
Oval Office
The White House

Susan sat on the couch across from Donghai with her legs crossed and a hot mug in her hand. They were both sipping green tea and munching on fresh-baked buttermilk cookies from the White House kitchen. Susan was glad the staff was oblivious to what had happened earlier that day. And not just because her appetite had returned so she could enjoy some warm cookies.

Her old friend was dressed down compared to their lunch earlier, wearing a long-sleeved oxford shirt, light beige trousers, and a leather belt. Donghai smiled at her warmly, and the crow's feet around his gentle eyes reappeared. "I'm sorry about earlier today. I was on strict orders not to say anything. At least not until my leadership had a handle on the situation. I know you must have been gravely disappointed. And for that, I'm sorry."

*If only he knew how close we came...*

"But you can tell me now?" Susan asked, sipping her tea.

Donghai nodded. "You were correct about the hack of the Chinese news handle and the deep fake videos. We experienced a series of cyber incidents throughout the day and will be investigating them thoroughly. When we have better answers, I will share them with you."

"Thank you. That would be much appreciated," Susan said carefully. She was still feeling blindsided by their lunch and not yet ready to resume familiar conversation as longtime friends. "My staff is also conducting its own investigation. I believe they have discovered the identity of the hacker and some potential connections to Russia."

Donghai raised his hand, signaling that he was not finished with his earlier statement. "I must explain the other part of the situation which led to a complete lockdown by my government," he said. "You asked about our two nuclear-armed submarines in the Northwest Passage at lunch..."

Susan sat up a bit straighter.

"I couldn't say this to you before... but one of the two submarines was unmanned. Due to some faulty programming, it went haywire. And for a time, we lost positive control over the submarine, along with all of its nuclear weapons. The other nuclear-armed submarine was manned and went after it, to make sure we didn't lose track of it. We sent a team of divers to retake control of the submarine."

Susan's mouth fell open. "You're deploying autonomous submarines carrying nuclear warheads?"

Donghai shook his head. "Not yet. This was meant as an initial deployment test, which failed with potentially catastrophic results for the plan."

"You had no way to recall the submarine when it went off track?" Susan asked.

"No," Donghai said. "We designed the submarine as fully autonomous to avoid the usual cyber vulnerabilities associated with network connectivity. Fully autonomous submarines can stay operational for much longer periods, are harder to track, and are better at evading anti-submarine weapons. We did ensure that the submarine was designed to return to the flotilla if there were any software errors. But apparently, that programming didn't work as intended. Anyway, we were too embarrassed about the matter to tell you earlier today."

Susan shuddered internally. *Embarrassed? China's attempt to save face could have been very costly.*

Still, she couldn't bring herself to tell him how close they'd come to blowing up the entire planet with nuclear weapons as a result of their embarrassment. If the Chinese had been more transparent about what was happening from the start of the day, Susan would have immediately taken the ARC system offline when it recommended taking offensive actions in response to China.

Donghai bowed his head to her. "I sincerely hope this didn't cause your government too much alarm. We did notice some recent mobilization activity, indicative of a higher alert status. For this reason, my government decided it was imperative to notify you right away. So there would be no misunderstanding."

*Better late than never?*

"Did you launch missiles from your submarines in the Northwest Passage by chance?" Susan asked.

"While we searched for the submarine, we wanted to keep up the appearances of our war game activities and conduct two test launches," Donghai said.

*Keep up appearances...*

Susan took a deep breath and was silent for a moment. "Thank you. I do appreciate the clarification," she said with a warm smile. "I hope that we continue to see value in full transparency between our two countries."

Donghai nodded.

"I do have one more question if you don't mind," Susan asked, touching her chin. There was something still nagging at her.

"Please ask," he said.

"You said that your unmanned submarine failed due to a programming error. You're certain it wasn't hacked."

Donghai stiffened his posture. "As I indicated earlier, we eliminated cyber vulnerabilities of the design through minimal communication."

"Yes, of course. I just wanted to be sure." Susan studied his face for a moment but couldn't detect any obvious signs of deception. Donghai had always been skilled at holding his cards close to his chest. And she'd already gotten more information than she expected.

Elise walked into the office with a deep frown. "Ma'am, I'm sorry to interrupt again, but Drew Hudson and Tori Scott from *The Counter View* are here for the interview you promised. I'm so sorry. It totally slipped my mind."

*Crap. The interview.*

Susan felt the blood drain from her face. She'd also completely forgotten about the autonomous weapons bill sitting on her desk, waiting for her signature. Susan rose from her chair, and Donghai followed suit, a wistful look in his dark eyes.

Although she understood the difficulty of his position, she wasn't quite ready to return to their friendship as it had been before. But she wasn't worried. They'd been friends for a long time and would overcome the small bump in the road.

"Thank you for stopping by this evening," Susan said. "It means a lot." She reached out to shake Donghai's hand. "I'll call your office soon to arrange a playdate between Lucy and Nianzhen, if that's okay."

"That would be lovely," Donghai said. "And thank you for seeing me. I know you might not have agreed to the impromptu meeting if it were not for our friendship. Please do not think for a second that my behavior today did not weigh heavily on me."

"I didn't think any such thing," Susan said, bowing her head.

Donghai bowed his head and took his leave.

# [ 56 ]

## TERMINATOR CONUNDRUM

DREW

1915

Oval Office

The White House

Drew gazed at the famous *Resolute* desk standing in front of him, still in utter disbelief at his surroundings. His chest tingled when he thought about how he'd started out the day—he'd gone from sleeping on the pavement outside the White House to having a sit-down with the president inside the Oval Office.

Of course, none of it would have happened if it weren't for Tori Scott interviewing him and making him famous with the video clip. She'd reminded him of that several times. And her huffy tone gave him pause about her real motivations for dragging him into all of it.

The Oval Office was even more grand than he imagined, and the pictures didn't do it justice. The cameraman situated a light stand behind President Tolley's empty chair and then turned on the camera that was facing Drew. The large, round black lens stared back at him, sending a shiver up his spine. Even though he'd spoken into one several times that day, he wasn't sure if he'd ever get used to the eerie feeling of being watched by millions of people.

*At least this interview isn't live like the last one.*

When they'd arrived at the White House, Tori had pushed the president's chief of staff hard for a live interview, claiming that was the deal she'd struck with her executive producer. But Elise Russell wouldn't back down, forcing Tori to accept a recorded interview or deal with a cancellation. She'd also insisted on having the final say on how the video was cut before it was released. Drew had heard Elise mutter something about the hack job *The Counter View* had done with Drew's interview earlier that morning, and he'd smirked.

Drew craned his neck to watch as the cameraman continued to set up the light and camera behind where Drew and Tori were sitting. Every minute of the discussion would be captured on the two cameras.

Behind him, Drew heard new voices, and he turned to see President Tolley walk into the office with her chief of staff. Drew and Tori jumped up, and the president smiled and shook their hands. Elise took a spot along the wall behind the president's chair. Tori and Drew quickly found their seats once more. Drew focused on steadying his breathing to calm his rapid heartbeat and avoided direct eye contact.

President Tolley was far more attractive in person than on TV. Even though she was dressed down in a pair of tan slacks and a short-sleeve navy top. Her dark-brown hair tied into a tight bun accentuated her bright blue eyes, which seemed to leap out and grab at him. Every time he caught her eyes looking at him, he got a fluttery feeling in his stomach.

Tori motioned for her cameraman to begin rolling the camera.

"Madam President, thank you so much for the opportunity to sit down with you this evening," Tori said.

"My pleasure," President Tolley said, her legs crossed casually. "But we both know why we're really here." She gave Tori a half smile and then turned to Drew. "Mr. Hudson, you caused quite a stir this morning that I can't say I was thrilled to hear about, even if *The Counter View* is my husband's favorite show and you are his favorite student." She grinned and gave him a wink, making his face flush. The president turned back to Tori. "Anyway, I was eager to meet this impressive young man you discovered today and to hear what he has to say. I'd like to have an open discussion with Mr. Hudson about autonomous weapons systems. But I don't have much time left this evening. So, shall we begin?"

Tori frowned slightly before launching into her first question. "Madam President, I understand the autonomous weapons legislation is currently on your desk and waiting for your signature. Have you decided what you're going to do?"

President Tolley ignored the question and turned to Drew instead. "Mr. Hudson, I was rather impressed by the arguments you made on *The Counter View* today. What do you think I should do?"

Drew jerked his head back. *She's asking me for my opinion?*

For a moment, his mind went blank. He hadn't expected to be consulted for advice. And definitely not on camera. Drew's heart pounded hard as he struggled to find something insightful to say.

President Tolley gave him an encouraging smile. "Imagine you were president for a day and had to make this decision on behalf of American citizens. Would you sign or veto the bill?"

"I guess I'm not sure," Drew said, scratching his head. "It's much easier to have an opinion when I'm not the one responsible for the decision." He grimaced at her.

President Tolley tilted her head and laughed out loud. "Touché. But you argued so vigorously against fully autonomous weapons systems earlier today. You don't think we should field such systems on the battlefield?"

"No," Drew said firmly. "I think it would be a grave mistake. But if I'm thinking about it from your perspective as the president, I'm not sure you have much of a choice. Ironically, I've heard the decision called the Terminator Conundrum. No one wants to build the Terminator, but everyone feels compelled to do it when one country goes down that road."

Next to him, Drew could feel Tori getting restless. She was crossing and uncrossing her legs and shifting around in her chair. He couldn't imagine Tori enjoying being cut out of the interview but it wasn't up to him.

"But don't I have a choice?" President Tolley asked. "I could choose to veto the bill and take a stand if I wanted. Isn't that what you demanded from me this morning?"

"Um, I didn't mean..." Drew stammered.

"It's okay," President Tolley said, reaching out her hand. "You were right to call me out. It's my prerogative as president to make the choice. If the United State refuses to field such systems, maybe other countries would follow our lead and refrain from developing autonomous weapons systems as well."

*She agrees with me?*

"And what if some don't?" Drew asked, suddenly feeling overwhelmed with the burden of responsibility.

*Did I convince the president to veto the bill?*

"That's my worry as well," President Tolley said. "I'm curious what you think about our history with nuclear weapons. Do you think the U.S. had a choice in developing nuclear weapons during World War Two?"

"No," Drew said quickly and then thought for a moment. "But that situation was different. Back then, we were in the middle of a world war, and Germany was winning. We also thought they might be developing nuclear weapons. The U.S. needed whatever advantage it could get in the war, and we needed to get there first. Today, we're not at war."

"But as you implied before, if we don't get there first with our own autonomous weapons systems," President Tolley said, "then Russia or China might beat us to the punch and win a key advantage on the battlefield. That's the thing I wrestle with most. If I decide to veto the bill today, am I causing harm to the American people in the future? Will I be responsible for the loss of lives in some future war?"

Drew shrugged. Now that he considered all the ramifications, he was no longer as comfortable with his black and white views about autonomous systems.

"There's something else," President Tolley said. "There's a disproportionate power in being first that can be used for good. We saw that with nuclear weapons as well. If the United States develops and fields autonomous weapons systems first, then the U.S. could help set global norms on restraint. But if our country doesn't have any of these autonomous weapons systems itself, it would be a lot more difficult for us to tell other countries how they should be used, controlled, and eventually eliminated."

Drew wrinkled his brow. "Are you saying we need to develop them first in order to one day get rid of them?"

*That would be ironic.*

President Tolley nodded. "Well, that's my fear. I also wonder if my energy is better spent dealing with an older problem which we might be more ready to fix."

Drew scrunched his face. "You mean, nuclear weapons?" He stole a glance at Tori. Her face said it all. She wasn't happy with the way the interview was going. But the president didn't seem to notice. Or maybe she didn't care. Drew suppressed a smirk.

President Tolley nodded. "If we can't solve the nuclear weapons problem, how can we talk about ridding the world of autonomous weapons systems? It seems we humans are finally ready to learn our lesson when it comes to nuclear weapons. I can't think of any country's leader who thinks nuclear war would be a good idea."

"Madam President, are you saying humans have to learn our lessons the hard way?" Drew asked. "That we have to develop autonomous weapons systems to experience how terrible they are before we decide to eliminate them?"

President Tolley nodded, and her face looked suddenly grim. "I'm worried that we do."

Drew felt a new surge of energy in his chest. "But what if instead of fearing that we can't stop countries from developing autonomous weapons systems, we decide to have the courage to persuade them not to," Drew said. He took a breath and then continued, "What if we do the unexpected? You could veto the bill and immediately call for arms control negotiations for autonomous weapons systems. Didn't you just successfully conclude the clean energy deal with China? I seem to recall many pundits claiming you wouldn't achieve any meaningful steps on that initiative. But look at what you accomplished. Maybe the U.S. and China could lead the world on this issue together."

"Mr. Hudson, you've given me a great deal to think about," President Tolley said, clasping her hands together loosely. She went silent for a moment and then looked back up at him. "I'm wondering if you might like to work for me."

Drew squirmed in his chair, his heart now pounding. "At the White House?"

She smiled. "Wouldn't you like to help me head up a multilateral negotiation to limit autonomous weapons systems? We need brilliant young people just like you to lead the way," President Tolley said, smiling broadly at him. "Of course, it would be an internship to start off, but then we'd figure out how to create a position for you."

Drew's heart felt like it was shrinking for a moment. "Ma'am, I'd be honored to work for you... but I can't afford to work for free. And I just lost my job because of—"

President Tolley laughed out loud. "For free? You don't think the president of the United States can find the funds to pay her interns? Don't worry, we'll pay for your time. An internship is just the fastest way we could bring you on board. Are you interested?"

"Yes!" Drew nodded quickly, his cheeks flushing red. "Yes, ma'am. Thank you very much. I'm sorry... I'm confused. Does this mean you've decided to veto the bill?"

Before the president could answer his question, Tori said, "Madam President, I have a source inside the Pentagon who claims that our early warning satellite network went offline today, nearly leading to a nuclear exchange."

*What?*

Drew turned to look at Tori, his face aghast.

"I don't know what you're talking about," President Tolley said, her face turning a few shades paler than before.

"My source at the Pentagon said we came within seconds of ARC launching a nuclear war against both Russia and China today," Tori said. "He also claimed that Centoreum Tech cheated on the test earlier this afternoon. Would you care to comment?"

Drew's mouth fell open. *We almost started a nuclear war today?*

President Tolley frowned, got up from her chair, and motioned urgently to her chief of staff.

"This interview is over," Elise said, rushing over to the first camera and fumbling with it, presumably looking for a way to remove the memory card. "Unfortunately, I'm going to have to confiscate the video footage," she said, finally managing to remove the memory card from the first camera.

"You can't do that," Tori said, leaping out of her chair to stop Elise from reaching the second camera. Drew shrank back in his chair and grabbed the arms, watching the chaos unfold. Tori's cameraman stood there as if frozen, apparently in complete shock at how the interview had fallen apart.

"This is not what we agreed to earlier today," Elise said, her eyes flashing with anger as Tori blocked access to the second camera in an apparent standoff.

"Well, I didn't agree to be sidelined for a one-on-one conversation with Drew, either," Tori said, her eyes narrowing. She put her hands on her hips and glared at Elise and then at the president.

"Would you prefer if I called Secret Service?" Elise growled.

Tori threw up her hands and moved to the side. "Fine. Go ahead and take the footage. I'll just run with what I have from my source, and you'll read about it in the headlines later this evening. And believe me, he gave me plenty to go on. There was something about you issuing the rescind order?"

President Tolley pointed with her index finger, her jaw clenched. "I have an inkling about who your source might be. Having just been fired an hour ago for insubordination, he'll come across as a disgruntled employee. I will also see to it that he faces charges for leaking highly classified information."

"But do you think that will matter to his base of support?" Tori asked, her arms tight across her chest.

For several moments, they stood face to face in angry silence. Drew's eyes darted between Tori and the president, wondering what either of them would say or do next.

"What if I were to offer you an exclusive?" President Tolley asked.

Tori's ears appeared to prick up.

"I'll give you your footage back," President Tolley said. "You'll air the clip between me and Mr. Hudson on your show tomorrow as agreed. But you'll not say or print a word about what you've learned from your source... that is, until we've completed a full investigation of ARC and Centoreum Tech."

Tori's eyes widened. "So, it was all true..."

"Do you agree to those terms?" President Tolley asked. "And I don't care if your source has gone to other news stations. You'll say nothing about it until the investigation is complete. Do you agree?"

"And I'll get the first look at the investigation report?" Tori asked.

"You'll get exclusive access." President Tolley pressed her lips together and nodded.

"Okay, it's a deal."

The president reached out her hand, and Tori shook it. As soon as the president released Tori's hand, she walked back over to Drew and said smiling, "Now, let's see about getting you that job."

# [ 57 ]
## DÉTENTE

MORGAN
2000
Oval Office
The White House

Morgan entered the Oval Office and stood still for a few moments, her heels sinking into the plush oval carpet. She rubbed her wrists and stretched her arms. They were quite sore from being tied up in zip ties behind her back for several hours. Morgan's stomach ached angrily from hunger, but she was more worried about other things—her uncle fleeing the country, her mother's involvement in Harrison's assassination, the mystery of her newfound sibling, and the prospect of getting fired from her job at the White House.

When she was finally released from custody, David had filled her in on everything that had transpired in the Situation Room with the ARC system. Her heart filled with pride when she learned about her friend Grace's performance in the midst of a nuclear crisis. Unfortunately, David wasn't able to reveal anything about Tolley's plans for her. That she'd have to hear from the president herself.

President Tolley sat stiffly at her desk and scribbled her signature on a piece of paper.

"Is that the autonomous weapons legislation?" Morgan asked tentatively, eager to ease the tension in the room.

Tolley nodded.

"You just signed it?"

"Actually, I just vetoed it," Tolley said, rising from her chair, walking around the desk, and offering Morgan a seat on the couch where they'd sat earlier that day discussing China's missile test.

Taking a seat, Morgan said nothing. She didn't quite know how to respond to the news. It was a surprising move, but then again not all that shocking. Somehow, deep down, Morgan had seen the veto coming since the cabinet meeting earlier that morning. Watching Tolley navigate the likes of Burke with ease and knowing the president's beliefs, she couldn't imagine the president would just roll over, cave to the pressure, and sign the bill because it was the popular thing to do. No, Tolley struck her as a woman of principle, and her decision would be based on her own judgment. For better or worse, she'd chosen a hard road for her presidency. Morgan eyed the president with a newfound respect.

"Are you surprised?" Tolley asked, appearing to study the expression on Morgan's face.

"Not really," Morgan said matter-of-factly.

Tolley raised an eyebrow. "Well, then maybe you know me better than I know myself. Because I didn't know what I was going to do until about thirty minutes ago."

"After your experience with the ARC system today, I don't think you had much of a choice," Morgan said in a reassuring tone.

"What about my decision to shut you out of the White

House?" Tolley asked, frowning slightly. "Did I make the right choice there?"

*Is this a trick question?*

Morgan grimaced, thinking about what might have happened if she hadn't broken into the White House to alert the president about the ARC system. "I'm sure you made the best decision you could at the time. You couldn't have known Grayson was attempting to marginalize me to keep you from learning the truth about him. Even I didn't see that one coming."

Tolley took a deep breath. "Well, I do regret my decision. I'm sorry I put you through the wringer today. I trusted the wrong person."

"Ma'am, it happens to all of us. After what I learned about my family members today, I could never hold it against you."

"Your uncle fled the country," Tolley said curtly, frowning.

"I know," Morgan said, a sharp pang of guilt stabbing her chest. She felt badly for letting her uncle escape and get away with whatever he'd done. Though at the time, she had other more important things to do. "Jack wanted me to come with him to avoid getting caught up in the mounting evidence against my family. When I refused and told him I was planning to get back into the White House somehow, he handed me that drive Elise gave to you."

Morgan had hoped the drive would curry favor with the president, but now she wasn't so sure anything could save her. Maybe it wasn't that valuable after all.

*How could Tolley ever trust me after all of this?*

"But you stayed behind," Tolley said. "Not only that, you got yourself taken into custody. Why?"

"Isn't it obvious?" Morgan asked. "I didn't want our country to turn into a pile of nuclear ash."

"Hmm…" Tolley murmured, unconvinced, and stared at the floor. "The FBI has evidence your mother was involved in Nightfall." Now she gave direct eye contact to Morgan, an unexpected fierceness in her eyes. "And I think you and Jack have been keeping that a secret from authorities."

Morgan flinched.

"It now appears your mother was behind Harrison's assassination as well," Tolley said. "Along with your sister? How could you know nothing of it?"

Morgan gulped. "Ma'am, I've suspected my family's involvement in Nightfall for some time, but I didn't have any tangible evidence to report to authorities. You may not believe it, but I only took the job on the national security staff to keep an eye on my uncle and President Monroe. At the time, it seemed painfully obvious to me that my uncle Jack and President Monroe were using the al Makhtar jihadist group as a cover story for Nightfall. I suspected there was far more to it. And I worried that they were hiding the true source and extent of the operation within the United States. Possibly even hiding their own involvement."

"What sort of involvement?" Tolley asked.

Morgan took a deep breath before answering. She'd never said the words out loud for fear that they might be true. "I'm not sure. But I've always wondered... if the nuclear device that was dropped from the International Space Station was developed using nuclear material from my uncle's company. But Jack has always denied any connection between his company and the bomb. Then again, he just made a run for it so maybe he knew about it." Her face fell, and she stared at the floor.

Tolley recoiled and exhaled sharply. Then she went silent for a few moments. "Do you think the Russians are involved?"

Morgan rubbed her forehead. "I have no doubt. Especially after hearing about the Russian space rockets headed for the moon. David said three of them launched today?" Morgan's thoughts drifted to the mysterious cocktail code.

*White Russian, black Russian, and a side car? Did the cocktails refer to each of the rockets?*

Tolley nodded. "Yes, three rockets launched from space pads belonging to a private company called *Green Dragon Pioneers*."

Morgan nodded quickly as she received a surge of adrenaline. "I know that name. Now I'm convinced more than ever that the Russians are up to their necks in Nightfall and possibly even behind the president's assassination. Before today, I'd suspected someone known as the Benefactor to be the driving force behind Nightfall. I only had an inkling of who it might be before, but now I'm certain of it."

"You think you know the Benefactor's identity?" Tolley asked.

"It's Anton Vega."

"What? The billionaire space technologist?" Tolley asked, her eyes bulging. "He's an American citizen. But why—"

Morgan gave her a half smile. "In full disclosure, it's just another one of my crazy theories at this point. I'm pretty certain that a company owned by Anton Vega called *Green Dragon* was involved in Nightfall. That name doesn't feel like a coincidence."

"The coincidences are definitely beginning to add up," Tolley said flatly.

"I found evidence today that Vega is linked to the Russian oligarch, Igor Koslov. He hired the individuals behind the cyber-attacks against China. And earlier today when I stopped by the Cyberthreat Intelligence Integration Center, I wondered if Vega's company also operated a satellite in highly elliptical orbit. But I didn't get a chance to dig deeper."

"You know how our early warning satellite network went down this afternoon?" Tolley asked. "You think Anton Vega hacked Polaris from his satellite and then took control of the entire network?"

"Ma'am, think about it," Morgan said. "The Russian government authorized the unannounced launch of three space rockets owned by a private company. They had to know we would receive alerts from our early warning system. To keep their plans a secret and prevent the ARC system from receiving a false alarm that might lead to nuclear war, they put us in the dark."

"For about forty-five minutes," Tolley said, finishing her sentence. "Just enough time…" She went silent for a moment.

*To bring about the end of the world.*

Morgan imagined the president was contemplating how close the United States, China, and Russia had come to an accidental nuclear war. To keep a few space rockets heading for the moon a secret.

*Whatever Anton has planned for them… it had better be worth it.*

The president looked up and stared directly into Morgan's eyes. "I still need to decide what I'm going to do with you."

Morgan swallowed hard. "Are you going to fire me?"

"Well, that's what Elise recommended," Tolley said. "She claimed you're a huge liability to my administration. She also thinks your loyalties remain with your family."

Morgan broke eye contact, and her shoulders dropped.

"But I disagree with her," Tolley said. Morgan breathed a sigh of relief and looked back up at the president as she said, "About your loyalties, that is. You've proven incredible loyalty to our country during its darkest hour. And at great risk to your own interests. As for posing a liability… I haven't decided about that part yet. Thus far, you've been quite an asset."

Morgan remained silent. There wasn't anything she could say at this point to persuade the president. Either Tolley would judge her by her own actions or determine her to be tainted by her family. And if she objected too strongly, the president might not decide in her favor.

"I had that drive sent over to FBI Director Laski earlier this evening," Tolley said. "He called me right away with some preliminary news that may be of interest to you. As I expected, the drive is an encryption key to a collection of sealed files about Nightfall. His agents have already begun poring over the evidence. An initial overview implicates a number of senior officials within the U.S. government including Grayson, your uncle, your mother, and sadly Harrison himself. I told Director Laski of your role in getting him the encryption key, your talent for

thinking outside the box, and of course... your stubborn determination. He had an interesting idea, but for it to work, it
would depend entirely on you."

Morgan sat up a bit straighter.

"Are you willing to help bring the perpetrators of Nightfall to
justice?" Tolley asked.

Morgan nodded without hesitation. "Yes, ma'am."

"No matter the cost to your family?" Tolley asked. "Your
close connection to Jack and Faye are the reason Director Laski
thinks you have special value to his investigation. Are you
prepared to turn your back on them?"

Morgan nodded solemnly. It was her only chance to prove
Jack's innocence.

"You realize I'm going to need you to help me bring your
uncle and mother into custody."

"I understand the costs, ma'am," Morgan said, swallowing
hard.

"Good." Tolley folded her hands. "Then I want you to head
up a small Top Secret interagency task force within the White
House. Its sole mission will be to discover the full truth behind
the Nightfall Incident. You'll work closely with the lead FBI
special agent assigned to the case by Director Laski. You will
report your findings only to me and Laski. We'll need to keep a
lid on this investigation until we're ready to reveal the truth to
the public."

"Yes, ma'am," Morgan said, feeling a new surge of energy
flood her body.

Elise marched into the Oval Office and tapped her wrist
urgently. "Madam President, Mike Palmer is here to see you
with some vital information about the Russian oligarch behind
the cyberattacks."

"Mike Palmer?" Tolley asked, furrowing her brow.

"Ma'am, he's your senior director for European and Russian
Affairs on the National Security Council staff."

"Oh," Tolley said.

Morgan suppressed a smirk. The president had yet to acquaint herself of her entire staff. Even though it was only Tolley's fourth day on the job as the president, she'd grown into the role as if she'd already been there for years.

"Put him on my schedule first thing tomorrow morning and beg my apologies. It's getting late. I really need to spend some time with Blake and Lucy."

Elise smiled. "Absolutely, will do. Have a restful evening," she said, rushing out of the office.

Then Tolley turned to smile at Morgan. "We'll talk about the task force more tomorrow. In the meantime, I've restored your full access to the White House, and you may leave without an escort."

"Madam President, thank you for having faith in me. I won't disappoint you." With that, Morgan rose from her chair and departed the Oval Office. As she walked down the hallway toward the main exit, her smartphone buzzed. She saw a text from Grace on the screen.

WANT TO GRAB A DRINK AT OFF THE RECORD?
JUST SPOKE WITH YOUR BOYFRIEND, AND HE'S GAME

Morgan smiled, typed a response, and turned around to head for the West Wing exit instead.

THAT SOUNDS AMAZING

Grace responded:

ALSO, MAY NEED TO CRASH ON YOUR COUCH TONIGHT
IF THAT'S OKAY
ZACH JUST DUMPED ME BY TEXT MESSAGE

Morgan touched her face in surprise. *Ouch.*

# EPILOGUE

TORI
August 10, 2033
1100
Homeland Network News
Washington D.C.

Tori glanced down at her script one last time and brushed a loose hair aside as the camera started rolling. "Hi, I'm Tori Scott, from the left," she said, smiling nervously at the camera. Though it was finally her big day, she wasn't looking forward to the shade her co-host would likely throw her way on the live show. They'd fought vigorously before going on air, and the source of their disagreement was not resolved.

"And I'm Emilio Valdes, from the right."

"Welcome to *The Counter View* on Homeland Network News," Tori said, glancing at Emilio and forcing a stiff smile.

"The news talk show that presents both sides of the issue and lets you decide," Emilio said flatly and glared back at Tori. "At least that's what it used to do..." he muttered under his breath.

Tori blanched, uncertain about how well his comment could be heard over the audio. "This morning, we have an amazing show lined up for you," she said, trying to muster as much enthusiasm as she could drum up while keeping her voice from shaking. "*The Counter View* was incredibly fortunate to receive an exclusive preview of the ARC investigation report coming out of the White House this evening. No other network has seen this report, and we'll highlight the key findings for you. We're also going to get a live response to the report from the one and only billionaire space technologist Anton Vega, who comes all the way from Moscow. So, you'll definitely want to stay tuned to the show." She turned to Emilio to ask him a question but then hesitated for a moment.

*Will he play ball?*

Tori glimpsed her executive producer urging her from the sound booth to keep things moving. "Emilio, you read the report. What do you think was the most important finding from your perspective?"

Emilio grimaced. "Personally, I'm most interested in *how* you got exclusive access? How is it that you're suddenly so cozy with the president?" He touched his face with his index finger and looked up at the ceiling. "Oh, I know... didn't something happen last month when you visited the White House with your protégé? Yeah... after that, everything changed. For example, you've refused to cover any of the obscene allegations against Centoreum Tech or anonymous reports we've heard about from inside the Pentagon over the past month. It's almost as if you've forgotten you're a journalist. And isn't that poster boy for killer robots working for the president now? Tori, tell me, what sort of drug deal did you make with Tolley to remain silent? That's what I'm most interested in hearing about."

For a moment, Tori was speechless, like a deer caught in headlights. She'd expected a hard time from her co-host. But she didn't think he'd attack her outright on live television. Ignoring the heavy feeling in her stomach, she swallowed hard, faced the camera, and read from the teleprompter. "With the ARC investigation report about to hit the streets, Dennis Warren, the CEO of Centoreum Tech, is currently facing charges of felony fraud for making false claims about the capabilities of the ARC system to the Pentagon and tampering with the system after its launch to deceive Congress."

Through the glass, Tori saw her executive producer signaling to go to the video feed from Moscow. "However, yet another CEO faces some close scrutiny given the findings of the report. And we're thrilled to have Anton Vega join the show to get his initial response to the allegations." She turned toward the video screen and saw Anton's chiseled face appear in front of a shelf full of books. "Mr. Vega, thanks so much for joining us today."

"Thank you so much for having me on the show," Anton said.

"You've received an advance copy of the ARC investigation report," Tori said. "I'm sure you have also followed the media coverage here in the U.S., suggesting your company may be liable for the close call we had with China and Russia last month. Thus far, you've been silent on the matter. But now that you've read the report, how would you respond to the allegations?"

Anton nodded. "Of course, thank you to Homeland Network News for the opportunity to comment on the report. It's very unfortunate that *Green Dragon Pioneers* got caught up in all of this. There's certainly plenty of blame to go around for the nuclear crisis with China, but I would push back against any assertion that my company bears responsibility. My company remains committed to bringing about the dream of commercial space travel. To achieve our vision, we collaborate with a wide range of private companies and foreign governments, including Russia."

"But your company did fail to announce the launch of your space rockets," Tori said. "And as you've read, this caused a false alarm within the Department of Defense's ARC system which led to the near-launch of U.S. nuclear weapons against China and Russia. Doesn't that make your company at least partially responsible?"

"Not at all," Anton said. "My rockets were launched from Russian territory. That means the Russian government had the responsibility for reporting the planned launches to international authorities. Now, I don't know why the Russian government didn't do that, but I'm sure it was due to a bureaucratic error. The real blame for the nuclear crisis should be placed squarely on the Department of Defense's ill-conceived automation of nuclear command and control. This report is intended to distract the American public from the terrible truths about the ARC system and the military and civilian leaders who succumbed to the siren call of artificial intelligence."

"Look, the ARC system wasn't entirely responsible for what happened," Emilio interjected. "If you really want to talk about what went wrong, then we have to consider Russia's cyberattack against China's unmanned submarines that were parked in our coastal waters. That's the sort of reckless behavior that will get us into a nuclear war, not an autonomous system."

"Actually, the report suggested that it wasn't the Russian government behind the alleged attack, but rather an oligarch by the name of Igor Koslov who acted independently," Tori said.

"So they say…" Emilio said, his tone skeptical. "I understand he's now under house arrest on the orders of the Kremlin. Seems like Koslov is a convenient patsy to me. Anyway, here's the point I wanted to make about ARC. Taking the system offline was extremely shortsighted on the part of the president. I admit it may have gone a bit awry, but didn't ARC detect that something unusual was afoot? Doesn't that prove the system is better at detecting an emerging nuclear threat than humans?"

"If I may add something to this discussion," Anton said, his forehead creased. "According to the report, the ARC system nearly started an accidental nuclear war on the basis of misinterpreted data. If the programmers hadn't been able to intervene in time, millions of innocent people would be dead right now."

"Yeah, yeah, yeah… we'd all be a pile of ash by now," Emilio said, flapping his hands dismissively. "But it didn't happen. Because someone stepped in to save the day. The system actually worked just the way it was supposed to. It provided us with strategic warning, and humans intervened just in time before it made a grave mistake. But with the system offline, the United States will no longer have strategic warning of nuclear threats. To me, we're much worse off than before. The report distracts us from what we should be focused on."

"Oh really? What's that?" Tori asked.

"As far as I'm concerned, the Russian government is covering up the real mission behind having Anton Vega send three space rockets to the moon. I don't buy the explanation of a moon base in the report for a second. The rationale is flimsy at best. There would be no reason for all the secrecy or the veiled threats from the Russians to steer clear of the moon."

"Well, what was the real reason then?" Tori asked. *Since you're so smart.*

"Isn't it obvious?" Emilio asked, giving her a dumbfounded look.

Tori remained silent.

"Let me lay it out for you," Emilio said. "A Russian oligarch hires a well-known hacker to mess with China and keep our eyes focused on them. The same hacker manages to take our early warning satellite network offline for a time so that we can't detect missile launches. The Russian government collaborates with a private sector company to launch not one, but three space rockets to the moon. And they do it in secret, raising the specter of false alarms and the risk of accidental nuclear war. To me, that suggests a mission of incredible significance to Russia. But our government thinks they're building a moon base?" Emilio shook his head and waved his hands again. "That's terribly naïve. No, the Russians would have carried off this scheme for only one purpose… to put nuclear weapons on the moon."

Tori's mouth fell open as she contemplated the implications. But she recovered quickly and asked their guest a follow-up question. "Anton, perhaps, you could explain Russia's intentions for the moon mission."

Anton smiled. "I admit, your colleague's suggestion gave me a good, hearty laugh. The Russian government has no plans to weaponize the moon. I personally checked the inventory of each rocket before the launch. I think I'd notice a few nuclear weapons lying around. Not to mention that would be a grave violation of the 1967 Outer Space Treaty."

"Then what do you make of the veiled threats coming from the Russian government about your new moon colony?" Emilio asked, his face scrunched. "Or the extreme secrecy around the launch?"

"Well, as I mentioned before, I don't know why the Russian government failed to announce the laun… What the?" Anton's eyes darted to the side and widened. His mouth opening, he jerked his head back as a large object moved in front of the camera, obscuring his face. Then suddenly, the video feed cut out and the screen went blank.

Tori stared at the screen, trying to hide the shock on her face at what she thought had happened. Then she turned back to face the camera and feigned a calm smile. "It looks like we've lost our feed at the moment. We'll go to commercial break while we try to reestablish a connection."

WANT TO READ MORE?

TRY THE LARA KINGSLEY SERIES BY NATASHA BAJEMA

You won't regret checking out this action-packed mystery series weaves together elements of mystery, techno-thriller, and science fiction and is set in the near future. Check it out at https://natashabajema.com

## ACKNOWLEDGMENTS

If you enjoyed reading this novel, even in the slightest, then it is all my friend Darren Cogan's fault, and you can thank him. If it were not for his prodding, I would have never written this novel.

I can remember the exact moment I decided to write *Rescind Order*. It was a weekday evening in early August 2019. Darren and I were on the phone talking about my research paper that explores the future impact of artificial intelligence (AI) on weapons of mass destruction (WMD). In what I thought was a stroke of brilliance, I decided to kick off the paper with a fictional scenario about an autonomous retaliatory capability (ARC) designed to launch U.S. nuclear weapons automatically when certain conditions are met. The scenario was intended to be an entertaining hook to draw readers into an otherwise abstract paper and get them to imagine how AI might shape WMD threats and responses in the future. And yes, I intention-ally chose the name of the automated system to be as bland and uninspiring as possible to parody many such systems developed by the Department of Defense. I also like the sound it makes when you say the acronym repeatedly; it reminds me of the seals barking in the distance when I lived in Monterey, California. To me, the seals always sounded like they were laughing hysterically. That's some meta-parody for you. Anyway, back to my anecdote.

It was an odd conversation for my friend and I to have. Darren is a screenwriter, not a national security expert. We usually talk about fiction stories, but I just had to tell him about the speculative scenario in my nonfiction paper. Developing an automated command and control system for nuclear weapons is a preposterous and extremely dangerous idea. Several days after I wrote it, two nuclear deterrence experts called for exactly such a system on a popular national security blog. When I first read the article, my jaw dropped in disbelief, and I had to read it again. Surely, they couldn't be serious. Sadly they were.

Would U.S. policymakers someday leverage artificial intelligence to build a system that automatically launches a retaliatory strike in response to a nuclear attack? After more than ten years of working in the Department of Defense, surrounded by many true believers in 20th century nuclear deterrence, I couldn't answer "absolutely not" with confidence. Rather, I could imagine policymakers claiming such a system was dictated by the logic of deterrence and arguing that it would keep us safe from nuclear war. These are the arguments us scholarly types hear all the time in nuclear policy circles in D.C. Many think nuclear weapons, the most destructive weapons in the world, must exist to keep us safe. Without them, we are in mortal danger. They also say we need to be able to launch them on warning—within less than thirty minutes—in order to ensure effective retaliation and prevent nuclear war. Basically because of nuclear deterrence, U.S. citizens face the chance of losing everything they hold dear to an all-out-nuclear war that could start in less than thirty minutes. As long as we have nuclear weapons, the U.S. threatens to do the same to the citizens of other countries with nuclear weapons. By living on this nuclear tinder box, they say we are safe. That's what they need to believe.

It didn't take long for Darren to convince me to write a novel about this scenario, though that wasn't his original intention. I think the dialogue went down something like this.

"That scenario would make a great short film," he said enthusiastically.

"You think so?" I rubbed my chin, considering the possibility.

"We could make the film the exact length of the decision-making window. The President has eight minutes and fifty-three seconds to issue the rescind order, right?"

"Yeah. You're right, that would be a cool short film…" I said, my voice trailing off. A moment later, I said decisively, "We should write it."

"Let's do it," Darren said quickly.

"I should probably write the novel first," I said, thinking about the technical complexity of nuclear deterrence, artificial intelligence, and autonomous systems. "To get my ideas worked out on paper."

"Good idea," he said.

This is how I got started on *Rescind Order*. A month later, I traveled to D.C. to start my one year stint as an NSquare Fellow and meet up with my fellow cohort of like-minded creatives. During this trip, I decided upon two things. First, that I would use the experience of writing novel as the basis for a dark comedy stage play called *American Doomsday*. Second, I decided to borrow the cast of characters from the first novel I've ever written but has yet to see the light of day. If you read the novel and have finished it, wanting to know much more about the Nightfall Incident, never fear. I've written an entire novel about Morgan and Jack Shaw and the sequence of events that led to Nightfall and plan to release it as a prequel sometime in 2021.

This novel benefited from the insights and skills of amazing editors. I would like to thank Brianna Boes for finessing the manuscript with her brilliant line edits and polishes as well as catching some important plot issues. Thank you to Christie Hartman who helped catch loose errors and typos.

Special thanks to a number of national security experts for their assistance with brainstorming the technical pieces of my novel: Dr. William Kennedy, Tim Westmyer, Dr. David Santoro, and Dr. Frank Sauer. Thank you to Rear Admiral (ret) John Gower for taking the time to read my book twice and provide vital feedback. I've based many of the concepts in my novel on writings by Paul Scharre, Michael Horowitz, Elsa Kania, Eric Schlosser, Scott Sagan, Thomas Schelling, and Herman Kahn. I am indebted to many other scholars who have produced serious work in this area and consider this novel my contribution to the debate. Also thanks to Erika Gregory, Morgan Matthews, and Tom Weis of the NSquare Collaborative for their continuous support.

Any inaccuracy in the novel is my own and should not reflect on anyone mentioned. Moreover, the views expressed in this novel are those of the author and do not reflect the official policy or position of the National Defense University, the Department of Defense, or the U.S. Government.

I am dedicating this book to my friend, Darren. Thank you for inspiring me to write this story and for messing up my planned writing schedule. Thank you for always being willing to brainstorm with me and even for listening to me explain nuclear deterrence and machine learning ad nauseum.

# ABOUT THE AUTHOR

**NATASHA BAJEMA** lives in Rockport, Texas with her dogs, Malachi and Charlie, and works as an independent consultant on national security. She has been an expert on national security issues for over 20 years, specializing in weapons of mass destruction (WMD), nuclear proliferation, terrorism, and emerging technologies. For ten years, Natasha worked for the National Defense University where she taught an elective course to senior military officers on WMD and film and led a research project on the impact of emerging technologies on national security. Natasha holds a Ph.D. in international relations from the Fletcher School of Law and Diplomacy at Tufts University.

*For more information:*
https://natashabajema.com